sex.
lies.
murder.
fame.

ALSO BY LOLITA FILES

Tastes Like Chicken
Child of God
Blind Ambitions
Getting to the Good Part
Scenes from a Sistah

sex.
lies.
murder.
fame.

LOLITA FILES

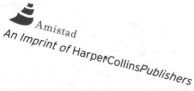

Amistad
An Imprint of HarperCollinsPublishers

HarperCollins books may be purchased for educational, business, or sales promotional use. For information please write: Special Markets Department, HarperCollins Publishers, 10 East 53rd Street, New York, NY 10022.

FIRST EDITION

Designed by Sarah Maya Gubkin

Printed on acid-free paper

Library of Congress Cataloging-in-Publication Data

Files, Lolita.
   sex.lies.murder.fame. : a novel / Lolita Files.—1st ed.
     p. cm.
   ISBN-13: 978-0-06-078680-9 (acid-free paper)
   ISBN-10: 0-06-078680-9
     1. Publishers and publishing—Fiction. 2. Music trade—Fiction. 3. New York (N.Y.)—Fiction. I. Title.

PS3556.I4257B66 2006
813'.54—dc22   2005045326

06 07 08 09 10 BVG/RRD 10 9 8 7 6 5 4 3 2 1

To the four wise men: Big L., for your constant encouragement and support; Bryonn Bain, for the African violets; Bill Hobi, for inspiring me, cheering me on, and keeping me uplifted as I made my way toward the finish line; and Eric Jerome Dickey, for always being available in cyberspace whenever I need to have a writer's rant.

To the five wise women: the superb Jennifer Pooley, for being my dream editor and a great new friend; Team Amistad (Dawn Davis, Rockelle Henderson, and Gilda Squire) for totally getting me and my book; and my agent, Elaine Koster, because it's high time I thanked her, by name, in print.

And to Michael DeLorenzo, a truly talented renaissance man with a heart of pure gold. For looking out for me. For everything. For just being you. You are my brother. You are my friend.

I.

actions

You can always count on a murderer
for a fancy prose style.
—Vladimir Nabokov, *Lolita*

There's something

. . . about the echo created by steps across a parquet floor. It's not like the sound of typical hardwood. Parquet resonates a bit deeper. Perhaps it's the arrangement of the interlocking wood.

Sound is everything. Intangible power.

Funny thing about sound. The same sound in the same space, all things being unchanged, can seem totally different based upon one important factor: the distribution of light, or the absence of it. A hundred-watt bulb. Looming shadows. The arbitrary flickering of a candle. Each creates a dramatically diverse effect that determines how sound is registered.

It's pure perception. A whisper in the daytime might be missed altogether. That same whisper, uttered the same way in the same space, in the dark, can inspire immeasurable fear.

This was Penn's only thought as he hefted the sack of thigh higher across his shoulder: the perfection of sound in accordance with light. The apartment and the moment were both fairly dark and required a pitch with the appropriate degree of gravitas. He adjusted his walk into a half-dance—stepstep*step*stepstep*step*. The cadence filled the entire hallway. He stopped. It wasn't right. The rhythm—anapestic dimeter, to be precise—wasn't ominous enough. He started again, this time losing one beat to make it iambic. Step*step*step*step*. That was better. That was more literary.

He wanted this to be a literary moment. And in the world of literature, when it came to beats and measures, the iamb was king. Anyone
with half a functioning brain knew that. One of his professors at Columbia had said that dactylic hexameter was the most important of the classi-
cal meters because it was what Homer and Virgil had used. Bullshit. Most
people wouldn't know a dactylic hexameter if it bit them in the ass, but
everyone had heard of iambic pentameter—and therefore the iamb—
even if they didn't know what it was. The iamb was a critical part of
Shakespeare's meter of choice, and Shakespeare was the ruling god of literature. Not Homer. Not Virgil. Shakespeare. End of subject.

The sack of thigh, a black trash bag stuffed to capacity with meat,
slapped against his back.

Hmmm.

Step*slap*step*slap.* Step*slap*step*slap.*

Yes.

He began a light whistle. "In the Hall of the Mountain King." It was
the fourth movement from Suite no. 1, op. 46, of Edvard Grieg's *Peer
Gynt,* incidental music written for Ibsen's eponymous play. Whistling it
now, of course, was not very original, but the tune had proven a sturdy
classic for moments like this. So what if it had been done to death since
Peter Lorre's turn as a murderous pedophile in *M*?

Ha. Done to death. He laughed aloud and lost his beat.

"Quit fuckin' around," yelled an out-of-view Mercury. "I'm just
washing up, then I'm gonna run downstairs. Give me about five minutes, then start throwing them in. And don't fuckin' dawdle. We need
to get this done. You hear me?"

"Of course," Penn mumbled, regulating his pace back to something
close to normal, although there was nothing normal about any of this.
He dropped the sack by the front door alongside four other sacks,
each one a trash bag stuffed with a pillowcase filled with rinsed flesh.
He wondered how he'd ultimately remember tonight. The objective
was for all knowledge of the events transpiring to evaporate like the
wind, but Penn had always been a lover of mythologies, and this was
clearly the creation of one. How would tonight, this night, go down?
Would it become a rumored part of his legend, or an indelible stain
on an unfulfilled dream?

He realized the Grieg tune had been a bad choice. It was tacky, clichéd. Penn was a Wagner man, after all. It occurred to him that he knew the right piece, had known it all along, one in line with the tenor of his actions. "Träume," from the *Wesendonck-Lieder,* that masterful five-part nod to illicit love.

He smiled and began to whistle again. Quick bursts of air this time, blown with gusto.

Ahhh.

Everything was perfect now.

Romanticism:

Love, that is all I asked, a little love,
daily, twice daily,
fifty years of twice daily . . .

—Samuel Beckett, *All That Fall*

She was

. . . late!

Late! Late! Late!

Beryl Unger was never late.

Not ever. Not for anything. She was a stickler for time, order, and precision. Every moment counted in life, none of it to be wasted. But through no fault of her own, she had wasted time, and now she was stuck in the gridlock of crosstown traffic. Her knee was shaking. She peered out the window.

"Let me out here," she squawked at the cabbie. "I'll walk the rest of the way."

"But it's just around the—"

"I don't have time!"

The cabbie closed out the meter.

"Four-eighty," he said as the receipt printed out.

She flung a fiver at him and jumped out. The cabbie had barely uttered the words "fucking bitch" when she opened the door again and handed him two dollars.

"Sorry," she said. "Have a nice day."

She slammed the door. Her pulse was racing, brow sweating, as she beat it down the street.

"Oh God, oh God, oh God," she said, checking her watch. Five fifty-seven. "Oh God, oh God, oh God, oh God."

This was Messier's fault. The bloviating blowhard had sat in her office, babbling on about himself as the minutes ticked by. She'd had no choice but to indulge him. He was one of her top authors, after all, and he'd dropped in unexpectedly, wanting to be coddled for no reason in particular. With every word that fell from his lips, her leg—the right one, the nerve barometer—shook a little faster, her mind raced a little more, and the tiny pits of sweat forming beneath her arms began to widen and drip as her eyes kept being drawn to the clock over his shoulder.

She rounded the corner now and raced up the stoop, tripping over herself, scuffing the left heel of a new pair of Alexandra Neels. She scrambled up the stairs to the tenant listings and hit the buzzer. She pressed pressed pressed, the buzzer zinging furiously. Someone zapped the door and let her in.

Beryl rushed to the elevator, checking her watch. Six-oh-two. She pressed the button. Pressed pressed pressed. Pressed pressed pressed.

"Oh God," she said, her whole body shaking.

She kept pressing as she watched the descending numbers above the elevator light up as the lift came down. The doors flew open. She rushed in, bodychecking the girl who was getting off.

"Sorry," Beryl said, her entire face sweaty with panic.

"It's okay," the girl said, regaining her balance. "Relax. He's running behind. I was supposed to let you know that he had to step out for a minor emergency. He'll be here at six-fifteen. I was coming downstairs to wait for you on the stoop."

"So I'm not late?" Beryl asked, panting.

"Of course not, Miss Unger," the girl said, a big smile on her face as she held the door open. "You're never late."

Ten minutes later, she was a bit more refreshed. She'd stopped in the bathroom and had cooled herself down with a splash of water to the face and a light retouch of her makeup. She had freshened her underarms, which were damp with panic. Thank goodness she'd worn a sleeveless chemise beneath a light jacket. It was late September. The weather would be growing colder soon, but for now, she still dressed as though it were summer.

Seven of the ten minutes in the bathroom had been spent trying to rub away the scuff in the heel of her shoe. It wouldn't budge. She kept scrubbing until it seemed she might rub some of the color away. She put the shoe back on, turned, and examined the heel. To someone else, it might go unnoticed. To Beryl, it was glaring. The scuff made her look tacky and cheap. It took away from all the care of her appearance.

She sat in the waiting area, the foot wearing the shoe with the scuffed heel tucked behind her other foot.

She was annoyed.

Ripkin was late. What if she'd had something planned immediately after? This was inexcusable.

She checked her watch. Six-thirteen.

She had a manuscript to read tonight. And what about dinner? Now everything had to be pushed back.

"C'mon, c'mon," she groaned.

Her right knee shook impatiently. She stuck out her left foot and looked at the heel.

"Ugh!"

She tucked the eyesore out of the way.

"He's coming," she said. "I know it, and when he gets here, I'm going to be ready."

She was fidgeting, always fidgeting. Even though she was lying down now, her right knee still shook like a racehorse at the gate.

"What exactly are you readying this time, and how will you know it? We've long established that there seem to be some challenges here about discerning when you think something is 'ready.' "

"Oh, Dr. Ripkin, don't be impertinent. You know what I mean. Spare me all your British doublespeak."

A rush of heat to the tips of his ears was Ripkin's sole discernible reaction to the affront of her comment. This . . . this . . . this . . . woman-child . . . was constantly making such statements to him. Impertinent indeed.

He would never become accustomed to her casual barbs. After six-teen years of variations on the same drill, Dr. Ripkin—Edgar Eugene Ripkin, M.D., fifty-eight, Old Etonian, Oxford-degreed, to the Dorset manner born, of excellent Saxon parentage, premier Upper East Side psychiatrist—realized he was aggravated by Beryl Unger's cheery infor-mality above everything else. Her words and tone perturbed him. She should be more respectful of him as an elder, he believed, but he remained the essence of patience and restraint, a stark antithesis to her high-strung bearing. He knew her tone was harmless. Still.

Ripkin abhorred the way Americans referred to him as "British." He preferred the term "English," for he was an Englishman to his core, English in the most old-fashioned sense. He took full tea at exactly four o'clock each afternoon, alone, always with the same items consumed in the same order: first came the savories (four very thin sandwiches, crusts cut off, one cucumber and cream cheese, two watercress, one salmon with dill), followed by two buttermilk scones with lemon curd, strawberry jam, and clotted cream (Devonshire), served along with his tea, Earl Grey (two scoops of loose leaves, one for him and one for the pot), and no milk (never milk). Then came one shortbread, followed by a fruit tartlet (mixed berry). His receptionist prepared this afternoon minifeast Monday through Friday, although she was never invited to participate. Solitude, Ripkin explained, was critical. This was a time to clear himself and relax. After that necessary break, he would resume seeing patients until seven. To compensate for not including the recep-tionist in his precious tea ceremony, he allowed her to leave an hour early each day, at six, after the arrival of the final appointment.

Ripkin was a traditionalist who favored ascots, bowler hats, and crossed the big pond annually for the yacht races during Cowes Week on the Isle of Wight. He was fond of silk slippers and sweet Black Cavendish tobacco smoked from a Becker & Musico dublin beside a roaring hearth. He liked rich things. More importantly, he believed rich people should be like steak tartare—rare. But that wasn't the case so much anymore.

And while Beryl, his last patient of the day, was in no way repre-sentative of the worst he had to deal with, Ripkin loathed her kind, that generation of American excess: self-serving, arrogant fast-trackers with no regard for time-acquired wisdom, credentials, and position.

Theirs was a generation of Madison Avenue gluttony, reality TV, tabloid celebrity, hip-hop hedonism, and pseudoheiresses. New Age carpetbaggers and scallywags, the lot. People who would have never been admired an age ago, during his grandfather's day. There had once been a time when social standing couldn't be bought. It was a thing afforded only by good breeding and refinement, and was cultivated and passed on with guarded dignity. Now the cretins melded with the cultured in a nasty wash he feared would drown civilization. Vulgarians everywhere, and he was part and parcel of it.

These vain young turks were ill-equipped to handle material excess and the access that came with it. Neuroses, psychoses, and full-blown dementia were the natural offspring of their success, which accounted for Ripkin's expanding practice. They were filled with moxie, these kids, and it was driving them all mad, even though that very moxie was making him quite rich. Richer. He'd always been rich. Perhaps, he thought, it was time for him to retire.

Beryl, the size-zero bag of issues stretched out on his couch, typified the bunch, although Ripkin, to his own surprise, had developed a tender, paternal fondness for her over the years that he did his best to keep under wraps. She was his second chance. He had a daughter from his first marriage who didn't know him at all. It was a source of deep regret. When Beryl came into his life, lost, alone, helpless, he found himself connecting with her beyond a professional level. He was hard on her because he'd come to want a lot for her, the best, if she would just let herself have it. But Beryl tended to get lost in fantasy. Ridiculous pointless fantasy. Things she believed were practical, but were in no way grounded in logic or common sense.

She was considered one of the most successful up-and-coming editors in the publishing world, an industry where the prestige factor often took precedence over salary. The business was notorious for its low pay, but many considered the chance to work with some of the greatest minds in the world and be a part of shaping the literary landscape a compensation that far outweighed anything monetary. The ones who came in at entry level, were identified as having editorial potential, and were willing to stick it out ultimately saw the promise of greater financial stability.

She was at Kittell Press now, but had gotten her start as a temp at Pale-Fire Publishing in 1989 after lying about her age to get the job. It was hard in the beginning, sometimes unbearable. Paltry pay, barely enough to survive on, and lots of filing, coffee-fetching, and copying. Entry-level employees were being paid more these days, somewhere between twenty-seven and thirty thousand dollars a year, but when Beryl entered the business, her pay was rotten. In the earlier days of publishing, editors usually came from families of social standing and wealth. Low salary wasn't an issue. Someone with a background as sketchy as Beryl's would have never stood a chance, but times had changed. Unfortunately, when she began, the salaries hadn't. She made only enough to buy food, pay the utilities, and cover less than half the rent. She had to take on a night job at Kinko's to make up the rest. When a group of publishing houses filed a copyright infringement suit against Kinko's for the company's unauthorized use of material, Beryl quickly quit. She didn't want anything to jeopardize her career plans in publishing. She got a job waitressing at Houlihan's to make up the rest of her rent.

After three initial years that saw her going from temping to well-liked receptionist to clerical work in the advertising, legal, art, and marketing departments, she finally landed a job as an assistant for Keri Porter, an editor who was on the fast track within the company. Beryl got the job on the recommendation of Keri's former assistant. The girl lived in Beryl's building and, while they weren't friends, they'd had a sort of smile-and-nod acquaintanceship that was taken a step further when the two ran into each other while doing laundry. Niceties were exchanged. Idle chitchat was made. Beryl happily prattled about how much she loved publishing and wanted to be an editor someday. The assistant confessed that she was planning to leave. Her boyfriend had gotten a job in Chicago and asked her to move with him. She was going.

"I know you don't know me that well," Beryl had said, suddenly emboldened, "but do you think maybe, since you're leaving, I could get a shot at working for Keri?"

"Uh, um, I don't know," stammered the assistant, surprised by the request. "Once I give notice, Keri might already—"

"But I'm a really hard worker. Really. You can ask anybody. I know my way around the company. I'm loyal, I'm committed, I'm diligent. I just want a chance, just a chance . . . please?"

The assistant couldn't get in a word as Beryl threw herself into earnest begging.

"Would you? Could you? I'm not saying you have to talk me up or anything. Just, you know, maybe see if I could get an interview with her. It would mean everything to me!"

"I'll ask, but I can't promise—"

"Oh, thank you!" Beryl said, throwing her arms around the girl's neck.

The assistant left the Laundromat to go for a cup of soup. She asked Beryl to watch her clothes. When she returned, they were fluffed and folded.

"Whoa."

"I had all this nervous energy," Beryl said. "I'm so excited you're going to do this for me."

The assistant arranged the meeting.

Keri met Beryl. Keri liked Beryl, particularly her enthusiasm, which seemed inexhaustible. In very short order, Beryl became Keri's new assistant.

Six months in, Keri gave her four manuscripts at once and asked for her gut opinion of them as a reader, not as someone in the business. They were books she'd inherited from an editor who'd left the company. No rush, Keri had said. Beryl could get to them over the next month or so. Eager Beryl saw her opening and plunged headlong into the project. She read all four in one weekend, and returned Monday morning with typed pages of commentary and editorial suggestions, the opposite of what Keri had asked for, but all of which the editor could see made sense.

All four books, published a year later with Beryl's two cents intact, went on to do well. Two were women's fiction, debut novels that made for great watercooler chatter and fun reading at the beach. One, written by a pretty but less well known CNN reporter, was a self-help piece called *Fear of Crying*. The book instructed women to wail more in order to free themselves of negative emotional weight from failed relationships. It was a modest hit among the single hand-wringing set. The last, a technothriller by a talented mid-level author whose last book had sold below expectation, became a runaway success that topped the *New York Times* fiction list for sixteen straight weeks.

Keri received a sizable bonus for the book's performance, and she shared with the publisher the value of Beryl's input. A week later, Anna Barber, then head of PaleFire, called Beryl to her office.

"So you've been with us four years," she said, going over her file.

"Almost five," Beryl answered with enthusiasm, awed by Barber's presence. The woman was one of the most formidable figures in the book world.

Barber continued examining the paperwork. Beryl's knee shook violently as she tried to keep herself composed. She was grateful her knee wasn't in plain view. She waited while the woman kept reading. Finally, Barber closed the file.

"Have you been going to college part-time?"

"No, ma'am."

"Not at all?"

"No, ma'am."

The chief executive sat back in her chair.

"Beryl, do you realize how competitive publishing is? Four years, almost five, as you put it, is long enough for you to be aware of the culture of this business. We have summa cum laude graduates from Ivy League schools doing menial labor just for a shot at an editorial position. It takes years sometimes to make any progress. Most people can't cut it and take their skills where they believe they'll be better compensated. This industry, more than anything, is a labor of love."

"Yes."

"I went to Barnard," Barber said. "Keri has a degree from Harvard. PaleFire takes the business of literature very seriously. We respect the word and those who have a command of it, and we do our very best to expose the world to the best material possible from the best writers, under the care of an excellent editorial staff. More importantly, we want to sell books. Lots of them."

"Yes, ma'am."

"So why are you here?"

"Because you asked to see me."

"No, why are you here? What are you doing in publishing?"

Beryl stared blankly at the woman. Barber waited for her to say something. A good ten seconds ticked by, and still Beryl was silent.

"Hello? Anybody home?"

"Oh. Sorry. I kinda zoned out."

Anna Barber was not one for games.

"Beryl, this is your life. You're sitting in front of the head of the company and you 'zone out'? That's not acceptable."

"I didn't mean it like that, Mrs. Barber, really," Beryl explained. "I feel honored just to get to talk to you like this. I would never take an opportunity like this for granted."

"I'm glad to hear that. I called you in here because Keri thought it was important that I know who you were. I make it a point of being aware of all our employees, but Keri insists there's something about you."

"Thank you, Mrs. Barber."

"So again, Beryl, I'm going to ask you, why are you here? Why would someone who didn't finish high school or choose to go to college seek a career in publishing?"

"Because I love books, Mrs. Barber. I read all the time. My whole life has been built around the promise I find inside of books."

Anna Barber fought back an approving smile.

"Then you can't stop learning, Beryl. If you're going to be in publishing, and I mean really be a part of it, you'll do your best to learn as much as you can. You'll read, and you'll read, and then you'll read some more. You'll meet people. You'll memorize *Publishers Weekly* and *Booklist*. You'll be aware of every new book about to come out and you'll read every magazine you can find, watching for emerging trends, trying to capitalize on them long before they've trickled down to the masses so that you can have books on the hottest subjects, ready to deliver to the consumer. I've accomplished a lot as a woman in this business because I care, truly care, about the line of work I'm in. It's rewarding work, but it's also very challenging, and

the less educated you are, the more uneven the playing field is going
to be."

"Is college mandatory?" Beryl asked.

"No, but it definitely doesn't hurt."

"Is high school? Are you saying there's no way I can learn this business from the ground up, the way I've been doing, and reach the levels I'm confident I can achieve?"

The publisher took a deep breath, weighing how to answer.

"I have to admit, Beryl, I don't come across too many people in
this business without degrees. Most are academics. English majors, lib-
eral arts."

"But I'm good at this," Beryl said. "I know what makes a story
work. I don't know how I know it, but I do."

Anna Barber contemplated the slight girl sitting across from her.

"Keri says it was your hard work that helped put *The Sun Giant* at
the top of the *Times* bestseller list."

Beryl smiled graciously.

"She said you even offered good marketing ideas."

"The author's six feet eight and really tan and fit. And he's from
California. It just seemed to make sense to take advantage of that as
we promoted the book."

"It made a lot of sense. Dollars and cents."

"Thank you, ma'am."

"She said you were a pretty good writer. I was impressed, considering your limited training."

"Keri showed you my writing?"

"Of course. I asked to see it."

Beryl glanced at the floor, gathered her confidence, and met Barber's eyes with her own. If she was going to convince this woman she
belonged, her bearing needed to reflect that. This was a golden
moment that she didn't want to ruin.

Anna Barber made a groaning sound, like she was tired.

"Well, young lady, it looks like all your helpfulness has put us in a
bit of a bind."

"I'm sorry, Mrs. Barber?"

"All right, first things first. Stop with the 'ma'am.' I'm not that old."

"Yes, ma'am. Sorry. Okay."

" 'Okay' is much better. Now, it seems our six-foot-eight best-selling author is asking for you specifically to edit his next book. He says that's the only way he'll do another contract. I knew we should have pinned him down to a three-book deal. These mid-list authors sometimes get a little cocky when they get a breakout book."

Beryl was simultaneously horrified and excited. It was February 1994, a time when it wasn't yet in her to do whatever it took to get to the next level.

"What does Keri think? Is she mad? Does she want you to fire me?"

"Of course she's not angry. And we're not just going to throw you to the wolves. But this will be a moment of truth for you, Beryl. I'm doing this on the strength of Keri's confidence, and because after talking to you, I sense a spark of determination that could really turn into something bright."

"Thank you, Mrs. Barber!"

"Keep in mind that you will be closely monitored. Just prove us right for taking this chance with you. And don't worry about Keri. She's a pretty happy camper right now. She got a nice bonus for how well *The Sun Giant* has been performing, and now she's getting the O.J. book."

"What O.J. book?" Beryl asked.

"O.J. Simpson. We did a deal with him last year for a book that we plan to release this summer. I was going to edit it myself, but I've decided to assign it to Keri."

"That's great."

Barber smiled.

"We're really excited about it. It's called *The Cutting Edge of Success: Principles of Leadership the O.J. Way.* We're positioning it with a Stephen Covey–type feel, with a whole line of *Cutting Edge* spin-offs . . . journaling books, calendars, an audio series. We expect it will appeal to a very broad market. There'll be a huge rollout with lots of press, and O.J.'s agreed to spend the next two years helping us develop the line. It'll be great. He's such an American folk hero."

————

On May 15, *The Cutting Edge of Success* began shipping to stores nationwide.

On June 9, three days before the official pub date, there was an elaborate book-launching party at the penthouse of a wealthy art collector on the Upper East Side. O.J. stopped in on his way from a board meeting in Connecticut.

June 12 was the slice heard round the world.

On June 14, PaleFire issued a global memorandum to stores regarding pulling the unfortunately titled books.

On June 17, O.J. and A.C. were in a white Bronco, doing the hokey-pokey down the 405.

On June 20, Keri Porter had had her fill. She resigned, citing her and her husband's desire to focus on starting a family.

On June 27, Keri's authors, to nearly everyone's surprise, were reassigned to a novice—Beryl Unger—who was quickly becoming an in-house enigma.

The no-degreed, no-GED'd Beryl was officially made an editor at PaleFire.

The initial backlash was enormous. Editors who felt they had much stronger clout and qualifications resented the fact that an uneducated former temp had encroached upon their hard-fought territory. Beryl was faced with a rash of cold shoulders, stony stares, and bitter whisperings. At first she attempted to win favor with treats. Fresh-baked cookies were followed by bottles of homemade jams and chutneys. Pound cakes. Fudge. Everything she brought in was delicious. Her goodies were happily accepted. Beryl, however, remained unhappily ignored.

In time, she stopped trying, determined to earn the respect of her peers through sheer excellence and commitment. She was grateful to Keri Porter and Anna Barber for having given her a chance. But she really had O.J. to thank for accelerating her career.

And what a career it was, with year after year of award-winning authors and commercial successes. She remained at PaleFire another five years, until 1999, when Kittell Press stole her away. Four of her top authors followed her when she changed houses.

Beryl's life was wonderful, give or take a few things, which was why she was now lying on a couch at the office of Dr. Ripkin, and had been lying on his couch for the past sixteen years.

What Anna Barber and Keri Porter and all the authors that came and went in between didn't know about Beryl was that she suffered from OCD—obsessive-compulsive disorder. It wasn't the kind that manifested itself in small ways like washing her hands too much or checking locked doors twenty times too many. Hers was on a grander scale, a hyper pursuit marked by extreme cycles of perfectionism. This also explained her reaction to the task Keri had given her as an assistant to read the four manuscripts over the course of a month. Beryl had pulled it all off in a weekend because of the severity of her OCD.

She would immerse herself in projects, devoting days, weeks, some-times months of intense preparation. At the eleventh hour she would panic, second-guess herself, destroy all her hard work, and start again. Ripkin recognized this as a coping strategy, of course, born of tragic loss and the fear that comes with it, but it had threatened her ability to function normally, which was one of the reasons she'd first sought help. Beryl understood that the extreme nature of her actions might be con-sidered self-destructive, even though she didn't think it was wrong to pursue perfection to its absolute. This was Ripkin's biggest hurdle. It was difficult to effect behavioral change if the patient didn't consider the behavior a problem.

"Things can always be better," she said. "Why settle for mediocrity when all it takes for excellence is just applying yourself a little?"

Her eyes would shine with a Mooniefied glow, so deep was her optimism and conviction.

"I like things how I like them. No one can fault me for that."

And then she'd smile. Always the smile.

The doctor knew it wasn't about things being better. For Beryl, better would never be enough.

It had been many years of dealing with the OCD, a problem that, on its own, was challenging enough.

But little Beryl was a loaded pistol. A double-edged sword of sweetness with two secrets too many.

She was also narcoleptic.

Ripkin had met with greater success controlling the narcolepsy than he had the OCD. There was no cure for the neurological sleeping disorder, but through collaboration with a sleep clinic she had visited under an assumed name, he was able to prescribe a cocktail of medications that allowed her to deal with the narcolepsy without having to tell anyone about her condition. No one besides him knew she was clinically obsessive-compulsive, either. People just thought she was a tad hyper.

After trying a variety of medicines, Ripkin switched her to the combination she had been using for the past year, with excellent results. She was taking 200 milligrams daily of modafinil—brand name Provigil—a newer psychostimulant that kept her awake. The drug was so effective, it was becoming increasingly popular among nonnarcoleptics, who used it as a lifestyle drug to get more mileage out of their day. It didn't cause jitteriness like amphetamines, didn't affect nighttime sleep, and there was little or no need for the body to make up lost sleep.

The modafinil even improved Beryl's memory, which had already been close to photographic. One of the keys to her professional success was her ability to recall a face, name, or factoid in an instant. The drug brightened her sunny disposition. Turned it into nuclear euphoria. Beryl was the kind of person who was so damn happy, it was borderline annoying. Her life was all sunny days. She was hope ad nauseum.

In addition to the modafinil, she was taking 100 milligrams of a tricyclic antidepressant called clomipramine, brand name Anafranil. She obviously didn't need it for depression. The drug was supposed to serve two purposes: control her obsessive-compulsive disorder and suppress cataplexies, which were the sudden loss of muscle control that narcoleptics sometimes had after experiencing strong emotions.

Ripkin had been encouraging Beryl for years to tell her employer about her condition, but she refused. There was no way she was going to tell Anna Barber after the woman had given her an opportunity to be an editor in spite of her educational handicap. To announce her other issues would have been a death wish.

And now, she decided, after so many years had passed without anyone catching on, there wasn't a need to tell anyone. The new drugs had made it so there were no glaring indications. The doctor suggested a narcoleptic support group, another idea she rejected. What was the purpose? But she did take his advice about napping whenever she could, even if it was just for five or ten minutes.

She lapsed into microsleeps, although they were rare. She'd be in an editorial meeting, at a book party, or on the phone in the midst of a discussion and would begin rambling about something that had nothing to do with anything. Her mouth would be doing what it was supposed to do, talk, but she would actually be in a deep microsleep. She might walk into a broom closet instead of the bathroom, her body on unguided remote control and needing to pee while the rest of her caught a quick snooze.

She never experienced a cataplexy in public. At least, no one ever realized that's what had happened. But there were times when she'd collapse after someone on the phone made her laugh too hard. Moments later she would regain muscle control and resume the call, the person on the other end of the line baffled at her sudden disappearance. The same thing might happen if she became angry, which was rare.

The medication made narcoleptic incidents so infrequent that, when they did occur, she was able to pass them off as something other than what they were, and people accepted it. That was just Beryl, they reasoned. She was brash and outspoken, in a cheerful harmless way, ambitious, and damn good at her job.

Even though she sometimes acted a bit loopy.

The narcolepsy was now the least of Dr. Ripkin's concerns. The clomipramine proved effective in doing half what it was supposed to. It all but eliminated the symptoms of narcolepsy.

It did nothing, however, for Beryl's OCD, which was, officially, off the Richter.

Despite the doctor's best attempts, all he had been able to do after sixteen years was shift her OCD into a sort of haphazard rotation. In the beginning, she used to obsess over making everything, and everyone, good, better, best. Now the attention was focused mostly on herself. Once she began making decent money, she sank a great deal of it into what she believed was self-improvement. She overleveraged herself financially in the pursuit of perfection, but she juggled it well, with meticulous care, rotating through a balance of credit cards, taking out loans, always paying just enough to be able to get more. She had excellent credit. She had excellent debt.

Ripkin had seen Beryl subject her body to endless harassment, all of which she confessed to while lying on his couch. There had been six weeks of frenzy about the cut and color of her hair. It went from a high-luster black to a lovely, much-complimented strawberry blonde. Then honey. Light copper. It finally ended where it began, high-luster black. Her brows and pubic hair were dyed each time to ensure a match.

She had developed friendships with a handful of prominent designers because of a series of style books she'd done. Because of these relationships, dull-faced Beryl slowly gained entrée to the New York fashion circle. She was invited to the best parties in town. She received minor mentions in a variety of magazines, from *In Style* to *Vogue* to *Jane.* Her name began to appear in the gossip pages. She caught the attention of the media because of her ever-morphing style, something unusual among the normally staid book publishing set. Her waifish frame made her a well-suited style horse. Hip companies offered her swag. The newest lowrider jeans, sunglasses, bags. Designers sent over dresses when she needed to attend upscale affairs.

She had a flair for putting herself together. While most editors tended to stay on the conservative side, Beryl eschewed the bookish look. She rocked jeans and fur-sleeved jackets, couture skirts with baby tees. She was always incredibly packaged, complete with four-inch heels, her style more befitting someone at a fashion magazine than CarterHobbs, the publishing giant. She got away with it, even though it was starkly different from the rest of her peers. The top dogs liked her. She was a hitmaker.

She studied the details of the rich and successful. She read magazines to learn what the rich wore, where they lived, how they decorated. She emulated it all by degrees, according to the constraints of her budget, then put her personal spin on it.

Beryl became someone to know. The designers had motives. They didn't just dream of clothing. They sometimes dreamed of book deals, too.

Even if it was just a coffee table book.

Men weren't flocking to be with her ("she's got a butterface"), but she was on the social radar of the greatest city in the world. It had been a marvelous stroke of luck on her part, but Ripkin and a handful of medical professionals knew that, behind all the stylish flash and flair, lurked a troubled (and sometimes troublesome) woman.

When Beryl's face and pubic region erupted in angry rashes as a result of all the hair dyeing, the obsessive behavior shifted to her skin. She believed the way to fix all the breaking out was by attacking her skin even more. She had sixteen facials inside of a month (at varying locations throughout the city in an attempt to avoid the embarrassment of repetition). She wound up at her dermatologist's office, legs agape in his mortified face.

"See?" she said, pointing. "See them there? The whole mound is covered!"

"I'm not a gynecologist," the man said with a frown.

"Doctor, please. It's so humiliating. I can't go to my gynecologist for this. It's a skin problem. I got it from dyeing my hair and shaving my bikini line. I know, I know, I shouldn't have been shaving once I got the rash, but now it's worse. I just need you to fix it. Please?"

Beryl's rash-ridden loins came a bit too close to the doctor's face for his liking. He backed away and wrote a prescription.

"I've never looked between a woman's legs in my entire post-intern career," the doctor said to his nurse after Beryl was gone. His head was over a sink as he splashed his face with cold water. "God help me, I don't ever want to look between her legs again."

Alpha and beta hydroxies. Scrubs. Ointments. Sitz baths. Beryl wasted thousands of dollars (charged, of course). The rashes at both ends were cured fast, but her face remained inflamed and peeling for weeks, unable to handle the stress of all the chemical assaults.

Her pubic hair fell out.

She was devastated. What would Mr. Right think if he should happen to show up?

She visited her dermatologist at once. He refused to indulge her.

"Look at it," she said, her skirt hiked. "All the hair is gone."

The dermatologist was cold.

"Come back in six months. Give your skin a chance to naturally heal."

Beryl flashed the only physical gimme the universe had allotted her: a dazzling smile. The man was unmoved.

"Six months," he repeated as he escorted her out of the examination room.

It didn't take long for Beryl to begin obsessing about something else. She was on her third nose, despite her plastic surgeon's warnings about the fragility of her septum and a dangerous diminishment of cartilage. After meeting with the voluptuous actress Carmen Electra to discuss a possible children's book, Beryl showed up at work a week later with a fleshy set of 34Bs, even though her chest had been flat before. The implants were removed two months later when a Marc Jacobs gown— a gift from the designer—didn't fall just right over her new Electras.

Page Six in the *New York Post* was the first to acknowledge the missing tits.

Just asking . . .
Which fashion-forward publishing wiz had a sudden case of the chest mumps that seems to have been cured overnight? According to an in-house source, the flighty plain jane is more concerned about her bra size than books these days.

Beryl was inconsolable when she saw the paper. It was the first time Page Six had taken a bite out of her. She spent the day locked in her office, refusing to show her face. She wore a coat for the next two weeks. She couldn't believe that her boobs warranted a mention in one of the most powerful gossip columns in the world. On the one hand, it meant she was someone to be watched, but Beryl was an emotionally fragile girl, an insecure girl, and the idea that her breasts were being ridiculed was like a knife to the heart.

But she got over it, and these days, the focus was on her abs. She was a gym rat now, even though, at five feet two inches, one hundred and one pounds, there wasn't much of her to begin with. Her stomach had been crunched into a spectacular six-pack. Upon seeing a smoother, more feminine belly on a model on the cover of *Cosmo,* she decided she didn't want to look like someone who was ab obsessed. She stopped cold turkey and let the muscle definition lapse. Then she happened across a couple jogging together in Central Park. Both were in great form with classic six-packs. As she watched them go by, it occurred to her that when *he* came—and, of course, all of this was about *him*—he might want a woman with good abs. It was on with the crunches again.

For now.

Ripkin found himself playing guessing games about where the compulsion would travel next. Her mind, of course, was in a perpetual state of reinvention, which guaranteed him years of guessing and reliable income.

Beryl made it clear right away, at the very first session with Dr. Ripkin, why she had sought psychiatric help.

"There's some things about me that might scare a guy off."

"Some things like what?" the doctor had asked, wondering to himself what kind of parents would send their daughter to therapy because of what some boy might think.

"Oh, it's nothing major." She was smiling. "Little stuff. Stuff a professional like you could probably fix real easy."

She was young then, just sixteen. She sat across from Ripkin, her legs crossing and uncrossing nervously. She kept smiling at him. He found it fascinating the way her smile seemed to turn an otherwise bland face into something rather electric. It was bizarre.

"Are you comfortable?" he asked as he watched the petite girl shift in the chair. "Would you like something to drink?"

"No," said Beryl. "I'm fine."

"Did you come with your parents? Would you feel better if I brought them in?"

"My parents are dead."

Ripkin had been jotting on a notepad. He placed the pad and pen on a stand beside his chair.

"Who brought you?"

"No one. I came alone," she said, gesturing with impatience. "But that's not what I'm here to talk about, Doctor. We can talk about that later. Not just yet."

Her words were casual, abrupt. Ripkin still bristled when he thought about it. She spoke as though she were the one in charge, still smiling that smile that looked as if it had been nabbed from a prettier face.

"My apologies, Miss Unger. What would you like to discuss?"

Beryl stared at him. Her legs had stopped moving.

He waited for her to speak, but all she did was stare.

"Miss Unger?"

He waited. Another teenage brat, he mused, ramping up for a lifetime of analysis.

"Miss Unger?"

Ripkin leaned forward.

"Miss Unger!"

Her face was frozen.

Ripkin's butt was halfway out of his chair and he was about to go over to her when she started speaking again.

"I'm concerned that I might be what's perceived as 'a little difficult.' "

Ripkin lowered his butt into his seat and leaned back, wondering what the frozen silence had been about.

"What do you think they mean by 'difficult'?"

Beryl was smiling again, shifting in the chair.

"Well . . ." She toyed with her hands, weaving the fingers together. "I tend to be really anal about stuff. One of my teachers said I was a perfectionist. I thought that was a good thing. It is, isn't it?"

"Where do you go to school?"

She exhaled.

"I don't go to school. I dropped out. But I don't want to talk about that just yet, all right? So stop with the sidetracks already."

It was funny in retrospect, the nerve of the girl. He might have terminated the session at that point, but her jigsaw smile saved her. It was a right piece that somehow fit into the wrong spot. It held his attention.

"I want you to help me fix it so that people don't think I'm weird." Her legs were moving again, *x*s and *l*s, *x*s and *l*s.

All the nervous crossing made Ripkin suspect that she might be manic-depressive or have OCD. It was only the first meeting and there was no concrete proof, but more than likely one of the two would bear out.

"So you hear that a lot? That you're weird?"

"Sometimes. I don't like it. I don't think I'm weird. Well, not for that."

"For what, then?"

"That's the other reason I came to see you," she said. "I need help with this thing. It's a family problem."

"What is it?" Ripkin asked.

"I think it's narcolepsy."

"You think it's narcolepsy?" The words came out harsher than he intended and startled the girl. She rushed over and stood in front of him in a panic.

"But you can fix it, right? It's gotta be fixed. I don't want to be like the rest of my family and not do anything about it. I don't want to miss out on him. I came all the way here, all the way to New York, just for him."

"Hold on, hold on. Calm yourself down. Take your seat, please."

"I don't want to sit."

"Then take a deep breath, relax, and tell me who you're talking about."

Beryl ignored the first two suggestions.

"I'm talking about *him.*"

She paced. Ripkin was thinking he would take a pass on this one. Refer her to another psychiatrist.

"I'm sorry, I'm still not clear. Who is 'he'?"

She stopped walking and gave him a full-on look of irritation.

"My husband!"

"You're married?" he asked. "But you're just a kid."

"No, I'm not married. And I'm not a kid, I'm sixteen. You're not listening to me. I'm telling you he's here and I know it."

Ripkin was doing a mental retreat at this point, getting his bearings in case the whack job in front of him did something rash like try to attack. He was large enough to subdue her if necessary. He wondered if she was carrying a gun. She had on a sundress. Didn't look like she could be hiding a gun underneath. Her hands were empty. It could be in her purse. Teenagers were crafty. He decided to remain cool and keep her talking until he could think of a way to get her out.

"Is he your boyfriend? Your fiancé?"

"No. I don't even know him yet. He's my soul mate."

"Your soul mate. I see."

That was it. The girl was certifiable.

She had calmed a bit.

"He's coming, and I need your help."

It had been a long day that day, sixteen years ago. Ripkin had seen six patients prior to her. His ex-wife had called to complain about the house in Cape Cod he was letting her use for two months for free. He was giving a speech at the Princeton Club in an hour. His head was throbbing, and this black-haired, mismatched-mouthed teen ranting in front of him was making it worse.

"I'm not sure I can help you," he said. "But I can make some excellent recommendations. In fact, one of my colleagues on the West Side has expertise in this very kind of thing."

Beryl's eyes widened.

"Of course you can help me. You're the only one who can help me. I read about you in the paper. They said you're the best. Please, Dr. Ripkin. I know I seem crazy right now, but I'm not. I'm really not. It's just that I'm young and, and, and, I'm kind of small for my size, but I'm not crazy. I just know what I want. I'm definitive. Definitive, Doctor. That's not crazy. It just means I know what I want."

Crazy people were always announcing how crazy they weren't. It was their battle cry before the chaos began.

"I've been waiting my whole life for him."

"You're just a teenager. You haven't lived your whole life. That may not make sense to you now, but in a few years—"

"But I don't know when I might meet him, and I can't afford to take any chances." She was frantic again. "I don't want him to reject me over something as stupid as narcolepsy. Or for being too anal, even though I don't think I am. I need you to fix me. Please, Dr. Ripkin. Please. You have to help me."

She was crying, hysterical.

Ripkin was about to open his mouth when she collapsed in an unconscious heap at his feet.

That was how it had started. This invisible man, the one who was coming, was the primary topic every week. Even as Ripkin worked steadily to help her get the more pressing conditions under control, it was all she talked about.

He got the backstory along the way. The narcolepsy had started when she was twelve. Her parents had done nothing to address it, even though school officials desperately tried to enlist their involvement. Beryl became a social misfit. Because of the collapses and erratic behavior that came with the condition, school friends began to distance themselves. Other kids, cruel kids, saw her as a comical oddity, a punch line for jokes.

"You're getting veddddddddy sleeeeeeeepy," one boy used to taunt.

"Sleep on this!" teased another, grabbing his nuts.

A group of boys peed on her when she dozed off in the stacks at the library. The librarian found her there moments later, soaked in tears and urine.

Her parents moved her to a different school, but that was worse. Four years later her parents were dead, victims of a car crash that Beryl survived. Narcolepsy ran in her family, and now the tribe was nearly extinct. She was the last of the Ohio Ungers, and she didn't know her mother's side of the family.

Her paternal grandfather had been run over by a tractor he was driving after having a cataplexy and falling out of the seat. His wife had been working with him in the fields, on foot just a few feet ahead, planting seeds. The tractor mowed her down as she tried to outrun it. After their deaths, Beryl's father, Neil, was raised by foster parents. He was also narcoleptic. His foster parents were embarrassed by it, but did nothing to help. Neil couldn't keep a steady job because of the fits. He went into a microsleep at the wheel as he drove his wife and daughter to McDonald's one Friday night, his typical way of celebrating payday. He veered headlong into a semi. His wife snatched the wheel but it was too late.

Neil Unger was a proud, simple man, just like his father. He chose to risk putting his family in harm's way to avoid the shame of having to admit he needed medical help.

Frightened, shaking, clothes tattered, knees skinned, suddenly alone, Beryl had made an instant decision right there at the hospital, even as she was still trying to process the fact that her parents were gone. Rather than be placed in foster care like her father, the sixteen-year-old had walked out of the hospital in Galena, the small town outside Columbus, Ohio, where she'd been raised, gone to the bus station, and gotten a ticket for as far away as she could with the money in her parents' wallets, which were surrendered to her by the attending nurse. It was five hundred and sixty dollars, the bulk of it from her father's freshly cashed payday check, which he never bothered to deposit in a bank. There was enough cash to get her to New York, a place she'd read about in books and magazines, a place where dreams were realized and destinies fulfilled. Someone at the Port Authority told her about the Harlem YMCA. Beryl didn't know much about Harlem, but a cheap room was a cheap room. She had enough money to cover a two-week stay in one of the economy lodgings (she got an even cheaper rate by convincing them she was a student, despite not having any proof). She was also able to buy a change of clothes, basic toiletries, and food. There was no extended family back in Galena who would come looking for her. She was the end of the line. She was on her own. She'd gotten a copy of the *Columbus Dispatch* at a newsstand in New York and found a write-up about her parents' deaths and the accident. There was no funeral. Beryl couldn't afford it, and, as far as she knew, they didn't have insurance. No one ever came back to claim their bodies from the hospital morgue. The nurses were puzzled by the emotionally rattled teenager who had arrived with the ambulance, taken her parents' wallets, and disappeared.

She considered surviving the car wreck as the intervention of fate. Ditto her arrival in Manhattan and getting a job (compliments of a fake ID) three days later, the following Monday, at a temp agency, which promptly placed her in a job at PaleFire, smack in the middle of the publishing world. She sought Ripkin's services the same day, after reading about him in the Sunday *Times*. She convinced him to take her on despite the fact that, with her new low-paying temp job, she couldn't

afford his exorbitant hourly rate. Ripkin had been stricken by conscience and moral responsibility. Especially after she collapsed at his feet.

"I think you've come to the wrong place," he said. "We should get
you the proper help. A young girl like you in a city like this with no
home, no family. I know the head of Covenant House," he said,
reaching for the phone. "I'll give them a call now and see if we can
get you situa—"

"But I'm not homeless," Beryl said. "I have a room at the Y. I've
only been in the city three days. I'm not some homeless street person.
I have a plan for myself. And now that I have a job, I'm going to try
to find somewhere permanent to live."

"I don't think I can help you," said Ripkin. "This is too much for
you to take on. The cost of living alone will be more than you can
handle. This is an expensive city. The last thing you need to be wor-
rying about is trying to fix yourself so you'll be right for a man. Perhaps in a few months when you've gotten settled you can give me a
call and I'll refer you to some state-funded clinics with staff psychiatrists who may be able to offer you affordable assistance."

"But Doctor, you're the best. Please. I'll work hard, I promise. I
won't take your help for granted. I just don't want the kind of life my
parents had. I never want what happened to them to happen to me."

Ripkin studied the girl. She was so young, so fragile, yet so determined. Even after having just cataplexied in front of him, she still
mustered the confidence to further plead for his help.

Something in him broke. The failed father. He could try again. It
wasn't the real thing, but he could offer her guidance. This little girl
needing looking after. He would help. For starters, he took her on pro
bono until she was able to pay.

She was a star now in the industry. Half her life had been spent in
the business. Her nonlinear ideas had proved a boon during a time
when books were losing momentum. She was a pioneer in cross-
marketing, going beyond what most editors did with her zeal for publicity and maximum exposure for her authors, never hesitating to
capitalize on the high-level relationships she'd cultivated from Wall
Street to Madison Avenue.

And today, that day, a day that already had sentimental value to her for other reasons, she had received even more good news. She had blurted it to Ripkin the second she walked in the door.

CarterHobbs was promoting her to a VP position, and although she would still be working at Kittell Press with Kitty Ellerman, there was the ultimate promise of her own imprint someday soon. But she wouldn't be just any VP. She would be entering the ranks of the most elite editors, those who existed in a world where the salaries were not based on logic, but hype and buzz. Beryl was aswirl in buzz and CarterHobbs wanted to show her their level of faith. At the tender age of thirty-two, her pay had just been raised to an astronomical three hundred thousand dollars a year, plus profit-based bonuses.

It might not have seemed like a lot to someone on Wall Street, but in Beryl's world, she was living a dream.

Half of her authors were the purveyors of what Ripkin considered a most insidious cancer: outrageous, fantastical tales of love and triumph—*Sex and the City*–type tonics—snake oil in print peddled to a generation of progressive women who should know better.

It was the fairy tale on crack, books that weren't content with just the traditional happy ending. These deadly works passed themselves off as authentic reflections of the real world, and rewarded their heroines with gorgeous, love-struck, deep-pocketed, commitment-hungry, jet-setting moguls/sex machines, blinding, multicarat flawless diamonds, haute couture ad infinitum, social status, beautiful Gerber babies who slept through the night, and high-powered careers that could be picked up and abandoned at will.

It was sick stuff, he thought, all of it, much more dangerous than the standard romance fare filled with Victorian settings and stock characters most women were able to distinguish from truth. The books Beryl hawked were present-day, set in major metropolitan cities, and peopled with characters living ordinary lives that suddenly turned extraordinary. Balderdash. To believe in it was lunacy.

Twice divorced, with three grown children (including that estranged daughter) and an immortal alimony, Ripkin was long over the allure of *l'amour*. It was a road to ruin that didn't need to be prayed up and prepped for; it had a dastardly way of throwing itself under one's feet. Yet Beryl, even as she helped shape the prose of her writers, bought into the dream lock, stock, proving herself, in Ripkin's opinion, to be a greater fool than the readers of such dreck.

"Suppose he's not here," he posed once. "What if your true love is somewhere else? What if there is no true love? Could you live with that?"

"This is where fate brought me. He has to be here."

Ripkin decided not to delve into the flawed concept of fate. She could figure that one out on her own.

It was by sheer luck that she wasn't a virgin. Six months into her job at PaleFire, a guy from the mailroom came on to her at a company party. It was the first time anyone had ever shown interest in her. They did it at her place. The coworker tore her clothes away and was on her with a startling wildness.

Beryl was so excited, so grateful and surprised by the attention, that she had a cataplexy in the middle of the act. Scared the fuck out of the poor guy on top. She had been thrashing beneath him, then suddenly went limp. Several scary seconds later, she was back, her thrashing renewed. The guy's erection was deader than Latin. He fled naked from her bedroom, his clothes bundled under his arm. Beryl was so embarrassed, she never spoke to him again, taking great measures to avoid running into him. A month later, to her relief, the guy left the company.

Other sexual encounters followed over the years, but they were sparse and more utilitarian in nature. Most were extreme cases for when she needed an adjustment, which wasn't often as she was an exceptional masturbator. The medications had diminished her sex drive by half. Having little interest in sex made it easy to wait for the One.

Sixteen years later, and he still hadn't shown up.

She was stylish, with a painfully ordinary face. Except for the jarring smile. When someone saw her, sex was not the first, second, or fifth thing that came to mind. It was the nature of her aesthetic that caught the eye. The sublime elegance and attention to detail, the order. The sheen of her hair, each strand a curved note in an impeccable symphony. An exquisitely worn scarf. The deliberate turn of an expensive Italian heel. The gentle whiff of something citrus.

Over the years, she had crafted everything about herself with great care. She was her own best product. Ripkin found it ironic that the same obsessive-compulsive behavior that had her lying on his couch once a week resulted in a magnificently engineered professional ascent.

No one in her life knew of these sessions every Thursday at six. Beryl made no note of it anywhere, paid in cash, kept Ripkin's phone numbers secure in her head, and never uttered his name outside the four walls of his office. Image was everything.

She was good on the surface at socializing and had a rather charming way with people, despite what most wrote off as somewhat neurotic behavior. But she never let anyone get too deep. With the exception of Ripkin, she kept her guard up. It would only come down for the right man at the right time, and that time had yet to come.

She could have found love long ago, thought Ripkin. Lesser women were doing it every day. Beryl was so exacting. Another sixteen years could pass and she'd still be waiting, morphing and remorphing every step of the way.

"So you'll never tell him about the narcolepsy?"

"Of course not. Why do you keep asking me that? I'm not going to change my mind. The man I marry doesn't need to know. The medicine has it under control, so there's nothing to discuss."

"It's been in three generations of your family. You could pass it on to your children. He has a right to know that."

"Narcolepsy's not that big a deal anymore. It's not like it's hemophilia. Relax, Doctor. Relax. Narcolepsy's not going to kill me."

This from a woman who had four dead relatives in her wake because no one in her family had acknowledged the condition. Ripkin shook his head.

"Not telling him about it will cause you to worry about being discovered. That will only make your condition worse. Your obsessive-compulsive nature will be aggravated by having to operate with such—"

She raised her head. Her eyes narrowed, a gesture she used sparingly for dramatic effect. He abandoned the issue. The girl was an idiot. A self-absorbed idiot. This was why he was not a good parent. He couldn't brook foolishness. Not like this.

He realized he was allowing himself to become too affected by his patients, even though he never showed it. Should he retire? This had become a charade. There were three other psychiatrists in his practice. He could transition his patients to them. The thought of no more droning, whining, nouveau riche brats was appealing, perhaps even necessary. Each week that Beryl came in and began her lament, his desire to shake her and scream *"He's not coming, you twit!"* intensified. What happened when the day came where he said it aloud?

Of course he would never do that, could never do that. His was the one profession where it was acceptable to attempt to fix something and get paid for sending it back home broken. What other job condoned such a thing? Week after week, month after month, year after year, the customers dragged their broken selves back for more nonfixing, paying the nonfixer each time, thus conditioning the nonfixer to continue nonfixing.

This was the precise pattern of many of his peers—keeping patients broken, creating cadres of static, unnatural dependencies, just to make money. Ripkin wanted to believe he wasn't like that. He had chosen this profession because he truly wanted to heal troubled minds. Especially patients like Beryl. He was supposed to be helping her, but the passing years had exhibited little change.

"So I'm back up to a hundred crunches in the morning and a hundred at night," she was saying now. "Do you think that's too many? Maybe I need to stave off a little. Muscles have memory, you know."

"Beryl, have you ever heard the phrase 'love comes when you least expect it'?"

"Of course I have," she said. "I'm an editor. I've heard every phrase in the book." She smiled at her own pun. "But that doesn't mean I should just sit around not doing anything. Is that what you're trying to say?"

"You've achieved a great deal in your life."

"You say that like my life is over, after I just told you I got a big promotion today."

"That's not how I meant it. You're an . . . you're . . . you're an attractive woman." He told himself it wasn't a lie. She was attractively packaged, if not in the face. "You're celebrated among your peers, one of the Who's Who of Manhattan. At thirty-two. Thirty-two, Beryl. That's quite an accomplishment. You must realize, of course, that any man would be fortunate to have you. It might sound clichéd, but it's true. You need to recognize this."

After sixteen years of protracted whining, will you ever recognize this?

"I know it," she said with confidence. "Why are you talking like this? I've never had any self-esteem issues."

Ripkin's face was blank.

"What? Why are you looking at me like that? I don't have self-esteem issues. Not real ones. Sure, I'm concerned about some things, who isn't, and I try to be better. That's self-improvement. But it's not like I don't believe in myself."

The Roy G. Biv array of hair colors. Old breasts. New breasts. Old breasts. Three noses. Her abs. Surely she wasn't serious. Ripkin's eyes met hers. Surely, tragically, unbelievably, she was.

"Right," he said. "Of course. Very well, then. Have you ever heard the phrase 'sometimes you have to take the bull by the horns'?"

"Yes, Dr. Ripkin. What's your point?"

"My point is this: it seems hardly likely that you are going to stop looking for love at every turn, which sends that first saying out the window . . . about it coming when you least expect it. You're always expecting it. I doubt it could ever sneak up on you. So since you're always looking, why not be aggressive about it? There are many reputable agencies in the city that offer exceptional matchmaking . . ."

Beryl sat upright, jaws rigid, arctic-blue eyes icily trained on him.

"Our time's up, Dr. Ripkin."

He glanced at his watch.

"My word. So it is."

He closed the notepad he was holding, took off his glasses, rubbed his temples with two fingers.

"Oh," Beryl said in an upbeat voice. "I almost forgot. I brought you something."

She reached into her oversized purse and pulled out a plant. She walked over to him and held it out. She flashed her specialty, the thousand-watt smile in the five-watt face, waiting for his reaction.

"Why, look." Ripkin was deadpan. "Another African violet."

"Sure is. I got it just for you."

"Your favorite flower. How delightful. You shouldn't have."

"Don't be silly. Of course I should. It's for my favorite psychiatrist. Today's our anniversary." She placed the plant in his regretful hand along with a wad of cash for the day's session, then made for the door, walking backward.

"See you next Thursday, Doctor."

"Looking forward to it," he muttered. "Why are you walking like that?"

She stopped, her eyes wide with surprise.

"Like what?"

"You're backing out of my office." He glanced down at her feet. She tucked her left foot behind her right one.

"Oh. No reason," she said with a girlish giggle. "I guess I just wanted to look at you as I walked away."

"Of course."

He watched her back away like a crab, an awkward grin on her face. Who knew what she was trying to hide. He turned away to help ease her mysterious behavior. There was obviously something she didn't want him to see.

Ripkin waited until he heard the ding of the elevator as the doors opened and closed. He counted to twenty. He stared at the plant in his hand.

"Once upon a time, I liked your kind."

The African violets were yet another manifestation of her anxious nature. Somehow, years ago, she'd gotten it into her head that since they were her personal favorite, giving them as gifts could be a definitive way of expressing her affection. Ripkin hadn't addressed it with her because the flowers were just another of her many, many tics. He knew she gave him the African violet in spite of herself, perhaps fearing that if she stopped, he wouldn't like her anymore.

He heaved a series of deep breaths as he took the plant over to the windowsill and placed it alongside the thirteen other African violets Beryl had given him before.

"Pretty soon there'll be no room for me to make a decent leap. Guess I'll just have to throw myself down the stairs."

He turned to find Beryl standing in the doorway staring at him.

"I'll never understand British humor," she said. "Throw yourself down the stairs. Is that supposed to be funny?"

"No, of course not. It was a joke for the plants. I talk to them from time to time."

"Really? I'm so glad. I had decided this would be the last time I gave you one. Well, I mean, maybe, I don't know. I wasn't sure you liked them. But now that I know you do . . ." She clapped her skinny hands together. "This is great. Hasn't today been a great day?"

"Splendid," he said. "Did you forget something?"

"No. You did."

Ripkin walked to his desk, imagining the horror of African violets that would soon be his office. He leaned back in his chair, emotionally beaten.

"I'm sorry, Beryl. I'm drawing a blank."

"You forgot to congratulate me," she said.

"Ah yes," he said. "I thought I did." He tugged his right ear. "Congratulations on your promotion, Beryl. You deserve it."

"That's not what I'm talking about, silly. I meant my new apartment. I move in tomorrow."

"Right. The new apartment. Of course. Congratulations, Beryl. Well done, indeed."

"I feel like such a grown-up. I own an apartment in Manhattan now. Can you believe it? I really have come a long way, Dr. Ripkin. Thanks to you."

"Yes, well, you've worked hard for it, Beryl." He was, admittedly, proud of her. It was a bit like watching one's own child grow up. "Triumph of the good will always prevail."

Beryl laughed.

"Okay. I'd better get out of here before you start getting deep. Later, Ripkin."

"Good night, Beryl."

He watched her leave, backing out again as she did before. Silly girl. This time he made sure he saw her get on the elevator, which she also backed into. He waited another pregnant second, then spun his chair toward the window and began to contemplate the ledge.

Realism:

A literary and philosophical movement emphasizing life as it truly is, without reliance upon idealized or romantic notions, often stressing social factors as key in the development of character.

You have to make every moment count. It's not easy to do, you know. I don't think that a day goes by when I don't turn my back on some small thing or some issue somewhere.

—Blake Edwards and Milton Wexler, *That's Life*

Four in

. . . the morning and Miles Tate was almost out the door.

"Where are you going?"

The voice was soft, unmistakable, filtering down at him from the shadows at the top of the stairs.

"No," he muttered.

And now she was coming, down, down, down the steps in bare feet, bringing her displeasure close, where it could be most effective.

Miles was a tall man, a dapper slab of meat that cast shadows even in the darkness. Splotches of moonlight covered him now as he put down his briefcase, the broad muscles across his back twitching beneath the Burberry coat. He made a quick signal outside, then closed the door on the heavy fog shrouding the Town Car waiting in the circular driveway.

"So you were just going to leave without telling me."

She was on the landing now, about to step onto the cold marble that led into the foyer. Such a treasure, he thought, as he watched her swing her sensuousness toward him. The tiny La Perla nightie was splendid advertisement for his wife's long lean body and perfect legs, her bosom heaving with every step.

She stepped into the dappled light of the entrance hall, her illuminated face staring up at him.

"You were, weren't you?" she said. "Right?" A crinkle in the swatch of skin between her eyes.

Miles cleared his throat, his standard battle prep.

"Now look here, Shar—"

"Don't even, Miles. You were just gonna go without saying a word."

Miles Tate was successful because of his foresight and business acumen. He was a masterful negotiator. "Everyone can have everything" was his mantra. That mantra didn't seem to be flying at home of late. Hence the need for a predawn exit. Rather, the attempt at one.

"Why'd you have me come out to the country if you knew you were planning on leaving again?"

"I didn't know I was leaving," he said. "Some unexpected business came up."

"Unexpected business is always coming up, Miles. Where to this time?"

Ah, there it was. The loaded gun. There'd be gale forces in the wake of his response. Miles put his hands on his wife, admiring all of her at arm's length. Then he pulled her close, nuzzling his face into her neck.

"God, you're so beautiful. Do you know how hard it is for me to leave you like this?"

"Don't try to play me, Miles. Just tell me where you're going."

He heaved a deep breath. Might as well be done with it.

"I'm off to Helsinki—"

"Helsinki!" She shoved him away. He staggered back a step, but didn't break his vocal stride.

"Looks like the board of Golarssen and the Finnish government have approved our bid and the merger's going to happen."

"You are such a liar." Her eyes were black lines with a flicker of rage, feline in the splotchy light of the foyer. "This couldn't have been an impromptu business trip. How in the hell can you just break out in the middle of the night, headed to the other side of the world, unless you expected this was coming?"

"I didn't expect it. Things have been so off and on . . ."

Sharlyn's body flushed hot as Miles kept talking.

". . . this wasn't planned, which is why I want to get there, get this thing hammered out, and get back—"

"Just stop it."

"Really. This trip comes as a complete surprise. There was the pos-

sibility that it might happen, but not so quickly. I had planned on taking you to Finland with me when the time came. I've been learning
quite a bit about the place, you know. It's really fascinating. You'd love
it. Do you know that fifteen-year-old Finns have the best literary skills
in the world?"

"This is a fucking Fellini film," she muttered.

"What was that?"

Did she just say the f-word? He bristled. No, she wouldn't do that.
It was a part of their rules. A random "shit" or "damn" was tolerable,
pushing it even, but he had a thing about women and swearing. Having a wife who did it was unacceptable. The sole exception to that
rule was in the bedroom, and then only during sex. And although
Sharlyn's books were filled with obscenities, he allowed her that folly.
The words were on the page, not in the air.

Sharlyn's temples were throbbing. She pressed her fingertips hard
against them.

"So what were you planning to do, drop me off at a Finnish high
school?"

Miles chuckled.

"No, baby. Don't be silly."

"Fuck you, Miles."

It was the f-word! All right, he figured, okay, he'd let it slide this
time since he was trying to make an uncomplicated exit. Sharlyn
moved in closer. He could feel her breath upon his face.

"I've been to Finland," she said, "which you seem to have forgotten. I have a Finnish publisher. I've had one for years."

"You do?" The f-word was still ringing his ears. "God, Shar,
you've done so much. I can barely keep up. And you talk about my
job—"

"Fuck you and your job."

And she dared to say it again!

"Maybe that's it," Shar smirked. "You're fucking your job, because
you sure as hell aren't fucking me these days. You're never on the
ground long enough."

The f-word clanged around in his head. She was trying to provoke
him, forcing a confrontation. Miles refused to let himself get drawn

into it. He gritted his teeth, determined to give her a pass, just this once, for urgency's sake.

"What are you saying?" He pulled her close, pressing her hand into his crotch. "Here. Feel this, Shar. Doesn't that tell you something?"

"What's the point in showing it to me," she said, yanking her hand away from the hard knot in his pants. "It's not like you have any plans to use it."

At those words, something in Miles snapped. The refined corporate mogul returned to his Atlanta roots, putting his Southern foot down in an outburst heavy with a usually undetectable hard-lined Georgia drawl.

"Now you look here, Sharlyn Tate, this trip can't be helped. I got word that Jussi Seppinen is ready to talk, and I'm the only one who can do this deal. I can't hand it off to someone else. That's just the way it is. This isn't just some job. I built this company from nothing, and now it's the third largest of its kind. In *the world*. Don't you understand what that means?"

Sharlyn trod the marble, her feet suddenly cold. He was about to resort to the speech.

"How do you think we can afford this lifestyle?" Miles's voice was a blade as he waved his arms around the vast foyer of the equally vast house. "You wanted the Hamptons, I gave it to you. The apartment in the city. The houses in L.A., Tuscany, Capetown. Vacations around the world, everything you ever asked for. An island, Shar. I bought you an island. Don't act like none of it hasn't meant anything."

"All I wanted was you."

"Well, that's not what you said last Christmas when you insisted on having that Maybach."

"You said you wanted me to have it."

"I wanted you to have it because you said it's what you wanted. You saw Beyoncé in one, so you wanted one, too. Beyoncé, for God's sake! But did I complain? Did I ask why the hell you were trying to keep up with the MTV crowd? Those people are kids. You're a grown woman. Three hundred thousand dollars and I didn't say a word. We already have a Rolls, but I got you that damn car. Even your driver thought it a ridiculous purchase."

"He did? He didn't say anything to me."

Miles took a breath, sheathed the blade. "Look, Shar . . . this stuff doesn't pay for itself. We got here because I made this happen. What I do pays for our lifestyle, and I know that's something you don't want to give up."

"Miles, you know you don't have to work like this. I'm one of the most popular authors in the country, in the world. I make more than enough money—"

Her words caught on themselves at her husband's granite expression. His scowl was apparent, even in the predawn shadows. Sharlyn swallowed, casting her gaze at the floor. She knew the type of man she was married to, had been married to for eighteen years. It didn't matter that her career as a writer had brought them millions or that she was an A-list celebrity. Miles was from a long line of traditional Southerners. Caretakers. Men's men. Men with clearly defined lines about the roles of women. Percival Milestone Tate would never be anybody's kept man, and he wouldn't let anyone, especially his wife, intimate such. She had already pressed his patience hurling the f-word around. Now, it seemed, she was exceeding all limits.

"Good-bye, Shar."

He turned and picked up the briefcase, triumphant in the way he found his exit. He'd flipped it on her and could now leave in a blaze of pseudoindignation.

Sharlyn rushed forward, reaching for him.

"Miles, honey, look . . . that's not what I meant."

She pressed her breasts against his rigid back, encircling him with her arms. He lingered a moment, hand on the door.

"Don't be angry, baby. Please. I'm sorry. I just hate that we never get any quality time together anymore. I miss you. I miss us. It's affecting everything I do."

Miles didn't move.

"I haven't been able to write. My concentration is all messed up. My manuscript is eight months overdue. Beryl's been on me every day. Readers keep posting on my website, harassing me about this book. 'What's it about?' 'When is it gonna drop?' I've stopped reading the message boards. It's too much pressure. More, more, everybody wants more. Eight months. Do you realize that's how long you've been on the road?

I asked for that car because I was bored. I'm reading magazines and going to stupid house parties and club openings with Diamond and Kimora and a whole lot of people I've grown tired of looking at and who must be growing tired of looking at me. You want to know how I spend most of my days? Watching TV. I can't stand TV. But what else can I do? I can't write, Miles. Don't you get it? What I do is directly affected by you."

She could feel his body soften under her touch.

"What do you expect me to do?" he said in a low voice. "I'm the first black man in history to run a company as global as ComMedia Wells. We're billionaires, Shar. Billionaires. I need you to understand what that means for me, for us . . . for our people. This is not about acquiring things and chasing the almighty dollar. This is about being examples for an entire generation."

He was doing the *our people* bit. She never knew how to fight against that.

"I know, honey. It's just that, sometimes, I feel like you're married to ComMedia Wells and I'm just your . . . I don't know . . . mistress."

His back was rigid again.

"Mistress? Why would you choose that word? Are you accusing me of having a mistress? Is that what you're trying to say?"

"No, baby, of course not, baby. I know you're not like that. But I feel like ComMedia is your real home and I'm the odd girl out. What am I supposed to do?"

Miles turned the knob and opened the door.

"You're supposed to let me do my job," he said. He turned to face her. "My home is with you. I always come back, don't I? I've been at your side for almost twenty years. Even though all you greet me with these days is a face full of shit."

Sharlyn's mouth was ajar, a jumble of unuttered words wrestling in the damp air as Miles stepped out into the morning. It was rare for him to swear at her like that, but she had pushed him to it, hadn't she? He wanted to let her know how it felt.

Miles didn't glance back as the driver held open the back door of the car, then quietly closed it once his charge was inside. The man tipped the brim of his cap at her, got behind the wheel, pulled off, and they disappeared into the thickening mist.

Naturalism:

A literary and philosophical movement emphasizing realistic, scientifically objective, often sordid and graphic accuracy in the portrayal of the human existence.

Everyone who has ever built anywhere a
new heaven first found the power thereto in his own hell.

—Friedrich Nietzsche

Killer Klowns

. . . from Outer Space.

He pressed the info button on the remote. A beige bar appeared at the bottom of the screen.

"Alien bozos snare earthlings in cotton candy cocoons."

Cotton candy cocoons. He was watching alien klowns and cotton candy cocoons. God. His life was shit and being parked on the couch like this was the proof of it. Fucking killer klowns. Klowns. With a capital *K*.

This is what happens to those who sit still, Penn reminded himself. People who did nothing ended up with nothing lives lived on nothing furniture inside a nothing space doing nothing watching nothing being nothing. They became supernovas of nothingness that turned into black holes of pathetic shit as they sank in on themselves and disappeared from existence. People like that were not even missed.

"I am not a nothing," he said. "I am a star."

These words were directed at the killer klowns, those dastardly demons of sugar-tomb spinning. The klowns didn't seem the least bit moved. They had earthlings to ensnare.

"Fucking idiot box."

He clicked off the TV. The transition of sound was seamless, as the yammer of the tube was washed over by the beckoning din of city life whirling around outside his window, filtering in as only a seductive, mild-temperatured Manhattan afternoon could. Honking horns, laughing people, crying babies, barking dogs.

All that noise, all those happy people. He placed his hands flat on the ledge as he peered outside. What the hell did they have to be so happy about?

He was feeling way too dark. Perhaps, he thought, he should get out for a while. It was Sunday afternoon. Half the day was gone. He needed to get his papers—the *Times,* the *Wall Street Journal,* the *Post,* the *Daily News.* Maybe he'd grab some takeout and stop by Merc's.

Another horn honked. Penn slipped on his shoes, shoved his keys in his pocket, smeared on some Kiehl's lip balm.

The city was calling.

•

Merc wasn't home and his cell phone was going straight to voice mail.

He must be with some girl, Penn thought. Or maybe he was working. He sometimes did on Sundays if a job was starting to fall behind schedule. Mercury King had been Penn's best friend since freshman year at NYU. He had an M.S. in architecture from Columbia, but instead of going straight to a firm as a draftsman, he chose to work as a contractor for his uncle's building construction company. The money was good, more than he would make as a newly licensed architect, and it was hands-on experience in building and construction.

He admired Mercury's willingness to take the long route to get to where he wanted. It was more than he would do.

Penn had a grand plan. And while it wasn't happening as quickly as he expected, he wasn't giving up. He already had the hard part handled. The masterpiece was ready. The rest was all execution. Soon enough. Soon enough.

He headed back home with his papers and sushi.

Adam stood

. . . next to Norman Mailer, Toni Morrison, Jason Epstein, and Salman Rushdie, all smiles at the Fifty-sixth Annual National Book Awards. Penn's hands shook as he held the paper. He still couldn't believe it. His eyes shifted right and there Adam was again, this time hugging a hot, leggy blonde, a Jessica Rabbit by the name of Seda Burstow, one of the sexiest, most talked-about authors of the moment, known for the As You Wish series, a line of books about the art of female submission. (What was *she* doing at the National Book Awards?) Adam's pocked face was perilously close to the swell just above the plunge of the front of her gown. Penn felt his stomach tumble.

Adam Carville hobnobbing with Salman Rushdie. Seda Burstow's double-Ds near Adam's face. What nonsense was this? It had to be some kind of joke.

But, alas, it wasn't. He scanned the top of the page. This was the Sunday *Times*—the *New York Times.* It wasn't Page Six. If it was, if this had been the *Post,* then there might have been another explanation. It could have been a mistake. The *Post* was prone to mistakes on occasion—that was half the fun of reading it. He'd fucked a girl who used to work there who'd regaled him with a tale of how, one night, she and a couple of disgruntled employees got drunk and made Photoshop pics that bogusly matched people together. They put fake heads on known bodies and fake bodies under known heads, and all of it managed to slip into production unchecked. People were fired, retractions were made, but it was the *Post*. They were used to taking heat. Penn remembered laughing really hard at the silly girl's story. It was post-coital laughter. He tended to be generous after sex, less intellectually exacting than usual.

But this wasn't the *Post*. It was the *New York Times,* just like the header said, and there was his graduate-school classmate, one suckass Adam Carville, in the company of the world's most renowned literati (and titterati). The *Times* had run an additional page of photos recapping the event, which had taken place during the week. Penn had heard that Adam was a nominee. He'd gotten a group e-mail about it from one of his former professors. But he'd rejected the thought, as though refusing to believe it would make it not so.

Penn found himself imagining what would have happened if some unupdated zealot had decided to carry out the rescinded fatwa on Rushdie and it went badly awry, taking out Adam Carville instead. Adam's blood, guts, and gore all over Rushdie, Mailer et al. Toni's mouth hanging open in horror, her panged keen frozen in time, captured for posterity. Jessica Rabbit's bloodstained boobs. Now that was a picture he would have loved to have seen. That kind of photo would have surely been in the *Post*. The *Post* only cared about the trashy stuff. Which was appropriate when it came to Adam Carville.

Penn crushed the paper into a tight ball, hurled it to the floor, and gave the spare wooden chair across from him a hard horizontal kick. The thing hit the wall and disassembled at once, a frail house of sticks. IKEA.

"Fuck!" he screamed, now standing over the broken chair. "You rickety piece of shit!"

He stared at a little white tag on the underside of a slat of wood from the rickety piece of shit. Like everything at IKEA, the chair had a name. Per the white tag, this broken creature had been dubbed Bernby. The fact that the chair was introducing itself at this inappropriate moment reignited his rage. Penn stamped his right foot down onto Bernby, snapping him into splinters. There was some relief in that. Some, not much. It still didn't erase the reality of those photos of the worst writer in his entire M.F.A. program at Columbia University in the *New York Times* (!!), beaming astride the lions of literature. Morrison! Epstein! Rushdie! Sexually submissive big-tittied authors! What the fuck!

He should just call it a night, he thought. He needed to. But sleep these days was a reluctant bedmate, making rare appearances, if bothering at all.

That he didn't wear such internal turmoil and restlessness was a testament to his impeccable genes. To see Penn in all of his lean, sculpted Nordic perfection was not to notice the heated thought weaving in and out, uncontrollably, as evidenced by how he now sat in front of his desktop computer with its oversized, illuminated flat screen, punched in "www.nytimes.com," and pulled up all the photos from that dreaded National Book Awards ceremony. He couldn't stop himself. It was a train wreck begging for eyes. He had to see more, even though he knew it would have his colon lurching for the rest of the night.

He got up, went over to the TV, and put in the DVD of Wagner's *Die Walküre*. It was the one conducted by James Levine at the Metropolitan Opera with the fabulous Jessye Norman, his mother's good friend, in the role of Sieglinde. Penn considered the great diva nothing less than a goddess. He had watched the DVD five hundred times too many, just for her, to the point that it was now one of his main soundtracks of solace. He had imagined himself Siegmund to her Sieglinde. Her soaring voice soothed him. He needed to be soothed right now. This Adam situation had gotten him stirred up plenty.

It was a long DVD, just over four hours, enough to get him through his continued investigations on the Internet. He adjusted the TV to a volume loud enough to appreciate the music and Jessye's voice. Not too loud. His neighbors had a tendency to get touchy at times.

He was barely back at his desk in front of the computer when stomping could be heard from the apartment above.

"Fuck you," he mumbled. "Just leave me alone."

Countless surfed sites later, he was still sitting at the computer, the back of his neck hot with sweat. He had the phone in his hands, punching the buttons.

"Yeah," came the familiar grunt. "It's late. What do you want?"

"Did you see the paper today?"

"It's two o'clock, man. It's two o'clock in the morning."

"Adam Carville is in the fucking *New York Times*. His picture's all over the Net. He's on the official website of the National Book Foundation."

"I'm hanging up."

"Merc, seriously. How could this happen? You know this guy. He's a bucket of rocks. And now he's being feted like he's the fucking Second Coming. What the fuck is that?"

"Three fucks in under a minute. That's my limit. Good night."

Dial tone. Penn called right back.

"Go to bed, man. Stop calling me. You knew he was a nominee. We talked about it. This is not news. Stop sweating some shit you can't control."

"But Merc, it's Adam Carville. This is a man who says 'mischievious,' 'sim*u*lar,' and '*ir*regardless.' "

"He's still in the paper." Merc yawned. "Irregardless of how he speaks."

"You're kidding me, right? You're just trying to fuck with me. Adam Carville blows. We've had a million conversations about that."

"What difference does it make? Get over it. Focus on making your own shit jump off. I don't know why you're even panicking. You know your stuff is good."

Penn was so discouraged from the pictures of Adam and Merc's cavalier response, he could feel his chest constricting. He cranked up the TV. The orchestra was deep into "Ride of the Valkyries," playing the song with vengeful gusto. Penn had lowered the music to appease the stomping earlier, but he didn't care now. He needed to hear something loud and booming. The three-hundred-pound gorilla in the apartment above him pounded the floor. The sound resonated throughout the room, above the music.

"Is that the fat man?" Mercury asked.

"Who else?"

"Turn that down and go to bed before he calls the cops on you again. What happens to Adam has nothing to do with you. His book struck a chord, and that's that with that."

"What did you say?"

"I said Adam's book struck a—"

Penn was halfway across the room. The phone had been thrown to the floor. He shot an angry glance at Bernby, still fractured in the corner, streamed some consciously pissed thoughts about how much he hated IKEA with all its sleek, cheap trappings and the fact that it was all he was able to afford, then made his way toward Ekeberg, his sleek, cheap IKEA bed.

Two hours later, he was fucking his neighbor from two floors up, a broad in every sense of the word, with fleshy gams and a rough tongue, which he liked her to flick around his bum, relishing the sensation of the cold wetness against his puckered flesh. She had twenty-four-hour availability, and a wide, sturdy back. She was flat on it, and he was Paul Revere.

Forty minutes later, he was writing in his journal.

Thank goodness for Eunice. If it wasn't for her deep pussy and low self-esteem, I might have gone stone postal today.

Pennbook A. Hamilton was that most tragic of things: a jealous genius. And he was, in fact, a genius, having scored at the highest end of the intelligence spectrum, ten points past two hundred, two hundred being the number where it became moot to continue to measure. It was a ridiculous score, one that his parents took great care not to reveal to him for fear of the pressure such an extreme number would bring. Theirs was a world immersed in academics and the arts, peopled with a wide range of talented individuals. They had seen the circus act that sometimes came with the celebration of prodigy and genius, and wanted their only child to enjoy as normal a life as possible, not one lived under a microscope of curious scrutiny. Penn was allowed to gravitate naturally to the things he enjoyed without being forced in any particular direction.

It had been obvious from early on that he was different. He had an ear for melody and could read both music and polysyllabic words before he was two. He entered his first piano competition at age four. The event was at Tanglewood, one of the most prestigious music centers in the world. It was a concerto competition for high school students, but he was allowed to participate because of his mother's close friendship with Harry Ellis Dickson, the late, venerable music director laureate of the Boston Symphony Orchestra. Penn wasn't considered a formal contestant. It was all just whimsy, really, as his mother tried to reinforce on the drive up to the Berkshires.

"So there's no pressure, darling," she said, mussing his hair playfully. "This is only for fun."

Liliana Clarke Hamilton was a mezzo-soprano at the Metropolitan Opera. At five nine, she was lissome and elegant, a graceful swan with classic features and lustrous blonde hair that fell upon her shoulders and around her face in a way that made her seem otherworldly. Penn and his father, Dane, considered her presence a fortuitous occurrence, as though she were a seraph on holiday and had somehow floated into their world. Dane, a theoretical physicist with substantial inherited wealth who served as a consultant for the United Nations, took great care not to do anything that might send her rushing back to whatever celestial place she had descended from. To her credit, Liliana acted as though she didn't recognize her own beauty or believe herself more entitled than anyone else, even though she held sway over every room she entered, every man within reach, and every woman who ever dreamed of possessing such ethereal luminosity. Penn adored her almost as much as his father did. She was his original measure of perfection. There would never be another on such an impossible par.

Almost everyone in their circle found it necessary to point out to Dane his tremendous luck in snagging Liliana. He was a man of letters, not looks. Not that he was a hunchback. Seeing the two of them together didn't drive passersby into hushed huddles of shock over their gross mismatching. Still, he wasn't her visual equal, not by leagues, and he knew it. But Liliana respected intellect, and he possessed it in great abundance. Their union, to her, represented a harmony of music and the mind. She didn't give the aesthetic issue much consideration until the birth of their son. When Penn arrived, he was gorgeous and golden, just like her, with her musical leanings and his father's brains, and he had it all in spades, at even greater, more accelerated levels. Seeing the way people reacted to the child's physical appearance alarmed Liliana and made her finally come clean about herself and how she had achieved much of what she had because of society's shallow fixation with beauty. She was determined to not leave to chance how Penn dealt with the way people reacted to his. She was equally insistent that his artistic and intellectual talents not be overindulged. If Penn believed he was special, it could prove more harmful than good. Liliana convinced her husband of this and he stood firm alongside her decisions regarding the boy. She read books on parenting children, she attended lectures and seminars. She was careful about everything when it came to her boy.

She had reminded Dane beforehand to back up her comments on the drive to the Berkshires for the piano competition. He didn't like denying his son anything and was secretly ecstatic to be the father of such a unique child. Dane knew Penn would want the spoils of victory, whatever they were, if he happened to win. The little boy was doggedly competitive. But Liliana always prevailed. She was the only god in Dane's otherwise scientific, atheistic universe. Penn would just have to accept that this would be one of those times when it wasn't about winning, and that needed to be clear before they arrived at Tanglewood.

"Son, there's no prize or anything," Dane said. "You understand that, don't you?"

"Yes, Daddy. Mommy just said it's only for fun."

"Very good. So if they like you and try to give you something, don't accept it. Just bow with respect and say 'Please, thank you, but could you give it to someone else?' Can you repeat that for me?"

"Yes, Daddy."

"Let's hear it."

"Please, thank you, but could you give it to someone else?"

"Good boy."

Penn looked up at his father. Dane and Liliana always spoke to him plainly. There was no need to dumb things down for a child with an IQ of 210. He didn't behave like a typical four-year-old.

"But why can't I have it if they want to give it to me?"

Liliana intervened.

"Because, dear, the kids in this competition are on the verge of becoming adults, and this is a chance for them to go on to scholarships and more public appearances, maybe even a serious music career. This event could be life-changing for one of them. You won't be an adult for a long, long time, so you can't even take advantage of what this kind of exposure brings. You'd be taking something away from someone who could really use it, just to please your ego, and that would be wrong. Very wrong. We don't want to be wrong now, do we?"

"No, Mommy."

She kissed the top of his head. The little boy stared at the road in silence, his hands folded in his lap. Liliana was relieved.

"But do you think I could win, Daddy?" Penn asked after a moment.

"Sure, son. Anything's possible."

Dane glanced over at his wife, anticipating the slight downward turn of the left side of her mouth. Their eyes met. She moved her head a fraction, just enough for her husband to recognize it as both a shake of disapproval and a command for him to amend his statement to the boy.

"Just enjoy yourself, son," Dane said obediently. "Play because you love it, not just to win. That's the only reason to ever do anything in life. Do it with zest, or don't do it at all."

"Do you think the people will love me?" Penn asked.

The question startled his mother, particularly his use of the word "love" instead of "like." Penn was not one to make casual slips of the tongue. When he said a word, he meant it.

"Don't worry about the people, Penn," she said, pulling him close. "Daddy's right. Don't just do things for prizes or money or to impress other people. Do it because the very thought of touching those keys and creating beautiful sounds excites you. Let that be your motivation, not adulation. Adulation fades."

"Yes, Mommy."

Penn was the last to perform at the concerto competition. He was the unexpected finale to an array of outstanding performances.

Everyone thought it was cute at first, the minimaestro in tails climbing onto the piano bench and bowing his head in quiet contemplation. A smattering of giggles and coos could be heard in the audience. Little Penn had already made up his mind after the conversation in the car. He inhaled and exhaled four times. Deep, slow breaths of fresh oxygen that filled his blood with a conviction of spirit. He lifted his head, raised his fingers in dramatic display, wriggled and cracked the knuckles, then launched into Franz Liszt's arrangement of Wagner's *Tannhäuser* Overture, one of the most difficult works for piano. It began slow and simple enough, then moved into a series of complicated runs and flourishes at octaves his tiny hands did not physically have the capacity to accommodate, yet somehow pulled off. Penn played it from memory, with remarkable execution and agility. He had played it a few times at home. His only exposure to the piece had been at a performance of the Berlin Philharmonic a year before, yet he had captured and retained every note.

When he finished, the crowd sat in a collective stupor, blown back by the sheer enormity of what had just happened. It was the kind of synaptic logjam that occurred when one saw a UFO, a check for thirty billion dollars, a giraffe at close range. It was the opposite of a gasp, which would have meant the body was still functioning properly with the ability to defend itself against surprise. Seeing a four-year-old play something most masters wouldn't attempt had brought about that arrested deer-in-the-headlights kind of moment where the brain, clobbered with disbelief, struggled to sync itself with what the eyes had just witnessed.

The little boy waited. The stupor swelled to its maximum capacity and exploded. A moment later, the audience was on its feet with thunderous applause, foot-stamping, and cheers.

He was proclaimed the winner. The teens looked on in shock.

Penn stood at the front of the stage, golden, glowing, awash in adulation. It was the greatest feeling he had ever known. He wanted to feel it again and again.

His hands lingered upon the prize as it was offered to him. He hesitated a moment too long, devastated that he couldn't take it. He heard a familiar sound coming from the front row. His father had a unique way of clearing his throat, in staccato clacks, almost a hacking sound.

"Please," Penn finally parroted, "thank you, but could you give it to someone else?"

The crowd was on its feet again, roaring with approval.

People who had been in attendance still talked about the beautiful towheaded boy, the "little Liszt" who wowed them that day. There was a standing offer for him to return when he could really compete.

Later that night, back at home in New York, Penn made his first journal entry in a diary his mother had given him for Christmas. He was an excellent speller. Even at four.

I won today. I played the piano and beat everybody. They were all bigger than me. I feel good. I want to win again.

He would keep such journals the rest of his life.

Penn had the astonishing ability to recognize complex patterns and immediately calculate probabilities and solutions within those patterns. Dane would often play chess by himself as a means of concentration, and after young Penn kept harassing him, he taught the boy how to play. By age six, Penn had won his first national championship. Five more followed. He eventually lost interest in formal competition, but it didn't stop him from being challenged by anyone who heard he had a knack for the game, especially when he was in college. He would trounce them in seconds, with swift, one-handed moves, sometimes while drinking a beer or watching a game on TV. He won twenty thousand dollars the first time he played Texas Hold'em with a group of trust fund brats at prep school. They tried to convince him to compete in the World Series of Poker, but Penn wasn't interested. Chess, piano, and poker were for sport. He would always toy around with them, but he had greater pursuits in mind.

He finally discovered his IQ when he was almost eighteen, after the plane carrying his parents went down over the Central Pyrenees, making Penn an instant orphan. They had been on holiday in France and were en route to Spain. Penn was away in boarding school at Choate at the time, just two months shy of graduation. He immediately came home upon hearing the news.

The executor of their estate, Peter Fleming, Esq. of Messrs. Fleming, Hunt, and Stein, informed Penn that all assets, properties, and monies, some seventy million dollars' worth, would be liquidated and given to charity.

Penn had been dumbstruck. He stared blankly at the executor, unable to process the meaning of his words.

"Mr. Hamilton?" said Fleming. "Do you understand what I've said?"

"You said something about charity. They're giving some money to charity?"

"They're giving everything to charity, Mr. Hamilton."

Fleming flipped through papers in a folder, avoiding eye contact.

"It was important to your parents that you have a full understanding of what it means to forge your own way, should anything ever happen to both of them before you came of age. They were people of principle who worked hard for what they—"

"I know what kind of people they were. I don't need you to tell me about my parents."

"Then you should understand that this is what they wanted."

Fleming opened and closed the folder. He would never get used to the delivery of bad news about money. People seemed to take it harder than they did death itself.

"There are provisions for a basic living allowance, and all expenses associated with your education will be covered, of course, as long as you choose to pursue it. The stipend will end once you've finished with school. The first semester's tuition to Harvard has already been paid."

"How much is the living allowance?"

"Three thousand dollars."

"Three thousand dollars!" Penn shouted. "That's nothing!" He took a deep breath, squared his shoulders, shook his head. "That's barely enough to get me food and clothing if I need it. God forbid something drastic comes up. At least I won't have to worry about rent. I'll just stay in the apartment in the city. I guess I'll just have to scrounge for everything else."

Fleming's brow was growing moist. This kid just didn't seem to understand.

"I'm afraid, Mr. Hamilton, that you will have to worry about rent. Not during your college years, of course, the dorms will be covered, but thereafter, once your formal education terminates, you're on your own. Everything is being liquidated. That includes the Park Avenue triplex, the estate in Lloyd Harbor, and the apartment in Paris. The will calls for them to be sold and the money turned over to various charities."

Penn stared at the folder in Fleming's hands, unconvinced.

"But I'm a charity! What about me?"

Fleming's face was hot. The beads of water on his brow were full enough to run down his face. He pulled a handkerchief from his jacket pocket and dabbed at his forehead.

"I don't believe I'm making myself clear."

"Well, speak up, then. What gives here?"

Fleming coughed, loosened the strangling knot of his tie. He coughed again. He still couldn't bring himself to look at Penn.

"Everything is being given away. Except for money for school and your living expenses while you pursue your education, you will get nothing else."

Penn's back was rigid as he sat across from Fleming, who was mighty glad there was a desk between them.

"What about the place in London?"

"The Belgravia town house is being sold. Everything is being liquidated."

Penn's head was swimming.

"There is good news, however." Fleming's lips lifted at the edges in what he hoped would be construed as a smile.

"I can't imagine."

"Your father left you his car."

Penn brightened.

"The Porsche? Awesome! I was beginning to think that he didn't give a shit."

Fleming wiped his face with the handkerchief. This was awful. He wanted it over.

"I'm afraid it's not the Porsche," he said, inadvertently correcting Penn and agitating him further. *POR-sha*. Penn had said *Porsh*. "He left you the Ford."

Penn's nostrils flared. He was borderline combative.

"That ten-year-old Taurus?"

He was standing now, his palms pressed flat on the desk as he leaned toward Fleming. "Are you fucking kidding me? That thing is a wreck. One pothole and it's over."

The Ford had been Dane's practical car. The one he drove everywhere for everything. The Porsche was for special affairs, rarely driven, and as such, was in mint condition. Why couldn't his father have left him that?

"What's going to happen to the Porsche?" Penn asked.

"It's being sold and the money is going to charity."

Penn stared at the man.

Fleming nervously slid a bulky manila envelope across the desk toward him.

"Here are the keys, along with the check for your living allowance. The checks will arrive every first of the month. The car is parked at the garage across the street. The valet ticket is in the envelope."

"What about my things? I have stuff at all our residences. Will I at least be able to go get them? C'mon. This is sick. It's cruel. Why would they do something like this to me? My granddad didn't do this to them. My father got all that money, all of it at once, when Grand-dad died. Granddad wasn't cruel enough to give it away to charity."

"Your father was an adult when your grandfather died. Your grand-father believed he sufficiently understood the value of money."

"I understand money!" Penn barked, slamming his hand down on the desk.

"Your things from all the houses have been packed up and placed in storage," Fleming said, refusing to be sucked into further debate. "The key and the address to the storage unit are also in the envelope."

Penn snatched the envelope.

"I don't have to take this. I'll contest the will."

"You have no grounds. This is the way they wanted it. Any court in the state of New York will uphold this document as legally sound."

Penn's chest heaved as he glanced around the room. Fleming feared he was looking for something to break or throw.

"I assure you," Fleming sputtered nervously, "your parents had only your best interests at heart . . ."

Penn's eyes were sky-blue icicles.

"I'm quite confident that you will be very successful in life, in spite of this . . ." Fleming couldn't stop himself. He wished his mouth would just stop working. "They spoke of you often, you know, of how proud they were of your—"

"Let me ask you something," said Penn. "What would have happened if just one of them died? Would I have come into any inheritance?"

Fleming hadn't anticipated this. He didn't know why. It wasn't an uncommon question.

"That's not really relevant now, is it? What good does it serve you to know something like that?"

"I'd like an answer."

Fleming went through the folder, shuffling through assorted legal documents until he came across the one he was seeking. He scanned through a few pages.

"Here it is." He didn't look up. "If one of them died before or after you were twenty-one, you would have received an amount equal to half the value of the estate when you turned twenty-five. If you were twenty-five or older at the time of death, you would have received your share of the inheritance immediately. If both died after you were twenty-one but before you were twenty-five, you would have received the assets in their entirety."

"At twenty-five." It was more confirmation than question.

"Yes. At twenty-five. But if they both died before you turned twenty-one, you were to receive nothing but the stipends for school. The rest was to go to charity."

Fleming knew this was torture for the boy. It was torture for him, so he could only imagine. There was no way to minimize the harshness of how things had played out.

Penn was still standing, disgusted by the entire ordeal. He shook his head, his lips pressed pencil-thin.

"I can remember quite clearly discussing this with Dane and Liliana," said Fleming, tapping the document with his index finger, still avoiding Penn's face. "The rationale was that as long as one of them was alive to assure you had a practical understanding of finances by a certain age, then you could be entrusted to receive your inheritance."

"Do you agree with what they've done?"

"It's not my place to set the dictates of my clients'—"

"Tell me the truth. What do you think? Do you think this makes sense?"

"Mr. Hamilton, these questions aren't going to solve any—"

"I just need to know," Penn bellowed.

Fleming's collar was ringed with sweat. It was at least sixty-eight degrees in his office. He liked it cold, although the paralegals complained. He wanted to buzz someone, anyone, to get the temperature lowered even further. A few minutes more and he would combust.

"Your mother in particular had some concerns about what it would mean for you to have that type of financial access without their guidance. They were confident in their ability to be your moral compasses into adulthood, but were unsure of what it would mean for you if they died before that. Liliana feared you would be unduly influenced by outside forces, or that perhaps you'd find the money a bit intoxicating, which, admittedly, it can be—"

"My mother. So this was my mother's doing."

"Yes, but your father agreed that—"

"Of course he did. He was her fucking slave. We all were."

The room was beginning to feel like a sauna to Fleming. He removed the tie. The stretch of silk that had encircled his neck was soaked. His underarms were circles of sweat. So were his back and his waistband.

"Your parents didn't want to see your future squandered. This is just a safeguard for your protection. You'll come to see that one day."

"They fucked me is what they did. They flat-out fucked me."

Fleming's mouth hung open.

"One last question for you," Penn said. "What would have happened if they both had lived? When would I have seen my inheritance?"

"Mr. Hamilton—"

"Tell me!"

Fleming swallowed a hot ball of discomfort and flipped through the folder. His voice was a monotone, robotic, when he spoke.

"You were to receive two million dollars when you graduated from college. Another fifteen million was to be released when you turned twenty-five, along with a transfer of the title to the town house in Belgravia. The remainder was to be disbursed in accordance with the deaths of either or both of your parents if it occurred after you were twenty-five."

"None of it makes any sense," Penn said.

He turned away abruptly, heading for the exit. His eyes were steamed over and blurred with rage.

"There's one other thing," Fleming said.

Penn stopped at the door, wordless, waiting.

"There were several cases of papers in the attic of the house in Lloyd Harbor. The will detailed in great length how everything was to be liquidated, down to clothing and shoes, but there were no provisions for the cases of papers. It was determined they should go to you. They've been placed along with your things in storage."

Penn chuckled bitterly. His hand was on the doorknob.

"Great. They shaft me when it comes to money and shelter, but all the meaningless shit comes straight to me." He turned to Fleming. "Papers, huh? And who knows what doozies are lurking in there. Maybe I'll find out I'm adopted. That'd be the perfect turn of the screw, don't you think?"

Fleming's entire body was sticky with sweat. Everything about the boy was giving him the creeps.

He was immensely relieved when Penn walked out. He raced from his chair and bolted the door for good measure, then poured himself a double of scotch.

Fleming hadn't been lying. There were papers. Many, many cases of papers.

One was filled with nothing but sketches. Drawings Penn had done when he was a child. They were filed by age. The first was a rendering of his yellow bath toy, Rubbiduck. Rubbiduck had been his favorite, in the tub and out of it. It was a decent sketch. The shape of the duck's bill was accurate, as well as the head and body. Flecks of red were drawn on the sides to indicate shading. Rubbiduck floated on a rippled surface of blue.

"This is cool."

He noticed his mother's delicate scrawl in the lower right corner.

"Pennbook A. Hamilton. Nineteen months."

"Shit."

He riffled through all the sketches. A self-portrait at five. A detailed drawing of the Louvre at six. A surprisingly exact picture of his father at work at his desk, done when Penn was three and a half.

He vaguely remembered liking to draw, but he hadn't done it in years.

He moved on to the rest of the stuff. Case after case of school-related materials, none of it of any real interest.

He was about to put it all off for another time when he came across a case filled with his report cards, medical records, and the results of psychological and academic proficiency examinations he had taken over the years.

There, in a folder marked CONFIDENTIAL: P.A.H., was when he first saw god.

Not the biblical deity.

Himself.

Inside the folder was his intelligence quotient, and the score, when he saw it, was so staggering, so gargantuan, so outrageous to behold, it seemed to rise from the page like a three-dimensional skyscraper. It was Willy Wonka's elevator, the one that had so much force, they couldn't make enough floors to contain it, so it burst up and out, beyond cables, shafts, and logic.

It was a pivotal moment. Like Clark Kent discovering he was Superman.

Penn was sitting on the floor of the storage unit when it happened. It took all the breath out of him. He stared at the number so long, his eyes glazed over.

210.

2. 1. 0.

Two-ten.

He could barely wrap his suddenly big brain around it.

This was why his parents kept telling him he wasn't special. This was why his mother had said, yes, he was gifted, but gifted children were not uncommon. The onus was on him, she said, to make the best of his abilities with hard work and applied learning and blah blah blah blah fucking blah.

It had all been a colossal lie.

"Awesome!" he said, slapping the ground. "Now it all makes sense!"

Chess, poker, the piano, the way he breezed through school. Math, physics, biology. English, Latin, Spanish, French, Portuguese, Russian, Norwegian. He could speak nine languages fluently, including Xoo, an African tongue comprised of clicks that he picked up in two weeks during a trip to Botswana with his parents. He was nine at the time. The Africans had been afraid of him. They thought he was an evil spirit that had returned in the form of a child.

If it had been left up to his parents, he would have never known. It was one thing for them to leave him with no money, but this was unforgivable. All the warm regard, respect, and adoration he felt for them was destroyed in an instant, as he realized his whole life might have been different but for the knowing of this one detail.

An IQ of 210 was just plain stupid. It was higher than the speculated IQs of Mozart, Darwin, and Galileo. Einstein's IQ was supposedly 160. Penn's score was beyond the range of Nobel Prize winners. It put him in the company of Goethe, Leibniz, and Stephen Hawking.

He fell back against the floor, rolling with laughter. He kicked his legs in the air.

There were other documents that confirmed the score. His mother's scrawl was everywhere, rebutting its value. He came across a letter where his parents rejected an opportunity for him to be skipped three grades, from fifth to eighth.

It is our belief such an action would give our son a distorted view of himself and create an environment where he would be perceived as freakish and unnatural. Nothing good could come of it. We would like him to follow the normal progression of his peers.

It was his mother's handwriting (again!) on a photocopy. She was the mastermind behind everything. *Our* belief. *We* would like. Had his father really agreed with all this? Why would he allow it? What an idiot Dane Hamilton, the theoretical physicist, had proved to be. The man was blinded by his wife's mesmerizing beauty. Liliana Clarke Hamilton was his mental kryptonite.

Penn was laughing, but it was derisive, more like outrage.

He thought he had known his parents. He was used to them trying to downplay his beauty, even though it proved futile. He knew he was physically exceptional. It was something his parents couldn't refute, short of having his face and body reconfigured. He excelled at athletics, and everyone fawned over his looks. His face and good body afforded him incredible access—access he was more than willing to avail himself of with the opposite sex. Being the best-looking male in the room for most of his life had been a big deal. But none of that could compare with the IQ thing. It was stupendous news. Reality-altering.

"I'm a genius," he said, clutching the paper with his score. "A fucking genius." He stared at the wall ahead of him, reveling in this new-found truth. "I'm a god."

He logged it in his journal that night.

Today I discovered that I have an IQ of 210. It is the best news I've ever had, even though it's outlandish. Two hundred and ten makes me a universal genius, with superior talent in almost everything I do. Da Vinci was a universal genius. I might even be the best-looking genius in history. All the ones I've ever seen look shot to hell. My thanks to whoever or whatever made that plane go down. I renounce my mother. She was a selfish bitch. I will never forgive my father for being so passive and letting her do this to me. I vow from this day on to never be like him. No woman will ever control me, especially not a beautiful one.

Penn's attitude changed drastically. Almost overnight, he developed the sense of arrogant entitlement his parents had worked so hard to keep at bay.

He aborted his plans to attend Harvard, opting instead to stay in the city and go to NYU. His mother had been against him attending school in the city, but he was determined to do everything in defiance of her. He lived on campus so that his housing would be covered as a part of his educational expenses. He prolonged his education even further by attending Columbia postgraduate. By that time he had already decided how his universal genius would make its public debut.

Many geniuses throughout time had been known to embody something called radical humility. It meant they were aware that their genius was not their own; that it came from a powerful source, something greater than them, and they were therefore instruments through which that higher power was manifested. Because they weren't responsible for this greatness, they didn't aspire to promote themselves or their gift. They were tools of God, and realized they would be used as such. Radical humility was a trait that had been present in some of the greatest spiritual and intellectual leaders in history.

Penn, apparently, was missing this gene.

He had big plans for his genius—*his* genius—which he attributed not to God, but to the excellent manner in which his parents' DNA had blended. There would be no radical humility for him. No way. There'd be lots of self-promotion, plenty of it. What was the purpose of having such a gift if one didn't plan on wielding it with flash and fanfare?

He would become a famous writer first. Not a theorist, like his father. Not a filmmaker, like so many attendees at NYU. He didn't want to be behind a lens. He wanted to be in front of it. The center of attention. He would mark his path from a place of intellectual and commercial respect.

But that wouldn't be the end of it.

Being a bestselling author was just the beginning, the first step in a master strategy, one which would effect the implementation of the theory of Richard Wagner, whose work he had come to idolize over the years, since that moment all those people at Tanglewood had lavished him with praise for playing the *Tannhäuser* Overture when he was four. Since then, Penn had become an expert on Wagner, well studied in the man's music and life.

In 1849, Wagner had introduced a concept called *Gesamtkunstwerk*. The translated meaning of the word was "total artwork," or, as Penn liked to think of it, "a total work of art." Gesamtkunstwerk proposed a comprehensive integration of music, song, dance, poetry, stagecraft, and the visual arts to create the ultimate synergy of expression. Penn planned to alter the components a bit, integrating literature, music, fashion, and film. It would still be Wagner's theory, with slight variation.

He would become a living example of Gesamtkunstwerk. The unification of many talents within a single interface: himself.

It would be a portrait of the artist as the perfect brand.

He had never discussed this grand scheme with anyone, not even Mercury. His best friend would give him the crazy look for sure.

But he knew it would work, and he would be adored by the world. He would be bigger than the biggest brand-whores. He would eclipse Martha Stewart and Donald Trump. He had studied what they'd done, but he was going to take it to an even higher level. The world would gaze upon him in wonder.

It had never seen the likes of someone like him.

He had

. . . a hard time keeping his resentment in check after discovering he had the genius factor.

It tortured him to see lesser souls like Adam Carville flourishing, getting National Book Award nominations (!!), when he was having to struggle. It defied natural order.

Penn believed in no gods. His father had been a man of science, not faith. Religion wasn't a part of their lives. Penn was taught to either create his own opportunities or maximize existing ones, within the boundaries of humanity and goodwill, natch. The goodwill part was dead to him now. His parents hadn't shown him goodwill when they chose to leave him practically penniless. So their teachings meant nothing now. To wait for intervention from a higher power was folly. Faith and higher powers were empty cloaks of comfort for the ignorant and weak. How could he have faith in a higher power? His parents had been higher powers of sorts, and as it turned out, they sucked.

He purposely chose not to write any short stories for submission to literary magazines over the course of his college career and after. He didn't want to build a career through appearances in *The New Yorker* or by writing for the school paper. He put all his effort into his novel, his most excellent untitled novel. He was convinced it would be a success.

He had written the book while still at Columbia and had received a

great deal of praise from one of his favorite professors, the very distin-
guished Ben Marcus, who had read portions to the class, lauding it as an
exemplary form of progressive literature. Penn's classmates had
responded with mixed reactions, but he knew much of it was jealousy.
The professor's encouragement had bolstered him substantially, enough
to map out the rest of his plan. He would graduate with strong credentials in literature, get an agent right away, watch the ensuing feeding
frenzy with the publishers, and then explode onto the literary scene to
stellar acclaim. This was how he figured it would happen. He was prepared for some difficulty, not much. He had a backup strategy, a Plan B,
if his first attempts to get the book published failed.

He didn't believe it would come to that. His work was strong,
clever, and socially relevant. Editors would be clawing each other for
the right to his masterpiece.

They weren't clawing. No one had even bothered with an idle scratch.

They were idiots, these people. That's what he decided. It was the
only reasonable explanation. His book was inventive, provocative,
downright smart.

And it was funny Funny-hmmm, not funny-haha.

So far the so-called experts had refused to see this.

In the in-box next to his computer were letters from the rejecting
agents who had even bothered to respond to his queries. There were
thirty-five letters. He was running out of agents to be rejected by.

The responses spanned the gamut of commentary:

"I found the distortion of such a classic work both offensive and disturbing."

And . . .

*"While the style is impressive and you apparently have talent, the story is
all over the place. Perhaps a class on structure would help. It would also be
advisable to give it a name."*

And this . . .

*"Your main character is one-dimensional and wholly unredeemable. I
couldn't connect on any level with him or his plight. Why is there no title?"*

And this . . .

"The concept is clever, although what you've written is too vulgar for what we represent. If you adjusted your greater metaphor, changed the locale, eliminated the extreme sexual element, made your main character more of an Everyman, and gave it a title, we'd be interested in taking another look."

Translation: write another book.

This was his favorite . . .

"This is shit."

Priceless. The agent had actually called his manuscript, his chef d'oeuvre, *shit*. What kind of person did that? Even on an agent's worst day, he didn't think they sent out letters like this. It would have been better not to respond than to write something so harsh.

That letter wasn't in the in-box. It was encased behind glass in an eight-and-a-half-by-eleven black-rimmed frame on the wall facing him, just above his computer. It was his fuel. Those three heartless words—"this is shit"—accompanied by just a signature on letterhead from a hugely successful agent—überrepresentative Spanky Katz— were the three hard, daily slaps in the face that urged him forward. She probably thought she was doing him a favor by writing it. Maybe she was one of those blunt Simon Cowell types who believed in quashing what they thought were false hopes.

Penn greeted that letter every day, saluted it and its audacious style, even as it kept him in angry knots. One day, he and the terse Ms. Katz would meet. She'd be clamoring for a heaping, scrumptious plate of his shit. And he'd hand it to her, happily, with a side order of unplucked crow.

Spanky would have her groveling moment under his sun.

It had been eighteen months since he first began sending it out. Eighteen long months of agent rejections and unreturned calls, wasted reams of paper, expensive toner cartridges, carefully crafted cover letters, postage, postage, and still more postage. He used NYU's computers and paper whenever he could in order to save money. Time kept passing and nothing happened. There had been brooding. Lots of brooding. It wasn't supposed to be like this.

He was twenty-five now, and had been out of school for almost two years. He lived in a small apartment at Amsterdam and 108th. The rent was fourteen hundred on a one-bedroom, one-bath space less than six hundred square feet. It was in a decent building with a part-time doorman, elevators, and laundry, but was nothing like the luxury and comfort he'd grown up with. He worked odd jobs to keep himself in money. He temped. He found the odd Texas Hold'em game and would hustle enough money to get him through for a few months. He used women. For money. For sex.

He refused to get a serious job, even though he was constantly approached by modeling agencies and probably could have walked into any business in the city and gotten an entry-level position based on his looks alone, even better if they knew his academic credentials. Mercury offered to get him work in building contracting, but Penn turned it down. He was too arrogant to settle for less than his original objective. He didn't want to start something he knew he wouldn't finish.

Sometimes Merc loaned him money. He understood his best friend. He was the one other person who believed in Penn almost as much as Penn believed in himself.

He had attended publishing events on his own limited dime. Book Expo America, the *Los Angeles Times* Festival of Books, the Miami Book Fair. His desperation hit its stride when he skipped paying rent for two months and sprung for a trip to the Frankfurt Book Fair to peddle his manuscript. These were all places agents and editors were known to haunt, on the possible prowl for the Next Big Thing.

Going to these events involved juggling and sacrifice. He was barely able to scrounge up much money beyond food, shelter, utilities, a MetroCard, and gym membership. He unloaded the ancient Taurus as soon as he graduated from Columbia. Gas, parking meters, and garages were too expensive. It would have been pointless to repair the car if it broke down, as it had done many times during his college years. He used the money from the sale of the car to buy two expensive suits. The rest of his clothing was casual and attractive, but cheap.

None of the book fairs, festivals, and conventions yielded anything significant, either. There were a few fake conversations and offers of cards from editors and agents, but in most instances, it was a ploy for sex. He saw Spanky Katz several times, but never said anything to her. He was willing to wait.

It proved futile to attempt to talk to the high-profile authors at these events. The ones who weren't buffered by publishing flacks and media escorts usually proffered a card as well, accompanied by a fake smile under empty eyes and a hollowly spoken "e-mail me," which he always did and none ever responded to. The ones that did tried to negotiate sex.

These were people on road trips, away from their mates, eager for a getaway fuck. He wasn't biting. That was not a part of the original plan. He would not fuck his way into publication. Not just yet.

It wasn't out of the question. It was the last resort.

That was Plan B.

During the eighteen months of trying to sell his book, he had had no need to go to Plan B. But the original plan was proving an uphill task and the dream of publication was becoming more distant than ever.

The Adam Carville incident in the *New York Times* had been a backbreaker. Penn stopped going to book signings in the city. Watching talentless bestselling dolts and the fans who loved them was killing him by infinitesimal degrees.

Times were lean. Sometimes they were leaner.

It was during these leaner periods that he used women. Not excessively. Just enough to get by. He was always being stopped, hit on, flirted with, goosed. It happened every day. On the street. In the store. On the subway. While doing laundry.

"Oh, my God," said one woman who was walking toward him on Broadway. She stopped cold, right in front of him. "You are so fucking hot!"

"Yum-my," said another standing next to him at the newsstand.

"Slurrrrrrp!"

It came from a round man at the gym who'd been eyeing his crotch.

A woman in a business suit cupped his balls as he stood in a huddle on the train.

There wasn't a place he turned where women and men weren't

giving him some sort of sexual cue. He had no interest in the men and, most of the time, didn't want the distraction of the females. His focus was on selling his book.

But he was undeniably beautiful, in a confident, masculine way, and he was exceptional in bed. Gifted even. And when money was short because he had spent it for an airline ticket to a book conference, or for copies at Kinko's and postage to send an unsolicited packet to an agent or an editor, well, it was then that women came in handy. Why shouldn't they, he reasoned. They threw themselves at him. He led no one on. New York women were aggressive, outspoken, sexually confident, and, more often, well heeled. If they offered to cook, take him to dinner, even pay his rent for the month, and times were lean, he didn't object. The women got what they wanted—sex, his brief attention—which was more than they deserved. His conscience didn't bother him when he discarded them.

Women were the great betrayers. His mother had been proof of that.

By Month Twenty of Plan A, his resentment had peaked.

He was fucking regularly, but not for the usual reasons. Not because he liked to, even though he did (like to). Not because times were leaner, even though they were. Sex had become a primal necessity to keep him sane.

He had a lot of angst, enough to disable a lesser man, and he needed a place to bury it. Sinking into a soft, wet hole with a woman wrapped around it allowed him the chance to unload some of his dark energy. The poor women on the receiving end never knew how karmically toxic the shot-wads of negativity were that flew out of him. One time, after a particularly fervent blow job, he came on a girl's chest and the semen was so hot, she blistered.

"Oh God!" she cried, scrambling away from him for the comfort of a cold shower.

Penn had given her time to soothe herself in the bathroom, but as soon as she was finished, he asked her to leave.

"Are you kidding?" she cried, three Band-Aids strategically placed across her torso. "Look what you did to me."

"It's your fault," he said. "You shouldn't have gotten me so heated."

He felt no remorse over using women as his rage receptacles. They seemed to like it. He even had moments of what could pass for tenderness. These usually set in right after he came, during that window of emotional and intellectual generosity, but they were fleeting. Once the nut was busted, crusted, and an appropriate amount of languor had passed (no more than ten minutes), he turned cold again. Kind-cold. Kind enough to not ruin the possibility of a future tryst, but cold enough to make the woman realize she needed to go. He couldn't offer more.

And while he could get women of every feature, size, and hue, he tended to go for those who were the least pretty. Not butt-ugly girls, although he was prone to mercy fucks upon occasion as a sort of sexual community service. Pro bono work.

Average girls and the subattractive tended to come to the table, literally, with a combination shock-reverence that always translated into a willingness to do just about anything. Most couldn't believe a man like him would shine his light their way and want to take it further. That introduced the shock element.

The reverence part entered once he got them into bed and headed south.

Then, then, then, their legs and the heavens would open and those women would see God. A man who ate their pussy, they reasoned, must surely be a man who was falling in love. They were usually wide open after that, literally, tunnels of opportunity offering the full palette of enthusiasm and exploration. Oral. Anal. He could stick it anywhere.

A pretty man's dick could go many places.

It amazed him that so many women weren't wise to the cunnilingus bit, no matter how many times it played itself out. A man who loved pussy loved pussy. That was that. It had nothing to do with the woman. It was an agenda unto itself, like using a public restroom. Just because a person took a shit in it didn't mean he wanted to buy the building. It was just a bathroom, a place to unload.

Pussies were life's bathrooms.

Warm, wet bathrooms with softer seats.

———

He finally buckled during Month Twenty-three of Plan A, twenty-seven days shy of two years. There was no getting around it.

It was time for Plan B.

He got a subscription to *Publishers Weekly*. It was expensive, as magazine subscriptions went, and he couldn't afford it, but he took the bold step. As soon as he made the decision to go with Plan B, the shadowy cloud began to lift.

It happened at once, with the arrival of the very first issue of the magazine, less than two weeks after he filled out a subscription card and mailed it in. He sat at his desk flipping through the thing, having tossed aside the rest of the mail. By either fate or coincidence, it opened to page twenty of the News section. The word "People" was in red, and beneath it, in black, was the headline UNGER MADE VICE PRESIDENT. A photo was next to the article. It was a woman, a young woman, with one of the homeliest mugs he'd ever seen. Her smile was unsettling, a wide curve of brilliance in the midst of gloom. It didn't fit with her face.

He scanned the copy.

Beryl Unger has been promoted to a vice president position at CarterHobbs. Unger has been in publishing since she was sixteen, when she started as a temp at PaleFire USA. Under the strong guidance of former CEO Anna Barber, Unger rose within the ranks of the company and was appointed editor in 1994, at the age of twenty. She joined Kittell Press, an imprint of CarterHobbs, in 1999, bringing with her several bestselling authors, including consistent chart-topper Sharlyn Tate and Pulitzer–Prize winner Canon Messier. As an editor, Unger's focus goes beyond her writers' material. She specializes in the total integration of all aspects of a book's development, with particular attention to inventive marketing campaigns and cross-promotion. Her new position is said to be in the mid-six-figure range with considerable performance incentives, making Unger, now thirty-two, among the highest paid editors in publishing.

Those two words—"total integration"—seemed to leap off the page. Penn read the article once more, then studied the woman's picture.

Just like that, there she was. Young enough, plain enough, perfectly primed for manipulation. Penn knew her kind well. The ambitious, underattractive workaholic who was married to her career because there were no other serious options. He could tell at a glance that she was single. A homely girl like this would abandon her job in a nanosecond if the right man came along and gave her some action. According to the article, Beryl had been fast-tracking her way up the corporate ladder nonstop for more than a decade. A woman that ambitious didn't have a steady man, and even if she did, Penn knew he could take her.

It would be easy. Granted, she'd be shocked by his interest in her, but women like Beryl—the well heeled and lonely—had a tendency to lose their sense of reason when a handsome man came into the picture. It didn't matter how successful they were on other fronts. An attractive man was their universal weakness.

Most of the time, the women got taken. They refused to listen to the warning bells their intuitions set off, and often ignored the advice of rightfully concerned friends. Having that pretty boy was everything. It was the final validation, the one that mattered most: proof they were lovable. Many of these women secretly doubted this, and that's what made them such easy prey. Some were shockingly beautiful. Those were the easiest to desecrate. Most were really smart, really successful, really fat, or really homely. Sometimes all four.

Fucking a woman like that wasn't a problem for Penn. Forget how she looked. That wasn't what he focused on during sex anyway. His hard-ons came from direct reflection. From seeing himself in the eyes of the fucked.

He ran his finger across her picture.

"Hel-looooo, Beryl. My sweet little deus ex machina."

Existentialism:

A literary and philosophical movement emphasizing the belief that an individual is isolated and totally free in an indifferent universe—not controlled by fate, higher forces, or preordained events—and is therefore completely responsible for what happens to him and what he makes of life.

It belongs to the imperfection of everything human
that man can only attain his desire
by passing through its opposite.

—Søren Kierkegaard

So what

. . . do you think the problem is?"

"I don't know."

Beryl studied the author sitting on the other side of the desk, one of her superstars. The woman was way over deadline, eight months over, and the publisher was on Beryl's neck to get her to produce.

"Sharlyn, come on. How many times have we had this conversation?" She was careful not to sound too harsh. Authors, particularly those on the top tier, could be so skittish. "You're always on schedule. That's your thing. What's going on? We've been waiting for almost a year."

Sharlyn glanced up, her long black hair falling forward.

"I know how long it's been. I'm a stickler for detail, remember?"

"So am I."

"Don't we know it."

"Then what's the problem?"

Beryl weighed her next statement and the effect it might have.

"Be real with me, Sharlyn. Do you want to leave the business? Is that what it is? Because if it is, just come out and say it, don't beat around the bush."

It was an attempt at reverse psychology that she hoped would work. The last thing she wanted was for Sharlyn Tate—author of nineteen number one *New York Times* bestsellers, screenwriter/producer of twelve blockbuster films based on her books—the last thing

Beryl wanted was to hear her say she planned to stop writing. The woman was one of their most-lactating cash cows. She was young yet, just forty-three, and hers was the only professional relationship Beryl had ever let turn into a personal friendship. Beryl had brought her over to Kittell Press and signed her to an eight-figure, three-book deal. Sharlyn had since signed on for two more books. Beryl was the best editor she had ever worked with, she said. And under Beryl's keen editorial eye and exceptional marketing ability, Sharlyn's books were performing at even greater numbers.

Hence the urgency of getting the next manuscript. Kitty Ellerman, head of the imprint, wanted to see that big advance earn out.

But Sharlyn was wealthy, quite wealthy, after years of success in both publishing and Hollywood. She didn't have to slave over the word anymore. She could stop working altogether if she chose, thanks to her husband. Miles Tate had come to represent the face of a new Black America. One that operated based on competitive performance, not color. When he sold the communications company he started as part of a merger with Wells Entertainment, he became a billionaire one and a half times over. The board voted him in as chairman and CEO of what was now a global powerhouse, and he and his superstar wife were one of the most powerful couples in the world.

Sharlyn definitely didn't need to work. *If I had over a billion dollars in the bank,* Beryl thought, *I probably wouldn't feel like working, either.*

"Congratulations on the big promotion," Sharlyn said. "We should go out and celebrate. Maybe I can plan a big party and invite all the—"

"No way, lady. The only thing I plan on celebrating is when you finish this book. Now tell me what you need from me to help move you in that direction."

"Hmmph," Shar muttered. "You happen to have a spare dick? Wait, what am I talking about. We need to be trying to locate one for you."

"Fun-ny," said Beryl. "Meanwhile, we're no closer to having your next book."

Sharlyn took a piece of Brach's candy from a bowl near the edge of Beryl's desk.

"You coming to Messier's signing tonight?"

"Where is it?" Sharlyn asked.

"The Astor Place Barnes and Noble."

"Why is it there? He'll have a big crowd."

"You know Canon," Beryl said. "He wanted a smaller space, even though he knows it'll be uncomfortable with all those people trying to cram in."

"The man lives to make people uncomfortable."

"So are you coming?"

"Nah," Sharlyn said.

"You've got plans?"

"Not really."

"Then that must mean you'll be writing," Beryl said enthusiastically.

Sharlyn smirked and shook her head.

"I don't feel like traipsing all the way down there. I'm tired. I think I just need to go home and lay down. Maybe I'll take a red-eye to L.A."

"I thought you were tired."

"Maybe I won't be after taking a nap."

Beryl pretended to glare at her.

"Maybe you need to stay close, maybe that's what you need to do. Going to L.A. won't solve anything."

"I could go to the beach house. Who knows, it might inspire me."

"The only thing you'll be inspired to do is hang out at the Ivy and, what's that club you like, Blue Velvet?"

"White Lotus," Shar laughed.

"Same difference."

"I don't even go there anymore. That place got old fast. Maybe you're right. I should just stay here."

Beryl got up and walked around her desk, over to Sharlyn. She grabbed her hand and pulled her up.

"Get out of here. Go write. You're being slothful, Shar. It doesn't become you."

Sharlyn dragged her feet as Beryl pushed her toward the door.

"But I can't write, B.," she whined. "I miss Miles. I can't stand him right now, but I really do miss him."

"Have you tried teleconferencing? It's not like the two of you aren't high-tech people. The man runs a global communications firm, for God's sake."

"Teleconferencing can't snuggle you at night. What am I supposed to do, spoon the computer?"

"Works for me," Beryl said. "Now get out. Go write."

She shoved the author into the hallway. Sharlyn stared at her a long moment.

"What? Why are you looking at me like that?" Beryl asked, suddenly unnerved. She skimmed her hand across her cheeks and lips. "Is there something on my face?"

Sharlyn laughed.

"God, you are so jumpy. I really do believe you need dick more than me."

She walked off, laughing.

Beryl stepped back inside her office and closed the door. She rushed over to her purse, pulled out her compact, and checked her face. She turned her head from side to side. Everything seemed okay. She closed the compact, threw it back in her purse, then looked at the clock on the far corner of the wall. It was five forty-five P.M. If she hurried, she could stop by the drugstore, pick up her prescription refills, and still get to Astor Place before seven.

Canon Messier wouldn't be at ease if she wasn't there. Of all her authors, he was the neediest. He didn't do very many signings, and when he did, they were only in Manhattan. He insisted Beryl be at every one. He always pointed her out to the crowd, which resulted in her having to fight off mobs of aspiring writers. She hated this, and had said so to Messier on more than five occasions. Each time she brought it up, he embarrassed her more the next time around. She finally caught on that she should keep her mouth shut.

Messier was considered an authority on whatever topic he wrote about, now that he had that Pulitzer to back him up. He was a good writer whose books made a lot of money for the company. His refusal to tour or do any kind of media was challenging at first, until she figured out the perfect tie-in that kept Messier's face, and his new book, *Apple Pie,* front and center. The book focused on the boyhoods of some of baseball's greatest, from Babe Ruth to Barry Bonds. Beryl had convinced McKee Foods Corporation (makers of Little Debbie snack cakes) and Major League Baseball Commissioner Bud Selig to partner with Kittell Press on a promotional campaign that would link the products and boost everyone's sales.

McKee Foods committed a million dollars and a million free Little Debbie apple pies for the chance to participate. The pies were given out at games over the course of the regular season. Beryl managed to work the deal so that CarterHobbs and Kittell Press didn't have to put up any money.

Everything was done with a discount of thirty. Beryl liked the number. The campaign was a partnership of three, so it seemed to work.

Tickets to games during the regular season offered thirty percent off the price of Messier's book and a thirty percent discount on a box of Little Debbie apple pies. Boxes of Little Debbie apple pies included coupons for thirty percent discounts to regular season games and thirty percent discounts for the book. The jacket of Messier's book was designed with a perforated flap extension with coupons good for thirty percent discounts for baseball games and boxes of apple pies. Every baseball stadium in the country sported a huge ad for Messier's *Apple Pie* and one of equal size for Little Debbie.

At some point during every televised game, viewers would hear:

Sponsored by the Major League Baseball Association, in conjunction with Apple Pie, the bestselling book by Canon Messier, and those incredibly tasty apple pies from Little Debbie, America's number one Snack Cake.

Baseball attendance was up by three percent, and sales of Little Debbie apple pies increased by a third. Messier's book was at 1.3 million and counting.

Canon Messier had loved the campaign. He wasn't even bothered by the perforated flaps on the book jacket or the articles that appeared in *Publishers Weekly* and *USA Today* speculating on what many perceived as a tacky turn for the book industry. Messier ignored it all. His popularity soared, and his neediness for Beryl accelerated.

Wouldn't it be nice, she thought, if my soul mate showed up and needed me the same way too?

Astor Place, for a brief time in the 1800s, was an area of import and wealth. Located between Broadway and Third Avenue, it was now home to Joseph Papp's esteemed Public Theater and "The Alamo," an enormous black cube that could spin on its axis and was situated on the plaza across from one of the busiest Starbucks in New York City (so busy, they had to build another one on the opposite corner to accommodate the traffic). But long before the legions of cube-loving skateboarders and extreme coffee-chuggers arrived on the scene, Astor Place had known its share of infamy, from two events in particular. One took place in 1911, when a notorious sweatshop at the corner of Washington Place and Greene Street caught fire, killing one hundred and twenty-five workers—a tragedy that resulted in new laws concerning workers' safety. A more violent affair, the Astor Place Riot, had occurred some sixty years prior to the 1911 fire, and has remained one of the bloodiest events in New York history. It was sparked by a tiff between former friends Edwin Forrest and William Macready, a New Yorker and an Englishman respectively, two dramatic actors living on different continents who had grown viciously competitive as each rose within the ranks of theater in their respective countries.

Their mutual venom escalated to the point of becoming an issue of nativism (foreigner-hating), fueled by the Order of United Americans, a powerful organization among working-class New Yorkers who saw Macready's nose thumbing at Forrest as a thumbed nose at America itself. When Macready arrived in the United States for an appearance at the Astor Place Opera House in the title role of Macbeth, he was promptly driven from the stage by flying debris hurled from a staunchly nativist audience. The indignant Macready had no plans for an encore, but he was urged to give it one more try by American luminaries that included both Herman Melville and Washington Irving. Foolishly advised, the Englishman returned to the same stage three days later, on May 10, 1849. The angry nativists couldn't believe the priggish thespian had the nerve to come back. An estimated twenty thousand people packed the streets of Astor Place from Broadway to Third Avenue. By curtain time, the area and the opera house were teeming with agitated agitators, ready for some anti–British action.

Ennobled, undaunted, Macready hit the boards, upon which the boards (along with a torrent of chairs, paving stones, and bricks) promptly hit him. Macready continued to perform, determined to keep his word and go on with the show. The mob outside began stoning the building and the police, who were stationed around the opera house in an attempt to contain the madness. Their efforts were futile; the place was besieged. Windows were smashed and the lobby was stormed. The National Guard was called in. They, too, were attacked by the mob and almost overtaken, until someone within their ranks gave the order to fire point-blank into the crowd in an attempt to calm things down. Hours later, thirty-one civilians were dead. Another thirty-some people had been shot and wounded, and more than a hundred policemen, national guardsmen, and civilians had been battered by stones, bricks, clubs, and sundry debris. Macready somehow made it out alive and fled back to England. He never returned to America again. Eighty-one people were arrested in the wake of the riot, including an author who operated under the pen name Ned Buntline. He had been one of the primary instigators of the fateful event.

These days authors and mobs could still be found convening together in Astor Place, on the upper floors of the big Barnes & Noble near the corner of Broadway. And while the crowds were no longer bloodthirsty stone hurlers, they could, on occasion, become a bit unruly when in the presence of the object of their literary affection (or scorn). Bookstore personnel kept the chaos to a minimum. No national guard necessary.

Yet.

Penn spotted her the moment she walked into the room. He was off to the side, near the area where Messier would be doing his reading. He wanted to see where she would be standing so he could make sure he was strategically placed. She was a lot smaller than he expected, in a pink Chanel jacket and skinny jeans. Her hair was beautiful, but her face was much plainer than it had been in the picture. It seemed like a stretch to even call it a face. It was more like . . . a knockoff Picasso.

Penn was reminded of the painting *Woman in a Hat*. That was Beryl's face. All geometric shapes and lines running every which way. Much ado about nothing. Dull disorder. One of those things that made a dog cock its head. He stuck his hand into his jeans pocket and pulled out a tube of Kiehl's lip balm, SPF 15. He smeared a dab across his lips.

He was ready.

His game face was on.

". . . and that's what led me to write this book. Well, that and my editor, who's trying to hide there in the back . . ."

Messier pointed, as expected, in Beryl's direction. The two hundred or so people crammed in the room turned to see who he was talking about.

"That's her there," he said, "in the pink jacket. And don't let her size fool you. She's a dynamo. A bit on the pushy side, but it's all worth it. If you want to write books, that's the person to have on your team. Beryl Unger. Wave at the people, Beryl! Let 'em know who you are."

"God," Beryl groaned as she flashed half her smile, raised her hand, gave it a quick shake in the air. She could hear people buzzing around her, could have sworn she felt a few closing in.

"You must hate when he does that," a voice beside her said.

Beryl looked up into the most beautiful face she'd ever seen. His eyes were the ocean, his hair was the sun. He was smiling at her.

She heard harps, real harps, and angels singing indecipherable songs in her head. Trumpets blared. Cupid drew back his bow with the bicep of a thousand quarterbacks, and released his weapon with malicious intent. It hurtled toward her in a rush of emotion, spearing her hard, right in the center of hope, with earthquake impact.

She grew dizzy, dizzy, and then she went down.

When she finally came to, she was lying on a couch. Penn was kneeling before her, clutching her hand. Messier was standing just behind him. Two hundred voyeurs crushed into his back.

"Are you all right?" Penn whispered, stroking her palm.

"Beryl!" shouted Messier. "You scared the shit out of us! What the hell is wrong with you?"

Penn flashed him a scowl.

"What?" asked Messier.

Beryl struggled upright, her eyes on Penn.

"I don't know. I'm tired, and I didn't eat lunch today. I've been pulling a lot of late hours. I'm probably just a little carb-depleted."

Someone handed her a giant Frappuccino.

"Are you gonna be okay?" Messier asked. "Do you need to go to the hospital or anything?"

"No, Canon. I'll be fine." She held on to the freezing drink with one hand and Penn with the other.

"Good." Messier turned to Moira, the B&N community relations manager who had organized the event. "Let's get going so I can sign books." There were two publicists from Kittell Press at his disposal, but he ignored them. They tagged along after him and Moira.

Messier cut a path through the throng. The crowd about-faced and raced after him, desperate to be among the first few in line.

It was just Penn and Beryl. He was still kneeling. He took the Frappuccino from her hand and set it on the floor.

"I get the feeling you don't want this."

"I hate Frappuccinos."

"Me, too. Your hand is freezing." He cupped her hands inside of his, rubbing them vigorously to warm her up. Beryl couldn't move. She was paralyzed with awe.

"Somewhere on an island in the South Pacific, there's a villainous scientist conspiring to destroy the world, one Frappuccino at a time."

She giggled.

"Seriously," Penn said. "And it's working. Since when were adults prone to casually guzzling down coffee covered with mountains of whipped cream and caramel? That was the kind of thing you only saw in ice cream parlors. Now you see people clutching Frappuccinos on the train, as they walk down the street . . . check this out . . . there was this one guy, I kid you not, he was standing next to me in the bathroom, at the urinal. He was taking a piss with one hand, and was slurping his Frappuccino with the other."

"You lie!"

"I swear to God. It's not natural. Frappuccinos are the work of an evil, evil man."

Beryl grinned, her mouth wide, showing all of her teeth.

"Wow. You've got a really beautiful smile."

"Thanks," she said, lowering her eyes.

He stopped rubbing her hands, placing them gently in her lap.

"There," he said. "That's better. Would you like some hot tea? I could run down and get it. That way you don't have to worry about walking."

"I'm okay, really, I'm a little hungry, but—"

"Would you like me to grab you some food from somewhere?"

She was staring at him again.

"I'm sorry," Penn said, getting off his knees and sitting on the floor at her feet. "You probably think I'm some kind of stalker or something. It's just that, well, I was standing over there talking to you one minute, and then you just—"

"It's okay. I'm glad you're being so helpful. Everyone else seems to have abandoned me."

Penn smiled, following her eyes toward Messier at a table in the back, furiously signing, smiling, and indulging photo ops. The line of anxious fans clutching his book snaked around the room.

"He's a monster of my own making, I'm afraid."

"I somehow doubt that," Penn said, his eyes meeting hers.

Beryl felt herself flushing all over.

"I'm Penn."

"I'm—"

"Beryl."

They both said her name at the same time. They laughed.

"I think everyone knows who you are by now. Your Frankenstein over there made sure of that."

A tall, skinny man approached them, his shoulders hunched forward as he tried not to seem too obtrusive. He cleared his throat.

Penn stood.

"Miss Unger," the man asked. "Uh, Miss Beryl Unger?"

"Yes."

"Uh, I was wondering, uh, Mr. Messier just signed a book for me and we were just talking and, uh, I told him about the book I wrote and, well, uh, he said I should come over here and, uh, talk to you."

Penn stepped aside, his hands folded behind his back.

"Yes," said Beryl, "well, now might not be a really good ti—"

"I brought a manuscript," the man said, reaching into a knapsack and whipping it out. It was weatherbeaten and much handled, with food stains and scattered splotches of something nuclear green. Beryl didn't want to touch it.

"I've been told it's pretty good. My mom's read it, and, uh, all my friends. Everyone thinks it'll be a bestseller."

Penn watched Beryl's face to see how she handled this type of thing.

"I'm not going to be able to take it, Mister, um, what's your name?" She proffered her hand.

"It's Temple. Adrian Temple."

"Nice to meet you, Mr. Temple. I'm afraid I'm not going to be able to take your manuscript. It's our policy not to accept unsolicited material."

"That's not true," Adrian said. "I know somebody who sent a manuscript directly to CarterHobbs with nothing but a query letter."

"It happens, but it's not something we recommend," she said. "Manuscripts like that usually wind up in the slush pile and most of us are too overwhelmed to be able to give it the attention it deserves. I would think you'd want your work to have the proper attention from an editor."

"The guy I know got a call a week later, and guess what? Carter-Hobbs bought his book."

Beryl squirmed. The man was a nuisance. On top of that, she could feel Penn watching her with those amazing blue eyes. She was suddenly aware of herself in a way that made her very nervous. Was her hair okay? Her makeup? Her mascara was probably smudged. What if she had a big mascara smear on her face? She had blacked out, after all. Shit. She needed to get her compact out of her purse. How could she do it without being conspicuous? She noticed a couple of girls standing off to the side, college-aged girls, pretty. They were whispering to each other, making eyes at Penn. Did he know they were there? God. She needed to get out her compact and check herself.

"Did you hear me?" asked Adrian. "CarterHobbs bought his book. So what do you have to say about that?"

"We bought his book?" Beryl said, casually rubbing under her eye and inspecting her finger for mascara. "Really? Well, I suppose you could risk it, but your best bet would be to get an agent. Why don't you try querying agents mentioned in the acknowledgments of books you feel are similar to yours. That's always a good approach."

"I've tried. I've been trying for over two years. Agents are jerks. They're all a bunch of bloodsucking asswipes."

Penn cut his eyes at the man, sickened to realize he had something in common with such a pathetic sort.

"So are you gonna take it or not?" Temple said, thrusting the disgusting thing under her nose. "I could be the next John Irving for all you know."

Beryl and Penn both fought back a snicker. This gangly creature was no John Irving. Several evolutionary life-forms from now, he'd still be off.

"I'm afraid I can't, Adrian. I'm just too busy to take unsolicited work. But if you can get an agent to submit it, I promise I'll—"

Temple snatched his filthy manuscript away, cramming it back into the knapsack.

"Forget it. This is probably the universe doing me a favor, saving me from a preditor like you."

"Hey, hey now," Penn said, stepping toward the man. "That's not necessary. The lady said she can't take unsolicited material. You're going to have to respect that."

"What are you, another overpaid preditor like her?"

"Predator?" Penn asked, growing impatient. "I'm nobody's predator, sir."

"You look like the type," Temple said with scorn, eyeing Penn. "With your Abercrombie and Fitch and the whole pretty-boy thing you got going." Temple had been stammering when he first approached, but now he was broadband. Continuous streaming.

"Everything's gotta be so perfect with you people. You're only interested in working with celebrities and writers who are already famous. Nobody gives a damn about nurturing real writers anymore, and it's because of preditors like you"—spittle flew from his mouth—"that someone like me can't get anybody to look at my book!"

The community relations manager rushed over.

"Is there a problem?" Moira asked.

"There's no problem," Temple said, storming off. "No fucking problem at all." They watched him leave. He glanced over his shoulder just as he was about to round the corner.

"Preditors!"

Penn and Beryl looked at each other and broke into laughter. Moira was lost.

"What was that about?"

"Some nut," Beryl said, still laughing. "He tried to give me his manuscript, then got really pissed when I told him I couldn't accept unsolicited material. He kept calling me a predator."

"A predator?"

"Yeah. He said something about me only being interested in working with people who were already famous."

"Oh," Moira said, then, "Ohhhhhhh. He called you a 'preditor.' With an *i*, not an *a*." She laughed. "Haven't you heard that term before?"

"No. What's it mean?"

"Think about it, Beryl," Moira said as she reached for the melting Frappuccino. "You don't want this?"

Beryl shook her head, still lost by the comment. Moira tossed the calorie-packed goop in the trash.

"I get it," Penn said. "Predatory editors. Preditors."

"Yeah, that's it." Moira gave Penn the thrice-over, although her words were meant for Beryl. "I can't believe you've never heard it before."

"I live in a bubble," Beryl said. "I can't believe he called us that. I can hardly go to the bathroom without getting stalked by somebody who's trying to pitch something. My manicurist pitched me the other day. She wants to do a book about acrylic nail art. You should see

what happens to Kitty, and God, the head of the publishing house.
They can hardly step outside without somebody pitching them. It's
ridiculous. And they call us 'preditors'? We're more like prey."

Moira laughed with exaggerated girlishness, cutting her eyes at Penn.
Beryl seemed visibly annoyed by the way she was looking at him.

Penn noticed her irritation. Here was his moment.

"I know we just met but, you said you were hungry. Did you want
to grab something to eat?"

"That'd be great."

"Moira!"

It was Messier, screaming from the back. "I need you! Get over
here!"

Moira looked at Beryl.

"You don't have to say it," said Beryl. "He's a handful, I know."

"But he sells a lot of books."

"Tons of them."

"Moira!"

"I better get back over there."

"He's got the publicists helping him."

"C'mon now," she smiled. "If it's not you or me, he doesn't really
care. Although I did hear him tell them they're taking him to dinner
since you're not feeling well."

Beryl laughed. "Good. Then I'm off the hook. Those two are in
for a long, long night."

Moira turned to Penn.

"Nice meeting you, um, I didn't catch your—"

"Penn Hamilton."

"Great name. Hopefully we'll see you around here again."

"Moira!"

"I'm coming!"

She rushed off.

"Let me help you up," Penn said, giving her his hand.

"I'm really okay," said Beryl as she took his hand and let him pull
her up. Their eyes met and she quickly looked down. She was nervous, almost afraid. Not in a bad way. It was kind of fear that comes
from seeing something prayed for finally materialize.

Meeting this man had been such a rush of emotion, it caused her to cataplexy. She hadn't taken her medication for the day because she had been late calling in the prescription. The pills were in her purse now, but they were still unopened. Her ritual was to pop them first thing, as soon as she arose from a full night's sleep, but this day had been crazy, filled with meetings and rushing around, and there'd been no pills to pop that morning. She had never waited this late to call in a refill. She usually did it a few days before. She didn't think anything drastic would happen if she missed a dose.

But something had happened.

Penn.

"So what do you feel like?" he asked.

"I could go for some mulligatawny soup."

"That sounds good. Since we're so close, do you want to go over to Indian Row?"

"Okay."

"You sure? We can take a cab if you like."

"I'm fine, really," she said. "Let's walk."

Indian Row was a block on Sixth Street between First and Second avenues in New York's East Village that was populated by a slew of dives specializing in Indian fare. That was "Indian" with a question mark, as many of them were Bengali- or Pakistani-run, but that was no matter as there was plenty of curry-this and tandoori-that, as well as lots of spicy vindaloos, naan, dal, and samosas to be had at dirt-cheap prices, all served up nice and greasy, in environments dressed with colorful lights and colorful music that ranged from the really bad to the truly awful. It wasn't top-shelf dining, although there were a couple of stand-outs on the block, but it was hearty sustenance in settings cool enough for first dates, cheap dates, old friendships, and newfound pals.

Beryl wasn't sure which of those she fell under, as she was just meeting this man, yet he seemed connected to her soul somehow. It was silly, this feeling, but it was clear, like a bell. It was the feeling she had been waiting and preparing for all those sixteen years between age sixteen and now.

They were dining at Mitali East, a Bengaliese restaurant that was one of the better joints on the block. She knew she should have been more cautious, taking off with a stranger the way she was doing. But this was Beryl, and Beryl had a dream, and the dream had materialized in front of her, fairy-tale style, just as she had been insisting it would. This was the work of fate, and fate, in her eyes, could never be denied.

It had been a quick walk over from Astor Place, barely five minutes. In that five minutes she learned he happened to be in Barnes & Noble looking for a book on Sartre when he discovered Canon Messier was scheduled for a reading. She learned his parents were dead, just like hers, and that he was an only child. Just. Like. Her. He was younger, five years younger, but that wasn't a deterrent, and he was tall, sweepingly tall, hovering over her by more than a foot. He made her walk on the inside, buffered from the traffic, and clutched her hand unthreateningly before they dashed across the street. He held the door for her. She was already smitten the second she saw him. By the time they reached the restaurant, she was thoroughly smote.

She watched him now, reaching for one of the three hot poori the waiter had just put on the table with a side of mango chutney. He tore it down the middle and placed half on her bread saucer without asking. Beryl liked that, the way he took charge. He plunked a spoon into the condiment and held it just above her plate.

"Chutney?"

"Yes, thank you."

He emptied the spoon next to her bread, plunged it back into the chutney, and heaped a fat dollop on his own plate. He dragged the other half of poori through the spicy relish and wolfed it down, his fingertips covered with grease and sauce.

"How's your soup?" he asked around bites.

"Good," she said. "It's hitting the spot."

"Better than that Frappuccino?" he kidded. "No way."

She laughed.

He reached for another poori and tore into it, giving Beryl a chance to really examine his face. His jawline was Grecian, clean and elegant, leading into a chin that squared off and merged in a gentle cleft. His deep-set eyes were crystal pools of azure framed with long, lovely lashes. His nose was a slope of—

"You're staring at me."

"Excuse me?"

"I can feel your eyes on me."

His gaze was penetrating. Beryl's stomach knotted.

"I have something on my mouth, don't I?" He wiped at the corner of his lip with a napkin. "How embarrassing. It's the poori. I lose my mind over the stuff every time I come down here, even though I know it's not exactly healthy with all that oil and everything. This place makes the best poori in the city."

"It was just a crumb," she lied.

He wiped again.

"Did I get it?"

She gestured at the right corner of her own mouth. He dabbed at his.

"Now?"

"Yes. It's gone now."

"Kind of uncouth, huh?"

"No, really, not at all . . ."

Penn began sucking the chutney from the tips of his fingers. There was nothing ill-mannered about it. It seemed like a natural, unpremeditated thing. Her eyes were riveted to his mouth as he inserted each digit, let it linger between his lips, did a slight pucker-pucker thing, then pulled it out. Slow. Clean. Glistening.

His finger wasn't the only thing glistening.

Beryl was wet. She hadn't been wet in months. Quite possibly all year. She squirmed inside her skinny jeans. Her knee shook. She wondered if her makeup was okay.

"Sorry," he said with a sensuous curved smile as he wiped his hands on his napkin. "The chutney's too good to let go to waste."

He took a big swallow of his Kingfisher beer, his head tilting back as he hurled a strong splash of the full-bodied drink against his throat. Her eyes rolled over the grace of his long neck, hit the hill of his Adam's apple, and settled on its peak.

She couldn't believe how hot he was. Model hot. Actor hot. Superhot. Beryl never got the chance to dine with men like this. Not casually. It happened quite often in business situations. She mingled with the beautiful all the time and was sleek enough to hang, if not equally pretty, and while she was welcomed, she was never mistaken for someone who naturally belonged.

She was so nervous right now. She didn't want to mess this up. She pressed her right hand on her knee to slow it down. What was he thinking? Could he be attracted to her in the same way? It was possible, wasn't it? He'd been so sweet back at the bookstore, and it was he who had suggested they have dinner. And what about his holding her hand on the way over? Even if it was just for a moment as they crossed the street, he had done it. A guy wouldn't do that if he wasn't interested, right?

Penn wiped his mouth with his napkin and plunged his hand under the table for something. He came up with a small tube of Kiehl's. He squeezed a tiny bit on the tip of his forefinger, then smeared it across his lips.

She sipped her Diet Coke, watching him, hoping he couldn't see how thrilled she was that this was even happening.

Men like this never dined with her casually. Men like this only paid her attention when they were trying to get a book deal.

It suddenly occurred to her that Penn might want a book deal.

"So what is it you do?" she asked.

The last piece of poori was on its way to his mouth. It hovered in midair a nanosecond, pinched between his forefinger and thumb. His lips were parted a fraction, and a burst of air was on its way up his trachea to push out the first word.

"One murgha tikka musalam."

The waiter slowly passed the creamy chicken dish beneath Beryl's nose with a flourish, then placed it in the middle of the table.

"One dildar curry with lamb."

The grinning man seemed to put special emphasis on the way he said "dildar." *Dilldarrrrrrr.* He waved the dish under Penn's nose, then put it on the table. Penn smirked at Beryl and made a slight nod toward the waiter. She giggled. He smiled and gave a seductive, conspiratorial wink.

The floodgates burst inside Beryl's skinny jeans. She smashed her little legs tightly together.

"One shaag bhajee."

Shaaaaaag. Again the dragging out of the word. The waiter was turning the arrival of their meal into a pornographic celebration. Beryl squirmed harder, tiny jolts of electricity igniting her loins. The cheesing waiter was about to orbit the spinach dish past her face, but she leaned back. His grin weakened. The plate orbit was his shtick, his moment of theater. He lived for it. This fraggle-faced girl was stealing his joy.

"Kashmiri pillaw."

The waiter was deadpan this time, though he still managed to stretch "pillaw" out into something obscene *(pee-lowwwwwwww,* heavy on the *owwwwwwww).* He set the rice mixture in the middle of the table without ceremony. The sweet aroma of plump, moist raisins and crunchy nuts flooded their senses.

"EnjoyyourmealthankyouverymuchIgonow," the man blurted with a bow as he backed away from the table.

Penn's face was frozen, then he broke into a full-fledged laugh. Beryl was too overcome for laughter. Between the *dilldarrrrrr,* the *shaaaaaag,* and the *pee-lowwwwwwww,* she was deep in the throes of a simulated food fuck.

"Would you excuse me for a sec? I have to go to the . . ." She made a weak gesture toward the bathroom.

"Sure," Penn said, leaping to his feet and stepping over to pull out her chair.

Beryl grabbed her purse and got up cautiously, convinced the back of her jeans were wet. She tried to pull her Chanel jacket a little lower, but it was one of those short jobs that stopped at the waist. She was riddled with nervousness as she walked away. She couldn't help looking back to see if Penn was laughing. He wasn't. He was still standing, watching her leave. Beryl couldn't stop shaking. She was overwhelmed by so many things. Too many things. Penn, the way he looked at her, the way she was feeling right now, the geyser action between her legs, panic at the thought of staining herself. It seemed as though everyone was watching her make this infernal trek to the bathroom. Eyeballs pressed against her. She looked askance. There was the supersexual waiter, grinning once again, his teeth towers of white cruelty. She quickened her step.

Beryl was barely inside the bathroom when everything she was experiencing merged in a wave of emotion that was no longer manageable.

She went down, down, crashing to the floor.

Her face was in a puddle when her eyes opened. Her right hand was on something cold. The porcelain base of the toilet. It took a second for her to register the environment, then she realized that her lips were resting in pee.

"God! Oh God!" she sputtered, scrambling to get up. She scuttled over to the sink and turned on the water. It was bitter cold. She pushed the button on the soap dispenser at least ten times, filling her palm with the stuff. She let some water mix with it, and furiously scrubbed her face. She scrubbed and scrubbed and scrubbed. Her makeup ran into the sink, mixing with the soapy foam as it swirled down the drain. She mashed the soap button again and scrubbed some more. She did it again. And again. And again.

She snatched up a handful of paper towels and rubbed her face dry. She was hysterical, unable to get the phantom taste and thought of the urine to go away. She pressed the button for more soap and plunged her face back under the faucet. Scrub, scrub, scrub. Pee and panic. Scrub, scrub, scrub. Neither one would wash away.

She stopped when she caught a glimpse of herself in the mirror. Her face was turgid pink, screaming for a reprieve.

"Look at me," she said. "This is awful."

She'd had two cataplexies in one day. Two. This kind of thing just didn't happen, hadn't happened in over a decade. She still hadn't taken her pills, even though it was now too late in the day. The reason for taking them in the morning was so she wouldn't be too alert at night and would be able to fall asleep. Not taking the pills had proved a grave error. Missing one day's dosage reduced her to a quivering, cataplexying mess.

"I should take them," she decided. So what if she was up all night from the jitters? It was worth it rather than risking another collapse.

She glanced around for her brand-new Pucci, a charming confection that was a gift from a friend at Apple, an exec she'd given advice regarding a ghostwriter. She had loved the purse at once, the moment she saw it. The signature Campanule print bag had silver chain-link straps and the fabric was a swirl of pink, green, burgundy, yellow, and white that coordinated beautifully with her jacket. Where was it?

She checked the counter and below. A flash of pink caught her eye. There it was.

On the floor next to the toilet.

Soaking in pee.

Mitali East had good food and amusingly distracting décor, but they were also the proud owners of one of the pissiest johns in the city. That day, anyway. Someone, presumably a woman, had come in and sprayed the floor and walls like a cat in season.

Beryl raced over to retrieve her precious Pucci, crying all the way.

"Why is this happening?" she sniveled, holding a corner of the bag with two reluctant fingers. "Why is this happening to me?"

The faucet was still running, wasted gallons rushing down the sink.

She looked at the water, then at her stained bag. It couldn't be helped. She thrust the Pucci beneath the cold stream. She was crying the whole time. She grabbed more paper towels, wet them, squished on more soap, and with manic zeal began to systematically ruin the delicate silk.

In the midst of her tears, she noticed something else. The knees of her skinny jeans were circles of pee.

Her mouth flew open in an unmitigated bawl. She wet more paper towels and began dabbing at her knees. Beryl scrubbed and cried and soaped and scrubbed, catching intermittent glimpses of her hysterical self in the mirror.

Someone banged on the bathroom door. The sound was startling. Whoever it was rattled the knob. They were about to come in.

Beryl rushed to the door to block it, as if her slight build were substantial enough to block anything more than the slightest of breezes. It flew open, hitting her in the face.

She went down.

———

She was cozy, peaceful, blissed out, cocooned within the rapture of down feathers and warmth. Yves Delorme sheets, three-hundred-thread counts of satin-soft pure Egyptian long-staple cotton, graced the front of her body in a gentle shroud and underscored her backside with equal attention. She floated on goose down featherbedding that topped a most exquisite mattress—a McRoskey Airflex, luxurious, made to specification, an experience in sumptuousness that defied the average wallet. Her head nestled in yet more down, flocked within elegant pillowcasings, plucked from the wings of airborne angels. The frosting, the agonizing pièce de résistance, was a Frette Demetra Foglie Arredo duvet, six-hundred-thread counts of brazen divinity. It covered her from chin to eternity, an epic expanse of material that promised paradise to anyone who dared venture underneath.

Penn sat beside the bed, next to a small table covered with potted African violets, enchanted and enraged by such extraordinary expression of decadent comfort. He was all man, and none of that manhood was metrosexual or remotely gay, but he knew high quality, and he knew it by name. He had been raised on supreme bedding like this. He was intimately familiar with every nuance of its elegance and feel. His mother had insisted upon Frette and Delorme bedding and bath linens in all their homes. She taught him that extreme thread counts didn't always translate to quality. A higher thread count was good, but the overall construction was key, and it was important to purchase the best. He sometimes went into the Frette store on Madison just to egg himself on in doing what it took to return to the lifestyle that had been so cruelly stripped from him.

The lush bedding wasn't the straw. It was the bed itself that broke his back with envy. He had recognized the McRoskey Airflex at once. To think that El Scrawnio, this less-than-lovely collapsible chick, the object of his grand scheme—she owned one. She was sleeping on something that should rightfully be his. It was probably just a really expensive bed to her. To him, it was a throne.

It had been Dane, his father, and Dane's father, Pilgrim, who taught him as a boy about the scientific significance of McRoskey beds.

Something about steel coils, innersprings, pressure points, resiliency. Grandfather Pilgrim, a man of enormous wealth and enormous quirks, had had the same McRoskey bed for sixty-three years. It had been made expressly to accommodate his six-foot-six frame. When he died, he was burned, per his request, on the indestructible thing like a funeral pyre. It had been an absurd ritual. All that was missing were the coins on his eyes and a ride up the river Styx.

Dane's bed had also been designed for him. So had Penn's. The Park Avenue apartment, the house in Lloyd Harbor, the Belgravia town home—McRoskey beds had been in each, made to spec for Liliana and Dane as a couple, and for Penn as a growing boy. McRoskey, headquartered in San Francisco, had been shipping beds thousands of miles for years for the Hamiltons' maximum enjoyment. Penn had imagined he would spend his entire sleeping life on one. He hadn't counted on his parents' death, his near-destitution, and Ekeberg, his bed from IKEA hell.

Dane would spin on his theoretical axis if he were alive and knew Penn was sleeping on something as mass-replicated and prepackaged as Ekeberg. Penn hoped his father was spinning in hell for having been the reason he was sleeping on Ekeberg in the first place.

Ekeberg didn't have it in him to evoke the kind of serenity Beryl's face wore now. This was a woman dreaming of heaven. Either that, or she was dead.

She moaned. Signs of life.

Beryl stretched her limbs about beneath the covers, smiling in her sleep. She snuggled against a body-length pillow. She was on her side now, facing Penn. She moaned again, exhaled, ground her loins into the pillow, and opened her eyes.

The breath she'd just blown out was quickly sucked back. She sat up in the bed, clutching the duvet close to her chest. There was no need. Penn wasn't threatening to come at her and she wasn't nude. She was still in the clothes she'd been wearing all day.

"What are you doing here?"

"Making sure you're okay."

"What do you mean? Of course I'm okay. How'd you get in my house?"

"The doorman let us in."

"What!" She pulled the duvet tighter.

"Calm down. Let me get you a glass of water."

He went into the bathroom with an air of authority. Small potted African violets lined the back of the toilet, the counter, and the sides of the tub.

"What's the deal with these," he mumbled as he ran some water into a glass he found on the counter of the sink. He took it to her.

"Here."

Beryl's eyes were Frisbees as she took the glass with both hands, paused with apprehension, then drank. He sat in the chair he'd been in for the last five hours and watched the rapid return of her senses.

"What time is it?"

It was an absurd question, given the apparent significance of time in the room. On the wall facing the bed was an enormous black digital clock with bright red LED readouts for five different zones. The top left corner was Pacific, the top right Mountain, the lower right Eastern, and the lower left Central. Square in the center, in even larger bright red, was Zulu time. It didn't fit the classic elegance of the rest of the room.

All she had to do was turn her head just a skosh, not even a full inch, and the time would have emblazoned itself upon her eyeballs. But she didn't, which Penn took to mean one of two things: either she was so high maintenance, she was too lazy to even check the time for herself; or, she was so taken with him she just couldn't look away. He was banking on the latter, but with all the mishaps she'd come with so far, he wasn't quite sure.

"It's two-eighteen."

"In the morning?"

"Yes."

He had the tube of Kiehl's in his hand, squeezing more onto his finger, smearing it on his lips.

Beryl glanced down at herself and noticed she was still wearing the Chanel jacket. She raised the covers a little higher and peeked at herself. The piss-kneed jeans were still intact. Penn watched her cacophonous face go through a series of twitches as everything began to come back to her.

"The bathroom at the Indian restaurant. I fell down in the bathroom."

"Yes. I got worried when you were in there so long, so I sent the waiter over. He banged on the door and tried to open it, but you must have been coming out or something because it knocked you in the head."

"The waiter?"

"The door."

"Oh," she said, then, "Oh!" and flung back the covers, rushing off to the bathroom. She was barely inside before he heard something hit the floor.

"Hey. You all right in there?"

She didn't answer. Penn hurried toward the bathroom.

It was Beryl. She was down. Out cold.

Again.

He was kneeling above her when she opened her eyes.

"You're narcoleptic."

In his hands were her bottles of pills.

Beryl shook so hard, the sleeves of her Chanel jacket flapped at the wrists.

"Wha—"

"You didn't want to go to the hospital when you hit your head at the restaurant. You made a big stink about it, even though all of us—the waiters, the owners, the other customers, everybody—we all thought you should go. You just kept saying 'take me home, take me home,' then you blacked out again. I looked in your purse to get your address so the cab could bring us here. That's when I noticed the pills."

"Oh God," she cried. Big blobs of water were falling out of her eyes.

"I'm sorry I went into your purse. I didn't know what else to do. I didn't know what the drug names meant, so I got on your computer and Googled Provigil. The drug modafinil's for narcolepsy. Suddenly your blacking out made lots of sense."

She stared into Penn's perfect face for what she feared would be the very last time. The truth was out. She'd finally found the One, and now this. He'd hang around long enough to make sure she was all right, then he'd be out of there. It'd be just like the boy from the mailroom years ago.

This was happening just the way she feared. Just as she first told Ripkin it would.

Ten minutes later, she was cradled inside his arms as they sat on the floor. He rocked her gently, brushing her forehead with feathery kisses of comfort and concern.

"It's all right," he said, "it's all right, Beryl, don't cry."

"But no one's ever known about it. Nobody's ever known."

"It's okay. No one has to know now."

She looked up at him, her wan face awash in wetness.

"But why would you protect me? I just met you. Why would you do anything for me?"

He hugged her closer, stroking her hair.

"I feel like I need to."

"But why?" she cried, pressing her cheeks into his firm pecs.

"I don't know." Penn's voice was low, almost a whisper. "I kind of feel . . . I don't know . . . connected to you. Like I know you already. Like I've always known you."

She opened her mouth, but he cut her off.

"I know, I know. It's crazy, it's cliché, it might even seem borderline psycho. It's every bullshit line ever said by every bullshit Lothario in every bullshit movie ever made."

She clamped her lips, chewing at the bottom from the inside.

"But it's the truth," Penn said. "I felt like that the second I spoke to you when we were in Barnes and Noble. It was crazy. Like this charge went between us or something."

Beryl's eyes were wide, and then so was her mouth. Her smile was fantabulous, fully flashing her teeth. All BriteSmile-zapped thirty-two of them.

She was crying again, but this time it was different. This was a happy cry. It was the I-just-hit-the-Love-Lotto squeal of cathartic release.

————————

"Here, take these."

Penn had opened the bottles and was handing her the pills.

"I usually take them in the morning," she said.

"It is morning."

"But I always take them around seven."

"I'm concerned about you collapsing again," he said.

She was mortified.

"It doesn't happen that much."

"It's happened four times already. That I know of . . ."

"One of them wasn't a cataplexy. I got hit in the head with a door, remember?"

"Right." Penn smiled. "Those blackouts, so that's what they're called? A . . . cataplexy?"

She cast her eyes toward the floor.

"Yes."

He lifted her chin with his finger, encouraging her to look at him.

"Don't be ashamed, Beryl. I'm not judging you. I'm staying, remember? That is, if you want me to."

There went that grin of hers. It was a rose amid thorns.

"Yes. I want you to."

He reached for her left hand, turned it so the palm was facing up, and dropped the pills into it.

"So take these already. It'll make me feel better. I'll get you some water."

"But then I won't be able to get to sleep."

"Right. Well. Perhaps we can come up with something to do."

They were in the Delorme sheets!

Beneath the promised paradise of the Frette Demetra Foglie Arredo duvet!

And he was on the McRoskey! At long last, he was on the McRoskey!

And he was impaling her, piercing her bony loins with the ferocity of every long-lost noble ever restored to the throne. Penn was Anastasia, Aragorn, Arthur—all the *A*s and more. He was back in the seat of luxury, and this sex-denied, sleep-disordered insipid little misfit beneath him was just the person to usher him into the awaiting laurels of fame and wealth.

He had chosen his prey well. The narcolepsy was a gimme from the universe. So was the obsessive-compulsive thing, which he hadn't mentioned but, when he found the second bottle of medication in her purse, he'd investigated that drug, Anafranil, on the Internet, too. Clomipramine was used for narcolepsy as well, he'd learned, but it was primarily a drug for obsessive-compulsive disorder. She was probably an ob-com. She had all the markings of it. He had studied obsessive-compulsive behavior at NYU, so he knew a thing or three enough about it to take a better than wild guess. This was most outstanding. He couldn't have asked for better. She had a defect. Defects. Which made her doubly desperate, doubly insecure. It had accelerated everything.

He'd found condoms, very neat and organized, in the cabinet under the bathroom sink, right where she said they'd be. Trojan Ultra Pleasure. Trojan-Enz Large. Lifestyles Ultra Sensitive, thin lubricated. The woman was nothing if not prepared. It was disarming at first, seeing such a stash at the ready, until Penn caught the expiration date on the side of one of the packets. July 2002. He checked out another. October 2000. The silver packs of Lifestyles were so old, they were curling at the seams. January 1998. Damn. This was the sign of either a serious fucker who'd suddenly staved off or a diligent planner who didn't score much. Ever, it seemed.

He had grabbed the ones most recent (fortunately for him they were the Trojan-Enz Large), then he got down to work.

And now he was giving the punch-drunk girl beneath him a most thorough thrashing, a thrashing in the best way, a beating of the body that rendered her a protoplasmic puddle. She was blubbering, hollering, crazed. Never had she been fucked like this. And he was looking at her, eye to eye. He instinctively knew no one had done that to her before. Most, he bet, just squeezed their eyes shut, or hit it from the back. She probably never had a man hold her gaze with longing passion as he pushed his way inside of her. Penn swooped down upon her with a determination he wanted her to believe was divine, preordained love. Fate had arrived. Fairy tales were coming true. *Sex and the City* and every tale of equal ilk women like her dreamed of were proving more gospel than fiction.

Penn speared her with purpose, gusto, and a finality designed to eclipse every thought she ever had of him in the future. He intended to do the job many more times in the days and weeks to come, but he wanted this first fucking to leave an indelible print on every cell of her being. He didn't want her to take a breath without feeling the lingering pleasurable pain of him on top of her. He wanted her lower lips to sting when she sat down or went to pee, a Pavlovian reminder of his sturdy meat, which he had positioned in her face with deliberate confidence an hour earlier as he kneeled above her on the bed. He wanted her to see how huge his proffering was (and it was), wanted her to realize that everything about him was grand—not just his face and his body, but his instrument of pleasure and propagation. She would be lucky to get this. This wanted her. This was a once-in-a-lifetime miracle. Outside of him, she would never get the chance at something like this again.

She misinterpreted why he had put his manhood so close to her face and, after an extended moment of shock and awe as she took in its size and beauty, she reached for the raging meat and pulled it into her mouth. He leaned down, taking her face in both hands.

"No," he whispered. "You've had a hard night. This is all about you."

He had removed himself from her surprisingly dry mouth and slid down her belly.

"Nice abs," he'd said, running his fingers over the six tight bumps.

He kept going down, pressing his face between the scarce meat of her thighs and into her wetness. He understood at once why her mouth was so dry. All the moisture in her body had beat it down south, having gotten the clarion call that something between her legs was about to give. She was glistening, leaking, oozing upon the bed, her pussy raining glee at so much attention.

Penn worshipped the area for what felt like forever, the better side of sixty minutes, giving his lips a good smear of Kiehl's first, then sending her over the cliffs of ecstasy eight times and counting. It was the first time she'd ever come with a man. She'd had lots of self-evoked moments, but had never experienced orgasm during the sex act itself. Sure, she had cataplexied during sex once, but that wasn't the same. And Penn was eating her like she was a most delicious meal. It was too much. She popped and popped and popped without respite.

The longest any man, including her gynecologist, could have ever been down there was ten minutes. Her genitals were actually ugly, if genitalia could be described that way. The inner lips, the labia minora, were large flappers, elephant ears that stuck to Penn's face like leeches as he lapped at her Frankensteinian clitoris. Her clit wasn't as big as a penis, but it was larger than anything he'd ever seen. The pinky of a five-year-old, that's what it was. The thing was at least that big. It was a rod that made him feel a bit uneasy at first as he sucked on it, but he soon gave himself over to the bigger picture, which was to get her to submit to his will. That alone was worth sucking her skinny clit-bone.

After he ate her, he thrust himself inside her slickness, no warning, no prep, just ramrod action designed to immediately break her will. She squawked and clawed at the air, then scratched at his back. Turned out she was a yipper, a screamer, first-class.

"Aaaaaaaaaaaaaiiiiiiiiiiyeeeeeeeyeeeeeyeeeeeyeeeeeyeeeee! Jesus, Joseph, and Mary! OhGodOhGodOhGod!"

"You feel so fucking good," he moaned, ramming her hard, his eyes locked onto hers. "Beryl. Fuck. Beryl. Fuck. Fuck."

Penn knew the power of repetition, what it would do to someone like her, just hearing her name over and over like that.

"Beryl, you're killing me. You feel so fucking awesome. Your pussy is so hot."

"Yeeeeeeeeeeeeeyeeeeeeeeeeeeyeeeeeeeeeeeeyeeeeeeeeeee!" she squealed.

He raised himself up on his arms, a foot of space between his torso and hers, and pounded her pudenda with a fierceness, angling his dick in and out, sometimes pulling it back just to the tip, then plunging it in, watching it knock the wind out of her chest.

"Yeeeeeeeeeeeeeyeeeeeeeeeeeeyeeeeeeeeeeeeyeeeeeeeeeee!"

He lowered himself, his mouth close to her ear, still pounding her, a butcher at steak.

"Tell me you don't have a boyfriend," he whispered. "It'll kill me if you can't be all mine."

"Yeeeeeeeeeeeeeeyeeeeeeeeeeeeyeeeeeeeeeeeeeyeeeeeeeeeeee!"

Her eyes were rolled back in her head, Linda Blair–style. She dug so hard into the meat of his back, she broke the skin.

"It feels like you're mine, Beryl. Tell me, tell me you're mine."

"Yeeeeeeeeeeeeeeyeeeeeeeeeeeeyeeeeeeeeeeeeeyeeeeeeeeeeee!"

She thrashed underneath him, her eyes pure white, pupils gone. Seeing himself wield such power over her gave Penn the extra wind he needed to close the deal.

"I fucking love you," he moaned. "I know it. It's crazy, but I already fucking know it."

Beryl came right then. Hard, solid, a cardiac arrest. Everything in her stopped. The thrashing, the rolling eyes, all of it. There was nothing but the pounding in her chest as she watched, catatonic, as Penn kept pumping above her. She held on to his back, pressing her face into his shoulder. She felt him shudder as he came. She clung on, refusing to let go of the moment, the insanity, the dream.

Penn's body went limp against her. He lay on top of her, stroking her hair, their loins a mess of melded stickiness.

Beryl's mouth was at his ear.

"Did you just say you loved me?" she asked.

"Yes," he whispered.

She hesitated, then, "Did you mean it?"

"Yes."

She was trembling beneath him. He could feel it. Her bones rattled like Ichabod Crane's. He wondered if another cataplexy was on its way. He could sense her struggling for words, words he already knew were coming before they were even spoken. He began a silent count. How long would it take her to say them?

One.

Two.

"I love you, too."

Women were the stupidest creatures alive.

Oops!!

. . . Hotshot Kittell Press editrix Beryl Unger sent everyone scattering when she literally hit the floor at the Astor Place Barnes and Noble last night. The drama took place in the middle of a book signing for Pulitzer prima donna Canon Messier. "She just collapsed," said a stunned spectator at the packed event. "It scared us all. Thank goodness I was still able to get my book signed." Some are speculating whether the fainting spell means Unger's in over her head at work, or if it's a sign of something else. "It couldn't be pregnancy," says our spy. "Her face is the ultimate contraceptive." Reps for Barnes and Noble and Kittell Press declined comment.

Sharlyn's mouth hung open, her bagel with a schmear poised just at the entrance. After the initial shock set in, she began to laugh. Hard.

She was sitting upright in bed reading Page Six. Beryl's face a contraceptive? That was beyond cruel.

Sure she was laughing. The phrasing was hilarious, even though it was bitingly mean. Beryl was a nice person. She couldn't help that Mother Nature had been kinder to her body than to her face. The woman was an excellent editor and a loyal friend. She was enthusiastic and enterprising. Everything a writer could wish for.

But damn. That was some funny shit.

Shar put down the paper, trying to decide if she should call Beryl and warn her about it. There were several editors, at CarterHobbs and outside of it, who'd been resentful of her fast ascent. They'd be snickering behind Beryl's back and in her face. She needed to be warned. A friend, a good friend, always gave the heads-up.

Sharlyn reached for the phone. It was early, just after six-thirty. She always had the papers brought to her at the crack of dawn. She figured Beryl would be up. She was always up. Shar sometimes wondered if Beryl slept at all.

She was awake, her eyes boring into the wall.

Aside from the medication, which was keeping her alert, she couldn't have slept anyway. She was walking through a dream and didn't want to do anything that might make it go away. His arms were around her midsection as he spooned her back. She could feel the soft heave of his breathing. Perhaps he was asleep.

"You gonna get that?" he asked.

"Oh. Um. You want me to?" She realized how silly the words sounded as they exited her mouth.

"It's up to you," he said.

She was unsure of what to do, not wanting to displease him or give off the message that she couldn't think for herself. Or that she didn't answer her phone. Suppose he called some morning, if he was still around, and she was unable to answer because she was in the shower or sleeping too hard? He might think it was because she was canoodling with someone. He might never call again. She couldn't let that happen. Not with him. He was . . . the one. The time to set the tone was now. She reached for the receiver.

"I don't know if I'm ready to share you just yet," he said, gently pulling her back. "It's early. Can't we have just a few more minutes? This'll all be over soon enough."

"What do you mean?" Beryl asked in a panic, turning toward him as the phone rang for the fourth and last time.

"Ssshhh," he said, covering her mouth with first his finger, then his lips. His kisses were light and spare, lingering over the tender mound of freshly injected collagen in the area that should have been her cupid's bow. "I mean sooner or later, we've got to get out of this bed, that's all. Relax. This isn't a one-night stand. Not for me."

"Me, neither."

He smiled, his blue eyes dancing.

"Awesome. I was hoping this wasn't just something you did. You know, stage blackouts so you can pick up guys."

"That's not funny, Penn. I'm still pretty mortified over you finding out."

"I'm glad I did," he said, kissing her left cheek as he leaned over her, pressing her back into the bed. "Otherwise I would have missed all this, you know?"

"Yeah," she said, choking with bliss. "I know."

Sharlyn decided against leaving a message.

"Oh well. I tried."

She pushed away the breakfast tray, swung her legs over the side of the bed, and stared at her laptop, which was sitting on the foot of her luxurious chaise just across the room.

"I'm going to write today. Yup. Today, I'm going to write."

She got up and walked her naked body past the chaise and the laptop, toward the master bath. The phone rang. Perhaps it was Beryl calling her back. She picked up the cordless extension in the bathroom.

"Hello?"

"Girl, you better wake up!" the happy voice sang.

It was Diamond DeLane, television personality, former circuit court judge, proud member of the African-American community (first and foremost, dammit, she was black!), ultra-celebrity (in her mind, anyway), and overall appreciatrix of living la vida opulence.

"Hey, girl. I was already up."

"You know I was gonna blast you if you weren't," Diamond laughed. "I got the early-morning call, so now it's your turn. I'm not going to be the only one snatched out of her beauty sleep. Look alive, girlfriend. We've got things to do."

"Parties to plan!"

That last comment came from a third voice, Aurora Kash, celebrated songstress, party giver, partygoer, and beloved socialite, whose last name was one of the biggest understatements of all time. Her spread in the Hamptons practically had its own zip code. She had once married very well, but she was single now and thrilled about it. Divorce had its privileges.

"Hey, Aurora."

"Good morning, Shar. Diamond and Shar! How adorable is that? Perhaps that should be our theme tonight. The Diamond and Shar Show."

"It's the Diamond, Shar, and Aurora Show," Diamond said. "I like that. It sounds intergalactic."

Sharlyn turned on the shower, letting it steam up the mirrors a while as she did other things.

"So to what do I owe this pleasure, ladies? What theme for tonight are you talking about?"

"We're throwing an impromptu party," both women replied.

"When?"

"Tonight," said Diamond.

"In honor of what?"

"In honor of everything," answered Aurora.

"And nothing," Diamond added. "It's in honor of the fact that we're all fabulous. Life and love are great. What more of a reason do we need?"

"It's nothing sprawling or overdone. Just a few friends getting together for a good time."

Sharlyn knew what "a few friends" meant. It could be anything from thirty people to three hundred. She stood at the sink in front of the steamed mirror. Neither of these women did anything small, and now they wanted to celebrate life and love? With an impromptu party? Life might be great but love wasn't all that. Miles was still gone, she was still horny, and all the partying in the world couldn't take the edge off. She reached for her sonic toothbrush and squeezed on a glob of paste.

"So why are you calling me so early? My husband is out of town, as usual, so I don't have any plans tonight. Count me in."

"No, girlfriend," said Diamond, sounding irrepressibly giddy, like she was getting more than her share of what Sharlyn wasn't getting at home. "We're hanging today while the planners put the party together."

"Hanging when?"

"After Diamond's done with the show," said Aurora. "We're having lunch, getting massages, manicures and pedicures, and then we're going shopping."

"But I was going to write today," Shar said, flipping on the toothbrush and polishing her teeth.

"You can write anytime," Diamond said. "The way you knock those books out, girl, you're like a machine. Give yourself a break."

Shar reached forward and cleared an area of steam from the mirror.

"She's right, you know," Aurora agreed. "Let's celebrate tonight. It will inspire you, trust me."

"I'onoboutalldat."

"Ooh, Shar. You could at least wait until we hang up before you do that. You know I got a thing about nice teeth, but I'm not trying to hear you brush yours over the phone."

"Rorry, rirl."

Shar spat the foam into the sink.

"Thank you," Diamond said.

"All right, ladies, enough of that. We need to coordinate our day. Shar, we'll pick you up a little before noon. Guess where we're having lunch?"

"Cipriani's?"

"Yep."

An easy lure. It was common knowledge that Shar couldn't say no to anything Cipriani. Harry Cipriani, one of several Cipriani restaurants throughout Manhattan and the world, was the one she loved best, even more than the original. She'd been a regular for years and had her own special table. The restaurant was inside her second favorite hotel and writing hideaway, the Sherry-Netherland (the Hotel Plaza Athénée was tops). Miles had proposed to her in Italy at Cipriani's flagship restaurant, the world-renowned Harry's Bar in Venice, well aware that she'd be most amenable to marriage with a bellini in hand and a tender piece of carpaccio sliding down her throat.

"Where's the party tonight?" she asked.

"Bungalow Eight," Diamond said. "So be ready to get your boogie on."

Good, Sharlyn thought. That meant it would be a smaller gathering, more intimate. Bungalow 8 could only hold a hundred or so people. She could handle that.

By now the bathroom was a thick stifling fog. Sharlyn could barely see the phone in her hand. Her feet were invisible. She enjoyed the steam. It was purifying. She'd been feeling so toxic lately, filled up with knotted thoughts and feelings that were better off released.

"I really do need to write, you guys. I'm so behind. Beryl's all over me."

"Beryl's all over the floor, from what I just read."

"That is so wrong," said Sharlyn.

"You're right," replied Diamond. "I shouldn't have said that. I know better than anybody how evil that paper can be."

"Perhaps you should invite her to the party," Aurora said. "She'll need a pick-me-up after dealing with all this."

Huge droplets of water were running down Shar's body. She wiped her brow and leaned against the counter.

"She won't come. She'll be too embarrassed."

"Invite her anyway," Diamond said. "It'll be good for her to get out. The worst thing you can do is go into hiding over a tabloid story. You've gotta keep movin'."

"Speaking of which, I need to get in the shower."

"All right. We'll call when we're downstairs. It'll be around eleven-thirty."

"More like eleven forty-five," said Diamond.

"Bye, ladies."

She could hear Diamond shrieking something as she clicked off the phone and laid it on the steamy marble counter.

"Invite Beryl!"

Shar opened the glass door, stepped under the way-too-hot stream of water, and let the extreme temperature punish her supple skin raw.

It was seven-twenty A.M.

Beryl and Penn were still in bed. She was tucked under his armpit, her arms entwined around his middle. They both stared ahead at the colossal clock.

"Why would you need to know Zulu time?"

"One of my writers likes to exile herself in Africa when she works. She hates it when I unintentionally call in the middle of the night. I got the clock so I could be sure to call at a decent hour."

Penn paused, still staring at the time.

"That's not the reason you got that clock."

Beryl giggled.

"All right, all right, so I saw the thing in one of those Skymall magazines on the plane and I ordered it during the flight." She squeezed her arms tighter around him. "How'd you know I wasn't telling the truth?"

"I don't know. I just know."

One of her bony elbows was digging into his side. He ignored it, willing to take the good with the bad. Ends justified means, he reminded himself. Ends justified means.

She let out a deep breath.

"I'm usually up and dressed by now."

He pulled away.

"I'm sorry. I'd better get out of here. I'm probably keeping you from all kinds of—"

"Nooooo," she said, pulling him back. "This is cool. I'm always working. It's nice getting to linger like this."

"Yeah?"

His smile was a twist that curled up on one side.

"Yeah."

She was grinning the broadest of grins. He was grateful for it. In the midst of all else, that grin made things much easier for him to endure. If she was just a bit fleshier, perhaps it would be even better. But a bad face and clanging bones? He was sure there were bruises on his temples from where her femurs had pressed through the slack give of flesh surrounding her thighs and crushed his head like a nut.

He reached for his tube of Kiehl's sitting on the nightstand on his side of the bed. He squeezed a bit out and swathed his lips.

"Can I ask you a question?"

"Sure," said Penn.

"Why do you use that so much?"

"What, the Kiehl's?"

"Yeah?"

"To keep my lips from chapping. What do you think I use it for?"

"I don't know," she shrugged. "I thought maybe you just liked glossy lips."

"My lips are glossy?"

"No, not really."

"It's just lip balm. Sometimes my lips dry out. I can't stand the feeling, so I use Kiehl's. Satisfied?"

He said it with a smirk and a gleam.

"Yes," she said, kissing his mouth. "I'd hate it if you had dry lips."

She ran her tongue around the side of his mouth, lapping at the coating of balm.

"Perhaps I'll play hooky today," she said.

"Can you do that?"

"Sure. I never do, but I can. I'll just say I'm a little under the weather, so I'm going to work from the house. Then we can spend the whole day together."

He didn't respond.

"I'm sorry," Beryl blurted, suddenly nervous. "I just mapped your day out for you without even asking. You probably have to go to work or something."

"I work from home," he said.

"Doing what?"

"Well, right now I keep the books for my buddy's uncle," Penn lied. He hadn't done a day's work for anyone in his whole life. "I've got a good eye for numbers, so I do it for the steady income while I'm working on some other things."

"Is that what you went to school for? Accounting?"

"No."

"Oh. Um . . . did you go to school? I mean, like, did you go to college? Not that it matters or anything. I didn't."

"Yes, I went. I got my bachelor's from NYU and an M.F.A. from Columbia."

"Wow. That's pretty impressive."

"Eh," he shrugged. "It's okay, I guess."

He left it at that, not bothering to go into what he had a bachelor's in or why he chose to get a master's in fine arts. The more mystique, the better. A woman like this would work extra hard if there was an element of mystery, something she could strive to attain access to. Women like this believed men like him had a sweet sensitive core, and that all it took was a few whacks at that hard outer shell, and then BOOM!—like some sort of mutant piñata, all kinds of warm and fuzzy goodness would come oozing out.

Crack on, he thought. There's nothing under my hard outer shell but layer upon layer of harder inner shells.

This was going to be fun.

"Where is she?"

It was the big boss, Kitty Ellerman. She was standing at Shecky Lehman's desk. The time was nine-thirty A.M. On the dot.

Shecky was Beryl's very pretty, very diligent editorial assistant. She had been at work for two hours already, reading manuscripts from the slush pile (something she'd taken upon herself in the hopes of coming across a diamond somewhere in the mountains of shit) and answering e-mail requests from authors regarding touring schedules and check status. She'd also been fielding calls about Beryl for the past half hour, and had an armful of galleys she was preparing to send out. She was in awe of Ellerman, a woman who, like Beryl, had started at the bottom some twenty-plus years ago typing contracts, then became a successful editor, and now had her own imprint. To Shecky, she was a god. Shecky stood at attention when Ellerman appeared. She might have even saluted if her hands hadn't been full.

Shecky was blessed with good height. At five ten, she was just tall enough to inspire awe in other women, but not so Amazonian that she intimidated men. She had a fine bone structure that was draped in the best clothing her parents' long showbiz money could buy. Her father was a successful Broadway producer who'd had hopes his brilliant and gorgeous summa cum laude Dartmouth grad would become a playwright and create material he could stage. Shecky couldn't be less interested. And despite the attempts of every major agency in the city to lure her into modeling, the erudite Shecky wanted one thing and one thing only: to be the head of an imprint, perhaps even a publishing group. She wanted to be . . . dare she think it? A Kitty Ellerman herself.

Her name, Shecky Lehman, was ready-made for it. It had that minimum three, maximum five, mostly four syllable rhythm that seemed to be the rule for heads of publishing. Son-ny Meh-ta. Phyl-lis Grann. Pe-ter Ol-son. Shec-ky Leh-man. It was a natural fit.

She'd get there. She was working on it by reading unsolicited material (something Beryl encouraged her to do as a way to possibly discover some gems of her own), being ickily agreeable to in-house authors, and getting to know the people that mattered. Beryl had even gotten her input on manuscripts she edited. Shecky relished the opportunity, envisioning her own fast track within the publishing realm. In the meantime, she was a paragon of efficiency as she strutted her stuff down the hallowed halls of CarterHobbs as though it were a catwalk and she was Giselle. She moved like a pony on the trot, knees marching higher than nature intended, hips asway, her gait full of restrained sexuality that never breached the bonds of propriety. Men and women stopped what they were doing just to watch her go by, all pomp and circumstance, two and a half feet of loose chestnut curls billowing in her wake. It was a real show, one to which nobody ever quite knew how to react, as most were unsure whether it was farce or form. She had been voted Most Likely to Fuck Her Way Up by a spiteful faction of her sorority at Dartmouth. They couldn't have been more wrong about her.

Shecky had the great misfortune of being a Puritan in a Playmate's body. It never occurred to her to use sex to advance. She was much too confident in her ability to get to the top on sheer brains and ambition. She believed a woman's real power lay in her thinking, not in her thong, and she resented the ones who used sex as a tool for advancement or manipulation. They made it harder on those with real ethics and commitment. She had equal scorn for those who could be manipulated by sex. Shecky Lehman was a woman with a rigid moral core—integrity, with a capital *Teg*—and that batch of mean-spirited girls in her sorority had had no evidence to support their salacious opinion of her.

The only reason she'd joined Kappa Kappa Gamma was because it was her mother's dream. Margaret "Maggie" Lehman, née Barrett, had desperately wanted to be in KKG when she was at Dartmouth twenty-seven years before, but she was a Jew, and KKG—a most excellent and prestigious sorority—was comprised of girls of impeccable WASP lineage. Maggie had tried to slide under the radar with her unassuming last name, a name that had formerly been Lipshitz until her father gave it an overhaul. (The name Barrett had been derived from the Middle English *barat,* a word that meant trouble, strife, and, ironically, deception.) The KKG girls weren't easily deceived. They'd smelled the Jew in her right off. Maggie had never gotten over the snub. When her daughter was accepted at Dartmouth, Maggie saw the chance to set things right, and, by golly, she was determined to see that Shecky did. After nearly two weeks of rush parties and events, on Preference Night Shecky had chosen KKG as the sorority she most wanted to join, not just because of her mother, but because she genuinely liked the girls that she'd met. Four sororities put in a bid for her, including KKG. They were impressed with her striking beauty and sophistication, and the fact that her name screamed Jew didn't seem to matter. Shecky sank her bid, agreeing to join. Mother Maggie was both vindicated and thrilled. It was a new day, and overt racism at the Panhellenic level was no longer condoned. But girls would be girls, and they had much more insidious methods of torturing each other than racism.

Like voting someone Most Likely to Fuck Her Way Up.

The Kappa Kappa Gamma girls had given yet another Lehman a chip to carry. Shecky was going to prove that she was more than just the butt of an ugly sorority joke. KKG would be clamoring to claim her as part of its ranks once she hit her career stride. She'd show them—every single one of those girls who'd called her "fuck up" behind her back (it was an abbreviated spin on "one who fucks their way up"). They'd see how wrong they were, and they'd be sorry. All of them.

"Beryl called in sick, Ms. Ellerman."

The CEO nodded with concern.

"Of course she did. She's seen Page Six?"

"I'm assuming so, Ms. Ellerman. There was a message from her on my voice mail when I came in. She said she was under the weather, but that I could e-mail her if I needed to. She didn't answer the phone when I called her at home."

Ellerman pursed her lips.

"She must have seen it. Poor dear."

Shecky reserved comment.

"It's just awful," Ellerman tsked. "Well, I hope she doesn't let it get to her. She's not the first editor to get reamed in the media. She certainly won't be the last. No matter what, you don't let this kind of nonsense bring you to your knees."

Too late.

Beryl was on her knees, and had been for the past ten minutes, taking it up the love canal doggy-style, head pressed against the cushy McRoskey Airflex, bare ass pointed toward the borealis. She'd never done doggy before (she'd never done anything, really), even though Snoop D-O-Double once gave her a drawn-out description of its merits as she worked with him on a book. She'd seen pictures in sex manuals and had watched porn movies in slow-mo (the better to perfect her skills, should they one day be called upon), but nothing could compare to being in the moment, getting reamed, and getting reamed *well*. Penn's smacks on her bony backside echoed around the pristine bedroom, resonating throughout the brilliant acoustics of the apartment. He leaned into her, slipping his hands underneath so he could ply and knead her meager breasts. Beryl was frenzied, her neck, shoulders, and back flushed with patches of red. The golden god was giving her the golden rod, and she was loving it.

And how.

"Is she there?"

"No, Mrs. Tate. She called in sick."

"Damn. She saw the *Post,* didn't she?"

"I'm guessing she did, Mrs. Tate."

"Is she checking her messages?"

"So far she hasn't, but she said she'll be checking e-mail."

"Right," Sharlyn said. "Hmmm."

"Mrs. Tate, I must tell you, I'm really looking forward to reading your new manuscript."

This bitch, Shar thought. Shecky knew damn well the manuscript was nowhere close to being read by anybody anytime soon. There *was* no manuscript. Fucking bitch.

"All right, Shecky. I'll just shoot Beryl a note on her BlackBerry to make sure she's okay."

"Sure, Mrs. Tate."

"Thanks." Shar's tone was sharp.

"I wasn't trying to be offensive, Mrs. Tate. I really am looking forward to your book."

Sharlyn couldn't believe Shecky mentioned the manuscript again.

The two women were at a nice-nasty impasse. A long pocket of dead air hung between them.

"I'll tell her you called then, Mrs. Tate."

"Bye, Shecky."

"Bitch," Sharlyn muttered once the phone was dead. She didn't like that girl, even though a lot of other authors, mostly men, seemed to think she was choice. That whole "Mrs. Tate" business. So egregiously deferential and helpful. It was irritating, bordering on condescension. Sharlyn could almost hear the gears turning in Shecky's mechanical head every time she spoke. The only person's opinion that seemed to matter to her was Kitty Ellerman's. Beryl was just a stepping-stone to get her closer to the Big Lady and the Bigger Job. Shar knew it, even though Beryl didn't seem to. Shecky knew just how to flaunt her good looks, ice-princess aloofness, and exceptional competence. Beryl loved her. Shecky's attention to detail was ideally suited to Beryl's personality. Kitty Ellerman thought she had great potential.

The girl gave Sharlyn the heebies.

"She's not that bad," Beryl had said, but Sharlyn didn't buy it.

Something about Shecky just didn't bode well. She was too perfect. People that perfect should always be watched.

———

Ten thirty–eight A.M. loomed in bright red LCD largeness, reminding them of the realities of existence. Things like hunger, a bath, coffee. Salve.

Beryl's cooch was burnt up. Fried. The friction from the ancient rubbers, coupled with her dryness, had torched her hole to cinders. She didn't have a lot of mileage in it anyway, what with the way her medication tended to affect her sex drive. Her physical enthusiasm had been, for the most part, a means of expressing overwhelming elation at meeting Penn, knowing he was the One she'd been waiting for, having him seem to mutually agree, then being able to commence with it all right away. She instinctively tried to convey that elation via sex, and she meant it, at least during the first two sessions. By the third round, however, her lower half was just going through the proverbial literal motions. She dried out somewhere between kingdom and come. Kingdom and ten comes. That's how many he got out of her, then the well ran dry. She didn't have any lubricants on hand to keep the show going. So somewhere around nineish that morning, a white flag shot out of her pussy and he eased up. He slid down, down, back into the abyss to offer her desiccated canyon the cool, comforting relief of his tongue, but once he got an up-close glimpse of how hideous her box looked postfuck, he eased back up with infinite grace and cuddled her into distracted conversation.

They talked of many things. He spoke a little, very little, of his college years and his best friend Mercury. She explained that she'd never had a best friend. He seemed moved by that confession and held her with heartfelt sympathy. He described meeting the Dalai Lama when he was twelve. She told him about the bestseller she'd done with Snoop, a book called *D-O-Double Deeds*. She said he'd taken her cruising through the streets of the L.B.C. when she went out to Los Angeles to go over the edits with him. Snoop had introduced her to Pharrell Williams from the mega-hitmaking producing team the Neptunes. Pharrell had been great, an instant buddy, and the two had maintained contact once she returned to New York. One night at a party for Donald Trump, Pharrell introduced her to On Fiyah, the wildly popular rapper/actor/mogul/fashion overlord who was the head of WifeBeater Records and W.W.B. (Worldwide WifeBeater, his global entertainment empire).

Beryl had liked Fiyah at once, she told Penn. He was funny, ambitious, intense, and much smarter than she'd expected him to be. The next day he sent over a gorgeous velour sweatsuit with real flecks of diamonds down the front and around the hood. It was from Rich-Bytch, the upscale line of his womenswear division, BurntBytch. On Fiyah, Fiyah, O-Fi, Yah—whatever he chose to be called at any given moment—seemed to have the magic touch with everything he attempted. When he made his foray into the fashion world under the brand name Skorched, he had exploded onto the scene with immediate success. In less than five years, the Skorched name and products were everywhere. A wide range of clothing, shoes, and bags for men, women, and children, plus home furnishings (Skorched sofas! Skorched beds!). Gross sales for Skorched International had reached an astounding five hundred million the year before, and the current year's sales were expected to swallow that number whole. Bentley Motors announced a limited edition Skorched version of their Continental Flying Spur. At the tricked-out yet reasonably affordable price of one hundred and eighty-five thousand dollars, it was a hip-hop wannabe's dream. The metal monster was already back-ordered, even though it hadn't even gone into production. Fiyah was big business. Beryl wanted to do a book with him.

Penn listened with great interest, eager to step inside her world. Penn asked about the African violets. Beryl explained that they reminded her of herself, her life. They thrived indoors and, despite their delicate appearance, the flowers were tough and had the capacity to flourish on very little. An African violet would last for decades, she said, if it was treated right. All it needed was a little light, not much water, and a gentle splash of love. They were hard to kill, having been used to living in the crevices of craggy rocks in their native East Africa, and were natural survivors. But a green, surviving version of the plant was the lowest denominator of its existence. A truly happy African violet was a blooming one.

"Yours are all in bloom," Penn said.

"That's because I love them. I talk to them." Her voice took on a softness, as though she were speaking of a child or a lover. "I have a friend, a business associate," she lied. "Every year, I give him an African violet. He's got them all lined up in a window in his office. All of them are green, but there isn't a bloom in sight. Not a single bloom. It's so tragic. He claims he likes them, but I'm not sure."

"Maybe he doesn't talk to them."

"He was talking to them the last time I dropped in at his office."

"What was he saying?"

"It sounded like he was threatening them," she said, her face scrunched serious. "He said they were blocking him from being able to jump out the window. It's no wonder they don't flower."

Penn laughed.

"What?" she said.

"C'mon now, babe, that's pretty funny."

"I didn't think so. He's British. I guess I don't always get their sense of humor."

"Right."

He could tell she had become defensive about the plants. Plants, of all things. She was turning out to be a real layered piece of work. She grew quiet. He could feel her body tensing.

"Don't you think this is all a little unrealistic?"

"What's that?" he asked.

"This."

"This what?"

"Us," she said, sitting up and looking into his eyes.

"I don't get what you're saying."

"I mean, this is ridiculous, don't you think? I had this, this freaking one-night stand with you"—her cheeks were flushed, her right knee was shaking, she was waving her skinny arms in the air—"and then you say you love me and now just called me 'babe' like I'm really your girl and here I am skipping work and I'm probably never going to see you again after this and it's just, it's just . . . it's insane is what it is. You know my secrets, you could hurt me, it's too perfect. It doesn't make sense!"

She was flipping out. Had his lighthearted remark about the plants set her off?

"Relax, Beryl," he said, reaching up and grabbing both of her flailing arms. "I told you, this wasn't a one-night stand for me."

"How do I know that?" she demanded.

"You don't," he said, now somewhat irritated. "You're just going to have to take my word for it."

She clamped her lips together. Her eyes were scary large, which made her sort of scary face even scarier. Her cartilage-lite nose was twitching. Her eyes began to fill up.

"Aw c'mon, babe," he said. "Don't cry. Please. It's all right, really."

The tears splashed out anyway.

"I'm sorry," she said. "I can't help it. I feel so vulnerable."

"So do I," he whispered, pulling her to him. "I'm scared, too. I wasn't looking for a girlfriend. I've got things I'm trying to do, things bigger than bookkeeping. I wasn't expecting you, but you're here. So what do you want me to do, just act like it didn't happen?"

"That's what I'm afraid of," she said.

"C'mon, man," he said. "Is it because we had sex so quickly? Or maybe you think I'm not good enough for you or something? I know I'm kind of crass and I have a tendency to swear a lot, but I believe in being who I am, right up front. I'm sorry if the way I talk and the way I am is freaking you out, but I'm not going to hide—"

"No, no, no. You're great. I think you're wonderful. Everything you did for me last night. The way you made sure I got home, and then you stayed here with me, and you've been so kind and good and—"

"Beryl, you think this is about you having something to lose, but that works both ways. It's not just you letting me into your life. I'm letting you into mine. I don't do that too easily. It's been hard for me to get close to people after my parents died. I have this fear . . . this thing, you know, where I feel like—"

"Like as soon as you get close to them," she whispered, "they'll leave?"

"Yes."

"Or . . . they'll die?"

He paused, dropped his head.

"Yes."

"Oh, Penn."

She threw her arms around him and began to bawl. He clutched her to his chiseled pecs and abs, letting her have her moment, a moment she assumed was also his.

"I've been the same way," she sobbed. "I'm always so afraid. There's so many reasons for someone to leave me . . ."

"Don't say that, babe."

"It's true. I've got narcolepsy. I've got o—"

She caught herself.

"You've got o-what?"

She breathed in a few times, sniffling back embarrassment.

"I've got old issues when it comes to my parents. I've got a really big fear of abandonment. It's why I've never had a best friend. I have lots of acquaintances and plenty of great business relationships, but I've been afraid to let someone get close."

He rocked her in a tight embrace.

"Then let it be me," he whispered. "We're both dealing with the same fear. That's not an accident. There are no coincidences."

"I know."

"Maybe we were brought together like this so we could help each other out."

He leaned back from her, lifting her chin with his forefinger.

"It's possible, you know," he said. "I believe in that kind of stuff."

"Me, too."

She rested her head against his shoulder.

"You said no one knows about your narcolepsy."

"No one except the doctor who prescribed the medication." She took great care not to mention Ripkin by name or note that he was a psychiatrist. "That's it. And the pharmacist, I guess."

"Okay, outside of them, you felt safe enough to trust me. That was bigger than sex. It's not like we met at some bar and hooked up. This was nothing like that." He breathed deep, in and out, rubbing his hand across his golden hair in frustration, seeming to speak more to himself than to her. "Of all the things I hate about the world, I think this is the thing I hate the most."

"What's that?"

"This. What's happening between us. Once upon a time, in my parents' day and my grandparents', people could meet and fall in love in an instant. Just like that. One conversation, one look, and that did it for them. The love would start right then, and would carry them forward for the rest of their lives. There was none of this hesitation and mistrust, no endless stream of lovers. Love was love. Simple. Honest." His gaze seemed somewhere far off, not just beyond the room, but beyond time itself. "My dad felt that way about my mom. My granddad was that way about my grandmother. I always imagined it'd be that way for me. I've always believed in it. And, lo and behold, it is. Right now. Just like I imagined it. But most people are too fucked up and fucked over to accept that something beautiful, something like this, can happen. It's become mythical. And scary. The world is full of danger and dangerous people. No one believes this can happen anymore."

She lifted her head, her eyes, nose, mouth close to his.

"I believe it can happen." She pressed her lips to his, tears of gratitude streaming down her cheeks. "I've been looking for you for most of my life. I was hoping, praying, that one day you'd appear."

They'd been napping for more than two hours, complicated origami folded into each other. The phone had rung several times, but Beryl let the calls roll over. When she said hooky, she meant it.

"I'm starving," he groaned, sequeing into a wide-mouthed yawn.

"Me, too."

"Wanna get something to eat?"

"Sure. We could order in. There's lots of places around here that deliver."

"I feel like getting out and stretching my legs. I'm not used to being in bed this late. Not that I don't like it, but—"

"But what?"

"But it's a bit much, don't you think? I was hungry earlier, and somehow I managed to fall asleep again. Do you usually sleep this much?"

"Not at all. Especially not with my medication. I'm usually up way early, then I'm off to the gym."

"Me, too," he said.

"This is the most relaxed I've been in a long time. It's like a burden's been lifted. Maybe that's why I slept like this."

"Do you need to take more pills?" Penn asked.

"No, I won't need any more today. The ones you gave me earlier will last me until later tonight. I can start from scratch tomorrow morning at my usual time." She stroked his hand. "But thank you for being so caring. I like that. I never knew I'd like it this much."

"That's what I'm here for," he said, sitting up and stretching. "Now let's get moving."

She pouted.

"But I wanted to just lie here with you for a while. I never get to have days like this."

He glanced down at her there, lolling amid the sumptuous pillows.

"If we lie here any longer we'll have bedsores." He threw the covers back and swung his legs over the side. He stood, then stretched again, his arms raised toward the heavens as he groaned. He leaned from side to side, knowing without seeing that she was drinking in the full span of his magnificent body. He turned to face her. She stared up at him like he was a dream. Penn reached for her hand and tried to pull her from the bed.

"C'mon, lazybones. Get up."

"Penn," she whined.

"We can always lounge around later, if you want," he said.

"Can we?"

"Sure, babe. But I need to get some coffee in me. I can't function without my Starbucks and my morning papers." He checked the time on the big red readout. "Though it seems the morning's shot to hell. It's after one o'clock."

"It was a good way to ruin a morning," Beryl said.

"Yes, it was."

She smiled. He wondered how it would feel inside that wide mouth the first time he shoved his dick into it. He'd given her a pass this morning, but she would be sucking some dick in short order. No question. There was no getting around that cardinal rule.

"I need to go home and get a shower."

"You can shower here."

"I don't like putting on the same clothes afterward. That's pretty gross. I had those clothes on all day yesterday."

She was pouting again.

"You wanna come home with me?"

She grinned.

"Sure."

"Awesome. All right, why don't we get out of here, pick up some Starbucks, hit the newsstand, and head to my place. I'll grab a shower and change, and then we can get something to eat. Cool?"

"Cool."

"Excellent." Penn grew quiet, glanced down at his hands, then looked up at her. "Just so you know, my place isn't all tricked out like yours."

"That's okay, baby. I don't care about stuff like that."

Put a fork in her, he thought.

"Well, you should. You should want to be with someone who equals you in every way. I'm talking intellectually, physically, emotionally, and he should have the same level of ambition as you. Or more. I just thought I should warn you about my place beforehand. It's modest, but that doesn't mean I'm content with it. I've got some big projects in the works. I expect in time all the hard work I'm putting in is going to start paying off."

"I'd like to hear about them sometime," said Beryl.

"I love this room," he said, looking around, deliberately not responding to her remark. "It's so cozy. That's probably why I keep falling asleep."

"Really?" she said, following his eyes, taking in the room herself. "I was thinking of redoing it. The whole place, actually. I haven't been here long. I just kind of moved my things in without much ado, but

I'd really like to get a good contractor in here and do some things. Put my signature on the place, you know? It's my first apartment. The first place I've ever owned, that is."

"You did good, little one."

Beryl looked up at him quickly, her cheeks flushed with pleasure. She glanced away, shy, thrilled out of her mind at any indication of meeting his approval.

"So let's get outta here," Penn said. "Bad things happen when I don't have my coffee."

He loomed over her, his arms raised, fingers crooked in a mock attempt at terrorizing her.

"Oh please, Mr. Hamilton," she squealed, "don't hurt me, please!"

"Then get me to Starbucks, and get me there now," he said with a fairly good pirate brogue.

"Whatever you wish," she said. "After I bathe first, of course."

"Suppose I want my woman dirty?" he said. "I like the way I smell on your skin."

She giggled.

"Be serious. I'm going to wash myself now."

"Fine," he said. "Then get to it, or I'll have to take my hand to your backside again!"

Beryl was taking a shower while Penn spent a few moments alone relishing the comfort of the great McRoskey. He could hear her humming a tune, but couldn't make it out over the roar of the shower.

He ran his hands across the duvet, breathed in deeply, relaxed. He took a longer look around the room. There was so much more to notice, now that the sun was fully up. There was an impeccable order and detail to everything. Colorful blankets, folded with military precision, on the seat of a cushy chair. Photos on a side table. Her with Canon Messier, a picture with Bill Clinton, her alone in a lovely black cocktail dress. More well-tended happily blooming African violets lining the sill. The most striking thing was a large portrait on the left wall. How had he missed it before? It was one of those hand-painted reproductions of the work of a famous painter—Peter Paul Rubens's *Head of a Girl*. There was a baleful innocence about it, something sweetly threatening in the way the flaxen-haired, rosy-cheeked kid with her wide Vandyke collar monitored him from across the room like a cherubic gargoyle. He stared at the girl's almond eyes. Her eyes stared back. She seemed to be withholding judgment for the nonce, even though she'd witnessed a great deal of debauchery within the past few hours.

Penn tipped an imaginary hat.

"Pardon me, m'lady," he said. "I should have introduced myself before I showed you my ass. Pennbook A. Hamilton, at your service."

He chuckled, sank back into the pillows. So Beryl wanted to change this room, did she? The whole apartment. That might be a gig for Mercury, he thought. Why not hook up his best friend in the process of hooking up himself? That's what friends did for one another. Merc would have done it for him. It wouldn't be just a hookup, either. Mercury and his uncle were excellent contractors. They could make a good amount of money on a job like this.

Right. Seemed like Beryl might turn out to be an all-around bonanza. Penn cozied his neck into the sweetest part of the pillow, fig-uring he'd give himself a couple more minutes before he got into his clothes. This had been so much easier than he'd anticipated. He knew she'd be charmed by his looks and attention, but he'd expected the path to her bedroom to have at least a couple of snags along the way. He couldn't have gotten here faster if he'd been shot out of a cannon. Beryl was better than desperate, she was an idealist. That trumped des-peration every time. He was the bolt from the blue she'd been wait-ing for, so he got an EZ-Pass straight to her panties and her heart. No tolls, no waiting, no application necessary.

His eyes were shut and he was just about to doze again when the tune Beryl was singing managed to rise above the beating water. This time the words and melody were clear, her voice a chirpy squawk as she soaped herself clean.

" 'Happy days are here again . . .' "

Penn opened his eyes.

Happy days indeed.

———

A Ukrainian woman with massive biceps pressed down on the piece of muslin, then snatched the snatch clean.

"Ow!"

"I don't know why you still insist on those brutal treatments," Diamond said from a nearby room. "With all the pain-free wax removals they do here, there's no need to go through all that."

"I like it old school," Shar said through gritted teeth, bracing for the next assault. "It's how I know I still have feeling down there."

Aurora laughed from another room.

Shar's Sidekick rang. She signaled to the Ukrainian technician to hand it to her. The woman had just put fresh wax on the muslin. She pressed it into Shar's crotch and snatched.

"Shit!"

Then the woman handed her the phone.

"Hello." Shar sounded more than angry.

"Baby?"

"Miles!"

"Hey, baby."

"You back?"

"No," he said, "that's why I'm calling."

Her moment of elation was gone in an instant.

"Shar?"

"Yeah, Miles."

"Listen, baby, now don't get mad—"

"Miles . . ."

"Talks here are going really well. Jussi and I have made so much headway. He's agreed to the ComMedia-Golarssen merger, but only on the condition that I spend a little time with him and his company to get to know its culture. It's very important to him that we don't make radical changes that destroy the esprit de corps . . ."

"How long is 'a little time'?"

"No more than a couple of months. Three at the most. I was thinking maybe you could come—"

The Ukrainian woman snatched.

"Fuck!" Shar screamed. Laughter could be heard from Diamond's and Aurora's rooms.

Miles was silent on his end of the phone.

"Hello?"

"You know how I feel about cursing." His voice was cool, even.

"What? You're admonishing me about the f-word after you just announce that I'm not going to be seeing you for three months? Stop changing the subject. Stop trying to control me."

"That's not what I'm doing. I was trying to tell you to come stay with me while I'm out here, but I'm not so sure I want that now. You're becoming so vulgar, Shar. What happened to the little lady I married?"

The Ukrainian woman came at her with more wax-on-muslin. Shar raised her hand. The woman ignored her. She needed to apply the wax while it was still fresh. She pressed and yanked.

"Shit," Shar mumbled.

"So that's how you respond," Miles said. "I tell you you've become vulgar, and you answer me with more vulgarity."

"I'm getting a bikini wax, Miles."

"That's no excuse."

"I don't want to argue with you again. I thought I'd get to see you. I was hoping for it."

"I was hoping that, too, but you've just ruined my whole mood with your swearing. I ask so little of you, Sharlyn. I give you every-thing, everything you want. Can't you at least show me that courtesy? Can't you at least show me respect?"

"You don't give me everything I want."

"What haven't I given you?"

"Time."

The Ukrainian woman was applying more wax to the muslin. Sharlyn leaned up to get a glimpse of her loins while the woman's back was turned. How much more hair was down there to get? The tech-nician made it seem like she had a bear between her legs.

"I've always given you time, Shar." The chip on Miles's shoulder had come down a bit. "I've given you all of it. We didn't have kids so that nothing would take away from the time we had for each other. That was important to me. To us. Don't you remember?"

"I thought you'd forgotten."

"How could I forget anything about us? You're my life force, baby. My soul mate. The company's at a pivotal point right now. It's not always going to be like this. I just need you to bear with me. We've been through two decades together, going on a third. This is just a moment in time. Do you understand that?"

Sharlyn sat up and shut her legs before the Ukrainian woman could touch her again.

"Done," Shar said to her.

"Done?" the technician asked, crinkling her broad brow. "No. Not done. Still hair down there."

"Don't worry about it."

"So you do understand," Miles said. "Thank you, baby. I need you to be on my side through all this."

Shar stared at the phone.

"Miles, I was talking to the—"

"All right, hon, I've got to run. I'll try to call you in a few days. I love you. I know you're not big on it, but maybe you could shoot me an e-mail if you get around to it."

"But what about me coming to—"

The line was dead. The fucker. Just like that, he was gone.

"Shar? You all right?"

"I'm okay, Aurora."

"Don't worry about it, girl," said Diamond. "He'll be back in no time. In the meantime, we're gonna shop till he drops."

"You mean 'we,' " Shar mumbled.

"I mean 'he.' There's always a penalty for leaving your woman alone too long. We have to console ourselves somehow. That's why they make diamonds and furs."

"She's right," piped Aurora.

"Of course," said Sharlyn.

Somehow, slapping a billionaire with the bill from an afternoon of shopping didn't sound like much of a penalty. She missed her husband.

She had a bald, raw cooch, and no place to show it.

———

Penn had his Starbucks. A Venti red-eye. Three shots of espresso in a large COD (coffee of the day). It was twenty ounces of scalding brown hell, strong enough to resurrect the dead. No cream. No sugar. Just pure-dee caffeine, uncut, inside a dark, fragrant roast. A satanic concoction that practically tore the skin off the gullet on its way down. He called it the Defibrillator. It was music to his veins.

Beryl had ordered a Defibrillator, too, which gave him some concern. She had already proved quite hyper, and she was on meds, to boot.

"I want to have what you're having," she'd said. God, he thought, his stomach clenching. She was imitating him already. She was one of *those* kind of women.

"You sure that won't get you too geeked-up?"

" 'Geeked-up'? What does that mean?"

"You serious?"

"Yes. I've never heard it before."

"I thought you said you did a book with Snoop."

"I did."

They were just walking up to a newsstand to get the morning papers.

" 'Geeked-up' means 'high,' really hyper. Like you've been doing drugs."

Beryl set her coffee on the counter and picked out her papers. She grabbed a copy of *USA Today,* the *New York Times,* a *Daily News,* and a *Post.*

"Then I guess I'm geeked-up by nature," she said, "so no need to worry."

"All right," he said, reaching for a copy of the *Daily News* and the *Post.*

"I got those already."

Penn looked at the stack of papers in her hands.

"You don't mind sharing with me?" he asked.

"No, babe. These are 'our' papers."

" 'Our papers'?" he said as he put his back. "As in, we're a couple?" There was a hint of camp in his voice.

Beryl cast her eyes down, then brought them back up with confidence.

"Yes."

"I don't know," he said. "You don't sound so sure."

"I am sure."

"Then say it again. This time with feeling."

Beryl took in a deep breath, paused, and bellowed, "Yes, we're a couple!"

A slender redhead, a real hottie, was paying for her *Post*. She looked at Beryl, then looked at Penn. Looked at Beryl. Looked at Penn. Looked at Beryl.

"Here's your change, lady," the cashier said.

"Oh. Sorry."

Penn could see the confusion in the woman's eyes. He was a rock star. It wasn't a statement of conceit. It was a fact with a long-substantiated track record. There were chicks all over the island and the outer boroughs with his skidmarks on them. And Beryl was . . . well . . . Beryl was Beryl. She was a girl with condoms so old and unused, one of them disintegrated before he could even get it out of the pack. She was a mouse at best. A mouse with great taste, granted. A mouse with an excellent apartment, the perfect job, superior clothing, but a mouse nonetheless. The woman staring at them was the first real indication of how people would react to them as a couple. Beryl saw the judgment in the woman's eyes and began to fumble with the papers. Penn put his arm around her and kissed her full on the lips.

"Cute," the woman muttered. She grazed close to Beryl's ear as she passed. "Don't let your hooks out," she said. "Half the city'll be on him. Including me."

Beryl was thunderstruck. Her mouth was wide open as she watched the woman walk away.

"Forget her, babe," Penn said, pulling her close. "I got what I want."

Beryl grinned. The cashier cleared his throat.

Penn reached into his wallet, pulled out a five, and put it on the counter. Beryl snatched the money and pushed it back into his hand.

"You got the coffee," she said. "I'll get these."

"C'mon, now. I'm the guy. I'll pay for the papers."

"No, babe. I'm not one of those women who thinks the man should pay for everything."

The cashier, a young guy with a twenty-five-o'clock shadow and tousled hair, gave Penn a full-on look of protest. Don't be stupid, his eyes said.

Beryl was already going into her oversized suede corduroy Miu Miu tote for her wallet. She pulled out the money and handed it to the cashier.

"You sure?" Penn asked.

"Yeah."

"Thanks, babe."

He sipped his coffee as she paid the man. This was great. So far, all it had taken was some dick and a smile, with a "babe" or two thrown in for good measure. The world was unfolding for him at breakneck speed.

Beryl scooped up the papers and tucked them under her arm.

"Give 'em to me. You're so tiny, these'll drag you to the ground."

"Thanks, babe."

She surrendered the papers and plunged her arm inside the crook of his. He realized the "babe" thing was going to wear on him quick.

"Don't forget your coffee."

"Oh yeah."

She let go, grabbed her cup from the counter, then stuck her arm back inside the crook of his.

"Where to now?" she asked.

"My place is uptown, near Columbia. Once I get showered and change, we'll grab some lunch."

"Okay."

"Let's take a cab," he said.

The cashier called out to them as they were walking away.

"Have a nice day," the guy said, giving Penn a wink.

"Right," Penn said with a smile. "You too, buddy."

They stepped off the curb. Beryl rushed ahead, Starbucks in one hand, her other arm stuck in the air, waving down an oncoming taxi.

His place . . .

. . . was nice, she'd said.

It was neat, clean, and very well done with its IKEA chairs and IKEA sofa and IKEA tables and IKEA rug and IKEA clocks and IKEA throw pillows and . . . well . . . pretty much everything IKEA down the line.

She'd asked for a drink of water shortly after they arrived. He knew without her saying that she needed something to take the edge off the bitter rush of the Defibrillator, which he was sure had burned the fuck out of her throat on its way down. He placed the papers on the coffee table, went into the very organized kitchen, got a bottle of Aquafina from the fridge, and poured it for her. He was polite, sweet, seemingly happy to have her in his space. He handed her the water in a sea-green IKEA glass.

"Thank you."

"My pleasure."

She sat on the edge of the couch, coddling her drink. Penn tapped the message button on the answering machine and let it play. He wasn't worried about the threat of messages from women. None were ever allowed to call or come over unannounced. That was his main rule. He was always the caller, the sole elicitor of plans. Anyone who dared break that commandment was cut off at once. The woman upstairs with the broad back knew it, and so did all the others. Everybody knew their place. Even if they saw him with another, no one ever dared to break the rule.

It would be different for Beryl, of course. The rule was mostly in place so women didn't mess things up for the one he wanted to believe she was tops. There'd been no one in that position until now. He wanted to make Beryl believe right off that he had nothing to hide. He knew that playing his messages in front of her was a sure means of establishing the foundation for her trust.

"Yo, P, where you at?" a voice blared from the machine. It was Mercury. "P? Penn? Nigga, pick up the phone." There was a long pause as Mercury could be heard brushing his teeth, gargling, and rinsing his mouth.

"He calls you 'nigger'?" asked Beryl. "That is so—"

"He said 'nigga,' not 'nigger.' He means it as a term of endearment."

"Still." She frowned. "I don't get how anybody would think that's cool. Is he black?"

"Uh, yeah, I guess. Partly. He's Dominican. Are you sure you did a book with Snoop? I would think you got n-worded to death. It's no big deal. Everybody calls everybody 'nigga' these days."

"I don't."

"All right then, holla." It was Merc talking again. "And get a cell phone, you penny-pinching muthafucka. You're the cheapest former rich kid I ever met."

Penn looked directly at Beryl, no readable expression on his face. He could see the glint in her eye. This more than compensated for his low-rent apartment. She was now a true believer. He knew he'd never have to produce a single cent to back up Merc's words. He was a former rich kid, whatever that meant. She'd heard Mercury say it. Penn knew what she was thinking. That he wasn't just attractive, great in bed, and into her—he also came from money. Not that it was about him having to be a rich guy. He was hot. That's all that mattered. He knew he could have had her if he was living on the street. But now this had become the full-blown American Female Dream, like one of those Hollywood movies where the girl loves the guy for just himself, the pauper with no car, skuzzy hair, and dirt under his nails, only to learn he was a Swollenwallet. This was that moment. She'd suddenly jumped castes.

The answering machine beeped again.

"Penn. Penn? Nigga, what the fuck? Oh, I get it. You're probably up in some a—"

Penn hit the button on the bleating box. He didn't check Beryl for a reaction. That would be the universal sign for guilt. He walked across the room, stepping out of his shoes, socks, jeans, and shirt along the way, giving her a chance to savor his body in all its golden backside glory. He wasn't wearing any underwear. He never did. Beryl was enthralled watching his ass, becoming lost in the dimples just above the firm cheeks.

"I'm gonna jump in the shower, babe," he said, stopping in the hallway and turning toward her. His penis was hard, raging, red, delicious.

Beryl blushed.

"You've got a shiner," she said.

"A shiner?"

"Yeah." She pointed toward his crotch. "Your . . . your thing. It's at attention."

"My thing. Yes." He put his hand on it casually, stroking the shaft. "I guess he's still got Beryl on the brain. He probably wants me to come over there right now and . . . well. I'd better get in the shower. Otherwise we'll never eat."

"Right."

"You don't have to stay in there," he said as he walked away. "Mi casa es, and all that shit. Bring the papers back into the bedroom if you want. Get to know the place. Hopefully you'll become a fixture after a while."

"Okay."

He disappeared into the bathroom, closing the door behind him. She heard the water turn on.

Beryl smiled, taking in her surroundings, hugging herself. Her boyfriend's apartment. She had a boyfriend. She was bursting inside, dying to scream out her great fortune to the universe.

She imagined herself cuddled next to him in his bed, reading manuscripts, watching DVDs, limbs entangled sleepily on long Sunday
mornings.

She couldn't wait to see Dr. Ripkin again, couldn't wait to point
out how wrong he'd been for always trying to burst her bubble of
hope. Ripkin had been beaten up by love, and that was all he knew.
He was a bitter man. A good doctor, granted, but a sad sack on the
inside who could probably stand a hug or ten. She was so glad she
hadn't bought into his cynicism.

It would have ruined everything she was feeling right now.

Penn stood under the stream of water, scrubbing lather into his perfect
pecs and rippling abs. He imagined Beryl strolling around the place.
Everything had been strategically positioned the week before, when he
first began to lay the real groundwork for the plan. She would be looking at things right about now, he figured. Running her hand across a
tabletop here, picking up a knickknack there. Fingering the Wagner
collection, noticing his high regard for all things Jessye Norman. She'd
be walking down the hallway, perhaps peeking in the linen closet, recognizing the repetition of the color teal and assuming, wrongly, that it
was his favorite. She would stand in the doorway of the bedroom, not
going in right off, getting her first glimpse of Ekeberg, wondering—as
all silly women did—just how many others he'd fucked in that mass-
produced slumber trough, knowing within her heart that such a
thought was a dangerous one, debating whether she should ask now
rather than later, deciding at last that neither time was worth the com-
plication, that she was the only one that mattered now. Silly woman.

He grinned, he couldn't help himself, steam sliding across and
around his pearly whites as condensation swelled against his palate and
tongue. He squeezed more of the cheap (albeit pleasant and effective)
St. Ives Refreshing Aroma Steam Body Wash onto his cloth and
scrubbed the lather into his face, making a mental note that, once the
money began to roll in, he would go back to his favorite indul-
gence—bath, hair, and facial products from Lush, especially now that
they'd finally come to the States and set up shop in New York.

In time, in time.

The sting of hot water beating against his flesh was as invigorating as an ecstasy rush. He opened his mouth wide, directly under the stream, letting the orifice fill to the point of expanded cheeks. He spit, shook the excess water from his hair, and placed the soapy washcloth on the shoulder-high ledge. He put his hands on his hips, leaned back, and took a long, long piss, watching the dregs of the Defibrillator swirl down the drain, on its way to the Hudson. This was a habit he'd developed after his parents' death, pissing in the shower. It was a direct defiance of yet another one of their rules. His mother had instilled in him very early that good boys—well-bred boys—only peed in toilets or urinals. Never in alleys or against a wall, or in a shower, a pool, or the ocean. It didn't matter how much he needed to go. He must always wait until he could make his release within the proper confines of a restroom.

He sprayed the wall with extra flourish.

Beryl would be inside his bedroom now, he figured, having recovered from the momentary catatonia of contemplating Ekeberg. After that, it was just a matter of nosiness. She might try to behave this first go-round. She was on medication for her obsessive nature, after all. It might take a while to get her to crack. Maybe more than one visit. Several even, he thought.

No worries.

He was prepared for the wait. He was already many steps ahead of the game.

Beryl placed the papers on the right side of the bed and set the glass of water on the (IKEA) nightstand. She didn't sit. Step by careful step, she made her way around the bedroom, keeping an ear alerted for the sound of running water from the shower, lest he come out too soon and discover her prying.

There were no pictures of his dead parents anywhere. She wondered why. She knew the reason she didn't have any photos of hers. They'd never taken pictures, had never been the kind of family that did things like that, had never even owned a camera. The photos in her home were of her with bosses, authors, associates, and people of other-

wise import within New York, national, and international society. But
Penn was a rich kid. Wasn't that what his buddy on the answering
machine had said? She would think he'd have his parents' photos
around somewhere. Or some pics of old girlfriends, at the least. What
kinds of women were they? Drop-dead models, she bet, the kind who
would make her feel so insecure, she would second-guess him ever
wanting to be with her when measured against their beauty.

"I shouldn't snoop," she said. "Better to not know than to torture
myself."

Right. Right.

She very, very quietly opened the first, then second drawer of the
nightstand. Nothing but paperbacks in both, all books on philosophy.
Philosophy? She moseyed over to the (IKEA) dresser, careful not to
make much noise. There was nothing on top but a sterling silver comb
engraved with what appeared to be his initials, P.A.H., more stacks of
paperbacks—dog-eared copies all—of Shakespeare's plays, and a dozen
tubes of Kiehl's in three very neat rows of four, four, and four. No
photos yet of his parents. Had there been bad blood? Was that the reason why he chose to live so leanly? Or perhaps it was too painful for
him to have them around. He said he had abandonment issues, just
like her. Could that be it?

"My poor baby," she whispered. "It must be so hard for him."

But what about the other girls? If she could just see what one
looked like, just one, for practical purposes only, so she would know
where the bar was set.

Beryl stood before the dresser, contemplating her next move. Nine
drawers loomed before her. Nine chambers of secrecy, potential
mother lodes of revelation. She hesitated, listening. The shower was
still running. Perhaps there was time. She had to know what was in
those nine compartments. The desire to peek was irresistible.

Ripkin had taught her that when she felt her compulsion getting
the best of her, when the urge to do something she was sure she
shouldn't do became unbearable, she should count to twenty very
slowly while tugging her left ear with one hand and rubbing her belly
with the other. She must focus all her energies on this exercise, mak-

ing sure she got to twenty, counting as though her life depended upon it. It would distract her mind, he said, reroute it until she could get hold of herself enough to overcome whatever irrational desire she was wrestling with in the moment.

She stared at the treasure trove of squares, trying to approximate how long Penn had been in the bathroom versus how much longer he might remain. He wouldn't just shut off the water and rush right out, she reasoned. He'd have to dry himself, deodorize, brush his teeth, lotion, perhaps even shave. She'd learned from one of Canon Messier's books that that's what men did—shit, showered, and shaved, in that exact order, although Penn hadn't shat, as far as she knew. Maybe he still had to, once he was done showering, and that would buy her even more time. Between the shitting and the shaving, that was a good ten more minutes, easy. She craned her neck, straining to catch any indication of what he might be doing. Still showering. Plus the shit and the shave. She was going to go for it. Against all logic, odds, and self-restraint (which her medication had no effect on any-way), she was going to look in the drawers.

Penn stood on the teal wide-looped pile rug from IKEA, his bath rug, letting the water drain from his body without the assist of a towel. He opened the cabinet and reached for the bottle of aloe-infused baby oil gel. It was part of his ritual. One of the inexpensive ways he kept his skin soft and supple, the stuff ladies dreamed of. She was awful quiet out there. Probably reading the paper. Or not.

She was eight drawers in and, so far, had come across nothing but well-ordered compartments of socks, T-shirts, more Kiehl's, folded jeans, more T-shirts, a book on Pilates, some Wagner CDs, and a glar-ing absence of underwear.

No photos of Mom and Dad. No girls, drop-dead or otherwise. No photos at all. Nothing revelatory, as she'd expected.

There was but one drawer left.

———

Penn's teeth were brushed and his face was half-shaven. He scrunched his cheek to one side, checking out his skin. Facials. Yes. He would start getting facials again.

It was going to feel so good to be rich.

Beryl was bent over, tugging at the very last square in the very last quadrant, the lower right one, of the so-far unmysterious dresser. She found herself half hoping for something juicy, something worth all this trouble. She'd feel ashamed of herself if there was no payoff. Shame. That was the negative benefit of an obsessive rush.

She could hear the faucet running in the bathroom. She went for it. She snatched the thing open with bald-faced necessity.

Untitled, a novel by Pennbook A. Hamilton.

Pennbook? His name was Pennbook? Penn*book*?

A tiny piece of her brain was trying to wrap itself around that. The rest of it was gagging, choking on the truth.

The Defibrillator was fucking him up. His stomach. It was in knots, the vicious brew proving better than any laxative. He shut off the faucet, reached for a hand towel, wiped the steam off the toilet seat, and sat his clean, aloe-infused buttcheeks down for a spell.

Fuck all.

He was a writer, another fucking writer trying to sell a fucking book.

Beryl was devastated. She'd let this man desecrate her, run his wanton tongue across the most intimate areas of her body, ram her, smack her many, many times on the ass, even stick his big . . . oh God . . . in her anus, that undiscovered country . . . although it was brief, just three or four pumps, five at the most, an accident, he'd said, so sorry.

And worst of all, he knew she was narcoleptic, knew she considered it a damaging secret. He could blackmail her now.

Oh, the shame! She was a sucker. A simple, simple sucker.

She felt her knees buckle with embarrassment and became frightened by what might possibly come next from such a rush of feelings—a medication-defying cataplexy. She breathed in, breathed out, deep, deep, grasping the edge of the dresser in an attempt to stave off the blunt edge of emotion. This man knew where she lived. She had told him she *loved* him!

The manuscript stared up at her.

Close the drawer, close the drawer, the sane side of her silently screamed. All it would take was one quiet move of her foot to kick it closed.

Untitled.

It was a force bigger than sense.

From the bathroom she heard the familiar spaz-fart that preceded a morning shit. He was doing it all out of order, the showering, the shitting, the shaving. She had time, she had time. She could kick the drawer closed and be out of there, out of his apartment, away from him and his irresistible beauty and shameless penis and extortionistic measures or whatever diabolical plot he'd come up with to get his stupid manuscript in the hands of a potential publisher, a plot where he was willing to stoop to something as low as fucking her, debasing himself for the sake of a deal. Not that she considered herself unfuckable, but who would want to get fucked on terms like these?

Ripkin, in all his British smugness, had been right all along. Her heart dropped through the floor, snatching her dignity along with it.

The toilet flushed.

"Sorry, babe," he yelled. "It's the coffee."

"It's all right," she said, her throat so thick she could barely squeak out the words.

Close the drawer, you stupid cunt! Close. The. Fucking. Drawer.

Her logical side had a forked tongue at times, nasty even, the better to get her to listen, it hoped.

The toilet flushed again. Beryl scooped up the manuscript, alarming herself in an out-of-body way by the gesture, then pressed her foot against the drawer to close it. The sound of shit-laden water swirling down the bowl drowned out everything but the pounding in her head. She raced to her oversized Miu Miu tote and tossed the thing in, flinging the bag on the floor next to the nightstand, out of plain sight.

Now she was a thief. A humiliated, demented thief.

She should have run out of there, she knew. Should have run like the devil was at her heels, run for cover, run for her life.

But curiosity was a big beast, bigger than shame.

And an unimpeded obsessive-compulsive disorder was the biggest beast of all.

Shar had already left several messages at Beryl's house and on her cell phone, which Beryl had apparently shut off.

"She must be so embarrassed," she said.

"Let it happen to her enough times," Diamond said. "She'll get over it."

"I'm not so sure of that," said Shar. "You don't know Beryl. She's a fragile sort, no matter how much she tries to downplay it. Maybe I should go by her place."

"Let her be, Shar," Aurora said. "She's probably just licking her wounds. Who knows, maybe she'll surprise us all and come to the party tonight. In the meantime, just give her some space."

Shar pursed her lips together, knowing Aurora was probably right, but still worried about her friend.

She was on the bed, flipping through the *Post,* when the bathroom door opened.

"Sorry I took so long," he said. "You must be starving by now."

"I'm okay," she said, her voice noticeably shaken.

Something's wrong, he realized. He surveyed the room quickly, but nothing seemed out of order. Still, he knew spooked when he saw it.

"You all right, babe? You mad at me for being in the bathroom too long?"

"No, no, I'm fine," Beryl said, her voice high, very, very high.

"All right," he said. "I'll just be a minute, then we can get out of here."

"Take your time, Penn."

Penn. He was Penn again. Something was wrong for sure. She wasn't calling him "babe."

He opened one of the dresser drawers and grabbed a pair of jeans. He shook them out and stepped into them. He opened another drawer, glancing back to check her out. She was staring at him, her eyes stretched with panic. At what? What had happened? He hadn't counted on this unascribable behavior.

"Beryl. Babe. Why are you looking at me like that?"

"Huh?"

"You're scaring me. Your eyes are all bugged out."

"Huh? Uh . . . oh. I think, um, uh . . . I don't know. I'm not used to being off like this. I guess I'm kind of freaking a little. I haven't talked to anybody at work all day. I think the guilt must be kicking in."

"You want to call the office? Use my phone."

"No, that's al—"

"Go ahead, call in. It'll make you feel better. It'll make me feel better. I'm starting to think I've done something bad by keeping you away from work."

"It was my idea, remember?"

Her tone was weak, shaky. Was she about to flip out on him again? Was this the whole insecure you-can't-really-love-me-so-fast thing, part deux, coming up?

"Call. Check your messages. Do it now."

"I'll check the ones at the house," she said.

She reached for the phone next to the bed and started dialing. He pulled on an olive-colored T-shirt that gave his golden skin an even bolder glow, if that was at all possible.

"I let you hear my messages," he said, his back to her.

He didn't want to prod her. He figured he'd just put it in the air.

"Oh."

She pulled the base of the phone onto the bed, searching for the speaker button. When she hit it, someone was already talking, mid-message.

". . . just worried. Call me, all right? You never take off, no matter what happens."

"Tell her about the party, Shar," a voice said in the background.

"All right, all right, just give me a chance. There's a party tonight, hon. Something Diamond and Aurora have put together on a whim. Come through, okay?"

"Pleeeeeease," said another voice.

"It's at Bungalow Eight. I'll probably get there around ten or eleven. I can come get you, if you want. Please come, Beryl. I'm worried about you. You can't let this kind of thing get you down. All right? Call me. It's Sharlyn. Of course. You know that already."

Beryl hit the speakerphone button, killing the call.

"I don't feel like listening to the rest."

"What's up, babe?" Penn asked, coming to her side. He sat next to her on the bed, his arm around her. "What's she talking about? What's got you so down?"

"Nothing. I don't know what she means. She probably thinks there's something wrong because I took the day off."

He turned her face to his, eyes narrowed, trying to squint out the truth.

"Don't lie to me," he said. "Something's wrong with you. You've been different since I came from the bathroom. Who was that? Was that Sharlyn Tate, the writer?"

"Yeah. That was her. It's no big deal."

He chucked her under the chin, trying to get her to make eye contact. She wouldn't. Her gaze was cast at the floor.

"Beryl, baby . . . what's the matter?"

"I . . . it's . . . I can't . . ."

Tears were now cascading down her cheeks.

"Beryl. What happened? Tell me. This is fucked up."

"Would you mind . . . would you be angry at me if . . . I just . . . is it okay if I just went home?"

"Okay, babe," he said, pulling her into a hug. "We can go back to your place."

She pushed away from him.

"Alone," she said. "I need to go alone."

Penn's mind was racing. Things seemed to be spiraling away from his control. She was arm's-length now, and there was that cryptic phone message. He searched his reasoning for the best way to handle this, the unknown. Step back. Let her breathe. To smother her now would only push her deeper into the freaky corner she was retreating into.

"All right. Would you like me to grab you something to eat first? I can order some takeout."

"No, no, really. I think I just need to go home and lie down. This . . . it's. Today . . ."

"Today was a lot. For both of us."

"Yes. It was."

She rose from the bed, grabbing her Miu Miu tote from the floor.

"I'll walk you out."

"No. Please. Stay. Really. Okay?"

Her eyes were pure enigma. Big blue batshields that told him nothing at all.

She was walking away.

"Hey," he said.

She turned around.

He was right behind her. He pulled her into his arms in a warm, comforting hug, kissed her forehead, put his mouth beside her ear.

"Whatever's wrong, babe," he whispered, "it's gonna be all right. Really. And I'm here. Whenever you want to tell me what it is, even if it's something I did, I'm here. Okay? Okay?"

"Okay."

"I love you, Beryl," he said. He chuckled awkwardly. "How stupid. I love you, and I don't even know your last name."

She looked up at him with vagueness, searching his eyes for something. What? he wondered. What the fuck was she looking for?

"It's Unger," she said, her voice wan, deadpan, as flat as her backside. "Messier said it at the book signing when he introduced me to the crowd."

"Oh. I guess I wasn't paying much attention."

"The guy who tried to get me to take his manuscript said it, too."

"Well, I was definitely distracted by then," Penn said. "I was too concerned with making sure you were okay."

"It's on my prescription bottles."

"So it is," he said. "Why are you hammering me on this? I wasn't looking at your last name when I found those bottles. I wanted to know what was wrong with you. So sue me. I'm an inattentive clod."

He wiped the tears from her face.

"Sweet baby."

"I've got to go."

She pried herself free and rushed to the living room and the front door.

"I love you, Beryl."

It was a quiet, unthreatening remark. Nothing oppressive to the left or the right. It was just . . . there. Hanging above her, a sword of confusion.

She stopped, just for a second, her thin shoulders squared as though bracing for attack.

Then the door was open, and she was through it, and, just like that, she was gone.

Penn sat at the foot of the bed, furious, wondering what could have happened to make his perfect plan come so undone.

Something nagged at him. A feeling. No. She wouldn't have gone there. Not just yet.

He leaned down toward the drawer, the one in the lower right quadrant of the dresser. Drawer number nine.

He pulled it open.

It was empty.

His masterpiece was gone.

He was drinking Grey Goose, cold, straight from the freezer, straight from the bottle. He was sitting in bed, wondering what to do now.

Plan B was screwed and there was no Plan C. She'd been nuts enough, quirky to the extreme, so absent of self-control that she'd raided his drawers and found the manuscript already. And she knew he was a writer, had assumed he was that commonest of things—another hustler trying to peddle his wares.

It wasn't supposed to go down like this. She was supposed to go through the philosophy books first, ask questions about those. Then she was to find his dissertation on Wagner and Gesamtkunstwerk, the one on top of the TV in his bedroom, hiding right in plain sight. She was supposed to see it, get a feel for how he thought. That would lead to a conversation about product branding, which would, in turn, lead him to discuss his views on himself as the consummate brand.

And then the book. In due time.

Not to-fucking-day.

The loon had gone straight for his jugular, ripped it out, and flown back to her loony roost, leaving him bleeding in the wind. With no recourse. No real one, anyway.

He chugged back the liquor.

He was fucked.

She'd taken the manuscript to let him know she knew, the cruel, bony bitch. She hadn't said a word, not one solitary word. She'd just welled up and gone all foolish on him, and then she'd split.

She'd played the player. She'd beaten the game.

He knocked back a third of the vodka in one gulp.

"Fuck it," he said.

Fuck it, indeed. What to do next? Next. There was no next. Nothing but drunkenness and derailed opportunity. His party was over. In less than eighteen hours . . .

. . . eighteen.

. . . eight.

8.

Bungalow 8.

Wait.

There was a party. A party with rich people. Diamonds. And cash. Aurora Kash cash. And probably lots of others with equally deep pockets. And a very, very popular author. A pretty author. Sweet, pretty chock-o-latte, almost as dreamy as that dreamiest of dreams, Diva Jessye.

Why not? he figured. What the hell did he have to lose? The Beryl plan was already shot.

He took another swig.

Enter Plan C.

Gregor Balzac

. . . awakened with a start. His head was throbbing and he couldn't see. The whole of him was hurting. He tried to move, but his flesh was so tight, so constricted, it defied anything beyond the horror of pain.

"Get up, man. We're gonna go shoot some hoops."

It was Neil at the door, inconsiderate as usual, already on his way in without invitation.

"What the—"

The door slammed and there was a rush of feet in the other direction. Neil was on the other side, shrieking.

"Pete! Pete! Come here, man! You gotta see this!"

Pete was their other roommate, the third man in the shared space that was their rented house in Van Nuys, a town on the early side, the southern side, of the San Fernando Valley, that vast bowl of suburban sprawl just over the hill from Los Angeles proper.

"What's up? What's all the screaming about?"

All one had to do was listen to Pete's voice and they'd have the Cliff's Notes to the man. He spoke with a lazy drag, the words reluctant boulders hauled out by ropes. His languor was a depressing infection. Just hearing him was enough to drain the energy from a room.

The two of them were just outside Gregor's door. There was a shuffling of feet, huddled voices, Neil's high, Pete's thick, low, and slow, and then the knob was turning again, one creak at a time. The sound made the throbbing in Gregor's head grow worse. He feared an aneurysm was imminent. He wanted to shout at them to either go away or come on in at once, but he couldn't get the words out.

He didn't have a mouth.

"Look at that," Neil whispered, both men now inside the room. "It's Gregor."

"That's not Gregor," Pete said, his voice higher, words coming faster than even he realized they could. He was smoking a joint. The fumes aggravated Gregor's already monstrous pain.

"It is him. It's got on his shirt."

"My God. It does."

The pulsing in Gregor's temples was so intense, he was crying. He could feel the leaking tears ooze thickly down his face. He needed a doctor, a hot rag, some Vicodin.

He wanted to tell them to call for help, but he was trapped inside himself. He couldn't move. He couldn't speak. He couldn't see. All he could do was feel and hear and ooze thick sticky tears.

"This is unfuckingbelievable," Neil said. "I've never seen anything like it."

"I have," said Pete, exhaling more fumes. "He's a big fucking dick."

Beryl's mouth was open, had been open for more than an hour.

She was deep into *Untitled* and it was good, damn good, even though she'd had no plans to read the thing ever, had flung it across the living room when she came home and cried for the good side of three hours until she'd run out of pity for herself and had been hit with the shits.

Compliments of the Defibrillator and an empty, stressed stomach.

She was sitting on the toilet, manuscript on the floor. She hadn't checked phone messages or e-mails or even read the day's papers. She'd left them at Penn's place anyway, and she didn't have any desire to go back out to get new ones. She never saw the write-up about her in Page Six. She was too caught up.

This story—this ridiculous story with no name—it was full of sadness and wit and a thousand natural shocks, and prurience and pornography and pussies and penises, and actors and models and freaks and greed and, of all things, Kafka. It was Kafka Redone. Penn had taken the man's masterpiece of classic literature, *The Metamorphosis,* and updated it, set it in modern times in the most unlikeliest of places—the San Fernando Valley, the porn capital of the world—and instead of making the main character wake up as a giant cockroach, he'd awakened as . . .

A giant prick.

A prick named Gregor Balzac.

It was crass. It was vulgar.

It was absolute genius.

consequences

Writers and whores. I see no difference.
—Salman Rushdie

Coke would

. . . never go out of style.

People could talk all they wanted about designer drugs, heroin, and crystal meth, but the powdery stuff—blow, snow, white girl, yeyo, toot, whatever one's term of fancy—it was stalwart, as reliable as the sunrise. It had stood the test of much, much time. Nations had been founded on it, while others had become war torn over the stuff. It was the bread of life, both the giver and taker of dreams. Cut just right, it could deliver a blast of I-don't-give-a-fuck-inducing numbness that was as liberating as a divorce decree.

Snuffed up in the right dose at a party, and it was on.

Snuffed up in the wrong dose, and the party was over.

Cocaine had gotten a bad rap in the nineties. Almost overnight, it had gone from being the rock star of narcotics to a shameful leper, much the way cigarettes were falling from grace. It was generally seen as an uncool habit for uncool people, even though the powerful and successful continued to do it on the sneak. For a moment, even heroin had become chic and crack wasn't as whack, yet cocaine was the dirty whore with a dirty past. But there was a new generation of Holly-wood hipsters, musicians, and celebutantes who were unabashed about letting the world peek into their sexual antics and recreational drug choices. Rappers and rockers alike bragged in interviews and videos about how much they loved weed, blow, and group sex, and

piles of white stuff were once again making appearances on the mirrored tables and plates of the better house parties, alongside big fat
blunts and rounds of X. People were once more dipping into their little vials of toot with their tiny silver spoons. "It" girls were pho-
tographed with insouciant traces of powder around the edges of their
noses. Yeyo had been relegated to the bastard position behind Ecstasy
and other amphetamine- and methamphetamine-based designer drugs
for nearly a decade, but now it was stepping back into the spotlight to
regain its rightful, time-weathering position.

Cocaine was, once again, the king of the room.

"Cooooooooooooke . . . is a many-splendored thing."

Sharlyn was singing as she dip-dip-dove her schnoz into a fluffy
white minimound of the stuff in a folded piece of plain white paper
she'd taken from her purse. She didn't snort often. Miles didn't know
she did it at all. He'd never seen that side of her and would disapprove
if he did, same as he frowned on the cursing.

Fuck Miles, she thought.

Diamond and Aurora didn't know, either. At least, they never let on
that they did. No one had ever seen her do it. Well, practically no one.

There was a knock on the door of her stall.

"Shar."

It was her friend Tina, who was also her stylist. Tina was the one
who'd hooked her up with the supplier of this most primo cocaine, a
guy called Titty. Really. Titty Mebane. Miles didn't like Tina. Natch.

"She's too much of a free spirit," he said, "and she's always cursing.
She's good with clothes, but there's something rather seedy about her."

Fuck Miles.

Shar opened the door and let Tina in.

"All I want is a little," Tina said, scooping a teensy bit with the
glittery-blue acrylic nail of her pinky. She snuffed it up. "Yum."

"I didn't know you were coming," Shar said, wiping her nose.

"I heard there might be cute boys here."

"But you've had all the cute boys."

"Not nearly enough," Tina replied.

Sharlyn smoothed the front of her low-rise Frankie B.s and opened the stall door. She walked out into the always packed bathroom and squeezed her way over to the mirror. Tina followed her.

"That's a cute top. Did I pick that out for you?"

"No, I got it today. I wanted something that made me feel good."

"That oughta do the trick. Are your tits warm enough?"

"You're such a whore."

They both laughed and made their way out of the bathroom.

Bungalow 8 was one of, if not the, most private nightspots in the city. Located in West Chelsea, it was the spawn of that entrepreneurial maven of club savvy, Amy Sacco, who also owned Cabana at the Maritime Hotel and the popular bar Lot 61. Lot 61 was a fun, funky, supercool lounge, with exquisite food, drinks strong enough to choke an ox, and damn good deejays playing damn good music. Over time, it had become less a gathering of the who's who of the celebrity world and ultrahip scenesters, and was now more bridge-and-tunnel, full of non-Manhattanites and regular folks trying to flex as though they were actual denizens of the city. Imposter was written all over them, but no one gave a fuck. People could get loose and have a good time. If one didn't mind hobnobbing with the hoi polloi, Lot 61 was a great place to be.

For those who wanted to leave the unwashed masses behind, Bungalow 8 was the antidote. Getting inside was a feat akin to winning a hundred-million-dollar lottery, although rumors (urban legends, perhaps?) were beginning to circulate of superattractive nobodies getting in on less-challenging Monday nights, the apparent Achilles' heel of the doorkeeper's week. There was a No Vacancy sign flashing in the window, lest anyone got the idea that they might have a chance at entry. Modeled after the glamour and style of the famous lair to the stars, Bungalow 8 at the Beverly Hills Hotel, this Bungalow 8 was an intimate setting filled with potted palms, murals, lots of big furniture, and skylights, all mixed with a tropical poolside theme. The place brought to mind images of everything from old Hollywood to something out of Brian De Palma's *Scarface*. One would not have been sur-

prised to see Tony Montana and his "liddle fren" burst into the room
at any moment. (Big-time Tony, of course, after he became a major
drug lord; the doorman would have never even made eye contact
with Mariel-boat-lift Tony.) There was a concierge and a nearby heli-
pad for the truly important who needed to lift off at a moment's
notice. Bungalow 8 put the "clu" in exclusive, and those who didn't
have a clue and insisted on trying to pry their way in were doomed
to doing the walk of shame, back, back, back to the nobody worlds
from whence they came, back to the tar pits and asphalt of the cruel
city, back with the rest of the non–Amex Black Card–wielding, no-
helicopter-having human dreck.

There would be no unwashed masses in Bungalow 8.

It was strictly the playground of the unwashed elite.

Penn was standing a few feet down the block, calculating his move.
A crowd of idiots hovered near the door, soon-to-be walk of
shamers all, blocked by a bouncer whose forehead looked as though
it could crush stone. These people had no chance of getting in and
they knew it, but this was New York, and people liked to dream,
and for some it was enough to be able to say they saw so-and-so
going inside or coming out of such-and-such club. Mindless frivol-
ity. Penn had greater things at hand, and it didn't involve crowding
around a door, begging entry. This would be a breeze. This kind of
thing always was.

Sure enough, a small group of two beautiful girls and three men
of assorted size and persuasion passed by him amid a cloud of ciga-
rette smoke and laughter. Penn noticed that one of the girls was the
actress Chloë Sevigny. He fell into step along with them as though
he belonged and walked toward the club. Chloë and her friends realized what he was doing and welcomed him in. As they passed effortlessly through the door, Chloë turned to him and said, "You're
beautiful."

"Thank you."

"You owe me," said Chloë. "I'll collect later. Not tonight."

"Done," he replied with a nod, and disappeared into the party.

———

"I want a lobster club sandwich," Shar said.

"No you don't. You want another Wardrobe Malfunction."

Sharlyn burst into a profound round of giggles. She couldn't stop herself. She kept laughing and laughing and laughing. Then she saw Diamond DeLane dancing with her husband.

"Look at them go," Sharlyn said, growing somber. "At least she's got her man." Her eyes began to well up and her lip was in a pout. "Where's Aurora?"

"I don't know. But we need some more drinks."

"Noooooo," Shar whined.

Tina raised her right brow.

"All right," Shar said, snapping out of her instant funk. "Just a couple more. Hey, I can't feel my nose. Is it still there?"

"Oh yeah," Tina said, pressing the tip of her client-buddy's snout. "You definitely still have it."

"And my cheeks. What about my cheeks?"

"Cheeks are in effect."

Sharlyn went into her tiny purse and pulled out a compact. She still had her cheeks, even though she couldn't feel them. And there it was. Her perfect brown nose. Not too wide and Negroid, but not so narrow that it looked retouched, which it wasn't.

"Miles loves my nose."

"Of course he does," Tina concurred in a deadpan voice.

"What?" Shar said, snapping the compact shut. "Are you saying he doesn't?"

"I'm saying you need another drink."

"He loves my nose. He loves everything about me. And I love him."

"Of course you do. Now let's have another drink."

Tina shined her pearly whites at Shar. The diamond stud in her left front tooth twinkled in the light. Shar stared at the sparkling jewel, cocking her head to the side.

"Did that hurt?" she asked.

"C'mon, Shar, you know it didn't."

"Are you sure?" She reached over and patted Tina's shoulder with concern. "It looks like it was painful. You can tell me."

"I was stoned when I got it. You ready for that drink? I told him to keep them coming."

"Oh, awwwwwriiiiiiiiiiight," Sharlyn said. "Gosh, Tina, you're such a bad influence."

Shar wasn't quite sloshed, but she was close. And she felt *gid-ddddddddddyyyyyy*, supergiddy, like maybe she could fly (or, at the very least, float around the room). It was that weird feeling that came from mixing drugs and drink. It was a combination that required great care. Too much, and a person was apt to do very bad or embarrassing things.

Their libations arrived.

A Wardrobe Malfunction, or WMD (the *D* was for "drink"), was a chocolate martini with a splash of Everclear and a Hershey's Kiss (faux nipple) floating on top. All it took was a few of them and bras inevitably came off. A fair share of starlets, A-list actresses, and their hangers-on had flashed their superbowls after one WMD too many.

Sharlyn grabbed one and drank it at once.

"Shar, slow down. You're gonna get sick."

"No I'm not," she said with a burp. "And you're a fine one to tell me to slow down when you're the one that's making me drink, you little skank."

Tina laughed.

Shar sat back against the seat, her brow furrowed.

"I can't stand Miles," she said.

"Miles isn't here," said Tina. "So party, bitch. Like it's 2005."

Shar gave Tina a prolonged blank stare. Then she brought her legs up on the banquette, stood on the seat, and funked to the music until her Giuseppe Zanottis punched a hole in the upholstery and she went crashing, laughing, onto the floor.

He spotted her across the room, over the sea of celebrity heads and reality-show throwoffs. Overpriced liquor was being sucked down like air and the scent of fame was rich, thick, and heady.

This is what it will be like, he realized. This is what it will be like to be one of them.

Random hands were feeling him up, faceless voices coming on to him at his ear. Someone snapped his photo.

"You're delish," the girl said as she clicked away. "Who are you?"

"You'll know soon enough," Penn said as he smiled and pushed past her. There was his dark horse, heading toward the bathroom. She'd been dancing on the seat in her booth for the longest, flinging her arms around, her breasts barely contained in a strappy silk top. And the way her jeans hugged her ass. Penn had a rock in his pants and just watching her made it grow more granite by the second. Sharlyn Tate, right there in front of him, a sexy beast in the worst fucking way. It would be fun to nail someone this beautiful, this powerful. He reached into his pocket for some Kiehl's, squeezed it on his finger, and smeared it on his lips. And then he was off.

Now was the time.

Shar was wiping her nose when she walked out of the bathroom right into a solid body in a solid black shirt. The force of the impact knocked her back a little and she stumbled. A strong hand caught her by the wrist to keep her from falling.

"My bad," she said, still not looking up. "I should watch where I'm going."

"No, it's my fault. I guess I was distracted."

Sharlyn glanced up into the face of the guy talking.

He was smiling. There was a twinkle in his pupils as he held on to her wrist.

"Whoa," she said. "Shit. Whoa."

"Whoa, yourself."

She staggered back a little, teetering on the stiletto Zanottis. He was still holding on to her hand as she ended up with her back against a wall. He was standing so close to her, right in her face.

Shar's head, the room, her emotions, all of them were atwirl. She was so fucking high, and drunk, and horny, and this kid, this kid, ooh-wee, this kid was hot.

"You sure you all right?" he asked.

Sharlyn's eyes were fixed on his lips. They were so moist, succulent even, like the flesh of some kind of juice-laden fruit. He had his hand pressed against the wall as he leaned over her. His hair was thick and blonde. She wanted to touch it, but those lips were calling first.

"Hey," he said, his voice low and seductive, "you looked really good dancing over there."

"Oh yeah," she said, her eyes still on his mouth.

"Fuck, yeah. You're gorgeous. But you know that, of course. I probably sound stupid even saying it. Everybody tells you that, right? You hear stuff like that every day."

"Not as much as I'd like to," she said. Which brought back thoughts of Miles. Miles and his mergers. Miles and his this, that, and everything else. Miles didn't have lips like this, hair like this, eyes like this, skin like this. Miles was sexy, granted, but Miles was gone. She'd never wanted anything but her husband, but her husband obviously wanted more things than just her.

Fuck Miles.

"I think you're really—"

Sharlyn cut him off as she pulled his face toward hers and pressed her mouth against those juicy lips. They were soft, fleshy, moist, delicious. And then his tongue was tangoing with hers and she was breathing him in and she was sure he could taste the WMDs on her breath and she couldn't feel her face because her whole sinus cavity had gone numb, but miraculously her lips hadn't, and neither had her tongue, and neither had that freshly bald place between her thighs because his hand was there now, pressing between the Frankie B.s, and she was wet, and getting wetter, and she was grinding against his hand and she didn't even care, because she needed this, needed this night, needed to be felt up and sucked on and dry-humped by someone who seemed like they at least might give a fuck, at least for a second, and although Sharlyn Tate had never cheated on Miles Tate before, right now, in this moment, it wasn't about him. This was going to be all about her.

Fuck Miles, she thought.

"Fuck me," she said.

———

And he was about to.

He didn't care. He would fuck her right there on the floor, in front of an Olsen twin, and all these celebs, models, and fashionistas. That would surely make a mark, get some attention. Look at what it had done for Paris.

But Sharlyn was apparently gathering her wits. He stroked his thumb across the jean-covered nub between her legs and she buckled a little, moaned a lot.

"We can't do this here," she said, looking around. "Too many people know me. I shouldn't even be kissing you like this. It'll be in the *Post* in the morning."

He stepped back from her, following her eyes. Everyone seemed to be into their own thing. There was Naomi in the corner, showing off her legs. The Olsens were laughing and shouting over the music. Owen Wilson or Luke Wilson or that other brother of theirs, whatever, in any case, one of the assorted working Wilsons was talking to one of the assorted working Baldwins. Alec maybe. Maybe not. There were a lot of well-known faces around. So far, what Sharlyn was doing seemed to be slipping under the radar.

"What's your name?"

"Penn. Penn Hamilton."

"Penn Hamilton. I could eat you up."

"Sounds like a plan."

"Shit," she said, talking to herself. He could see her thinking, could tell she was weighing the matter of next moves. He could touch her right now, touch her in a place of weakness, but that might be a bad move. Just let her be, he thought. Let her sort the what–ifs out for herself. This had to be her decision. It had to be all on her.

She reached into her tiny purse and pulled out a pen.

"You got some paper?" she asked.

"No."

"All right. This is so high school, but here . . ."

She grabbed his right hand and jotted down a number.

"That's my cell. Can I trust you to have my cell?"

"Of course, but don't you think you should have asked me that before you wrote the number down?"

"I'm a little discom—"

"Bobulated?"

"Yeah." She smiled, her lip pressed into a tight curve. "I'm a little discom–that."

He cast his eyes toward the floor, a practiced move of sudden coyness, then lifted them again and gave her the full-on gaze. He knew his lashes would be framed just right, showcasing the inviting luminosity of his baby blues.

"Are you a spy for anybody?" she asked. "Page Six? Gawker.com?"

"Do I look like a spy?"

"Yes. You're too perfect. This must be a trick."

"I suppose I should say thanks, but I'm not sure that's a compliment."

"It is."

"Well, I think you're pretty perfect, too."

It was Shar's turn to cast her eyes to the floor. He could tell she probably hadn't done the flirting thing in years. Penn realized this was a woman who was used to getting what she wanted and always had her needs attended to. Something must be missing. Her pupils were dilated when she glanced up at him. Just how high was she? Was she completely aware of what was happening, or would this be a blip, the dregs of an afterthought when the hangover kicked in? He'd tasted the chocolate and vodka on her breath and her tongue. She was steeped in drink. But Penn didn't believe it was just the drugs and alcohol making her behave like this. This was a deliberate woman, a very intelligent woman, a woman whose work he'd read and recognized within that writing a shrewdness and an eye for detail that meant not much got past her.

There was something more going on here. Despite the fact that he needed something from her, Sharlyn Tate obviously needed something from him, too.

"Hold out your arm."

He did.

She rolled up his sleeve and wrote the following:

I, Penn Hamilton, want nothing from Sharlyn Tate and have no plans to exploit or sue her.

The writing was wobbly and crooked, but legible. She was high, but not so high that she didn't want to cover her ass.

"Now write the same thing on my arm," she said. "Verbatim."

"Damn. This is pretty elaborate, don't you think? Next you're going to want me to sign my name in blood."

"That's a thought."

Penn gazed long into her eyes. He really did want to fuck her something fierce. And a plan was a plan.

He took the pen and wrote the same words on her arm.

"Now sign them both. My arm and your arm."

He shook his head and laughed.

"You're crazy."

"People are crazy. I've got to protect myself."

He signed both arms.

She reached into her purse and took out her Sidekick.

"Now hold up your arm."

He did. She snapped a picture of it.

He was still laughing. This woman was smart.

She snapped a picture of her arm.

Then she snapped a picture of him. His face.

"I need something to look at to remind me why I'm doing this," she said.

"And what, exactly, are you doing?"

She glanced around.

"Meet me at the Sherry-Netherland in thirty minutes. You know where it is, right?"

"Of course."

"Ask for Tina Turner's room. They'll give you a key."

"Suppose it's the room key of the real Tina Turner?"

"Then lots of luck. She's got legs of steel."

———

The Sherry-Netherland was a landmark in New York City. Located on Fifth Avenue across from the southernmost entrance to Central Park, it was a historic piece of architecture from the Jazz Age, a gorgeous testament to luxurious living.

Sharlyn's suite, the Grande Deluxe, was a study in moneyed elegance. There was the (standard) chandelier, a sumptuous cream-colored sofa, chairs done in a delicate salmon, an inviting chaise in a rich burgundy brocade, and a desk, the desk where she wrote, facing the window overlooking Central Park. A vast mirror hung over the fireplace, and a short-legged coffee table in deep mahogany sat just in front of the sofa. Fresh flowers were everywhere—just inside the door, by the window, on the mantel, in the center of the classic round dining table, in the bedroom, next to the sumptuous king bed, and inside the marble bathroom.

This was a place where she could find comfort and creativity. A place that brought out the best in her, when the best was there to be found. She hadn't been very creative at the Sherry of late, but things, it seemed, were about to change.

They were in the bathroom. She was standing on the toilet, the agile minx, in the Zanottis and nothing more.

His face was between her legs. She was biting her lip, moaning, her eyes tightly closed.

He was wet with her, pressed into her satiny brown hairless netherloins of wonder. He was eating book pussy, movie pussy, superstar pussy, and it was soft and scrumptious and should have come with a glass of nicely aged tawny port, because this was dessert, sweetness, heaven, the antithesis of the bony hell of Beryl's mean snatch with its alien labia and sideshow clit. Penn realized that it was going to take everything in him not to fuck Sharlyn tonight. He had to wait, do this exactly right. Tonight he would eat her, there in the bathroom of her hotel hideaway, eat the shit out of her, and then leave her there, wobbly kneed, but just turned out enough to want to know him more, to need him more, to buckle every time she thought about his tongue darting in and out of her tight wet canyon, and lapping around that sea of brown softness. He would do what he had planned to do to Beryl, only this time he would get it right.

She was coming now, coming loud, on his cheeks, in his mouth. He grabbed her legs and carried her, crotch still in his face, into the bedroom and laid her down on the coverless bed, onto the cool, welcoming sheets. She was gasping, choking, spastic, reaching at him and his incredible hair, coughing, coming, and coughing some more. He was on his knees at the foot of the bed, still working on her, even though she was in the throes, in many throes, throes and stilettos, all kicking in the air.

Sharlyn couldn't feel her face.

None of it.

All the sensation had traveled out of her head and was down between her legs, which felt like some sort of dormant volcano that had at long last erupted.

When was the last time Miles had eaten her? She searched her mind, but couldn't remember. It was a long time ago, whenever it was. So much time had passed, cunnilingus almost felt brand new.

"You all right?" the handsome boy asked. He wasn't a boy, Shar thought, correcting herself. He was a man. God. And what a man. He was lovely, golden, glowing, and he had a magical tongue.

The Magic Tongue. Yes. That could be the name of her next book.

No. That was silly.

The Magic Boy.

No.

A tune danced in her head.

Try, try, try to understaaaaaaaaaaaaaaaaaaaaaaaannd . . .

The Magic Man!

There.

That was better.

"Hey," he repeated. "You all right?"

He was stroking her face, her breasts, her thighs.

"You've inspired me," she whispered. She was in a reverie, her body throbbing and her mind refreshed. It was the first creative moment she'd had in months. She wanted to run to a computer, a laptop, some paper, something, and write it all down.

"Inspired you?" he asked. "How's that?"

He was lying alongside her nakedness, but he was still clothed. Sharlyn realized she hadn't even seen his dick. Hadn't even felt it. Yet she was happy, sated, had experienced tremendous, necessary release. And he was so pretty, this guy.

And she'd just cheated on Miles! And she didn't care!

Fuck Miles!

This was business, not personal. Her husband shouldn't have been hunting down the Finlandian dollar and neglecting his business at home. See what happens when you set pussy free? Premium pussy? Ukrainian-yanked hairless pussy, the most exotic in the world? Miles had left his unattended. When you do what you do, you get what you get.

Fuck Miles!

"How did I inspire you?"

"Huh? Oh. You're making my brain work. It's been stuck on stupid."

"You? Stupid? Never. You're the shit." He placed fluttery kisses on the side of her neck. "You're a goddess . . . [kiss] . . . a beautiful . . . [kiss] . . . amazing . . . [kiss] . . . delectable goddess." His lips were against her ear, his voice a gentle, barely audible wind. "A goddess with a pot of honey so sweet, I could drink from it forever."

A jolt of electricity shot through Shar. Was it the drugs that were making her like this? she wondered. The alcohol? She still felt lucid, and yeah, her face was numb, but she was aware of everything around her. She knew she had cheated on her husband, and she had done so willfully. There were no pangs of conscience.

Fuck Miles indeed.

He was getting up off his knees.

Shar opened her legs wider, expecting to welcome the rest of him in.

He went to the bathroom instead. Took a piss, checked his face in the mirror, turned on the faucet, washed his hands and splashed some water on his face.

He was fixing his clothes when he came out.

"What are you doing?" Sharlyn asked. "Get your sexy butt over here."

"I've gotta go," he said.

She bolted upward, her legs still splayed.

"What do you mean, 'go'? We're just getting started. Get over here."

Penn walked to the bed. She pulled him closer.

"Now let's get these slacks off," she said, tugging at his zipper. "You have condoms, right?"

"No, seriously." He took hold of her hands. "I have to go."

Penn leaned down and kissed her on the forehead.

"So you're just going to, to"—she swallowed—"to do what you just did and that's it?"

"Believe me, I'd like to do more, but I've got to be somewhere really early—"

"Oh brother," Shar said, flopping back on the bed, "tell me you're not going to run that oldest of lines on me." She clasped her forehead. "I can't believe it. The first time I dare to do something like this, I get blown off."

Penn sat on the bed.

"I'm not blowing you off. I so want to be here. I want to feel what it's like inside of you . . ."—her ran his finger along her thigh—"slide in and out of your . . ."

"Then why are you going?"

"Because I have some important business to take care of in the morning, and if I don't go now, I'll never leave. I know myself."

"Shit," Sharlyn said.

"But I'd like to see you again."

She was looking at him, scouring his face with those dark, sexy eyes. He really did want to fuck her. Damn.

"You know I'm married."

"Oh yes."

"My husband is a very—"

"I know who your husband is."

She wriggled her nose.

"He's a very powerful man."

"He's not the one I want to fuck."

She sat up, her face very close to his.

"But you will be fucking him," she said in a low voice. "We both will."

Penn pulled her mouth to his and kissed it hard, his tongue playing with the tip of hers.

"I can taste myself all over you." She exhaled, her shoulders going limp. "Why can't you just do me and be done with it? Let me get this out of my system."

"You really think one time would get whatever 'this' is out of your system?" He shook his head. "I don't think so. Not for me, anyway, and I'd dare to guess that it wouldn't for you, either. We're attracted to each other. All you did was bump into me, and look where it got us."

"You bumped into me."

"We bumped into each other."

"Right," she said.

She was playing with her hands. She glanced up, her eyes full of gravity.

"Not in public. Never in public."

"We can do this however you want."

"And I'll need to see an AIDS test."

"So will I."

She leaned back, surprised.

"I've gotta protect myself," he said with a smirk. "I've heard how wild celebrities can be."

He was at the door, about to leave.

She had all the pertinent information, where he lived, his phone number, his name, his cunnilingual abilities. She'd given him no further information of her own than what he already had: her cell number and her Tina Turner alias at the Sherry. She was a public personality. It wouldn't be that hard to find her.

Her whole body was tingling as she watched him. She'd just had a tryst. That was the kind of stuff she wrote about, not the kind of thing she did. She was a bad girl, bad girl, such a dirty bad girl.

Beep, beep. Uh-huh.

"Keep the key," she said. "Use it tomorrow. I'll still be here."

Penn nodded.

"Do you need me to send a car for you?"

"That's not necessary," he said. "The less spectacle the better."

"I like that."

"Awesome."

" 'Awesome,' " she said with a laugh. "You're such a white boy."

"And you're quite the black girl."

"Girl?"

"Boy?"

"Young man."

"All right then. Woman."

"That's better. There's nothing girlish about me, young man."

He was contemplating her now, checking the whole of her out. She was suddenly aware of her nakedness and the Zanottis, and the way she was sitting at the edge of her bed with her legs open. This was a porn pose. She wondered if she looked the part as much as she felt it. With her legs showcased like this, she was even feeling a little like the real Tina Turner, a pseudonym she'd come up with after her stylist suggested she go with something more inventive than the name she'd been using, which was Ben-Hur.

"I get tired of asking for that," Tina had said after she'd come up to Shar's room at the Four Seasons in Milan so she could get her dressed to attend Roberto Cavalli's fall show. "Every time I say the name, images of Charlton Heston dance in my head."

"That's not a bad visual," said Shar. "He was sexy in that movie."

"That's not the Charlton Heston I picture," Tina said.

"Yecchh," said Shar, who had been standing in nothing but a bra, panties, and strappy heels at the time. "Perhaps I do need to come better than that."

Tina was opening garment bags and taking out clothes as Sharlyn pranced about the room, unable to keep still, high on a quick whiff of some local blow.

"Look at you," Tina had said. "Look at those legs. What a tall drink of water you are, Mrs. Tate."

And Shar had checked her reflection in the mirror and looked at Tina, and put two and four together and, like that, her next all-purpose hotel pseudonym had been born.

"So what happens when you wake up tomorrow," Penn was now asking, "and realize you were just a little too high and maybe drank a little too much? How do you know you won't regret all this?"

"Because I'm forty-three years old, Penn Hamilton, and at forty-three, you know yourself and take full responsibility for what you do. No matter how high or drunk I get, which isn't often by the way, I don't lose my sense of awareness. I'll remember what I've done. If I'm not here tomorrow when you put your key in that door, it won't have anything to do with regret."

"That's good," he said. "I think."

"You just hold up your end and I'll worry about mine."

"Done."

He opened the door and turned.

"Tomorrow."

"Tomorrow," she said. "Hey, wait a sec. What are you, a model? An actor? You have to be someone to have gotten into the party tonight."

"I'm a writer."

"A writer?"

"Yes. A writer."

Sharlyn was laughing now, and shaking her head.

"Of course. Of all the men I could have messed around with, it's just my luck to find another scribe."

"Is that a bad thing?"

"Not necessarily. You published?"

"No."

Sharlyn laughed again.

Her Sidekick was ringing. At this hour? It was probably Tina, hunting her down.

"You going to get that?" he asked.

"I'd better," she said. "Good night, Penn."

"Good night, beautiful."

The door was barely shut as she crawled across the bed and grabbed her purse from the nightstand. She pulled out the phone.

Miles.

She laughed again, this time even louder.

Fuck him!

She was zinging, every pore of her, full of liberation and rebelliousness and rich, rich thoughts. She waited until the call had rolled over to voice mail, scrolled through the directory, and found her assistant's number. It was late, very late, but hey, that was what assistants were for. The groggy girl answered after three rings.

"Wake up, Brookie."

"I'm awake, Mrs. Tate. Are you okay?"

"I want my laptop. I need you to go get it."

"Yes, ma'am. Where is it?"

"It's in my bedroom, sitting on the chaise. I need you to go over there and pick it up, and then bring it to me at my spot."

"Your spot, ma'am?"

"You know, Brookie, where I hide out to write."

"The Plaza Athénée?"

"I'm at the Sherry."

"The Sherry, of course."

Shar could hear the poor girl fighting back a yawn, trying to bring herself around. It was late. Or early, depending on how you saw it. After two in the morning. So what? she thought. It wasn't like she made a whole lot of demands on Brookie (whose real name was Brookland, which ranked right up there with Milestone). Most of the time Brookie skated by, enjoying far more perks than she did practical labor. The girl, a twenty-three-year-old graduate of Spelman, was the daughter of one of Miles's favorite cousins and was quite efficient and full of endearing charms and Southern ways, most of which Sharlyn appreciated, although she occasionally found that Southern graciousness grating when she needed to cut to the chase and Brookie insisted on being formal or going through unnecessary pleasantries.

The girl couldn't help it, she'd been trained by legions of suppliant Southern women who believed in catering to others with beguiling civility, always making sure everything was "okay." Shar had heard the phrases "Are you okay?" and "Do you need anything?" come flying out of Brookie's mouth more times than she could count. One of these days, she had decided, she was going to say "No, Brookie, I'm not okay," just to see what would happen. The girl's head would probably fly off. Or not. Ol' save-the-day Brookie had more tricks than a Swiss army knife. It didn't help that she spoke with one of those sickeningly sweet, eye-batting twangs. The kind that, outside of the South, enslaved any man within earshot and made an independent woman's skin do a crawl.

"How long do you think it'll take you to get over here?" Shar asked.

"Is an hour all right?"

"Try to make it in thirty, forty-five at the most."

"Yes, ma'am. Is the laptop all you need? Would you like me to—"

"Just the laptop, Brookie, and make sure you bring the power cord."

"Yes, ma'am. Do you need any—"

"You don't have to bring it up to my room. Just leave it at the front desk. They'll be expecting it."

"For Tina Turner, Mrs. Tate?"

"Yes, Brookie, for Tina Turner."

Why was the girl taking her through this? Tina Turner was the only fake name she knew. Brookie hadn't been around in the Ben-Hur days. Shar was sure Brookie was purposeful when she did stuff like this. It was standard passive-aggressive Southern-girl nitpicking. Breaking your will with sweetness under the guise of trying to be helpful.

"Mrs. Tate, do you need me to—"

"Thanks, Brookie. Hurry, hurry."

Sharlyn clicked off the call before the overaccommodating Brookie could squawk out anything else. She already knew the girl would come with more than just the laptop. There'd be some ghetto shit like an ice-cold pineapple Fanta and a bag of crab-flavored Utz from the bodega on the corner of her block in Harlem.

Shortly after her arrival a year before, Brookie had somehow divined that Shar craved low-brow stuff as much as she did high-end, and the girl appealed to that yen with a quiet maliciousness that Shar-lyn didn't know how to fight against. Shar was mortified the day Brookie "accidentally" left a greasy sack of cracklins on her desk, tasty pieces of salted fried pork fat with thick crunchy skin (far more low income and lard laden than those popular bags of air-puffed pork rinds that had somehow jumped class and become Atkins favorites). Shar had scarfed the cracklins down in toto, only to be stricken with an abysmal case of shame immediately afterward. Brookie had tapped into a weakness Shar didn't even realize she had, but Brookie never said anything, she just kept, literally, feeding the guttersnipe in Shar, taking a bit of Shar's dignity every time she did it.

Since then, Brookie, who also possessed superb culinary skills, had left Shar everything from popcorn with hot sauce on it to fresh-cooked hog maws (Shar didn't even know what a "maw" was, but, damn, it was good!). Shar never ate the items in Brookie's presence, but she never sent them away, either. The exasperating girl was always doing something, anything, to show Sharlyn that she wasn't just another assistant, but one who paid attention to the little things, the ones that mattered, like what Shar liked to munch on when she was writing, treats that had a surprising way of making Shar creatively bet-ter, especially when she was properly motivated and the sex was great between her and Miles. But the sex hadn't been good, even though she was still eating all the snacks Brookie brought around.

Shar wasn't a big fan of exercise. She was lucky she had good genes and a high metabolism, even though she had put on a couple of pounds since Brookie's arrival. Not enough to cause alarm, still, those unsolicited, unexpected ghetto snacks had the potential to do real damage, not just to her appearance, but on the health front—all those fried pork skins and hoghead cheeses and pickled entrails, disgusting shit, really, if you considered it objectively—which was why she did her best to deter Brookie from bringing them anywhere near her.

Shar picked up the room phone and pressed the button for the front desk.

"Yes, Miss Turner."

"I'm expecting a laptop to be delivered shortly. Will you ring me before you send it up?"

"Yes, Miss Turner."

"Make sure you ring me first."

"Of course, Miss Turner."

"Thanks."

Shar hung up the phone, her legs stretched out in front of her. She studied her calves, which were lean and shapely. Her skin was smooth and blemish free. Funny how she hadn't noticed how attractive her legs were, not lately. She was almost as bad as Miles, the way she'd been ignoring herself. Diamond and Aurora had done her such a favor, getting her out of the house like that. She ran her hand across her thigh. It was butter-soft in the wake of her afternoon at the spa.

She could still feel a gentle throb between her legs. The thought of what she'd done made it throb some more. The alcohol/coke buzz had mellowed into something quite nice. And she had a title now (and, perhaps, a muse?).

The Magic Man.

It was a start. That was all she needed.

After that, the rest would come easy.

Penn was

. . . deep in thought, rubbing Kiehl's on his lips with his right forefinger, thinking about how cool it was the way Sharlyn Tate had responded to his balls-out up-front statement that he was a writer, when he saw her there, sitting in front of his building.

She was in a Dolce & Gabbana sweatshirt with the hood pulled up. It swallowed her tiny head, which was set so far back under the generous cloth, all he saw at first was faceless shadow, shadow that could have been harboring the Grim Reaper or the Ghost of Fucks to Come. But he knew it was her. Unmistakably. She was holding his manuscript in her lap. Her right knee was shaking.

So here it was. The showdown. She'd gotten up the nerve obviously to come back and blast him. He had to give it to her. The girl had balls.

Fine, he thought. He had other options now anyway.

"Hi," she said, her voice small but steady.

"What are you doing here?"

"I've got something of yours."

"I see," he said, stepping forward, reaching for it. "May I have it back?"

She clutched it close.

"Can we talk first? I need to clear some things up."

He noticed the writing on his skin. Sharlyn's penmanship. That silly contract on his arm. Her cell number on his palm. Beryl hadn't seen either. He rolled down his right sleeve and thrust his hand into his pocket.

"Things like what?" he said nonchalantly.

"Inside. Can we go inside? I'm not used to"—she glanced around, nervous—"you know, being outside like this. On a stoop in the middle of the night."

"How long have you been here?"

"A while."

"Why didn't you just try to buzz your way in or wait for someone to come out?"

"I didn't want to do that. I didn't want to come in without your permission."

"Right," he said, rubbing his chin, "yet you took my manuscript without my permission."

"Can we go inside? Please?"

He wasn't up for this. She was going to give him a tongue-lashing for using her, and top it off with a brash attack on his story. She'd read it and torn it to pieces and had come to make the pronouncement in person. It was the only means of retaliation she had.

"If you've got something you want to say to me, then just say it."

She was standing now, still holding the manuscript. The hood was still pulled way over her head.

All she needs is a sickle, he thought. He almost laughed. Beryl the Reaper, come to lay him to waste.

"I owe you an apology," she said. "I shouldn't have run off the way I did. And you're right, I had no business taking your manuscript. Your very good manuscript, I might add."

This, now this he wasn't expecting. It was a dropkick to the chest. All those months, twenty-four of them, full of rejection after rejection after smug-ass rejection, and someone was finally seeing things right.

"Wha . . ." His breath was coming short. "What did you just say?"

"I said your manuscript is very good," came her voice from the shadows of the hood. "It's brilliant. It's like nothing I've ever seen."

And Penn was smiling now, his feet doing an invisible Snoopy dance of long-awaited glee. No one had said these words before. No one that mattered. No one that could make it matter, that is.

"Are you shitting me?"

"Not at all. But I don't want to talk about that out here. If it's all right, can we please go inside?"

"Of course. I hope you don't mind, but I need to take a shower first. It's been a rough day. After that, we can talk."

He'd written Sharlyn's cell-phone number on a piece of paper while he was in the bathroom, then he soaped the writing off his arm and his palm as he stood beneath the hot water.

What a night, he thought. This was amazing.

Like something out of a book.

He smiled as he turned his face upward, directly beneath the stream of hot water.

She was sitting on his IKEA couch, drinking a hot cup of microwaved oolong tea, and he was sitting in an IKEA chair across from her in a T-shirt and a pair of gray sweats, wanting to know everything, particularly about his book.

"Could you just answer a few questions for me first," Beryl was saying now, "before we talk about your manuscript?"

"Okay," he said, sounding guarded again.

Beryl didn't want to make him feel too pressed, she just needed to know the truth. She already knew what to do about his book, but everything that had led up to the moment she'd discovered it, that's the part she needed clarity about.

"Did you know I was an editor?" she asked.

"No," he said, a slight crinkle in his beautiful forehead. "Not until I heard your author say it when he announced you to the crowd."

He was so convincing, she thought. And more gorgeous than she remembered. How could a man be as gorgeous as this?

He was biting his bottom lip, lips that had been all over her less than twenty-fours earlier. She couldn't stop remembering their sweet taste.

"So why were you in Barnes and Noble?"

"I told you why. I was getting a book on Sartre."

"What for?"

"Because it's a free country, and Sartre's books are for sale."

She would have laughed if her heart wasn't aching, but it was aching, breaking, quaking for him. She just wanted to hear him come out and say it—that he had stalked her on purpose, just like every other writer who'd done the same thing, and that was all he'd wanted from her, a book deal, and he'd used sex to do it.

"Beryl, I didn't stalk you, if that's what you think." The prescient words blew her back on the couch. "Imagine how embarrassed I felt when I saw someone actually do that to you. That skinny guy who came over with his crappy, stained manuscript? The way he tried to force his work on you, then got all hostile when you told him the rules? Do you think that's the kind of person I am? Do you think that's the kind of person I want to be? That guy made me ashamed for writers everywhere. I mean, there's hustle, and there's hustle. I would have told you everything sooner, but for that guy. After the way he came at you, me telling you that I was a writer too was the last thing on earth I wanted to do, believe me."

She searched his quantum-blue eyes, sinking into them, wanting to do just that, believe.

"Why Sartre?"

"Because I love philosophy and theories and crazy stuff like that."

"And Wagner."

He smiled, suddenly coy, dropping his lovely cleft chin.

"Yes, Wagner. I guess you noticed all that stuff when you were in here before."

She felt flush, fully aware of his implication. She knew he knew she'd gone through his things, how else could she have gotten the manuscript? But he seemed to be cutting her slack on that, just letting it hang over them, a huge bubble of hot confession, waiting to be popped. She'd have to be the popper. She was the one who had chosen to put him on the defense.

"I'm sorry I went through your things," Beryl said.

He was silent, which rattled her more.

"It's just that, you know, everybody always seems to want something, always trying to hawk their books, and each one gets more creative than the next. No one's ever tried sex before. I have to admit, it scared me."

"So you think my angle was sex?"

Beryl wanted to run out of there. Her legs were shaking. She reached for her steaming cup of tea, clutching it with both hands, oblivious to the heat. He would tell her the truth now, that, yeah, he was using her—what was she, nuts?—he'd never have someone like her as his girlfriend. He was a god, after all, and she was most definitely not a goddess. She had narcolepsy, among other things. She was a chockablock of defects.

He had his head in his hands now, quiet. Beryl watched him, waiting for him to lay into her, tell her about herself, deride her for dreaming beyond her station.

His lashes were wet when he lifted his head. And his eyes were red.

"Penn?"

"How dare you," he said, his voice low, almost a growl. "How dare you come here and accuse me of that."

Oh no! she thought. What had she done! Look at him. The poor boy was stricken!

"Penn, I—"

"So that's why you ran out of my house like that today? You go through my things, my personal things, and you see my manuscript and you figure that's who I am? That I'm just another dickwad like that guy at Barnes and Noble? That I'll fuck for my supper, because that's the only way I can get ahead?"

And she was up now, her hot cup of tea back on the table, and she had thrown her arms around him, even as he cowered away from her. What kind of horrible person was she? she thought. Look at how she had upset him so. This was not her intent. It was never the plan.

"I'm sorry, Penn, really. I didn't mean to imply—"

"Yes you did, babe, you did. That's what you think of me. But what's even worse, that's what you think of yourself. That I couldn't just want to be with you for you."

She hadn't heard his last words. Everything had cut off at "babe," which was ringing in her ears like the bells of Notre Dame, clanging crazily upside and inside her head as she tried to absorb the fact that he had slipped into vulnerability, and in that state of weakness, he had called her his "babe."

He did love her! It wasn't a ruse!

"Oh, Penn, babe, I'm so sorry. I'm so, so sorry."

She squeezed him close, the hood covering her face thrown back, and she was rubbing his flaxen hair now, the hair that she had fallen instantly in love with, the hair on the head of the body with the eyes and mouth and mind of the man, her man, with whom she had fallen in love at first sight.

"Stupid me," he was saying, "I had some ridiculous romantic notion that maybe fate had brought us together. I mean, what are the odds of it? Me seeing you and you seeing me and both of us having a fucking *coup de foudre* like that, and then it turns out we have even more in common, both of us being fans of the word? I mean, what are the fucking odds of us being simultaneously struck down by love? Shit, when you collapsed, I was like, fuck, love struck her down for real!"

Penn had a wild look in his eyes, a flame of hope and mad, mad passion. Beryl wanted to thrash herself for questioning it before.

"And there I was," he ranted, "believing it could happen, that fate was bigger than coincidence, because that's how it happened for my mom and my dad, and that's how I had always dreamed it would happen for me, and then you pull that shit this afternoon, just run out on me like that, and now you come here, you, you, you have the nerve to come back to my house and tell me I fucking used you . . ."

He was talking so fast, so hard, he was panting.

"You tell me that I used you, when you were the one I should have been keeping an eye on all along. You were so busy thinking I was trying to fuck you over, that, without a second thought, you fucked me over."

Beryl wanted to crawl into the ground. She was a clod, a heel, a cad(ette?), the scum on the bottom of scum on a shoe. She was fucked up. Really. If Ripkin was here, he would tell her that, tell her how she put the loon in loony, and she'd know he was right, because she was loony, a full-blown looney tune. Her man was here, right in front of her, an Adonis extraordinaire, with not just looks, but brains to back it up. And what had she done? She'd gone out of her way to humiliate him and run him off.

"Please, Penn, please," she sobbed, her arms still around him, "say you'll forgive me? Please. I was scared. I was so scared."

"Don't you think I was scared, too?" he asked, still cowering away from her. "I wasn't looking for you that day. I was looking for a damn book. If I could scratch that whole—"

"No," she cried, "don't say that. I don't want to scratch it. That day changed everything for me. I love you, Penn. I love you so much I didn't know how to . . ."

He got up from the chair, leaving her there, babbling erratically, terrified that her future, her whole life, was now slipping from her grasp. What an idiot she was. She'd had love on a platter, perfect love, beautiful love, and she'd practically beaten it away with a stick.

No, she thought. She couldn't let that happen. Not after sixteen years. Not after sixteen long years.

He was standing in the middle of the room, his back to her, very, very still. She ran over to her man and faced him. Because he was her man, and she was going to make sure he knew she wouldn't make that mistake again.

His eyes were red, beet-red, and his cheeks were flushed and wet, wet, wetter than wet. He was gushing with love for her. All his love was gushing away.

She threw her arms around his middle.

"Please, babe, say you'll forgive me." Her tears were coming hard. "Please, babe, please, please, please say you won't turn me away. I love you so and I know you love me. I know that now. I believe it. I'm sorry."

And his arms, which had been limp at his sides, were now wrapped around her, tight, tighter, tightest, and the two of them were sobbing together, letting it all out, and *coup de foudres*—the kind of bolts from the blue that resulted in love at first sight—were coming from every direction, as Beryl realized that, when fate was ready and the heavens decided to open and shed goodness one's way, that goodness came with a vengeance, as lightning bolts of love were hurled from the sky without respite, back to back to electrifying back.

"It's so funny and sad," she was saying. "I was laughing really hard in some parts, but when they started exploiting him in all those porn flicks, it was awful. His roommates were pigs. I was in tears. They made all that money off of him, yet he was just this . . . thing . . . even though he had once been a man. He wasn't always a thing, but everyone around him seemed to forget that."

"Wow," Penn said. "It sounds like you really connected with it."

"I did. Poor Gregor Balzac. Everybody either used him or treated him like a freak. I spanned the entire emotional landscape. It was totally cathartic."

"Really? It really did that for you?"

"Oh God, yes. This book is going to win awards, and plenty of them."

They were in Ekeberg, beneath the covers, naked, limbs entwined, cuddling. They hadn't had sex. She was a little sore, she'd said. He was more than relieved. He still wanted to bask in his memories of Sharlyn's luscious body and what awaited him the following afternoon. If he'd had to mount and service Beryl before that, it might have tainted the dream. He would have done it if he had to, but he didn't. Which was good.

"How did you come up with it?" she asked. "What made you decide to redo Kafka?"

"I don't know," Penn said, thrilled to be talking about his masterpiece this way. "It just seemed like the logical thing to do."

"It's going to be the biggest hit I've ever had."

Penn leaned back from her.

"What do you mean?"

"I mean, I have to do this. You have to let me do this. There's a few things I could help you fix. You know, tweak the story just a smidge so that everything's just perfect. This book is such a gem."

Penn started to sit up.

"No, Beryl, c'mon. Not like this. Not after everything we just—"

"Sshhh," she said, pulling him back down, her finger on his lips. "There are no coincidences. We're supposed to be together, and I'm supposed to have this book. Who says good things can't all come from the same place?"

"But don't you think I owe it to myself to show it around a few places? If it's so good, shouldn't I get an agent to shop it?"

"Do you have an agent?"

"No."

"I know the way this business works. I could help you. I guarantee you that whatever offer an agent gets, I'll best it. I'll make a preemptive offer."

"What's that?" he asked, feigning far more ignorance than she could imagine. He knew what a preempt was. He was curious about how she would explain it, wondering if she would downplay the money.

"If your book goes to auction where several houses can bid on it, a preemptive offer is one that's enticing enough to take the deal off the table before the auction can ever happen."

"Interesting. What if someone goes really high, I mean really, really high, higher than what you plan on making with your preemptive thing."

"Trust me," she said. "No one's going to top me. No way. I've had a string of bestsellers, so I've got some capital to spend, so to speak. I can go pretty high."

Penn pulled her into his chest, crushing her close, his broad hands rubbing her skinny back.

"So, babe, what do you think a book like this would fetch?"

"Something high concept like this? It's got all the right angles, and we could do some really good tie-ins with it. I've got a friend over at Apple. I'm thinking some iPod stuff, and maybe Starbucks, and, I don't know, there's a lot of things. I could go crazy with it. Leak the manuscript to Hollywood, maybe get a movie deal to further hype things up."

"A movie," he said. "You could see this as a movie?"

"Yes. And it would be tasteful, not pornographic. This could be something really bittersweet, like *The Elephant Man*. It's a real testa-

ment to American culture, and all the obsession with money and sex
at the expense of human emotion and concern."

"Wow," Penn said. "Wow."

This was extraordinary, he thought, almost scary, the way she had
jumped, full-bodied, into the idea of it all. She had taken the ball at
the ninety-yard line and was running it all the way to the end zone,
oblivious of everything else. Beryl was laying out the blueprint to his
dream, and she was coloring in everything in between. Her obsessive
mind was on a tear, and master schemes were spilling out of her faster
than he could keep up with. He'd always had a grand vision for himself, but hers was grander, if that was even possible.

"You should definitely be on the cover. People need to see you as
a part of the total concept."

"Total concept?"

"Hell yeah. You've got model written all over you. I was thinking
about that this afternoon as I was reading. I've got a buddy at Calvin
Klein. I think if I pitch it right, we can get you in one of their ad campaigns. Your body's perfect for it, and your face. The people at Calvin
will go nuts, and so will the rest of the world, once they see you."

"Uh-oh. Now you're talking about exploiting me. Am I your Gregor Balzac?"

"Not exploiting you, babe. Branding you. Before the book ever
hits the shelves, people will know who you are. They will have seen
you and lusted for you and idolized you, and by the time this book
drops, you'll be a star."

"A star, huh?"

"Yeah. A star. My star."

She was smiling. That was the thing he liked best. That nuclear
smile. It was the first time he'd seen it all night.

"Can you handle that, babe?" he asked. "Me as a star?"

"Can you handle it?" she said.

"I asked you first."

She suddenly grew serious, considering his words.

"Maybe this afternoon I couldn't. But I was afraid then. I wasn't
sure of you. Of us."

"But you're sure now."

"I'm sure now."

"Are you sure you're sure?"

"I've never been surer of anything in my life."

He was showing her his paper now, the one on top of the TV that she was supposed to have seen when she first came to his place, the dissertation on Wagner and his theory of Gesamtkunstwerk, and she was awestruck by it, thrilled that they were so simpatico about even this, cross-promotion and the concept of branding.

"Can I have this?" she asked. "I'm going to sell my boss on it. I'm going to get everyone so hyped on the possibilities that when I make my preemptive offer, no one's going to balk at how much money it is."

"You never said how much you think it'll be," he said.

Her face grew somber again.

"We won't be able to be a public couple, though. I could lose my job. If anybody found out I got you a deal this way, it could ruin everything, even though I know this book is going to make all of us rich."

"Do you mind us not being able to be out in the open?" Penn asked.

"No. No one really knows my business at work anyway. We can just keep everything on the low. I like that phrase, 'on the low.' I think we can do it. We can still have our relationship, we just can't show it off to the world. Not just yet."

"I don't know, babe," he said. "I don't want to have to hide my feelings. I mean, if it's a choice between fame or you, I don't think—"

"It doesn't have to be a choice," she said. "Don't you see? We can have it all."

"How's that?"

Beryl fixed her eyes on his.

"Where do you see us in the long run?"

"How do you mean?"

"I mean, as a couple. In the long run, where do you see us?"

Penn was smiling inside. This must be how David Blaine felt when he saw his magic (rather, his nonmagic) working; that jedi mind trick stuff where he hung in midair for days at a time and people would start out ridiculing him, but by the end, they were in captivated awe. No matter how exhausted or food-starved he was, when he was in that extraordinary moment in time where he knew everyone who was witnessing him believed, Blaine must have felt invincible. That kind of power was intoxicating. It was really heady stuff.

"Do you see us together?" she continued. "As a couple? Are we just dating? In a serious relationship? What?" She was looking up at him, wanting to be in that David Blaine moment. Wanting to believe.

"I see us married, of course," he said. "At least, that's how I feel. I want what my parents had. I won't settle for less than that. I can't. That's the gold standard to me."

"Ooh, me too, me too!" she squealed. Penn could feel her trembling now, as the intensity of it all really began to sink in. "Oh, I almost forgot. I brought you something. A peace offering, just in case you didn't want to see me again."

She rushed over to her big purse and pulled something out.

"Aw, babe, you brought me one of your African violets."

"Yes. A blooming one."

He hugged her.

"Thank you, babe. I'll make sure it stays that way."

He placed it on the nightstand, next to the bed. Beryl smiled with approval.

"So what about this," she said, "what if we get you out there, expose the world to the amazing Pennbook Hamilton, get you a book deal, turn you into a star, keep our relationship 'on the low,' and after you're on your way, I'll quit."

Quit, he thought. Fuck no! What the fuck?

"Quit? Quit what?"

"My job, silly. I'll quit my job."

"But babe, you're one of the best editors in the business. Why would you wanna do something like that?"

Beryl's eyes were smiling, as much as her eyes could, as she looked adoringly into his, then kissed his forehead, his cheeks, his chin, his lips.

"Because I love you, and because I want to be a real wife, full-time, not somebody chasing deadlines and up to her eyeballs in manuscripts and meetings. I want to be your editor exclusively, at home, the one whose opinion matters most to you, the way Tabitha is for Stephen. I love publishing, but it's a rat race, and the rats keep getting bigger and bolder, and the race is overcrowded. I'd trade life in the literary grind for domestic life with the man I love any day of the week."

He liked the idea of her being his personal editor. The marriage thing was an all-out lie, but he could deal with that later. After he'd gotten everything that he wanted. First things first.

"I like that, babe," he said, "but only if it's what you really want. You don't have to leave your career for me."

"It's what I really want. I've spent half my life in publishing. It's time for something more. This could be my swan song, and oh, what a swan song it would be."

"Wow," Penn said. "This is . . . man, I don't even know what to say. God is so awesome. It's like he's giving me everything I've ever asked for, all at once. I almost don't want to go to sleep tonight. I'm afraid this whole thing might just be a dream."

"It's real, babe. For both of us. We're both getting our dreams."

She melted into him, planting wet kisses all over his face.

That was a good one, he thought. Please. He'd never asked God for anything. He believed in Him about as much as he believed in the lottery. Less, actually. The lottery operated by a system of odds, odds that operated against most people, but odds that had a payout nonetheless. He'd met a woman who'd hit the lottery once. She was the mother of a girl he had messed around with briefly at NYU. The girl had gotten a fair share of money from her mother and given it to Penn.

So yeah, the lottery was real, but he had yet to meet anyone who'd ever met God. Met him for real, flowing robes, white hair, überwisdom and all, not the kind of "I've seen God!" that born-agains always proclaimed. That was just change-of-heart shit. If someone really saw God, it would be all over the news.

But then again, he had hit a bonanza that defied natural possibilities.

He had cracked the code on Sharlyn Tate, and would be hitting that in a few hours, less than twelve, per the silver IKEA clock on the wall. And he had gotten Beryl back. Beryl, the one he'd feared was a lost cause if there ever was one. She had returned of her own volition, and had done so with visions of love, a lucrative book deal, and marketing genius dancing in her head.

A twofer. The universe had given him a twofer.

Hardly. The universe had given him nothing. This was the result of hard, hard work. Opportunity meeting preparation.

Two doors had opened, and he had entered both at once.

No cosmic assistance necessary.

He chuckled at the way it was all unfolding.

"What's so funny, babe?" Beryl asked.

"Life, babe. You just never know how it's gonna turn."

"No shit," she said. "Meanwhile, we have to get you an agent. A real player, someone everyone knows. Even though this'll be rigged a little, we still need a pro to run everything. A pro who won't know what's up, of course, but who'll know a good deal when he sees it."

"Any ideas?"

Beryl stared up at the ceiling for a moment, her lips pressed together. Her face lit up.

"Ah. I've got the perfect person."

"Who's that, babe?"

"Have you ever heard of Spanky Katz?"

Brookie had

. . . brought her a pig's foot, one of those fuschia-tinted kind that sat in a giant jar on a bodega counter, steeping in red-dye-number-three-colored pickling juice, jammed up with more red-dye-steeped porcine hooves. And Shar had eaten it, eaten it while she was standing, had bitten through all that thick, bristle-covered skin that covered even thicker fat, and had sucked it clean, all the way down to the bone, pickled pig juices running down her chin and arm, dripping past her elbow, and she was ashamed, ashamed in the way she should have been ashamed for letting that stranger gnaw at her genitalia an hour before, but wasn't.

She glanced up nervously, looking around the room for hidden cameras. In an age of spies and hackers and an Internet gone wild, she couldn't imagine the embarrassment of having this image of herself blasted all over the Web.

The bellman who'd brought up her laptop bag was practically recoiling as he handed Shar the paper sack with its raging vinegar fumes, fumes that were probably still polluting the elevator and the rest of the hall. She had snatched the bag, humiliated as she crammed a fifty into his hand and slammed the door. She'd intended to ask for change for that fifty. Not that she was cheap, but fifty dollars was much too egregious a tip by her standards. For a bellman delivery. If she gave him fifty now, he'd spread the word that she'd upped the ante and all the employees would expect at least fifty every time they brought something up.

She'd planned to give him twenty, which was generous and what she was known for doling out freely to the staff at both the Plaza Athénée and the Sherry, but once she'd gotten a whiff of that pig's foot, she was too embarrassed to do anything that might cause the guy to have to linger and be aware of the fact that Someone. Like. Her. Dared to stay at the Sherry-Netherland and have pig's feet sent up. Even though she had a reputation for fabulousness and had been on the cover of every magazine from *Ocean Drive* to *Vanity Fair,* she knew that, from now on, in the mind of this person of supposed lesser station, she would only be . . . the pig-foot eater. He had sniffed his nose at her. Word would spread within the liveried nerve center of the Sherry-Netherland. Soon the rest of the staff, behind her back, would be sniffing their noses at her, too.

Damn that Brookie. Fucking passive-aggressive bitch.

But between that embarrassingly delightful pig foot and her happy snatch, Shar had written and written—oh, how she had written!—and *The Magic Man* was taking shape. Between the hours of three A.M. and seven-thirty A.M., she had knocked out thirty pages. She took a break to call Brookie to get her to bring a printer, some paper, and a change of clothes over to the hotel.

"What kind of clothes would you like, Mrs. Tate?"

"Some jeans and a big, loose top. A hoodie or something. And some sneakers. And socks. Something I'll be comfortable in, but can wear on the street if I need to. And oh, I might spend the night here again, so bring enough clothes for two days, and some lingerie. Something sexy."

"Any preference? The La Perla? Or maybe some of your Victoria's Secret?"

"Hmmm. No. I think I want the Agent Provocateur."

"Ooh, yes," Brookie drawled, "those are nice. Which ones?"

Shar kept her lingerie separated not by type, but brand. She took it even further, with drawers for different lines within the brand.

"The Virginie," she said. "The bra and panties. And the Fifi. The bra and the briefs. And some black fishnet thigh-highs. And a nice pair of sexy black shoes. Pumps, not sandals."

"Which ones?"

"I don't know. Be creative. You've got excellent taste."

"Why, thank you, Mrs. Tate."

Shar was so relieved none of her requests would come as a surprise to Brookie. The girl was accustomed to her boss playing lingerie dress-up when she wrote, or pretended to write, just to get in the mood. Cosabella for when she was writing glitzy tales. Victoria's Secret was for more pedestrian stories. It wasn't unusual for Shar and Miles to have trysts at hotels (not at her writing hideaways, of course), just to keep her in the creative spirit. Miles didn't know the Hotel Plaza Athénée and the Sherry were Sharlyn's secret writing places. Having private, interruption-free writing zones was necessary for her to produce. Miles understood that, and had never given her any kind of problem about it. Even Beryl didn't know where Shar slipped off to when she churned out her work. The only one who knew was Brookie, and despite the fact that Miles was her cousin, Brookie had been sworn to professional secrecy, and Shar believed Brookie took that oath to heart.

It was the perfect setup for an affair. Shar had never realized that until now.

"Would you like a scarf?" Brookie asked.

"A scarf? For what?"

"The weatherman said the wind's going to be a little high today and—"

"No, Brookie, no scarf. Just the clothes and the printer and some paper."

"Yes, ma'am."

"And Brookie?"

"Yes, Mrs. Tate?"

"Do not, I repeat, do not, bring anything other than what I asked for." She was firm, stern, determined that Brookie obey her this time. "You understand what I'm saying?"

"Yes, Mrs. Tate." The girl was sweeter than ever, her words dripping with deference.

Shar knew this was a passive war of wills. Brookie heard what she wanted when she wanted. They never spoke directly of the appetizingly gauche foodstuff, but Shar knew Brookie knew what she meant.

The items arrived at the front desk less than an hour later. Brookie had brought, as instructed, the printer and paper, a pair of 501s and a dark blue Phat Farm hoodie, some white Nikes and white footies, a grass-colored Juicy Couture velour sweatsuit, the requested Agent Provocateur items, and some standard-issue patent leather Stuart Weitzmans. But she'd also had the insight to see that a better shoe would go with the lingerie, so she'd brought a pair of Kate Spades, the heart satin open-toed slingbacks with a three-and-a-half-inch heel and a sexy bow. Smart girl.

She also left a brand-new cartridge of black ink for the printer, just in case the other ran out.

And a Pucci scarf.

And a tasty fried bologna sandwich, smushed together, the edges of the meat dark and crunchy, nearly burnt, with just the right amount of mayonnaise to smooth it all in.

She heard the card key in the door.

It was exactly three o'clock.

She had showered and moisturized and preened her body to dainty perfection. A masseuse had come up two hours earlier and beaten away the tightness in her shoulders that came with pecking away at keys.

She'd written sixty pages so far. The laptop was closed. The Fifi line of Agent Provocateur lingerie was working her curves like someone had threatened them if they didn't. She was in the fishnets and Kate Spades. And, like Marilyn Monroe, was touched with just a few drops of No. 5. Something classic. Something simple. A timeless beacon of familiarity in the midst of imminent sin.

It was a different scent than what she wore with her husband. She'd had the concierge fetch it. She didn't want to smell the same.

Moments later, after the Chanel had been delivered, she'd remembered something else, and had thrown on the 501s, pulled on the hoodie, tied the suddenly useful scarf around her head, and slipped downstairs, walking until she found a Duane Reade drugstore, where she discreetly purchased condoms and Astroglide. Just in case he didn't

have any. Just to make sure. Because she couldn't send the concierge
for condoms and Astroglide. Not when her well-known husband was
out of town. Not as long as there was a Page Six, whose faceless, ubiq-
uitous spies were legion.

The door slid open and he stepped inside, golden, resplendent, as
lovely as she remembered. Nothing followed him in. Not remorse,
not dread, none of the ghosts of the day after that haunted the characters inside her books. Those ghosts had yet to make an appearance.
Perhaps they never would.

There was nothing but him and goodness. She felt a Pavlovian rush
between her legs.

He was right on time.

She was right on ready.

Beryl was

. . . exultant.

Penn had said the m-word! He wanted to get married!

He said that was his ultimate plan, just as it was hers. She couldn't wait to get started on the planning. There would be no definite date anytime soon, of course, but she could start, couldn't she? After years of hopeful waiting, her life could begin. Her world was finally complete, as Ripkin soon learned on the Thursday she announced,

"He's here!"

"What's that? Who's here?"

He was sitting in his chair and she was in her ritual pose, stretched out and yammering. Admittedly, his mind was adrift, fixed on the duck confit he would be having for dinner in just shy of an hour, an hour and a half at the most, and he was so ready for it, starving even, because it had been a particularly depleting day. He was contemplating what wine might go best with the bird—a pinot noir, or maybe a nice Riesling. He didn't want to rely on the sommelier's recommendations, which tended to be hit-or-miss. Perhaps he should go with an Australian Shiraz. And maybe he would have the pear-and-apple tarte tatin for dessert, with a semisweet Blanquette de Limoux. Ah yes. He could almost smell the sparkling wine's bouquet paired with those succulent pieces of carmelized baked fruit. That would be deli—

"Doctor, you're not listening to me!"

"What? Yes!" said a salivating Ripkin, swallowing the moisture that had gathered in his mouth. "Of course I am. You said 'he's here,' and I've been trying to get some clarity about what or whom you might mean."

What a superb liar I am, he thought. Perhaps it really is time to retire.

"Dr. Ripkin, who else was I expecting?"

She was staring at him in that impudent way of hers. He bit back his exasperation. Dinnertime couldn't come quick enough.

"Are you trying to tell me your Mr. Right has arrived?"

"Yes. Finally. Some comprehension on your part."

There was silence as Ripkin counted in his head and tugged on his ear.

"Why don't you tell me about it," he said after a time. "You seem quite excited. How can you be so sure it's him?"

"*Becauuuuuuse,*" she said, "it happened just like I always thought it would. It was so obvious. It was fate."

"Ah yes. Our dear friend fate. At long last, he has decided to rear his head."

Beryl's expression was stern.

"I knew you were going to do this. I was all prepared for your cynicism. I told myself, 'Dr. Ripkin's going to try to ruin this for me, but I'm not going to let him do it.' And I'm not. Just because you're jaded—"

"This isn't about me, Beryl. My beliefs and values are my own. We should be using this hour wisely. Tell me about your Mr. Right. How did you meet him?"

"At a book signing," she said, grinning. "It was so weird. I was there for one of my authors, Canon Messier, you know, the one with that book, *Apple Pie*—"

"Yes, yes, go on," said the hungry Ripkin, pushing away the image of apple pies of any sort.

"He was just standing there next to me," she babbled, "I don't know, it was like he just materialized there, like some sort of genie—"

"Materialized, you say?"

"Yes, materialized. Don't be sarcastic."

"My apologies. I wasn't aware that was how I was coming across."

"So anyway, he said something to me and when I turned to look at him . . . Oh God, Doctor . . . this was so embarrassing . . ."

She was all atwitter, Ripkin noticed. He wasn't going to interrupt.

". . . it was awful. He was so good-looking. I really do think he's the most beautiful man I've ever seen."

Ripkin adjusted himself in his chair. A beautiful man and Beryl? This was interesting indeed.

"I was so shocked by how attractive he was, and how he was just, you know, right there, you know, in my face, out of nowhere, that I"—she laughed nervously—"I still can't believe I did this—"

"We've less than an hour, Beryl."

"All right, all right. I had a cataplexy."

"You had a cataplexy."

"Yes, Dr. Ripkin, I had a cataplexy. The very thing I feared exposing to the man of my dreams was the very first thing I did the second I met him."

"Interesting."

"Interesting?" she said, sitting up. "That's all you have to say?"

"Had you taken your medication on schedule?"

"No. Not until late. I hadn't picked up my new prescription."

"Oh dear. And were you under great duress or some sort of extreme pressures that day?"

"No, Doctor, that's just it. It was just one of those moments. It was that bolt from the blue, lightning striking, love-at-first-sight thing that people like you don't believe in. It actually happened, just like I imagined it would. It happened for both of us. He feels the same way, too."

"Really."

"Yes. Really."

"And he told you as much."

"Yes. He said the words. 'Beryl, I love you.' There was nothing for me to have to guess at or read between the lines about. He made it very, very clear."

"That he's in love with you."

"That he's in love with me."

Ripkin rubbed his right eyelid. His stomach growled.

"Pardon me," he said.

"I suppose your stomach's a cynic, too."

"Does this man know why you had a cataplexy?" he asked, ignoring her comment. "Does he realize what actually occurred?"

"He knows everything," she said.

"What do you mean by 'everything'?"

Beryl stretched out on the couch again, her hands behind her head.

"I mean he knows about my parents and he knows about me. He knows I'm narcoleptic."

Ripkin was startled.

"So you actually took my advice and chose to tell him the truth? That's great news, Beryl. Quite a bit of progress for you. Does he know about your obsessive-compulsive disorder?"

"Yes," she lied. "And he's fine with it. He's perfectly fine."

"Interesting."

She jumped up from the couch, stamping her foot.

"I wish you would stop saying that. I know what you mean."

"I don't mean anything, Beryl. I'm just listening and asking pertinent questions."

"Well, you're doing it with judgment. I can hear it in your voice."

"I'm not judging you, Beryl. That's not my modus operandi. Please, do sit down."

She did, planting her bottom on the edge of the chair.

"I don't need you to judge me," she said, her eyes flashing with restrained anger. "This is a happy time for me. I wasn't expecting you to do backflips, but no one likes a pie in the face, either."

Ripkin's stomach snarled on cue at the pie.

"I would never minimize the significance of your feelings, Beryl."

"Hmph," Beryl sniffed. "Okay. We'll see."

"So when, exactly, did this portentous meeting occur?"

"Tuesday."

Ripkin's throat caught. He cleared it. She was kidding, of course.

"*Tuesdaaaaaaayyyy* when?" he asked, dragging out the words in the hopes that, surely, she was not going to say what he feared would be the obvious, that she had *just* met this man.

"Tuesday the day before yesterday."

"Right. Yes. Of course."

He cleared his throat again, a simultaneous gesture that blended with a fresh chortle from his belly and created a bizarre gurgle of a sound.

"Tuesday. The day before yesterday."

"Yes."

"And now you both are in love."

"Yes."

For once, Ripkin didn't know what to do with his body. He wanted to cross his legs, but the girl was so hair-trigger, she might read something further into the move. He coughed instead. His stomach yodeled, demanding the duck confit.

"Are you comfortable with this?" he asked.

"Quite," Beryl said. "He's great. His name is Pennbook Hamilton. He's a writer."

"A writer?"

"Yes, a very good one, too."

"That's quite a coincidence. Looks like kismet's delivering you the full monty. 'Editor meets writer.' A real headline for the heavens."

She was grinning. Ripkin couldn't believe she was smiling at his words. He'd broken form, of course. Said something conspicuously biting. Yet here he was being his most ironic, and she didn't even . . . whatever.

"He's a genius, Dr. Ripkin," she said, gushing. "He's got an IQ of two hundred and ten."

"Two hundred and ten? I say, that's an extraordinarily high number. Are you sure you're not mistaken?"

"Two hundred ten is two hundred ten."

"Right. Of course."

Beryl was shaking her head.

"Marvelous," Ripkin said. "Well then, I suppose congratulations are in order, young lady. This has been a long time coming."

She looked up at him.

"Do you mean that?"

"Of course. We want the best for you."

"We?"

"Yes. You and I. We both want the best for you. If this is it, then I'm happy to see that it makes you happy."

"Really?"

"Really."

She reached into a big purse she had sitting on the floor.

"You're the reason I'm even able to have a healthy relationship, Doctor. I owe you so much. This has been sixteen years in the making."

Ripkin's stomach roared.

"Yes, it has."

"I know I've given you a lot of these, but this will be the last."

She pulled one of her dreaded African violets from the bag. It was in full bloom, bigger and louder than the ones that lined the sill. Something snapped in Ripkin's nape. At least, he thought it did. Was it the cord that held his neck and torso together? It was, wasn't it? Finally, after years of tolerating fools, his head had rebelled and was about to fly off. What was this ridiculous talk about this being the last plant? Surely she didn't mean . . . ?

"I wanted to give you something to mark all the hard work you've put into me over the years," Beryl said. "You've done so much and I'm so very grateful. You've practically been a surrogate father to me."

He could feel something breaking inside of his chest. No! Not this! She couldn't be leaving him.

"Yes, well," he stammered, "I've watched you grow up practically, from a delicate teenager, who was a little on the brash side, I must admit—"

"I won't be coming back anymore," she said, handing him the plant. There. She'd said it.

Ripkin's stomach made a long, hissing sound that tapered off into a high squeal.

"Beryl. Surely. You must realize that now is not the time to—"

"I don't need to anymore, Doctor."

"But what about your medication? You'll need to keep taking them."

"I've got a few more refills. Then I plan to wean myself off. He gets me, Doctor. I don't need to hide behind pills anymore." She smiled.

It was the whitest, most fabulous smile he'd seen from her. Ever.

She was downright beautiful for one shining moment. Ripkin had to blink a few times to assure himself it was her.

"Mission accomplished," she said. "Well done, Doctor. Well done."

She wrapped his hands around the plant.

"Beryl." He laughed nervously. "I think this is a mistake. You shouldn't just end your sessions like this. There's so much still to explore. We're not even sure of how you will integrate into a normal relationship after years of never having one—"

"I've got faith. I want to try this on my own."

She stood on her tiptoes and hugged him.

"Thank you," she said. "For taking such good care of me."

"Of course," he mumbled, staggered by surprise. "I'm here if you ever need to call on me. It's your choice. No pressure."

"I know." She leaned back, her eyes connecting with his. "Be happy for me," she whispered. She kissed him one last time on the cheek.

He watched her walking out the door, her perfect hair and perfect clothes making a perfect exeunt out of his life. The back of his throat felt thick.

He looked down at the radiant plant, blooming with life.

Much to his amazement, he wasn't hungry anymore.

She immediately subscribed to all the appropriate periodicals: *Bride's, Modern Bride, Elegant Bride.* She registered at www.theknot.com. She began building her database of who to invite (and who not to), picking out places where they could register for gifts, all manner of exciting things. There were so many choices.

"Would Mercury be your best man?" she asked Penn.

"Best man for what?" he said, lost in Sartre's *Being and Nothingness.*

"Best man for the wedding, silly."

"Wedding?" he said, looking up.

"Yes. When we get married." A thought suddenly struck her. "You still want to get married, don't you?" she asked in a panic. "You haven't changed your mind?"

"Of course not," he said, smiling. He buried himself back in his book.

She stared at him, needing to be sure. He glanced up at her and winked, then resumed reading.

Thank God, she thought. At least that was settled.

So who would be in her wedding party? She really didn't have close friends who could be her bridesmaids. Perhaps she could get some of her professional acquaintances. Maybe Shecky could even be one of her girls.

But who would walk her down the aisle?

She thought of her parents and felt saddened that they wouldn't be there to see her special moment. Her father had been a strong, quiet man, sparing in his praise, but loving, protective. He would be proud of her, so proud. So would her mother. They would be pleased to know their daughter had gotten such a prize, and Penn was indeed the prize of a lifetime. She was going to have a chance at happiness, a real chance, after so much tragedy had befallen her family. Beryl knew they were watching over her. They would be with her in spirit.

She could ask Ripkin to give her away, but he was so damn cynical. Maybe he'd be different by the time their nuptials approached. Penn's book would have to go into the publishing production schedule, he'd have to tour, they'd have to allow enough time to pass for her to quit her job. So many things.

There was plenty of time for Ripkin to soften.

And plenty of time to ensure she had the wedding of her dreams.

A deal

. . . was a deal, and Penn finally had his.

And money. A fat advance of two-point-three *meeeeeeeeeeeelyun* dollars, to be paid out in increments divided in three, upon signing the contract, after delivering an approved manuscript, and upon publication. The deal made all the New York papers, *Variety,* and all the relevant gossip sites, Gawker.com et al., were blogging about it. The buzz about the book, which had remained untitled, was already starting to build.

And Spanky Katz. Turned out she was really cool and damned good, really good. Oblivious of a connection between Penn and Sharlyn, Beryl had convinced (so she thought) her star author to recommend Penn to her agent. Shar was represented by Spanky, and any request from one of Spanky's authors always got top attention. The agent reread the manuscript and enjoyed it this time (after Beryl had gone through it with Penn in a preedit). Spanky was going to take it to auction. She created a storm of interest, treating the manuscript as top secret information, requiring editors to sign statements agreeing to keep the subject matter confidential if they wanted a chance to see it and bid. Even if they passed on it or didn't win, they couldn't divulge its content prior to the book's publication. Just when it appeared things might get crazy, Beryl came in with her preempt and shut it all down.

Spanky became one of Penn's biggest champions, impressed by his charisma, attractiveness, and pluck.

And if anybody knew from pluck, it was Spanky Katz.

Owner of one of the most powerful literary agencies in the world, Spanky Katz had been in the book business for more than thirty-five years. The first half of those years were spent as an editor, where she turned burgeoning voices into blockbusting superstars and literary giants. The second half was spent repping blockbusting superstars and literary giants, many of whom were some of the very authors she'd developed as an editor.

She was tiny, tony, elitist, and abrupt, with short jet hair, narrow brown eyes, and rosy chipmunk cheeks. The narrow eyes served her well, the better to see through bullshit and effect lucrative deals. The rosy cheeks, however, were most deceptive. They looked pinchable, almost cute, but only a fool would pinch the cheeks of Spanky Katz. If anyone was going to do any pinching, it was Spanky, and Spanky alone. Only Spanky didn't pinch cheeks, she pinched checks, and was a master at pinching big checks for those fortunate enough to become her clients.

Penn was as impressed with her as she was with him when they finally met. Sharlyn had arranged for their formal introduction to take place over lunch at Cipriani's. She was present to make sure everything flowed well. Penn expected to feel smug and self-satisfied now that Spanky was coming to him, but that wasn't how it went at all. What he experienced instead was a kind of mutual guarded fearsome awe, like two prize dogs sniffing each other.

"Spanky Katz," she had said, pumping his hand with a Popeye grip. "A pleasure. A pleasure."

Her clawlike shake nearly squeezed the feeling out of his fingers, but it gained her instant respect. Her grip was like an arm wrestle, some sort of dare to take her on. He got the feeling she rarely lost a challenge.

"I've read your manuscript several times now," she said. "I think it's extraordinary. There's a lot we can do with this. A lot."

"Really?" Penn said. "I'm surprised at that."

"Spanky," Sharlyn interjected. "Penn has read quite a bit about your impeccable reputation."

"Of course he has," Spanky said. She turned her skinny gaze on Penn. "So why are you surprised that I like your book? Why wouldn't I? I know good work when I see it."

Sharlyn cleared her throat. She had warned Penn to let any resentment go. He told her he would, but now that he was in the moment, he felt he at least wanted an explanation.

"I sent you my manuscript before. A couple of years ago. You sent me back a letter saying it was shit."

"That's ridiculous," Spanky sputtered. "Ridiculous. I would never do that. That's not my style."

Penn produced the letter, still in the frame. Spanky's eyes traveled from Penn to Sharlyn to Penn again. She snatched the thing from his hand, simultaneously donning a pair of glasses that hung on a chain around her neck. She peered at the letter, scanning it with her fiery gaze. She thrust it back at him.

"What is this, some kind of a joke?"

"That's what I thought when I got it," Penn said.

"Well, I didn't approve it," she said, removing the glasses. "It probably came from some overeager assistant."

"Is that your signature?" he asked, pointing to the scrawl on the page.

Spanky lifted the glasses again and glanced at the letter.

"Looks like it," she said, dropping the glasses, "but that doesn't mean anything." She signaled for the waiter, snapping her fingers. "Pellegrino, please. Pronto."

"Are you saying they send out letters without your approval?" Penn pressed.

"Put that thing away," Spanky ordered. "I said I never sent it. Besides, it's moot."

"Moot how?"

"Because it is. The bottom line is I represent you now, if that's what you want. I'm the best in the business. If you read up on me like Sharlyn said, you know that already. Anything else is bullshit and shouldn't come under discussion at this table. Do you understand?"

Penn, for once, was speechless.

"Do you want me to represent you?" she asked.

Her tapered eyes were locked onto his. Sharlyn sat between them, unsure of what was about to go down.

Spanky and Penn held each other's gaze for a long moment, then Penn smiled.

"I guess I have an agent now."

"Of course you do," Spanky declared. "And I'm going to make you rich."

Penn had what he wanted.

More importantly, he had what he needed: the love and affection of two women, and a great degree of power over them both. Sharlyn was doing everything to help him, in addition to the efforts that Beryl put in.

Beryl had done what she did best, stoked the interest of other companies in a grand synthesized plan to promote one of her books. This time, it would be bigger than what she had done with Canon Messier. This would be her biggest feat yet.

Four major corporations had already signed on. Beryl had called on her connections at Calvin Klein, Apple, Starbucks, and Tower Records and had brought them together in a huge pitch meeting where she rolled out her version of the concept of *Gesamtkunstwerk* as it related to Penn.

"It'll be more than just the book, but the man as the brand," she'd said. "He's young, blonde, tall, beautiful, talented. Everything America loves. This man, this new breed of writer"—her arm was outstretched as though she were a circus barker about to lift the curtain on a bearded three-headed lady—"this, ladies and gentlemen, is the American Dream!"

And she had brought Penn out to pose and squeak and signify on cue, a modern-day King Kong who wowed the room and gave the executives and their minions a glimpse of marketing perfection.

"But it's a book about a man who wakes up as a giant penis," said the Apple exec. "That's not exactly the kind of thing we want to align ourselves with. We want hip, fresh, progressive, and fun, but not vulgar. The subject matter of this book borders on outright pornography."

"Not at all," Beryl had said. "There's a reason none of you have been given the entire book to read just yet. We wanted to keep it shrouded in secrecy. We plan to do that until the very moment we launch, which is something we've never tried before. There'll be no galleys, no advance reviews, no blurbs. Just hype. But it's a hype we believe will fully pay off."

"That's absurd," said the Tower rep. "It'll never work. Why would people buy a book they know nothing about? Why would the media participate if they can't get an advance copy? This is a give-and-take business. There'll be a backlash from the press. You can't sell what you don't know about."

"No disrespect, sir," Beryl said, strolling over to the man, "but I believe you can. I've studied this considerably. I've looked at all the possible angles. Sure, we're living in morally stringent times. Sure, people like knowing what the product is they're promoting or reviewing or considering buying before they sign on. But this is the age of the buzz. Pretty soon it won't matter what the product is. All any of us will have to do is represent it with confidence. That doesn't mean we should take that as a license to sell garbage to the American public. Not at all. But there is something to be said for mystery when there's an excellent product to back it up."

She wandered back to the front of the room, making eye contact, one by one, with every exec.

"With each of you on board, we can create a synergy that benefits all of us. The consumer's imagination will be fueled by the desire to know why four such powerful corporations would get behind an unknown artist with an unknown product. The curiosity will drive them mad. We live in an age where people need to know, have to know. That's why we Google everything. We TiVo stuff so we won't miss out. We have to know what's what and why. By simultaneously branding Penn through the buzz of secrecy behind his book, consumers will be compelled to know more. I'm confident of this. They will buy, and buy in droves."

"But it's about a *penis,*" another exec reiterated. "When people finally discover that's the core of the content, who knows what the reaction will be? It's a crapshoot. This is an incredible risk. We're talking decency here. These days people get up in arms over risqué clothing catalogs. We're liable to be open to all kinds of lawsuits. It's dangerous, very dangerous."

"I can understand your concerns," Beryl said. "We're living in an age of moral conservatism. This book isn't about what it seems. On the surface, yes, it's about a man who wakes up as a giant penis. That's easy to dismiss as pornography if you haven't read the book. But at its core, this story is an argument in favor of decency, an allegory for what's tragically happening in the world today, what with all the focus on excess, self-absorption, the lack of personal accountability, and the pursuit of money at the expense of the human spirit. Penn Hamilton has written an extraordinary story that examines the horrors of sexual perversion and moral complacency. It's a cautionary tale that will have all of America talking, which is difficult to do in an age when people don't exactly run out to buy books anymore."

The execs glanced around at one another. Their attention was piqued.

"So will any of this branding have to do with the book's content?" asked the Starbucks exec. "Are you asking us to tie into the whole penis theme?"

"No, no, definitely not. I think what's happening here is that everyone is getting hung up on the penis imagery. That's a minor metaphor for the greater concept. It in no way gets to the heart of the book and who Penn Hamilton is as an individual. Our initial focus will be on the writer himself, capitalizing on his visual appeal and market positioning as a focus for the consumer. Everything else will radiate from there."

Beryl was in her element at the front of the conference room at CarterHobbs. She had them transfixed.

"All of us are aware that image is everything. Image is what sells. Everything else will naturally follow. The content is already there."

"So where do we fit in?" asked the Tower representative. "What can Tower do?"

"I'm glad you asked that," Beryl said. "You see, in addition to the book, Penn will also have a hip-hop single and music video costarring and produced by rap mogul On Fiyah that will be released a few months before the publication of the book, both of which will further cement his image and broaden his demographic beyond the literary realm. This means tremendous opportunities for Tower Records and Apple iTunes," she said, looking at the Apple rep, "both individually and combined."

It was an egregious lie, but one she knew wouldn't be a lie for long. She already had the meeting with Fiyah set up. It was to take place the next afternoon. And he would sign on. She was sure of it. She knew she was walking a dangerous line, but the executives were now even more compelled. The smell of money was in the air, and everyone was suddenly doing silent computations of just how much could end up flying into their coffers. Penises be damned.

The idea to make a record with Fiyah had come about quite accidentally, as she discovered yet another fascinating talent in her beau.

It had happened at the Canal Room, at a party Beryl was invited to and had brought Penn, on the low, to attend as her date. They didn't sit together, hang together, do much of anything together—just in case—but they'd made eye contact across the room and had somehow managed a casual dance.

At one point during the night, the deejay let people come up and take a turn at the mic. Penn had been knocking back drink after drink, his spirits high on all the good fortune he'd been riding of late. He took a turn with the deejay and had freestyled over the music of Biggie's "Hypnotize" for a full ten minutes. The crowd, which included Mariah, Mos, and members of the Roots, packed the tables, the floor, and the banquettes, shaking their shit as he rocked the beat.

Pharrell was at the party that night and was digging Penn along with everyone else. Beryl's head began spinning with ideas. The next day she was on the phone with Pharrell. She wanted to reconnect with On Fiyah again. She wanted him to do a song, any song, with Penn.

"Can he rhyme?" Pharrell asked.

"Yes. You saw him last night."

"Who?"

"The really good-looking blonde guy who was rapping over that Notorious B.I.G. song."

"Yo, that kid? He was tight. All right, all right. I'll set it up. But Yah's gonna want to hear something. Why don't y'all roll by tomorrow. Maybe we can lay something down right quick."

Penn was just as good in the studio, kicking clever street rhymes that flew off the top of his head with ease. He'd been freestyling for

years. It was something he did for the amusement of his friends during his college years. Music was a strong suit. He'd been a piano
prodigy, after all.

Pharrell put him on the spot, just to see what he could come with.
He kept changing the beats. Up-temp. Slow stuff. Twista-type rapid-
fire beats that required serious lingual calisthenics. Much to Pharrell's
shock and amusement, no matter what he dropped, Penn could spit.

"Where you been hiding, man?" asked Pharrell.

"Just biding my time, man, biding my time."

"Why didn't you ask me to do a joint with him?" Pharrell asked
Beryl. "I could have produced something sweet. Everybody would
have been bumpin' his shit."

"Uh, um, uh . . ." Beryl stammered.

"That's all right," Pharrell laughed. "The lady wants Fiyah. We'll
go get you Fiyah."

For Beryl, the landscape was growing wider and wider. She didn't
know much about hip-hop, being more of a pop and rock kind of girl.
What she did know about rap, she'd experienced with Snoop and
Pharrell. There were names she'd heard in the media like Jay-Z and
P. Diddy (both of whom she'd seen at parties), and Biggie and Tupac,
who she was pretty sure were dead. But On Fiyah seemed to be in
virtually every single form of media there was. That's why she wanted
to get to him. There was another rapper she'd heard of. Eminem. He
was immensely popular. Penn had the potential to be like that, but
glossier. Teens would love him. The girls would go crazy.

Pharrell recorded the impromptu session and sent it over to Fiyah.

The meeting was set.

She would make it all come together. But these execs in front of
her now didn't know that, and didn't need to. It was just a matter
of transactions now.

"We see opportunities with iPods to download audio versions
of the book or individual chapters," Beryl said now, turning to the
Apple exec. "We also plan to do audio interviews introducing Penn.
These will take the place of galleys. They'll go to the standard review-
ers, as well as radio stations around the country, packaged along with
an advance of the rap single. It'll employ the newest scrambling tech-

nology, so the music can't be bootlegged on the Net. Once the song is released, the only way to get it will be to pay for it. But iTunes has already proven consumers are willing to do that."

"This sounds like what Martha Stewart did," said the Apple guy. "Co-opting all types of media. What makes this any different?"

"Martha made a lot of money for the companies she worked with," replied Beryl. "Cross-promotion is a bonanza within itself. But Martha took one thing—raising the standard of domestic living—and that's what she parlayed into an empire. We're talking about a man who will parlay multiarts across multimedia."

"How so?" the Calvin rep asked.

"Through fashion, by being a model for your company, Calvin Klein. Through literature, via his book with us. Through music, with his song and video, therefore allowing a tie-in with both iPods and Tower Records, and as an accessible Superman who drinks coffee, strong coffee, from the king of all coffees, Starbucks. Starbucks and their Defibrillators are what keep him going. How about that as a message! Starbucks makes the fuel that keeps our engines churning throughout the day, but if you drink Defibrillators like Penn Hamilton, just imagine the things you could do!"

The Starbucks people were smiling, imagining it all.

"And that's just the beginning. There will be film opportunities based on his literary material . . . television. He'll already be a star by that point—in the book world, the music world, and in fashion. The difference is he won't just be one of those celebrity dilettantes who piddle around in every genre of everything, spread paper-thin just for the sake of personal gluttony and naked consumerism. Penn Hamilton is a true talent who brings extraordinary things to the table. His writing is genuinely impressive, the kind that garners critical acclaim and wins awards. He's a musical prodigy, a six-time national chess champion, all before the age of twelve. He has an IQ of two hundred ten."

A gasp cut through the room. If all eyes weren't on Penn before, they were certainly on him now. Beryl allowed the "two hundred ten" to hang in the air for a long moment, long enough for them to consider the vast implications.

This was no ordinary King Kong. This was a monkey genius.

"Imagine the press that will precede him. His backstory is amazing. It's right there, in that packet in front of you. Everyone will be dying to do a story on this man, even if they don't know what his book's about. It'll be a feeding frenzy. A feeding frenzy from which we can all directly benefit."

Beryl realized in that moment that she should have been a manager. The Kittell Press crew, who were also present, were damn lucky she worked for them.

"Product placement will be woven throughout the text of his upcoming book. It's a very simple editorial tweak that in no way affects the quality of content. Characters won't just go into a record store, they'll go into a Tower, and they'll listen to their music on iPods while they're drinking Starbucks"—she turned and made eye contact with the Calvin exec— "and wearing Calvin Klein. Once the book is released, potential buyers will be able to download sample chapters from kiosks at all of your stores. Kiosks where they can dock their iPods. We'll do CDs, compilations of songs Penn Hamilton loves to listen to as he writes. Starbucks can sell them as point-of-purchase items. As the public connects with Penn Hamilton and the characters in his book, they'll simultaneously be connecting with all of your products!"

The entire room was one unified grin.

"And we plan to have ads," she said, "right inside the book. At intervals, so as not to be too obtrusive, but they'll be there. Bright shiny ads for iPods, Calvin, Tower, and Starbucks. Unlike magazines, which people tend to toss after a certain amount of time, books are forever. They're never thrown away. If anything, they get passed on, traded, checked out of libraries. Imagine the shelf life of a book in the library! Imagine the shelf life of an ad in a book in the library. That same ad touching people over and over and over again!"

She was flashing her megawatt smile, her arms outstretched. She was completely running the room in her impeccably tasteful cream Dior suit.

"Imagine if we had all of you on board with this. It's a wide-open arena, people. All you have to do is be willing to play."

She let the electric silence hang over them as they pondered the potential riches they'd reap.

"We'd need to see an advance copy of the book, of course," said the Starbucks rep. "We can't just take your word for it. Even if the rest of the country is going to be kept in the dark, those of us who decide to sign on are going to require full disclosure."

"Yes, yes," said the other execs.

"Our legal department will have to review it," said the Tower guy.

"Of course," Beryl agreed. "We have packages prepared for each of you. I'm sure we all understand, of course, that they are extremely proprietary. The way we plan to launch this book is unique to us as a publishing house and unique in the world of business in general, so to have its content leaked would greatly jeopardize our strategy."

The execs nodded.

Beryl clasped her hands together in happy, infectious excitement.

"But again I must say, I'm confident that, once you read the material, you will be just as enthusiastic as we are about the tremendous possibilities that lie before us."

"From what I understand," said the Tower guy, "you don't even have a title for this book."

"Of course we do," said Beryl. She ignored Penn's quizzical look. "And it's very much in keeping with our desire to keep things shrouded in mystery."

She was smiling, her eyes dancing with mischief.

"Well, what is it?" asked the Starbucks exec.

The room stared at her in anticipation. Even her boss was confused.

Beryl basked in their gazes for an extra moment before she spoke.

"The title of Penn Hamilton's first book is . . . *Book.*"

All four companies were in by the end of the week.

And so it was that Beryl had been able to rah-rah Calvin Klein into putting Pennbook Hamilton in a major ad campaign where he wasn't even wearing any underwear. Apple and Tower would be a part of that same ad, with both iPod and Tower logos on the cover of the book he would be holding. There would be separate iPod and Tower campaigns as well, all integrating the other companies. Starbucks would sell the CD single of Penn's new song, and they would introduce a new coffee, the Defibrillator, the strongest they had to offer, in an ad featuring Penn and his book. Dump displays in bookstores would have logos for Apple, Tower, Starbucks, and Calvin Klein, and offer discounts for their products with the purchase of Penn's book. Customers would be able to pay to download Penn's new song into their iPods at music stations in Tower Records all across the country. The song would come with an audio bonus of Penn talking about his creative process. Previews promoting the book's release would be run as a coming attraction at movie theaters.

Twenty-five million dollars. That's how much in combined dollars and co-opted services Beryl had been able to coax out of the four companies to help kick off the great Penn Hamilton cross-marketing campaign. It was a first in publishing. Kittell Press was throwing in a couple hundred thousand. There wasn't a need for them to put up much more. The plan was for sales to be bigger than big, somewhere in the millions, that rarefied place saved for books like *The Da Vinci Code* and anything with the title *Harry Potter.* Everyone involved with *Book* was daring to dream. Between Beryl, Kittell Press, Apple, Tower Records, Starbucks, and Calvin Klein, everything would be done to ensure Penn became an American icon.

On Fiyah was everything and nothing like Penn expected.

They were at Worldwide WifeBeater. Penn expected the place to be crawling with hardheads and thugs and have a rough, ghetto edge that would be instantly palpable.

Fiyah was a professional. He greeted them personally and escorted them back to his office, but he wasn't as stiff as they'd expected he'd be. Pharrell had given him the heads-up. Fiyah's conversation was very accessible, as though the three of them were already friends.

"Thanks for taking the time to see us," Beryl said.

"Not a problem," he said. "I remember we met before at that Trump thing, I think. I've read a lot about you in the press."

"Really?" Beryl asked nervously.

"Good stuff, good stuff. Relax yourself. How'd you like that diamond sweatsuit?"

"I loved it," she said. "It's my favorite."

Once they were settled in Fiyah's office, Penn couldn't help study-ing the man. He was charming, magnetic, quite sleek and sophisticated in an expertly tailored suit and enormous diamond studs in both ears. Lots of shiny bright things. Watches, cuff links, rings. Neatly trimmed hair. A kind of sublime elegance, despite all the blinding jewels. He was alternately soft-spoken and reserved, then full of raucous laughter, which could, just as quickly, turn into pensive intensity.

"I'm usually more casual in the office," he said, explaining the suit, "but I got a thing uptown I'm doing this afternoon."

"You look great," Beryl said.

On Fiyah nodded.

"So my man Pharrell was talkin' you up. Y'all got this book deal and all, and the Calvin thing, and what, what else?"

"Starbucks," Beryl said, "Calvin Klein, Apple, and Tower Records."

"For real? That's hot. Yo, I checked out the tape and, yeah, you got something. You definitely got something. I mean, you could be a white boy doing hip-hop, but you won't come across as just another hip-hop white boy, know what I'm sayin'?"

"Yeah," Penn said. "I like hip-hop, but I'm into a whole bunch of—"

"He can do anything," Beryl said. "He plays the piano and—"

"The piano? Yo, that's crazy." Fiyah nodded, the wheels in his power head visibly turning. "Here's the thing: see, I don't just put my name on stuff just to see my name on it, you know what I'm sayin'?"

Beryl opened her mouth. Fiyah held up a finger.

"Lemme finish. What I was gonna say, though, is I'm seeing this, you know, the possibilities. There's like a million ways we can flip this thing. You got that look, that blonde, blue-eyed, pretty-boy-next-door kinda thing. Brad Pitt and shit. Everybody's all-American. Peo-ple like that."

"That's the idea," said Beryl.

"Yeah, yeah. And what I really like about it is that it speaks to the heart of how I get down. I'm all about the cross-promotin'-multiplexin'-product-maximizin' thing. This is straight-up how I like to do it." He was intense now, almost talking to himself. "Yeah. White chicks, black chicks, Eskimos, Aborigines . . . everybody's gonna flip over you. You got the perfect American look. Gay, straight, you won't alienate nobody. It's like every demographic in one fell swoop."

Beryl was thrilled at On Fiyah's enthusiasm.

"See," he said, "marketing is all about identifying the facts, spinning off some new ones, and making the people believe. Look at you, kid. Everything about you is user-friendly. And this book you got coming out . . . what's the name of it?"

"Book," Beryl said.

"Yeah, the book. What's the name of the book?"

"That is the name," Penn said.

"What's the name?" asked On Fiyah.

"Book is the name of his book," Beryl said.

Fiyah sat back, silent, checking out both of them. He rubbed his chin.

"Y'all fucking with me, right?"

"No," said Penn. "That's really the name."

Fiyah's face was blank. He leaned forward, his expression unchanged. Then he sat back, shaking his head.

"Now that's some brilliant shit," he said with a laugh.

"That's my editor," Penn said. "She's a marketing machine."

Fiyah looked at Beryl.

"I admire people with hustle," he said.

Beryl smiled, basking in his approval.

Fiyah leaned back in his chair.

"You know I heard it's a whole big secrecy thing surrounding it. Like some spy shit. No reviews, no samples. I like that. How'd you come up with that idea?"

Beryl jumped in before Penn could speak.

"Actually, we're revealing a little info, but not much. People will know it's an update of—"

"Yeah, yeah, Kafka," On Fiyah said. "I know. *The Metamorphosis.* With the big-ass cockroach. That shit was crazy."

"I've always liked Kafka's work," Penn said. "I started out just having fun with it, and it kind of turned into something real."

"That means you hit the zone."

"The zone?"

"Yeah, the zone. When you're writing, or making music, or producing, or creating, at some point you start hitting everything just right. That's the zone, man. That's the best place in the world an artist can be."

"Hopefully I'll do it again," Penn said. "This was just my first book."

"Yeah, but you'll write more," said Fiyah.

He was connecting with Penn. Beryl was very pleased.

"I like this," Fiyah said, turning to Beryl. "I like how y'all are thinking. Nobody's ever come to me before about doing something on a level like this. I like the creativity behind it. You gotta play that shit up. Ride that wave, 'cause let me tell you, waves crash, and you gotta make sure you don't crash with them. You gotta always be thinking, be thinking"—he tapped his temple—"ready for the next wave. Diversifying. Going to the next level."

"Right," Penn said.

"I read an article a few years ago . . . funny, I can't remember where I saw it. Some magazine. Mighta been *The New Yorker.*"

Fiyah's face performed the above-the-neck equivalent of an abdominal crunch, a sort of spasm/shudder/blink where his eyes rolled upward and off to the side as he lapsed into fiery concentration, as though the heat of his thought would pressure his gray matter into spitting forth requested data. It was over in a nanoinstant.

"I can't remember," he said. "Anyway, it was about the zeitgeist and reinvention. It offered this theory that I think makes a whole lotta sense. It said all the celebrities who've had longevity reinvented themselves every three years. Three years." On Fiyah held up three fingers. "It's a cycle. It takes about that long for your popularity to rise, crest, and ebb, and the ones who ain't got no Plan B die out, but the ones who keep flippin' it, flippin' it, see, they keep going. Every three years you gotta flip it. Remember that. Madonna perfected that shit. She showed the world how to work the three-year flip. She did everything from simulating sex on stage to dancing around a black Jesus in flames and shit on a cross. Now she's the bestselling author of children's books. That girl is a damn zeitgeist zen master. Tell me she ain't."

Penn and Beryl both nodded.

"See, you got that thing, and it overlaps a whole lotta genres. Ain't too many people got that, and on top of that, ain't too many of the ones who got it know how to keep it. That's why it's not good enough for people like us to just have a Plan B. We gotta have a Plan Alphabet, and I'm not just talking about the regular Latin alphabet."

Penn had been astounded to learn that On Fiyah was this deep. The regular Latin alphabet? Who, outside of English teachers, linguistics experts, and extraordinary nerds remembered what the standard alphabet of the English language was called?

"See, that's not good enough," Fiyah was saying. "When we get to Z, see, that's when we go Greek, and kick it with Plan Alpha, and work our way all the way to Plan Omega. Gotta keep it movin', baby."

Penn and Beryl stared at him, dumbstruck.

"So let's do this," he said. "Let's maximize and multiplex. Let's make some hit records."

"Oh, Mr. Fiyah, thank you!" Beryl squealed.

"Yeah, Mr. Fiyah," Penn added. "I almost don't know what to say."

"That's all right, kid. Save your breath for the record. We're about to make you a star. You could be my new buddy. My cool white boy. Every brother needs one cool white boy in their camp."

The Calvin Klein national print campaign was the first to roll out. It included an enormous black-and-white billboard of Penn in Times Square. He was naked, his body absolute sculpted perfection, his book placed strategically in front of his larger-than-life business.

In the lower corner of the ad was the logo for Tower Records. In the lower right corner was an iPod and the Apple logo. Their placement in the ad didn't seem to make much sense, but they were there nonetheless. The words "Calvin Klein" were in giant print above Penn's head. The ad was traffic-stopping. It was as though Times Square had its very own god.

"What's this word? I'm not familiar with it."

They were at Beryl's office, deep into a line edit of *Book*. She'd been in there with him for the past three hours and had Shecky holding all her calls. Even though she worked with Penn during off hours, she wanted to make a good show at the office as well.

He leaned over her shoulder. She angled the page so he could look.

"Oh that," he said, sitting back. "It means 'goat sucker.' It's a creature that's been blamed for the deaths of thousands of goats in Mexico and Puerto Rico that have been found with puncture wounds in their necks. But no one's ever seen one. Kind of like how no one knows who's making crop circles. It's considered an ABE."

"What's that?"

"An anomalous biological entity. That's what UFO experts call creatures for which there are no scientific explanations."

"I see," Beryl said, her brow crinkled. She was beginning to wonder if Penn was an ABE. Everything about him was so very . . . different. She loved him for those differences, but in cases like this, they got in the way.

"What does it have to do with the story?"

"Nothing."

"I don't understand."

He shrugged.

"There's nothing to understand. I just always wanted an excuse to use the word *chupacabra*. I was writing a book, so there it is."

Her brow was an accordion.

"Right." She paused. "I think we should lose it. It's silly and distracting. I had a hard enough time trying to learn how to pronounce 'Gesamtkunstwerk' and say it right at all those pitch meetings. Just because you've got a big brain and know a lot of weird stuff, there's no need to show it off without cause. It'll annoy the readers."

"No," he said. "The *chupacabra* stays."

"Surely you're not serious. This is your career."

He stood and walked over to the vast window overlooking the city, his hands clasped behind his back.

"Penn."

He glanced up Sixth Avenue. The street was a tight bustle of moving flesh and metal. And pigeons. Always the pigeons. A group of them caught his eye as they flapped themselves airborne from the top of a shorter building across the way. Such disgusting creatures. Flying parasites that served no purpose. He could never understand why things existed in the world that didn't serve a purpose.

"Penn, really," Beryl pressed. "This word is just stuck in the middle of the text and it's not relevant to anything. We're positioning you to be a serious author. The last thing we want to happen when people read your work is for them to be able to dismiss you as another dumb blonde model throwing words around without any respect for the craft. We have to do this right. You're going to change the paradigm for beautiful blondes everywhere."

Penn watched an enormous pigeon on a ledge, the epitome of feathered nastiness, a Jabba the Hutt among his peers. The bird was so big, all it could do was squawk and coo, but not much else. It had attempted flight a couple of times and apparently said fuck it. There was too much girth to become easily airborne. The bird probably only flew under extreme, necessary conditions. Another pigeon dropped some bread in front of the stuffed bird and flew off. His bitch, Penn assumed. The fat fuck sat back, letting the chick do all the work. Penn felt bile gathering in his mouth, he was so offended by the useless creature.

"Take it out," Beryl was saying. "People will know how smart you are. I'll make sure of that. You won't have to announce it like this."

He tore his gaze away from the lonesome ghetto dove and looked at her, letting the command she'd just made hang in the air. Her expression was firm. This was not the face of his adoring lover. This was the intense gaze of an editor on a mission.

"Fine," he said. "Get rid of it."

He was writing in his journal with great fervor, now that things had begun to accelerate.

My life is finally on track. Beryl has taken this whole thing on and she's gone ballistic with it. She's the perfect fit for this. If only we were able to do it without the sex. I guess I should be grateful she doesn't need it that much, although all the damn cuddling she wants to do is killing me. It would be so good to have her in my corner just

*as my friend. She really is a good editor and an awesome marketer. I
see why she's up there with the best.*

The musings were almost childlike in their simplicity of tone.
Sometimes they went on for pages. Other times, he expressed himself
in clean, simple, abbreviated strokes.

Calvin Klein!

Or . . .

*I'm holding a check for six hundred and fifty-one thousand six hun-
dred and sixty-six dollars. The last three digits are six-six-six. I
suppose there's some humor inherent in that.*

His favorite notation of all was the height of perfect brevity.

Sharlyn Tate has the best pussy I've ever had.

When he wasn't journaling, scheming with Beryl, savoring Shar, or
spending his new stream of money, he was angling over other concerns. They weren't as heavy, but they mattered nonetheless.

Next on his agenda: hooking up his boy Mercury so he could cash
in. He already had a plan for it. Beryl was taking out some kind of a
loan. She'd already been approved. She wanted to rehab her place.
Penn was going to convince her that Mercury and his uncle were just
the team to do it.

Sharlyn's creativity

. . . was back. She was satisfied and sunny, full of a lust for life, fueled by a lust for love. She was done with *The Magic Man* by the time Miles returned, which was two weeks after the first time she and Penn did the do. Beryl couldn't believe how quickly Sharlyn had gone from having nothing for almost a year, to suddenly producing a manuscript.

"How'd you . . . I don't understand . . . I'm delighted, but where did the—"

"It just popped out of me," Shar said with a grin.

It was late October, plenty of time to push the book through the production schedule for a summer release. The art director was already hard at work trying to create a cover that would match its highly erotic nature.

"It's very Anaïs Nin," Beryl said. "It's good, but very different for you. My hands got sweaty just reading it."

You should have seen me writing it, Shar thought.

"If I didn't know any better, I'd say you had yourself a Henry Miller somewhere, stoking you full of ideas. Miles must be back."

"Are you saying it's cheesy? Is there too much sex?"

"No," Beryl said. "The amount of sex is fine. It feels organic, not forced, which is what makes it work. Nin's writing was filled with very intellectual, literary eroticism. This reminds me of *Spy in the House of Love*. There was poetry in her prose, an elegance in the midst of all the sex. It was beautiful. That's what this is like. Dangerous, edgy, poignant, but it's all you. I think it's your best work yet. If this is why it took you so long, then I must say, it was worth the wait."

Shar was pleased. She thought this was her best work, too. The devil was in those pages. The dark side of her had been freed. Good and bad had melded together into what she felt was a perfect symmetry of artistic expression.

The sales force at Kittell Press had rushed forth to create an advance stir.

> *In the spirit of the bold, provocative prose of the giants of erotic literature, Sharlyn Tate, the Queen of Pop Fiction, has crafted a searing tale of sex, love, and power among the ruins of the Manhattan demimonde. Fans of Tate will love* The Magic Man, *and she's sure to win even more loyal readers with every turn of the page.*

Barnes and Noble, Borders, and others responded by pre-ordering in bigger numbers than ever. *Cosmopolitan* bought the first serial rights. *The Today Show* had her scheduled to appear on May 23, one week before Memorial Day, to help launch *The Magic Man* as the read of the summer.

Meanwhile, Shar had become Rumpelstiltskin, churning away at her laptop, turning words into gold. She was already at work on her next manuscript, oozing with inspiration. The more she was with Penn, the more she wrote. Pages were flying out of her faster than she could keep up with.

She had read Penn's book, which she thought was remarkable, like nothing she'd ever seen. She wanted to be a part of helping him break out as a writer. She knew Harvey quite well, she told him. He'd turned four of her books into movies, all of which were commercial successes. If Penn didn't mind, she wanted to send a copy of *Book* over to him. It would make a great film, and this story was just the kind of thing big Harvey was good at.

She even tried to convince Beryl to release Penn's book around the same time as hers.

"I don't know if that's a good idea," Beryl said. "I don't want to do anything to take the attention off either of you. His book is going to be a big deal. You always get a lot of attention. *TMM*'s going gangbusters." Beryl often abbreviated the names of books with more than one word in the title. *TMM* was her shortened version of Shar's new book. "You both deserve to have the limelight on your own," she said. "We're going to publish his book in September. It'll give us time to get everything rolled out the way we want."

"But don't you think it would be great publicity, the two of us doing some TV and radio together and maybe a few signings? It'd be a good way to help build his momentum."

Sharlyn watched Beryl as she sat behind her desk. That nervous knee of hers was shaking, she could tell. Beryl was trying to come up with a solid reason for why it wouldn't work. She could be so close at times. What did Beryl think she was going to do, try to steal her thunder and take credit for Penn?

"I don't know. I'm afraid you might cannibalize each other's sales."

"How? My audience is my audience. They're going to buy my books no matter what, as long as I keep trying to tell a good story. My sales are consistent and my fans always wait—enthusiastically, I might add—for the next project from me."

Beryl was frowning.

"But it won't be fair to Penn. Don't you think? It won't give him a chance to build an independent identity if he's automatically linked to you."

"Automatically linked to me?"

"That came out wrong. What I mean is, our plan is to roll out his book by building a distinct, well-crafted image for him. Advertising and publicity are working hard toward that end. It's a delicate balance. The public is so unpredictable."

"But aren't you going to have all that other stuff? The Calvin Klein ads and Tower Records and, what, iPods? Shit, I'd like a signature iPod. Apple could make one inspired by me, with cheetah print, or maybe leopard, and they could put diamonds around the edges of it." She leaned forward, excited at the prospect. "I know . . . there could be a limited-edition Sharlyn Tate iPod, customized by Jacob the Jeweler. I could have a billboard. How come you're not doing that kind of stuff for me?"

"How do you know about the iPods and Calvin Klein?" Beryl asked, blinking rapidly.

Sharlyn's insides felt wiggly as she thought of the moment in bed when Penn had told her what was being planned for him.

"C'mon, Beryl. Word gets out. What's the big secret anyway? This is me. We're friends."

Beryl was up, pacing the room. Sharlyn watched her fidgeting around. Beryl really needed to relax more, she thought. She was such a flutterbudget.

"So how come I don't have any iPod deals? How come I'm not in a Calvin Klein campaign?"

Beryl turned toward her, a tiny crinkle of exasperation in her brow.

"So now you're mad," Shar said.

"I'm not mad, Sharlyn."

"Oh, yes you are. You called me Sharlyn."

Beryl heaved a deep breath.

"Shar . . ."

"Fine," Sharlyn said. "I don't want to tour with your precious writer and steal any of his limelight."

Sharlyn got up from her chair.

"I'll just take my black, no–iPod–deal–having self home and try to write your indifference out of my system."

"Shar, I was not being indifferent—"

"You're being all protective of your new rock-star white boy."

"I am not," Beryl protested, realizing the last thing she needed to do was alienate one of her biggest stars. "I'm just trying to make sure you both get the attention you deserve, and the only way I can do that is by—"

Shar was laughing as she walked out the door.

"Shut up, Beryl," she said. "I'm just fucking with you."

Beryl was crying.

They were at Penn's place, in bed, watching *Primetime* on ABC. It was a funny segment about women drivers. Out of nowhere, Beryl had erupted in tears.

"What's wrong, babe?" Penn asked, startled, annoyed. What could it be this time? he wondered. Her emotions could be so hair-trigger at times.

"What about kids?" she sobbed. "What if our children have narcolepsy, too?"

Penn cringed inside. He set the Red Bull he'd been sipping on the nightstand. The only reason he was drinking it was because he thought it might be one of those nights when he needed to perform for Beryl. He was feeling a little low on energy, and way, way low on motivation. Now she was crying, which succeeded in killing any remote chance of an urge. More and more, she was coming up with bullshit.

He put his arm around her.

"Our kids will be fine," he managed to convincingly say.

She looked up at him with her wet eyes and her crooked face. The corners of her lips trembled.

"But we don't know that," she whimpered. "I had it. My dad had it. My grandfather. Look at all the devastation in my family because of it."

"That's because they were ashamed of it, babe," Penn said, rubbing her back. "If our children had narcolepsy, we would educate them about it. I would make sure I knew as much as possible so I could take care of all of you. There's no reason why we have to treat it like some crippling disease. It's a shame you spent so much of your life embarrassed about it. It's really not that big a deal."

"Really?" she said, her face turned upward, toward his, like he was the sun. "You mean that?"

"Of course," he said, leaning down to kiss her.

She smiled luminously, and for a moment, just a moment, she was downright pretty.

He felt the stirrings of an urge. Perhaps he could still fuck her tonight.

Just as quickly, the urge went away as the thought of making narcoleptic babies with Beryl entered his head and strangled his loins.

Miles nibbled

. . . on Brookie's neck.

She giggled.

"Stop it," she said. "You're just trying to change the subject. I want to know when you're going to deal with this."

She was at the stove cooking a low-fat seafood stir-fry. Snow peas, baby corn, broccoli, and shrimp. The shrimp was high in cholesterol, but she'd done some research online and found that it could still be part of a healthy diet. Brookie was very antifat. She didn't dare to allow such toxins in her body. Far too many of her Southern relatives had died from eating all that greasy food.

Miles was standing behind her. Now his hands were coming around to her front, slipping something around her neck.

"What's this?" Brookie asked, looking down. She was blinded by the glimmer. She fingered the thing. "Miles! What is this? What have you done?"

She dropped the spatula and raced into the hall beyond the living room where there was a mirror. A series of perfect endless stones encircled her neck, an eye-popping array of carats. Brookie welled up.

"Oh, Miles!"

He waited for her in the kitchen, feeling like Kublai Khan. An overlord of love.

He was full of confidence and pomp these days. Tickled money

green. He had successfully wooed Jussi Seppinen, and that elusive
Finlandian fish Golarssen had joined the growing number of once-
elusive fish that now flapped around in the bottomless belly that was
ComMedia Wells, whose apparent objective was world domination.
Milestone Tate would see to that.

He had been back home in New York a whole month before his
wife was aware of it. He didn't have to worry about her finding out.
Even though they were both on the island of Manhattan, Sharlyn
lived in a bubble. When she wasn't writing, she was trying to cling to
the celebrity lifestyle with her friends. Miles wasn't into that scene.
His friends were power brokers, and unless power brokers were fucking pop stars and actresses, they weren't of much interest to the rag
sheets of the world. No one at the office ever contacted Shar without
his express direction and Sharlyn didn't much care for ComMedia
Wells of late, so there was no threat of her ever stopping by.

So Miles had spent the month undetected, living uptown with his
passion, his pet, the pride of his resuscitated manhood, Brookie. She
wasn't really his cousin, not per se. She was in the family, but strictly
by law. She was the stepdaughter of his favorite cousin, Ian, which
made her his cousin, but not by blood.

Brookie had turned his head on its axis the very first time he saw her,
when she was but a nubile fifteen. She had long flowing hair, rosy
cheeks, succulent breasts (small mounds, just enough), skin of silk, and a
bottom so incredibly round it could have been bounced down a court
and rocked a perfect three-pointer. She had haunting green eyes that
held him hostage every time he looked into them. Brookie had owned
him from that very first day, even though she didn't know it, couldn't
know it, and he couldn't show it, her being fifteen years old and all.

But now he could, and did, and would, every opportunity he got. It
had taken him some effort to crack her. Eight long years. During that
time, he had suffered mightily, watching her ripen into gorgeous fruit.
Deadly fruit. This girl was going to be his making and breaking, and Miles
Tate knew that, but he had to have her. He'd never wanted anything, not
a business, not even Shar, as much as he'd desired Brookland Ames.

She had almost married a Morehouse grad during her college years,
but Miles had called up a friend on the quiet, a Japanese electronics

mogul, and had gotten the boy a high-paying two-year stint overseas. Miles made sure there were plenty of sexy distractions to amuse the young man, so it came as no surprise to anyone but Brookie when he called up and said he planned to make Japan his permanent home. He wasn't ready for marriage, he said. There was still so much (sideways pussy) to see. Brookie had been stricken. She stopped eating, closed herself off, cried, cried, and cried herself sick. Her stepfather Ian didn't know what to do.

Miles Tate, to the rescue!

"Send her here," he had said. "She needs to get out of the South any-way, away from all those girls who feel like they need to get married as soon as they're out of school. She'll come into her own in New York. Sharlyn needs a personal assistant. Brookie can meet lots of people and get some exposure to a bigger world. It's the best thing for her. I'll make sure she's taken care of, Ian. You know you can count on me for that."

And so the oblivious Brookie had flown to the North and had lived with the Tates at first, until Miles realized that just wouldn't work. He could barely function with the girl in the house. He found himself hov-ering outside the bathroom in her upstairs suite, listening to her shower, sneaking into her room, smelling her things. Erections plagued him unmercifully. He was jacking off everywhere, in the shower, the car, his private bathroom at ComMedia Wells. Shar would surely catch him if he kept this up. He got Brookie a place in Harlem.

"It'll be good for you to have a sense of freedom," he said to the girl, "without having to worry about being pushed up with us." She was looking at him with those eyes, snatching his soul out of him like a reaper. "You'll be fine. I'm always just a call away."

"We both are," Sharlyn assured the pretty young girl. "Remember, Brookie, it's not many girls your age who can have their own place in Manhattan, all expenses paid, car service on demand, with an expense account. You really do have a wonderful life."

"Yes, Mrs. Tate," Brookie had said. "I'm not worried. I'll be okay."

She had been in New York for three months when Miles finally broke her down. Sharlyn was away at the London Book Fair. Brookie had a bad moment, thinking about how she'd been abandoned by her Morehouse man. They were having dinner at the Tates' Upper East Side apartment. Just her and Miles. It was an evening he had planned with quiet care. After the meal was prepared, the staff was dismissed. Miles served the food himself, something Brookie found exquisitely endearing. Somewhere between a bite of the arctic char with horseradish cream and a sip of the Pouilly Fuissé Cuvée á l' Ancienne 2002, things went terribly awry. She had fallen into pretty pieces, a tearful, sobbing, mournful mess.

"Why me? What makes those Japanese girls better than me?"

Of course Miles wouldn't say the many things he'd heard, things about the incredible submissiveness of (non-American) Japanese women, their willingness to please and accommodate their men, and, purportedly, the sweetest private parts in all the world. He would never tell her that. That, at the time, had nothing to do with anything.

"Brookie, my darling," Miles had exclaimed. "Please don't do this. That boy was trash to abandon you like that. Why would you bother to spill any tears over him?"

He had rushed to her side and was kneeling, pulling her into his arms.

"But what's wrong with me?" she asked. "Why wasn't I good enough? I gave him my virginity. He was the only man I've ever been with. He was the only man I ever thought I'd need."

"Pshaw!" scoffed Miles. "That's ridiculous. I would never encourage you to sleep around, but I can certainly tell you the first guy you have sex with is usually not the one with whom your destiny's bound."

"Really?" she sniffed. "You think so?"

"Brookie, I'm certain of it. He was just somebody for you to cut your teeth on. I'm just sorry you had to get hurt in the process."

She leaned into his shoulder, her tears wetting his shirt, her lustrous hair falling over him and beyond.

"He wasn't a man, Brookie, he was a boy. There's a huge difference. A real man knows how to take care of a woman. A real man would never abandon someone he loves."

He was rubbing her back in a way that was neither avuncular nor cousinly. It wasn't threatening, but it was the stuff that boners were made of. Brick ones. This was no regular rub. This was the rub of lust.

"But I let him . . ."—her wet lashes shrouded her downcast eyes—
"I let him . . . do things to me."

"What kinds of things?" His voice was soft, strong, comforting,
close to her ear, even as he continued to stroke her back, his hands
moving lower, just a little lower, somewhere between her lumbar
region and a bit too far.

"I can't tell you that," she said, looking up at him shyly, shooting X
rays of power from her green eyes. "I'm too embarrassed."

"You don't have to be embarrassed with me, Brookie. I'll always
look after you. I would never judge you about anything you did."

"Really?"

"Really."

Fresh tears covered Brookie's lashes as she leaned further into his
shoulder.

"He made me . . . he had this . . . oh, Mr. Tate, please don't make
me say these things!"

"Miles, dear. Call me Miles."

She leaned back, looking into his face.

"But I feel funny calling you that. You're my elder. I was taught to
show respect to my—"

She never got to finish. Miles Tate and his elder lips were all over
her.

Brookie couldn't come.

Miles had carried her to his bed, his and Sharlyn's, even though
there were other bedrooms he could have taken her to. He laid her
down and pored over her, his eyes wet at the prospect that he was
finally getting to worship at the temple of Brookland, a mecca he had
been journeying toward for eight solid years. He had taken Viagra earlier that evening to ensure, should things get this far, nothing stood
between him and consummation. But he didn't count on Brookie's . . .
issue. She had given herself over to him rather willingly, the thought of
her cousin-not-cousin Miles taking care of her, showing her love.

But Brookie couldn't come.

She was too mentally fucked-up for that.

Until visions of Japanese girls stopped dancing in her head and whatever her ex had done to make her so sexually ashamed, she wouldn't be able to, no matter how much Miles stroked and tasted and penetrated and probed. She was accommodating enough, lying there in the bed in all her goddess splendor, hair strewn about, lithe limbs, ample flesh in only the pertinent places, looking at him with those eyes. Those eyes. Miles was willing to do whatever it took to fix things. He was just happy to finally have her.

Miles loved Sharlyn. He really did. It just wasn't with the passion he felt for Brookie. Shar had been his best friend, his (half) life partner, a steadfast, faithful lover for more than two decades. They'd had a dedicated love that the two of them managed to keep stoked over the years. Even during the years Miles silently longed for Brookie, he was still able to channel that longing into lust for his wife. Shar kept herself up and was sexy, sensual, and fun. But that was over now. He was entering the next phase of his life.

There came a time when fun—the childish, attention-seeking kind—needed to be put aside. His wife was beautiful, but older. She even seemed a little softer around the middle since his return from Finland, not as toned as she used to be. And she was into things he wasn't. Brookie was young and completely pliant. He could shape her into whatever he wanted.

What he felt for her was bigger than love. It was a burning, a yearning, a desire for something so strong, he was powerless against it.

Brookie was young, tender, sweet, the essence of everything, so delicate in demeanor that it would offend her sensibilities to ever curse or swear, as Sharlyn did so freely. She was the reward for all his hard work building an empire. Women like her were the pot of gold at the end of a mogul's rainbow, the second wife who offered a second life, with babies this time, babies Sharlyn hadn't given him. He would have Brookie, the whole of her, with her young skin and young hair and young eyes and young essence. That youth would sustain him through the end of his days. That was his right, after all, wasn't it?

Every man was entitled to such things, especially if he could afford it. Warren Beatty had summed it up neatly, that a man should be able to change a forty-year-old wife for two twenties. Miles didn't think his desire to do this was unreasonable. After all, he didn't want two twenties.

He only wanted one.

Brookie would be all that he'd ever need.

Since his return from Finland, he and Brookie had been going to an orgasm therapist at an exclusive private practice that guaranteed them the utmost secrecy. Three days a week. She was going to have to learn how to come. She still hadn't told Miles what things the Morehouse man had done to her, but whatever they were, they had scared the living feelings out of her snatch.

Miles would fix her. He would use his billions and powers and influence and body to that singular end.

Because a cumless Brookie was still better than a thousand cumming Shars.

Any day.

He would break the news to Shar when the timing was right. He didn't want to do it just yet. Now was not a good time. He couldn't focus on this sex therapy thing with Brookie and corporate takeovers and conflict with his wife. Everything in stages, everything in stages. But he couldn't get as hard with Sharlyn anymore. Not enough to sustain the entire sex act. They tried four times after his "return," but nothing seemed to move him. He tried his best, but it was as though his penis had decided it would remain faithful to Brookie by no longer getting hard for his wife.

It was frustrating and awkward for both of them. So Miles did whatever he could to avoid it altogether.

"I'm going out to the country," he said a few weeks after his "return."

"I'll come with you," Shar said.

"No, no, don't worry yourself. Stay here in town. I'm going to play some tennis this weekend."

"Tennis?"

"Yeah. With that young writer at the cocktail party. He looked very athletic, so I asked him if he played. He claims he's halfway decent, so I've set up a few games of doubles for us on Saturday."

"He's staying at the house with you?"

"Yes. Is that a problem?"

"No," she said. "I just didn't know you'd asked him out to the country. I'm surprised he didn't tell me."

"I wouldn't get so upset over it. He probably didn't think it was a big deal. It's just tennis. If he's any good, I might have myself a regular partner."

"I see."

Look at that expression, Miles thought. He couldn't tell if she was pissed or puzzled. Sharlyn couldn't just take what he'd said and leave it alone. Everything was a debate now. She would probably give that poor writer useless grief over not telling her about the tennis thing. Her behavior would only grow more complicated with time, he knew.

Which was why he'd begun eyeing his next takeover.

He needed another reason to get out of the house. There was a Wi-Fi company in Brazil he'd been investigating. Perhaps this time, he could find a way to get Brookie relieved of duty for a few days to accompany him.

Brookie had been nervous about her affair with Miles from the start. Not because she didn't want to do it. She couldn't believe her great fortune in getting Milestone Tate, a man she had looked up to with awe since she was a teen. A billionaire. A man of international power and authority.

From the beginning, when her life was still pure, she had believed she would be with a powerful man, but she would have never imagined it to be Miles. She'd had high hopes for her college boyfriend, Mr. Morehouse, Mr. Perfect, until he showed himself. She'd done everything for him. She'd done the ugly thing. The ugly, ugly thing.

It was right after she'd finished pledging. She had just joined Alpha Kappa Alpha, and suddenly guys who'd been merely flirting before were aggressively trying to step to her. Having a pretty girl in a popular sorority was like a status symbol for some guys. Brookie wasn't just pretty. She was drop-dead.

Darren, her boyfriend, had just graduated from Morehouse and was going away for an internship. He was worried someone would steal her affection while he was gone. She'd been under his control for nearly four years. He needed to make sure he owned her, that he could manipulate her enough to ensure she'd stay put until his return.

"You say you won't cheat," said Darren, "but that's what all women say. I see those guys coming at you. I see you checking for them. I'm not blind."

"No, Darren," she'd cried, "that's not true. I love you. I don't want anybody else but you."

"I'm not stupid, Brookie. As soon as I'm gone, you'll be pushed up with the next man. Who is it? Tony? Dennis? I've seen how you look at my boys. I see how you flirt. Maybe I should just break this off now."

"Darren, don't do this!"

He had watched her tears, knowing how much it hurt her for him to suggest she could ever be unfaithful. He had been her world. Darren was handsome, highly intellectual, from an excellent family, and the president of his fraternity. He had been a perfect match for her, she believed, and she wanted nothing more than to start a life with him and pop out as many babies as he wanted. She'd given her virginity to him. She had prided herself on that. She'd only had sex with one person, and that was the way she wanted it to be.

As she tried to defend her love for him, Darren had walked off, disgusted by the thought of what she might do, and she had chased after him, begging.

"Please, Darren! I love you! I don't want anybody else, I swear!"

He had stopped, but he didn't turn around.

"Prove it."

Six hours later, she was in a three-way. Darren, her, and a stranger, a stripper from some skanky Atlanta gentlemen's club. The woman did unspeakable things to Brookie, with objects, toys, some sort of egg-shaped thing, and some kind of vibrating business with ears like a rabbit. Darren had done things to the woman. Brookie watched them fuck, frightened, horrified, but obedient, determined to prove her love. Then Darren did things to Brookie while the woman watched. Then the woman joined him and Brookie. It was a nasty, messy scene.

She'd done her best not to cry. She wanted to prove to Darren she would do anything for him, and this, he said, was how she could do it. They were at the Westin in Buckhead. When it was over and the woman was gone, Darren held Brookie as she lay violently shaking, fighting against tears.

"Now we have a secret together," he whispered. "We can't be broken. We have something that's just between the two of us. This is the kind of thing I would only want to share with my wife."

"You mean you'd want to do this again?"

"No," he said, hugging her tight. "Never. I didn't do this because I wanted a three-way. I did it for us. I needed to know we were solid. I needed to know your word was your word."

He kissed her forehead.

"I know that now, and I love you for it, Brookie. I love you so much. As soon as I'm done with this internship, I want to get married right away."

And he had gone into the bathroom, run a hot, sobering bath, come back into the room, and carried her lovingly to the tub. He had bathed her, caressed her, cared for her, until she understood why he had done what he had to do, had forced her hand this way, and she realized that she would have done it again, again and again, a million times over, if it meant keeping Darren.

But Darren was gone. The Japanese girls got him.

She couldn't lose another man. Not after the kind of humiliation she'd gone through just to try to keep one. She had to make sure Miles was hers, and she wouldn't do it with three-ways. She would do it her way, with one-on-one heterosexual sex, once she could get her head straight.

She would learn to satisfy Miles, even if it meant having to suffer through therapy.

She would make him happy.

This time she'd win.

What worried her was Sharlyn. How could she, Brookland Ames, compete with such a superstar? The only advantage she had over

Sharlyn was age and a different kind of beauty. And Miles's attention, which she couldn't lose, no matter what. She forbade him from having any more sexual relations with Sharlyn. She couldn't lose another man again. It would kill her. She knew it would kill her for sure.

Sharlyn Tate was a snacker. The whole time she was writing, she would snack, snack, snack.

That was the way, Brookie had realized. She would feed her boss those nasty foods, those killer foods, the type of stuff she knew Miles couldn't stand, but his wife was apparently weak against. Those foods sickened Brookie, but she knew how to prepare them with expert skill. This was the cuisine of her mother, her grandmothers, and all of her aunts. Deadly sustenance. That's what she would give her.

And Sharlyn Tate would grow fat and ugly. She was too distracted to stick with a trainer and too vain to submit to undergoing lipo. She'd turn into a cow, and Miles would hate her, and there would be no threat of him ever leaving Brookie again.

She would learn how to have sex with Miles. She had to.

Because she couldn't be alone.

There was no way she could ever be abandoned again.

Fiyah made

. . . the video.

They had already cut the song in the studio, a clever ditty simply called "Book." Penn had cowritten it with On Fiyah. It was a catchy tune that would blaze throughout the summer.

The Calvin Klein billboard had been up in Times Square since March. People were already stopping Penn about it. Girls were making public displays of themselves. A few had flashed him, right there on the street.

The song was out a month before the video hit. It was already in heavy rotation on the radio and On Fiyah had already worked the remix, which had become a club favorite, the kind of song that got asses on the floor the second people heard the first beat hit. After a while, the song was like air. There was no getting away from hearing it pour out of every car, truck, and stereo system across the U.S.

The video shoot took place on the Universal lot in L.A. Brett Ratner directed. A host of people mentioned in the song came through and made cameo appearances. The A-list chicks hit on Penn. So did a couple of A-list guys.

". . . and . . . *action!*" Ratner barked.

The beat dropped and Fiyah strutted around, mugging for the camera, Penn at his heels, mirroring his moves.

"Not Penn and Teller . . ."

Penn and Teller, the satirical magic team, stood against a vivid white background, fighting against a giant hook that was trying to snatch them off.

"Not pen and paper . . ."

. . . close-up of a gold-tipped Montblanc fountain pen touching down on vivid white paper . . .

"This ain't your regular . . . moneymaker . . ."

"No, I ain't Justin . . ."

The real Justin Timberlake mugged for the camera.

"No, he ain't Mark . . ."

The real Mark Wahlberg stood wide-legged, arms crossed, in front of his original Calvin Klein ad, wearing a T-shirt that said ORIGINATOR.

"It's the original Wonder Boy rockin' the charts . . ."

The verse went back and forth, on through to the hook, which was . . .

"And yo, check it out, you gotta get the Book."

The scene moved to night in Times Square, with Fiyah and Penn busting moves on a huge stage. Penn's Calvin Klein ad was lit up in the background.

"Get the look!" a huddle of celebrities shouted.

"Get the Book!" the masses packed in Times Square shouted in turn.

". . . aaaaaaaaaaaaaaand cut!" Ratner yelled.

People took their advice.

The pre-orders on Amazon had passed the one million mark, even though *Book* wasn't scheduled for release for another four months.

Even though people had no idea, other than the Kafka connection, what it was about.

The video debuted at number ten on *TRL* the second week in May.

A week later, it was number one.

Penn Hamilton—Calvin Klein guy, Defibrillator drinker, iPod hawker, star-fucker extraordinaire—was on top of the world.

"Yo, Fiyah, can I ask you a question?"

"What's up?"

They were sitting on a couch in an editing suite at R!OT Studios in Santa Monica, watching the colorizing guy adjust the tint on the video. Brett sat next to the guy at the boards. On occasion, On Fiyah would give his approval or disapproval of the direction they seemed to be taking the edit.

"I was just wondering . . ."

"Speak."

"What made you call me 'the original Wonder Boy'?"

"That's some clever shit, right?" Fiyah said with a grin. "See, that's one of those things I figured people would either get if they get it, and if they don't, they'll just think I'm calling you a superkid. And it's catchy as hell. People are gonna start calling you that."

"They already are. How'd you come up with it?"

"From that movie *Wonder Boys*. It was about writers and shit, you know, and I always liked that movie. Tobey Maguire and Michael Douglas was Wonder Boys, you know, smart cats who was, like, geniuses with the word at a early age and shit—"

"Yeah, I saw the movie."

"But they was fucked up and shit. Tobey was trippin' all through the movie and Michael Douglas's shit was all fucked up. They weren't exercising their powers right. But see, now, you . . . you look good, write good, dress good. That's the ticket. You working it in every direction, baby."

"You think so?"

"Hell yeah. Now all you need is a clothing line."

"You know, I was thinking about that. I was going to ask you about it."

"Seriously?" Fiyah said, turning toward him. "What would you call it?"

"Scribo," Penn said.

"Screebo? What the fuck is that?"

"It's Latin. Spelled with an *i*. It means 'I write.' "

"Scribo," Yah said, thinking about it, nodding his head. "That's hot. It sounds kinda hip-hop. I could see people rocking that shit."

Penn liked this guy. He had a keen eye for business and he spoke his mind without hesitation. On Fiyah thought like he did. They were branding birds of a feather. Big men with big ideas and big plans on how to turn those big ideas into big realities.

Except Penn would be bigger than Fiyah.

For sure.

Beryl had found her dress. Well, not exactly found it. It was going to be made.

By Vera Wang.

The designer Zac Posen reintroduced them. Beryl had met her once before at a launching party for the wedding book Vera did a few years back. Beryl told Vera of her plans. It was all very secret for now, she'd said. There was plenty of time.

Vera was in. Besides, she'd been thinking of doing another wedding book. Perhaps a series of them. Beryl could return the favor.

Getting Defibrillators was no longer an easy thing.

Customers recognized him as he stood in line. It happened all the time. People boldly sweated him now. All kinds of folks were coming out of the woodwork. Old classmates from Choate, people who'd never spoken to him at Columbia, friends of his parents who'd forgotten about him once Dane and Liliana died in the plane crash. They were everywhere. Like rats, they were.

Tabloids and gossip columns began pairing him up with people. Scarlett Johansson. Angelina Jolie.

"I've never even met Angelina Jolie!" he laughed the first time he saw it mentioned in *Us Weekly*. Beryl had been bothered by it, but what could she do? It was the backlash of growing fame.

"Would you ever want to be with Scarlett Johansson?" she asked him one night when they were in bed.

"Don't be silly," he said, thinking that he certainly wouldn't mind being *in* Scarlett, now that Beryl had brought up the subject.

"But she's beautiful and you're going to be shooting that new Calvin campaign with her. How do you know you won't fall for her?"

"Because I'm in love with you," he whispered, holding her close. "And stop with the knee shaking. You're such a worrywart. I'm where I wanna be, and it's not with Scarlett Johansson."

"Are you sure?" she asked. "Is my body good enough for you? Is there anything you'd change?"

"Yes," he said, "there's something I would change."

She stared at him, stricken.

"What? My nose? My breasts? Is it my hair? I can always change my hair."

Penn watched her ramble nervously.

"I'd change your mouth," he said.

She clasped her hand over her lips.

"What's wrong with it?" she said, her words muffled. "It's my teeth, isn't it? Should I have them fixed?"

"No. It's your lips. They're always flapping. You need to relax. Be quiet. Everything between us is fine."

Websites and blogs had begun to pop up all over the Net. The most popular one was called SoccerMomsforPenn. Dot-com. They had become the most vocal group among his growing fan base. He was the object of lust for desperate housewives all across the country, with many of them posting their fantasies daily. (Another site, a bit seedier—www.Milfs4Penn.com—offered even raunchier fare.)

An ex of his from Columbia started a blog called I Fucked Penn Hamilton (dot-org). (I Fucked Penn Hamilton dot-com had already been taken, but whoever owned it hadn't put up any online data as yet.) The IFPH dot-org site received thousands of hits, mostly from women who wanted to know what it was like to be with him. The girl who ran the website encouraged others to write in with their own accounts of having been at Penn's sexual mercy. Penn's ex from NYU, the one whose mother had won the lottery, was one of the most frequent posters on the site. She'd had an emotional breakdown after dating him, and she listed all the gory details of what came along with it, including photos of cuts she'd made on her body to purge herself of the pain. Another woman boldly exposed her naked chest. There were three scars across her breasts, like small raised splashes. Burn marks, she wrote, compliments of Penn's evil semen.

Other girls wrote in about equally dark things. Penn's penchant for rim jobs (getting them, not giving) came up. Beryl had been terribly bothered by it all. She didn't even know what rimming was.

"It's analingus," Penn said, stretched out on his couch.

"Huh?"

"Ass licking, babe, ass licking. I can't believe you're even talking about this."

"So that's what this means?" she asked, turning red. She was sitting at his computer, her back to him. She scrolled through the web pages she was reading. "These women are saying you like having your ass licked?"

"You'd know better than anyone. You're my girlfriend. Have I ever asked you to do it?"

"No, but—"

"Then drop it, babe. It's ridiculous."

"But Penn," she complained, "there's hundreds of them who've written in. Have you really been with that many women?"

"C'mon, babe. It's the Internet. People make up things just so they can feel important." He was channel-surfing. He landed on Comedy Central.

"But one of them described you perfectly," Beryl said, turning around in her chair to look at him. "She even mentioned the kinds of sounds you make when, you know, when you're doing it. And she was accurate. You do make those sounds."

Penn gave her a stern look.

"I wasn't a virgin when you met me, babe. You knew that. I thought we weren't going to go through this kind of stuff anymore. You're the one who warned me that people would start talking about me once I began to get more press. You said they might lie in the absence of having total access to me. They've already dug up photos of my parents. They've been writing articles about my dad, talking about his days at the U.N., interviewing his old colleagues, showing pictures of the wreckage of their plane. I wanted to keep that stuff private, it's my personal life, but I can't. Some of the things I've been reading about my mother aren't even true. People have been saying she was difficult and high-strung. That she was a diva with excessive, extravagant tastes. She was a lot of things, but not that. She liked nice stuff, but she was never excessive. Her friends loved her, my dad worshipped her, but the media's been twisting it all. She's dead, but that doesn't stop them from fabricating lies."

Penn couldn't believe he was defending his mother, but it was a convenient subject to hide behind to deflect Beryl's probing.

"So you haven't been with all those girls?" she asked. Her right knee was shaking.

"I'm saying I'm not going to keep answering questions like that," said Penn. "If I do, you'll never stop asking them. They're pointless. I'm with you now. You're the woman I love. Everything else is irrelevant."

Beryl was sullen. He went over and knelt beside her.

"You understand that, don't you?" He grabbed her hands, his hypnotic eyes searching hers. "I love you. Just you, babe. There's nobody else for me, no matter what you might read on a blog or in a magazine or on Page Six. You got that?"

"Yes," she whispered.

"Good," he said, kissing her palms.

"Penn?"

"Yes, babe."

"Do you like . . . rimming? Is that something you'd like me to do?"

"Babe!"

"I'm sorry."

"I don't ever want to hear you say that again."

And that had been it. She stopped bugging him, even though the online fascination with him increased, as more and more people began to chatter about Penn sightings, Penn myths, Penn the man.

He ran into his share of cloying people every time he stopped in Starbucks. He'd met more of them than he had real literati. He knew that would come in time, but for now, it was mostly coffee and rats.

He never had to pay for beverages and snacks at Starbucks anymore. All he had to do was flash a special card. He could hear the whispers around him now as he waited in line to get his fix at the Starbucks near Fiftieth on Sixth.

"Yes, it is."

"Are you sure?"

"Definitely."

"He is so fucking gorgeous."

"Look at that cleft."

"I'm gonna go over and say something to him."

A finger tapped his shoulder.

He turned around to see a man, an important-looking man, smiling at him.

"Penn Hamilton?"

"Yes?"

"Harold Gersh. Brecker Books."

He was a big guy, solid build, six two, six three, slightly balding, mid- to late fifties. He could have easily been a politician or a Hollywood mogul. He had that kind of look. Like somebody with power. Lordly yet accessible, spiffy, sleek. Penn knew him at once. Gersh was mythical for his ability to turn books into hits. Authors loved the man, and his editors were brutally loyal.

Gersh stood in front of him now with his hand stuck out. Penn shook it. A pretty blonde came toward them, then abruptly turned away.

"Nice to meet you, Mr. Gersh."

"You know, we really wanted your book."

Penn smiled and nodded, unsure of what to say.

"It was off the table before anybody could even get their bearings," Gersh said.

"Yeah. It went kind of fast."

Gersh gestured for Penn to move forward. People passed, gawking at the fair-haired model.

"What kind of deal they got you in over at CarterHobbs?"

"It's a one-book."

"A one-book? Really. I'm surprised at that."

"Yeah. My agent thought it was a good idea."

"I see." He gestured again. Penn moved up. "So what's next on your agenda? How's the rap thing going? Seems like you and On Fiyah are everywhere."

"I know. It's amazing."

"It's like you just exploded onto the scene out of nowhere. Books, music, fashion ads. I've never seen a writer market himself the way you have."

Penn was now up at the counter. He flashed his card.

"A Defib, please."

"Name?" the cashier asked, a slight curve to her lips.

"Penn," he said, poker-faced.

"Told ya!" said someone a few feet away.

"I'm afraid to try one of those," Gersh said. "That's a helluva lot of caffeine."

Penn laughed.

"I need it," he said. He moved to the side to wait for his java.

"A regular coffee," Gersh said to the cashier. "Venti." He reached into his pocket. Penn stepped up and flashed the cashier his special card.

"On me," he said, smiling at the publishing exec.

"You didn't have to do that."

"It's my pleasure, sir."

"Thanks."

Gersh stepped out of the line and waited with Penn.

"So maybe we can sit down one day and talk about your next project."

"Penn! Defib!" the barista yelled.

He stepped up and grabbed his coffee.

"Have a great day," he said, smiling at the barista.

"I just did," the frumpy girl purred.

He turned to Gersh.

"I'm sorry, I'm running really late. It was nice meeting you, Mr. Gersh. An honor, really."

"Let's talk. See if we can put our heads together."

Penn was already halfway out the door.

"I'll tell my agent," he said, and took off.

———

Mercury was now deep into the rehab on Beryl's apartment. It hadn't taken much for Penn to convince Beryl to kick some business his friend's way. She was more than willing to do anything to please her man. Mercury was Penn's best friend. Besides, it wasn't like he didn't have any credentials. He had a degree in architecture with excellent hands-on experience. Of course she would hire him. She couldn't wait to get started with her ideas for the place. She had planned to do the bathroom, bedroom, and living room at the same time. That would mean she'd have to spend most of her time at Penn's, including overnights, which was exactly how she wanted it.

"I can't believe this shit, man," Mercury said. "This bitch is crazy. As soon as we get a room all torn up so we can start on it, she changes her mind about what she wants us to do. We never get a chance to get it started. What kind of nonsense is that?"

"You making money?" Penn asked.

Mercury took his Yankees baseball cap off and wiped his brow.

"Yeah, we're making money. This job is never-ending. The more she changes the plans, the more days it adds, and the more it's gonna cost her. We finally pulled up everything in the living room, bedroom, and the bathroom, but now she's not sure about flooring and the walls. So we wait until she makes up her mind. We're redoing the wiring now until she tells us how she wants to proceed."

"Tear it up as much as she wants. This gig could keep your pockets lined for a long, long time."

"Why do you say that?" asked Merc.

"She's obsessive-compulsive."

"No shit. That's a fucking understatement."

"No," Penn said, putting his hand on his friend's shoulder. "She's obsessive-compulsive for real. It's clinical. She takes medication for it."

"Well, the shit ain't working," Merc said.

"It is for you."

————

"I'm going to have to call off the job for a little while," Beryl said.

They were in bed watching *Dateline*. She had a manuscript in her lap. Penn was munching a slice of pizza.

"Call off what job?" he asked, halfway listening.

"The rehab at my apartment."

He looked at her.

"Call it off why?"

"Because . . ." she said coyly. "I'm running out of money. My funds have dropped kind of low."

"That's because you keep changing the plans," he said.

"I know, I know," she whined, leaning into his shoulder. "I couldn't make up my mind. I didn't expect the architect to charge me so much. I didn't think it'd be so complicated. Every time I ask him to adjust one tiny thing in the blueprints, he charges me. And the interior decorator. She doesn't come cheap, and she hasn't even really done anything yet."

"Interior decorators are expensive, Beryl."

"I know, I know. Don't talk to me like that."

"Like what?"

"Like I'm a child."

"I'm just saying, I figured you had this thought out."

"I did," she said, her voice barely a whisper.

Penn chomped on his pizza. This was fucked up. After he'd told Mercury everything would be cool.

"So now what? Your place is all torn up. They haven't rebuilt it because they don't know what you want."

"I'm still going to do it," she said. "I just figured I'd pay some of the loan down first and then try to get it increased. I've got a really good relationship with my bank. And maybe I can do some of it through my credit cards. I can get cash off them. I've got it all worked out. I can make it balance."

He stared at her.

"How long are you talking about calling it off for?"

"Just a couple of months. Maybe three. Not long."

What the fuck? he thought. Three months?

"So what about your place? You're just going to let it stay ripped up like that? Where are you going to stay?"

She gave him a quizzical look.

"You're joking, right?" Beryl said.

Penn blinked, rapid-fire. Great. She probably had this shit planned.

"I can stay here, can't I?" she asked. "We're always together."

What choice did he have? He needed her. For now, anyway. Damn. It was one thing for her to be over because her place was being worked on. It was another for her to be officially living with him.

"So what, are you going to move your stuff here? Is this where you're going to take your calls?"

"No, babe," she said, smiling now, leaning into his arm. "I'll still go home every day to get clothes and stuff. I need to at least act like I still live there. I definitely can't take my calls here. People at work can't know that I'm here, remember?"

"Right. Well, I guess you'll just stay here then until we can get your place together."

He said "we" on purpose. He knew it would score him some points in the wake of his seeming hesitant about her moving in for three months.

Beryl flung herself upon him, kissing his cheeks, his nose, his mouth.

"Thank you, babe! Thank you, thank you, thank you!"

"Cut it out," he laughed. "You're such a silly."

"I'm not a silly," she giggled. "I'm a happy! A happy! Aren't you happy!"

"I'm thrilled." He kissed her. Enough already.

"This is going to be so good," she said, settling back into the pillow, tucking herself under his arm. "It'll be like we're married, sorta. Like a test run, you know?"

Married, he thought. Oh hell, no.

"Look at that car," he said, pointing to the TV. "That's a Maybach, isn't it?"

"I guess," she said. There was no car on the screen when she turned to look.

Penn bit into his pizza, his mind on fire. He would be playing house with her for the next three months.

"Oh, oh," she exclaimed, "I almost forgot! Guess who wants you to give him a blurb?"

"Who?" he asked, still reeling from the thought of round-the-clock Beryl.

"Adam Carville! He loves all the hype that's been built around *Book,* and even though he doesn't know what it's about, he'd love to have your endorsement for his next book. He says he went to school with you. That would be so good, you giving a quote to a National Book Award nominee."

Penn's teeth were immobile, still planted in the pizza.

"Everyone's so excited about it. Kitty was really hyped when I told her."

"No way," Penn said, freeing his teeth from the cheese.

"Way!" She was pure giddiness, delighted to be delivering good news. "He wants you to give him a quote. Isn't that cool!"

"No," he said. "No way would I give a quote to that guy."

Beryl's face froze.

"What? I don't understand. Why wouldn't you? Adam Carville is, like, so hot right now."

"Because he's a talentless fuck, that's why."

His face was stern.

Beryl searched his eyes, unsure of herself.

"Are you joking?"

"No, I'm not. I don't want my name anywhere near that bastard's books."

Beryl cast her eyes down at the manuscript in her lap, utterly confused.

"I don't . . . uh . . . I'm not sure . . . I mean, what should I do? I already called him and told him to send over a galley so I could get it to you. He was so excited. I was so excited. I called Spanky. She was excited, too."

"You should have checked with me first."

He threw back the covers and got out of bed.

He could feel her watching his naked splendor as he walked away. He took his time, strolling slowly to the bathroom in silence, allowing her to drink in his magnificence, realize that she was lucky to be in the presence of it, and adjust the error of her impetuous ways.

He took a long, long piss, compliments of three Heinekens. When he returned to bed, she was filled with apology.

"I'm sorry, babe. I didn't know."

"You should have checked with me first."

"I . . . I didn't know it would be a problem."

"So tell him I said no blurb."

"No! I can't do that! I'll just lie and say we've gotten so many requests that I'm not sure you'll have time to do much reading. I'll tell him you're under a crunch with things winding down to your pub date. Something. I don't know."

"Don't lie," Penn said, looking at her. "Tell him the truth. Tell him I don't want to give him a fucking quote. Tell him I hate his work. Tell him I think he's a first-class hack."

The bed was shaking. He knew without looking that it was because of her right knee. That damn nervous knee.

"I can't tell him that, Penn," she said, her voice low. "I would never say something like that to another author. I'll just leave it alone. I won't follow up on it."

"No," he insisted. "I want him to know."

"But I don't want you to get a bad reputation or anything. I would hate for people to think you're this arrogant writer, because you're not. What if there's some kind of backlash against you?"

"I'm not worried about it," he said.

"But I am—"

"Then have Shecky do it if you're afraid." He was firm. Blunt. "I just thought you had my back on things."

He watched her squirming now, unsure of herself. She liked being the one to save the day for him, to show him that she was always willing to do his bidding.

"Okay," she said after a long moment. "Okay. I'll call him tomorrow and tell him what you said."

"That he's a hack?"

"Yeah. That he's a hack."

Penn smiled. He believed her. She was the little engine that could. He knew she would do it. Good girl. Good girl.

"C'mere," he said, pulling her close. He kissed her hair, then mussed it with his hand. "Do you know how much I love you?"

"Really?" she asked, doe-eyed again.

"Really. You're always there for me, no matter what. You're my little angel. My Beryl angel. My babe. My baby. My angel-baby-Beryl-babe."

She giggled, wrapping her arms around his waist.

"I love you, Penn. I'll do anything for you."

He pressed his face into her hair, burrowing deep into the roots. He belched.

"Ew!" she squealed, pulling away. He pulled her back.

"You said you wanted this to be like a test run for marriage. Well, this is it. Belches and all."

He tickled her. She kicked up her knees, the manuscript pages falling everywhere.

He was going to have to distract himself with silliness like this. How else would he get through the next three months of living with her?

"So how long of a delay is it?" Merc asked.

"Just two or three months. She's getting more money together. She'll do it."

"So why don't you front her some loot," Merc joked. "She's been dishing out cash to you left and right."

Penn laughed.

"Nigga, please. That's what a chick like her is for."

"I've got a surprise for you," Beryl said, peeking inside the door of her office.

Penn had been in there alone, flipping through the galleys of upcoming books.

"What's up?" he said.

She flung the door open.

Jessye Norman.

Penn sprang from his chair.

"Shit!"

The great diva stepped back.

"Beg pardon?"

"I'm sorry," he stammered, the ocean roaring in his ears. "I . . . I . . ."

"He's a big fan, Ms. Norman," said Beryl. "I think he's got every recording you've ever done. The DVD of you at the Met in *Die Walküre* is always on at his apartment. He blasts it. The neighbors go crazy, banging on the floors . . ."

The great diva looked at Penn with alarm.

"That's not good."

Penn wanted to pimp-smack Beryl, smash her clean through the floor, but he was too out of his head to make rational moves.

"I adored your mother," Ms. Norman said. "She was an incredible singer and a dear, dear friend. I'm sure she would be very proud of your accomplishments."

Penn couldn't get words out of his mouth.

The great lady stepped forward and clasped his hands. She kissed him on both cheeks.

"Such a beautiful child you were. You've grown into a beautiful man."

She was a vision. All he could do was stare.

"Turn the volume down on that DVD," she said. "We wouldn't want the neighbors to hate my voice now, would we?"

"You couldn't say anything?" Shar asked.

"Not a word. Except for 'shit.' I can't believe I finally meet Jessye Norman and all I can say is 'shit.' "

He pressed his face into a pillow and groaned.

"Get over it, baby," she said. "People like her get that all the time. Just be happy you didn't faint."

He groaned again. She pulled the pillow off his face.

"So why don't you meet me in L.A.?"

"I can't," Penn said. "Fiyah and I are on *TRL* in two days."

"Aw, baby."

"I signed a contract with Worldwide WifeBeater. We're going to do a whole CD. Fiyah's going to try to get it out by the time the book drops, so we can capitalize on the momentum on the song. MTV's talking about building a reality show around me. One of those follow-my-life-for-a-few-months kind of things. Fiyah might produce it."

"Yay, Fiyah" Sharlyn said.

She draped her legs over him as they languished in bed. She reached over for the warm glass of Dom on the nightstand and finished it off.

"So since you're gonna be on *TRL* in two days, that means I won't see you for at least three weeks," she said.

"How will I live?" Penn said, smiling, cozying his nose into her neck. He stroked her breast. Sharlyn moaned.

"Why . . . are you fucking with me?"

"Because I can," he said. He rolled on top of her.

"What are you doing?" she said with a mischievous grin.

"The hokey-pokey."

"But we just did the hokey-pokey."

She had her arms around him, moving her hips against his. He was hard again, for the third time. He never tired of her. They had started living dangerously. He wasn't even using condoms anymore. Penn had been tested. Shar was on the pill. She'd never wanted babies. Not in all her years of marriage. But now, with this man, this beautiful, beautiful man . . . the possibilities . . . something inside of her was changing.

"Open your legs," he whispered.

"They're open."

"Wider."

She did.

He put the tip in, just at the entrance, and hovered around there, exciting the nerves. He faked a few in-and-out moves, watching her arch her back toward him, believing he was about to go all the way in.

"Do it," she groaned. "Don't play with me, baby."

He stayed at the shallow end, refusing to get wet.

Shar moaned and writhed underneath him, her hands pawing at his back, taking care not to scratch.

"Penn, do it!"

"Say please."

"Please, Penn. Do it. I'm going to explode."

He plunged all the way in, up to the balls, and banged her hard, fast, and vicious, the way they both liked it best.

He bit down on her shoulder.

"No . . . no marks."

"Fuck that," he said, and bit deep, then softened the bite, sucking at her flesh. He knew she could cover the mark. It wasn't like Miles was fucking her and would get close enough to see it.

"Do it, do it, do it, baby!"

He did it, did it, did it, running his tongue over and around her nipples, pulling on them, sucking her in. In and out, in and out, he stormed her like a trooper as he held her gaze.

Her breathing rose higher and higher until it was almost a full-out pant. He could feel her coming and wanted to come with her, leave her with a reminder of their synergy before she headed out on tour.

"Penn!" she cried.

"C'mon, baby. Give it up."

They popped. It was one of those movie pops, except better choreographed and real. Her whole body was flushed and tingling. He lingered inside her, savoring the wave of contractions, letting their togetherness enjoy the rhythm of the moment.

"I'm on *The Today Show* tomorrow morning," she said.

Penn chuckled.

"How did *The Today Show* suddenly get in the room?"

He pulled up and halfway out. She stopped him.

"Could you stay there for a while? Just a little bit?"

He slipped back in.

"Am I squashing you?"

"Squash me all you want, baby," she said.

They lay there for another quiet moment.

"So what are you going to do while I'm gone?" she asked.

His face was pressed into her shoulder. He loved the way she smelled. She wasn't wearing No. 5 this time. There was just a light sesame scent that was sweet and hypnotic.

"I'm making the rounds, promoting the song. Oh yeah, and playing tennis with your husband again."

He felt Sharlyn shift.

"He called you?"

"Of course."

"Do you think he suspects something?" she asked.

"I hate to say this, baby, but no. He's all into these games of doubles we play. He loves the fact that we win so much. He's so damn competitive. I can see why he's on top."

"He's not on top now," she said.

Penn lifted his head and looked at her.

"You're such a bad girl."

She kissed him.

"I'd rather be bad than lonely."

"You'll never be lonely, baby. Not as long as I'm around."

An hour and a restful nap later, they were at it again.

Penn was rimming Shar.

He'd never done that for anyone before. He was always the rimmee (the rimmed?), but he enjoyed the way she gave herself over to absolute pleasure. He wanted to explore every part of her, leave no skin untouched by his tongue. It was a logical natural segue for him to go there.

"*Ohhhhhhhhhhhhhhh, baby!*" she screamed. "*Oh . . . my . . . g . . . ooooooooooooh!*"

He flicked his tongue briskly at first, then slowed to long, generous lapping.

Sharlyn flapped and lurched and buckled until he could feel her almost becoming spent. He quickly slid above her and plunged himself in. She burst the moment he entered. She screamed, clinging to him tightly, afraid to let go.

"God, I love you," she finally whispered.

He looked into her eyes and the feeling mirrored his own. Dreamy, fulfilled.

"I love you, too," he said.

And he meant it.

A few hours later, he was at a nearby Starbucks, getting a Defibrillator before he returned home to a waiting Beryl.

"Penn Hamilton."

Penn had just stepped up to the counter. He turned around.

He laughed.

"Adam Carville."

Adam extended his hand. Penn glanced down at it. Adam let it hang alone in midair, then shoved it into his jeans pocket.

"So I'm a hack, am I?"

"With a hatchet," Penn said, turning back to the counter. He was about to open his mouth when the cashier said, "One Defib, right?"

"Right." Penn flashed his special Starbucks card. The cashier nodded and called out his order.

"I guess membership has its privileges," Adam smirked, peering at the card. "How can I get one of those? Pose naked for a billboard in Times Square?"

Penn smiled.

"I doubt anybody'd pay to see that," he said, stepping aside to wait for his coffee.

A pretty woman in her late thirties holding the hand of a young boy followed closely behind him. One of his many soccer mom fans.

"One Defib," Adam said to the cashier as he stepped to the counter. He turned to Penn. "Believe it or not, I actually drink them. They're great for all-nighters when I need to write."

"You mean you actually stay up nights creating that stuff? I figured you could fire off shit like that in a matter of minutes."

"Hey, hey, buddy," Adam said, making a time-out sign with his hands. "What's the deal? I have no beef with you. We're colleagues. We're in the same business. We had classes together."

"We were never colleagues," Penn said.

The soccer mom with the little boy moved in closer.

"Mr. Hamilton," she said nervously, "I'm such a fan. Both me and my son Angus. We love your song with On Fiyah."

"Get the Book!" the little boy chirped.

"Thank you," Penn said with a broad smile, clasping her hand. He glanced sidelong at Adam. "Thank you so much."

"I've already pre-ordered your book," the woman said with fuck-me eyes, despite the ring on her finger. "So have all my friends. We just know it's going to be a big hit."

"Thank you. I hope so. I have a website. Double-u, double-u, double-u, dot-Penn-Hamilton-dot-com. I'd love to hear from you once you read the book. E-mail me. Be sure to mention where we met. I never forget a face."

Penn kissed the back of her hand before he released it. He mussed the little boy's hair. The woman flushed red with unbelievable lust and glee. Little Angus jumped up and down. Adam Carville rolled his eyes.

"Penn! Defib!" the barista yelled.

Adam followed Penn as he went to get his coffee. He was in Penn's face when he turned around.

"So how about a truce?" Adam said, holding out his hand again.

Penn stared at the hand, then looked up at him.

"No truce necessary. You're not in my league."

"Ha!" Adam scoffed. "I'm the one with the National Book Award nomination, buddy, and a score of other awards to back it up. Talk to me when you've accomplished *that*. One naked billboard and hanging out with On Fiyah does not an author make. Anybody can show their nuts to the world. Show me some soul, and then we can talk."

"Hey, you jerk!" the soccer mom snapped, rushing over with her boy. "Don't you yell at Penn. Who the hell do you think you are!"

"You jerk!" Little Angus gave Carville a quick kick in the shin.

"Ow!" Adam hopped on one leg as sharp pain shot up through his knee.

"Defib! Adam!" barked the barista.

Adam reached past Penn for his coffee, his eyes glaring, his lips pressed tight. He took the hot drink and limped off, muttering to himself.

"We'll see who the real hack is," he said. He turned when he reached the door, his anger boiling over.

"You're an arrogant fuck, Penn. You were arrogant in college. I figured you would have grown out of that. It's a fucking shame that nothing's changed."

Penn was in the shower the next morning as Beryl lay in bed waiting for Sharlyn's appearance on *The Today Show.* She was scribbling notes in the margin of the Gesamtkunstwerk dissertation, which had become her bible. She consulted it to strategize everything. Katie Couric appeared onscreen, making a brief introduction of the new book. Beryl sat up. The camera cut to a wider shot of both women. Shar's legs were as sexy as Katie's.

"Penn! Shar's on!"

He didn't respond. She figured he couldn't hear her over the shower.

Shar looked good. Not too trashy, but attractive, smart, and erotic, just like her book. She was such a professional. She really knew how to work her public image.

"The book is number one on Amazon and the *New York Times* list," Katie said, adjusting her glasses to better see a piece of paper she was holding. *"Publishers Weekly,* in a starred review, says, quote: 'Best-selling veteran Sharlyn Tate's newest novel really turns up the heat. The self-appointed Queen of Pop Fiction puts the "ooh" in la-la with an erotic plot filled with unpredictable twists and turns that are sure to leave readers exhausted and fully satisfied at the end.' " Katie peered over her glasses at Sharlyn. " 'Exhausted and fully satisfied.' Yowzah! That's some endorsement."

This is great, Beryl thought. Katie's happy banter was really show-casing the book.

"We were all pretty excited when we saw the review," Sharlyn said. "I'm really pleased to see that readers trust me enough as an evolving writer to follow me in this particular direction."

"C'mon." Katie grinned. "It's almost Memorial Day. This is a steamy summer read if there ever was one. You went right for the jugular. We can't even do an excerpt."

"It's not that steamy," Sharlyn said with a coy smile.

"My glasses are fogging up just reading the reviews!"

The Today Show crew could be heard laughing off camera.

"Well, if you think my book is hot," said Shar, "wait until you see the one coming from Penn Hamilton."

"What the—" Beryl leaned forward. "What is she doing?"

Katie looked a little awkward, her eyes darting, blindsided by the unexpected plug.

"He's the Calvin Klein guy, right?" she said, obviously seeking a way out. "The one with the mysterious book that everyone's talking about?"

"Yes, and it's going to be one of the best, hottest books to come out in years."

"Right. Have you read it? Do you know what it's about?"

"That's a secret," Shar said with a smile.

"Well, we'll look forward to that," Katie said, extricating herself. "In the meantime, you're hitting the road on a major tour."

"Yes," Shar said. "Forty-five cities."

"Yikes," said Katie. "That's some tour. We should add that you'll be at the Borders Books in Columbus Circle at noon today and the Barnes and Noble at Astor Place this afternoon at five o'clock."

"Yes," Sharlyn said. "People can come by, say hello, and pick up the perfect read for the upcoming holiday weekend."

"Sounds like it's going to be a long, hot summer," said Katie, fanning herself. "Again, the new book is *The Magic Man,* in stores today. Sharlyn Tate, thanks for joining us this morning."

"Thanks for having me, Katie. Remember Penn Hamilton."

"Right. Up next, dog weddings and honeymoons, the newest craze in canine mental health." Katie laughed. "I can't wait to see that. But first, this is *Today* . . . on NBC."

Beryl stared at the screen. What was the matter with Shar, plugging Penn so foolishly? His book was four months off. The *Today Show* people might not even want to have him on after an outrageous stunt like that.

It just didn't make sense. Shar was acting like a silly schoolgirl.

Beryl sat back against the pillows, her mind churning. She was suddenly overcome by a strong sense of fear, followed by the ghost of suspicion. She wasn't sure what she suspected, but Shar's behavior had been egregious and unprofessional, completely out of character.

She decided not to say anything to her. All she would do for the time being was watch. Maybe there was something to see. Maybe there wasn't.

Maybe it was just an aging author's crush.

Sharlyn did the same thing on *Live with Regis and Kelly, Larry King Live, Charlie Rose,* and at both her signings in the city that day. The next day, Kitty Ellerman sent Beryl an e-mail with "Sharlyn" as the subject line.

ARE THESE COMMENTS PLANNED? IS THIS SOMETHING YOU'VE ASKED HER TO DO AS ADVANCE PROMOTION FOR P. HAMILTON'S UPCOMING BOOK? WE SHOULD CONSIDER ASKING HER TO TONE IT DOWN, PREFERABLY DROP IT ALTOGETHER. IT'S VERY AGGRESSIVE.

Beryl's fears took further root.

Something was definitely up.

"I think she's becoming obsessed with Penn," she said aloud, the sound of the words resonating back at her like a dare. Her heart was racing. What if Sharlyn got it in her head to take Penn away? She was beautiful, sexy, famous. She had way more money than Beryl could imagine.

But she was married! She had a husband!

Beryl sat at her desk, the fingers of her right hand tapping with anxious rage.

Sharlyn Tate would *not* take her man.

She would do everything in her power to make sure of that.

Throughout all

. . . the affairs and intrigue going on between Penn and Beryl and Shar and Brookie and Miles as the months went by, Page Six had been quiet, oblivious to everything, missing the hotbed of action right under its omnipotent nose. Its spies had their hands more than full with all the half-baked heiresses, starlets, songstresses, rockers, rappers, talk-show hosts, rehab rescues, and reality-show rubbish clinging to the last nanoseconds of their fifteen minutes.

Add to that the mismatched, ill-fated unions between haphazard A-listers, addled Oscar winners, Tony toters, Emmy wielders, and attention-hungry billionaires, and there were scarcely enough spies to cover it all, the loads of breaking news in their knapsacks too heavy to even drag.

The giant was sleeping.

But soon it would feast.

Nihilism:

A literary and philosophical movement emphasizing a belief that human life, religion, laws, governments, and moral codes are meaningless.

A man without ethics is a wild beast
loosed upon this world.

—Albert Camus

One week

. . . before the official release date, news came that *Book* would come in at the top of the *New York Times* bestseller list. Penn's new CD, *Wonder Boy*, had just debuted at number one on the *Billboard* charts.

Five studios were at war over the film rights. One of them wanted Penn to star.

Beryl had gotten her loan increased to finish the rehab at her apartment. Merc and his boys were back on the job. Soon she would be able to go back to her own place.

Penn spent that night, the week before he was scheduled to hit the road, partying with Mercury, On Fiyah, Pharrell, Snoop, and a gaggle of supermodels at Bungalow 8. Everyone drank lots of Crissy and popped much shit.

"So how they gonna ask you to star in a movie if they don't even know what it's about?" Fiyah asked. "That shit is crazy. It's brilliant. You jacked the shit outta Hollywood. Let's give this nigga a toast. That's some genius shit right there! I wish I woulda thought of it."

Everyone raised their glasses.

"To Penn!"

One of the models, a bit too happy, teetered and slipped off the banquette, hitting the floor, knocking down a bottle of Cris on the way.

"Hey, hey now," one of the guys shouted. "That shit ain't water."

"Relax, they got more," Pharrell said. He held up four fingers. A waiter rushed over with four more bottles.

The guest deejay that night was Cameron Douglas. He played hit after hit after hit from Penn's new joint until, after a while, it turned into a big ol' Penn party.

He was floating now. This was it. He had money, fame, incredible pussy, and more of each on the way.

Beryl was back at his place, strategizing last-minute details of his tour and things he should say during interviews. He had no problem leaving her there alone for long stretches. She was living there, after all. Besides, she'd already snooped and found the thing that mattered. There wasn't much else for her to see. His most important computer files required passwords to open. His journal was behind a loose brick in the wall of his bedroom. She would never see that.

Sharlyn was at the Sherry-Netherland, waiting, just in case he could come by. She didn't feel like partying out that night. She wanted to party in. With him.

"Please, baby," she'd said, "try to come over. Miles got on my last nerve. I need you tonight."

He didn't know if he'd make it over there. He was having the night of his life.

He was famous. In his element with the beautiful people.

He'd been an outcast in some ways his whole life. Always different from everyone else. But now things had changed. These people, these rich, famous people, they were embracing him as one of their own.

He finally belonged.

It was five-thirty A.M.

She'd been up since three, when the phone began ringing again and again. The caller was relentless, refusing to accept that no one was going to answer.

After the second time, she was wide awake, curious. It wasn't Penn calling. They had a signal for that. One ring. One ring. Two rings. Three.

Whoever was calling now let it ring until the answering machine picked up.

Beryl had gone into the living room where the machine was. Penn always kept the volume turned down. When the third call came, she turned up the sound.

"Penn, baby, where are you? I know it's late and I never call, but I need you. I need to feel you inside me so bad. I'm so wound up. Miles is off in Brazil for six weeks, and Brookie's gone back to Atlanta for a few days. I've got all this shit going on, and she just takes off. I am so pissed. You know, the only way to get this feeling out of me is to fuck it out. Call me, baby, all right? Or better yet, just get over here the second you hear this. I'm at our place, but you know that, right. Shit. It makes no sense you don't have a cell phone. It's mandatory at your level. You have to stay connected. I know, I know, you hate phones. Still . . ."

Beryl clutched her throat. She thought she was going to gag. She was coughing, hacking, running her hands up and down the front of her neck. She was still coughing when the next call came in, just moments later.

"You know what I just realized? I'm leaving all these messages on your machine. I probably shouldn't be doing that. I'm a little tipsy. I've had nearly a whole bottle of Dom. Come over, baby, okay? We could get a few hours in still. I'm having a late lunch with Beryl to go over the paperback cover. Whatever. I might cancel. She can be such a pain in the neck. Especially the way she acted about me plugging you this summer. Hahaha," she rambled, "I think I got that backward. You're the one who's plugging me. So get over here and do it already. I'm wearing something new. Something tiny. Something wicked. Just call me, okay?"

Beryl began to convulse, her breath coming fast. She sat on the edge of the couch. The phone rang several more times. More messages were left.

In a compulsive fit, Beryl deleted all of them, one by one. No more came in.

As of six-thirty A.M., Penn still hadn't returned.

Beryl had been crying for hours, examining and reexamining everything she'd done, everything she'd thrown away. Her career. Her ethics. Her relationship with Dr. Ripkin, a man who had been steadfast to her for half her life. A man who had taken her on for free when she had nothing. She just walked out on him, spurned him, pushed him away.

And all the time he had been right.

Her right knee shook. Her whole body shook. She'd been pulling at her hair, going through wads of tissue. Her eyes had bowling bags beneath them.

Penn was everything those girls on those catty websites said he was, and worse. She'd fallen for him despite all those warnings. Despite everything, she'd been completely taken in.

"I'm a fool," she said. "I'm such a damn fool!"

She had been planning marriage! Oh God! Vera Wang was making her dress! Vera Wang! Vera-fucking-Wang!

She'd talked about having his babies and he had let her! He'd gone along with it, like he wanted babies, too!

She cried and cried and cried some more. Something inside of her—an entire foundation built upon fantasy and hope—collapsed, caved in, and sucked her soul away.

She managed to stop her hand-wringing long enough to write him a note.

> *I left a little early to get some things done. Meet me at my apartment around eleven so we can go over the key points for the interview with Entertainment Weekly.*

She wrote the note several times, tearing up each until her hand was steady. She didn't want to give off anything to indicate her broken state of mind.

She'd deal with that when she saw him again.

God. How would she be able to see him again?

Shar was snoring, full of Dom, sleeping so hard, even dreams didn't invade. She forgot her late-night barrage of phone calls to Penn—calls that had been made under a coke-assisted high. She slept well into the next afternoon, way past her meeting with Beryl.

———

Beryl was so stressed from the revelation about Sharlyn and Penn, all she could do was pace once she was back at her apartment. She'd been pacing for hours, too shaky and distracted to even remember to take her pills.

It was raining outside. The contractors had taken the day off. Her living room, bathroom, and bedroom were a mess of stacked tiles, rubble, loose flooring, scattered nails, plaster dust, and exposed wiring. This was probably why she wasn't at peace with what direction to take with the rehab of her apartment. Her spirit had known better, had known it was all a farce. Everything about it had been wrong all along.

Penn wasn't in love with her. He'd been sleeping with both her and Sharlyn.

But Sharlyn was married. Why would she even risk doing something like this? All this time, Beryl thought they were friends. Sharlyn was just another star-whore with no morals, values, or concern for anyone other than herself.

She kept brushing her hand across her forehead, pushing away imaginary strands of hair that were irritating her skin. She was disheveled. Her face was a train wreck.

She had done everything for him. Put her career on the line by prearranging his deal, going to those corporations and bringing everything together, editing his work and coddling him as an artist way beyond what the job required.

She'd spent a great deal of her own moncy on him. His whole wardrobe, down to the finest shoes. She'd paid for that. Even though he had his own money, she'd been spending hers, because she believed they were going to be together. He was going to be her husband. But he wasn't. He was lying. He'd been lying. He was a liar. Why did he feel the need to be with another woman? Was it simply because she couldn't give him enough sex? Why Sharlyn? Why?

"I explained to him why my sex drive was low," Beryl said to the air. "It was the medicine. What was I supposed to do?"

More crying and hand-wringing. More why, why, whys.

She meandered from corner to corner in the living room, trying to accept the obvious.

She'd been used. She should face that truth and just deal with it.

She wandered through the rubble and loose materials, making her way down the hallway on the still-intact parquet floors, into her bed-room. More rubble and materials. All the expensive bedding had been put into the closets. The Rubens painting (rather, knockoff) was in storage. She glanced around at the wreckage in her room, a perfect mirror of the wreckage in her heart.

She glanced at the small table of African violets and the ones on the sill.

Some of them were naked from neglect, their petals on the floor.

Beryl was standing in the living room when he opened the door and walked in.

"Hey."

"Hey," she said, jumping back. "The doorman didn't call up."

"He wasn't there. I came in behind somebody."

She looked awful, Penn thought. Her hair was a mess and her eyes were all red. She'd probably spent the whole night working on things for him.

"Sorry I didn't get in before you left. Me and Fiyah were at Bun-galow Eight, and next thing you know, it was this big-ass party for me. I got on the mic and everything."

She turned away from him and began to pace.

"You eat yet?" he asked. He was starving. "I know it's not lunchtime, but it's close enough. I could go for one of those giant pas-trami sandwiches at Carnegie Deli."

Beryl didn't answer.

"Hey," he said. "What's up? Where are you?"

She was facing the wall now, not speaking at all.

She's mad I didn't come home, he thought. Great. He couldn't even enjoy one fucking party. It wasn't like he did that a lot.

He walked over to her and touched her on the arm. She spun away from him, screaming.

"You're fucking Sharlyn!"

"What?"

His heart sped up.

"Don't 'what' me, Penn! You're fucking her! You've been fucking her all along!"

He stepped toward her, reaching out to grab her hand. She backed away.

"I don't know what you're talking about. I thought we were past these kinds of jealous tirades from you. Sharlyn's been a mentor, like Fiyah. Fuck, forget that, she's happily married, so why would you even say something as ridiculous as that?"

She was hyperventilating now, her eyes bursting with red vessels and tears. He could see the bags beneath them clearly. She'd been crying for a long time. She hadn't found the loose brick in the wall, had she? That was impossible. That brick was imperceptible to even the sharpest eye. This was panic. She was just having a separation freak-out.

"Is this because I'm leaving next week on tour?" he asked. "Do you think I'm going to neglect you when I'm on the road? That's not gonna happen, babe. That could never happen with us."

Her whole face was turning red. She was still backing away.

"You lying bastard. You fucking dog. You think I'm stupid. Maybe I am. But you're not going to get away with this. I'll ruin all of us before I let you get away with it."

Her breathing grew heavier. Penn's palms began to sweat. Not now. He didn't need this to happen right now. He was right on the cusp of greatness, and she was pulling this shit.

"I'll go to my boss and tell her what happened," she said, her breast heaving, "and I've gotten to know Miles pretty well. Wait until he finds out what the two of you've been doing. That fucking bitch!" The heaving had turned into gasps. "Pretending to be my friend all these years. Just wait! I'm going to tell Miles ev—"

She collapsed, her head bouncing off a piece of rubble on the floor.

"Oh shit!" Penn said, racing over to her.

He knelt beside her, turning her head to the side. Her temple was bleeding from where it had landed on the rubble. There was a nasty gash along the side.

Beryl moaned.

This was so fucked! She was fucking up everything. She was going to ruin his whole career before it had a chance to see daylight, and now she had this fucking gash on her head. He'd have to take her to the hospital and it would certainly make the gossip news. Beryl would squeal to everyone, even though he didn't know how she knew what she knew. She'd make him out to be some kind of a monster.

Beryl moaned again, her eyes closed.

This couldn't happen.

Penn picked up the piece of rubble she'd fallen on. He raised it in the air and, without a moment's hesitation, he bashed her skull in.

She's not

. . . breathing."

"Of course she isn't."

"Did you check her pulse?"

"Yes. Hours ago."

Mercury squatted beside Beryl's body. A small pool of blood had gathered beneath her head. A jagged piece of concrete was under the cracked part of her skull. The concrete was stained with clumps of brain. A little more brain had oozed onto the floor.

Mercury looked up at Penn.

"So she fell on this piece of concrete and it fucked her head up like this?"

Penn's eyes met his.

"Yeah."

Mercury turned his attention back to Beryl's mangled cranium.

"Damn. She must have fallen really hard. Her head cracked open like a walnut. You gotta fall with some serious velocity to get an injury like this."

He looked up at Penn again. They held each other's gaze, long enough to acknowledge the unspoken contract being effected between them.

"So we handle it," Mercury said. "That's all there is to it."

He stood and walked over to the front door. He peered through the peephole, turned the knob, stuck his head out into the hallway, looked both directions, then came back in.

"Did she scream?"

"No, but she was yelling."

"Yelling about what?"

"Crazy stuff. A magazine interview, the tour."

"You think anybody heard her?"

"I don't know. I don't think so. A lot of people aren't home that time of day."

"What time did it happen?"

"Around eleven, eleven-thirty."

Merc walked around Beryl's body, checking it from every angle. "Damn."

He went over to the window facing Central Park. He watched a rush of taxis whiz by. The night glimmered with flickering lights.

"Why'd you take all day to call me?"

"I was kinda freaked out. I've been sitting here for hours, since this morning. I can't believe this shit. I just can't believe it."

"This is a prewar building," Merc said, turning around. "There's thick firewall in here, not that cheap stuff." He stood in the middle of the living room, his hands on his hips.

This was Mercury King the professional talking now. The problem-solving project leader.

"It's probably cool. If someone had heard something they would have knocked on the door or called the cops right off. So you didn't call 911?"

"No, Merc," Penn said with irritation. "I called you. What the fuck."

"Look, man, don't 'what the fuck' me. I'm just doing due diligence."

"I know. This is just . . . it's crazy."

"You need to relax," said Mercury.

He was standing in front of Penn now.

"This ain't nothing new. Shit like this goes down every day. You might not have seen it before because you had a privileged life growing up, but I didn't. I've seen some shit."

Mercury was an intense man of medium height with a burst of fuzz that coated his dome and the space of flesh just above his top lip. Dark brown eyes hovered above a thick nose and a horizontal slice that passed for his mouth. His neck was almost as wide as a thigh, and massive hairy guns and forearms burst out of the sleeves of his beige T-shirt like he was some kind of brooding brown Hulk. His calves were hairy stones jutting from the openings of his long saggy khaki cargo shorts, stumping down into a pair of broad feet that terrorized the weathered Tims he was wearing. This was an intelligent man with a postgraduate degree in an elite profession, but on the street, at first blush, he seemed a natural bone-crusher.

"When I was five, my pops killed my uncle Pito, his brother, right in front of me. You wanna know why?"

Penn waited for him to say.

"Because Uncle Pito told a joke that made my moms laugh too hard. Harder than she ever laughed at anything Pops ever said." Mercury's eyes had a far-off look. "So he shot Uncle Pito right in the face. Blood spattered all over me. I'll never forget that shit for as long as I live."

"Damn, dude."

"That was the first death I ever saw. That's the kind of shit that went down in my neighborhood. What you gonna do? You can freak the fuck out and get killed your damn self or go to jail and get killed in there, or you can be cool and do what you gotta do. I learned a long time ago how to do what I gotta do."

Their eyes met.

"You got that?" Merc said.

"Yeah."

"I need you to be cool."

"First we gotta get this blood up."

It was ten minutes later. Mercury had gone from room to room, negotiating the logistics of what would come next.

"We've got a distinct advantage here," he said.

"What's that?"

"The construction. We've been tearing stuff up and rebuilding in here for months. The doorman's seen our work crew come and go. There's rubble all over the place. All we gotta do is take care of the body, and then we can have the crew carry off anything in here that might have blood, DNA, whatever on it. We'll take it down to the landfill we use in Jersey. And that'll be that with that."

"Has your crew done something like this before?"

"We're from Washington Heights. We've done a lot of stuff."

Merc paced, rubbing his chin.

"You called my cell from here. You probably don't even realize what a good move that was."

"How so?"

"Because it's consistent. Beryl was always calling my cell, first thing in the morning, different times throughout the day. She often did it from here whenever she stopped by to check on the work and I happened to be out. She was always trying to track me down."

"So why is that good?"

"Phone records, man. The police will check everything."

"The police?"

"Yes. The fucking police. Don't even sweat that shit. Dealing with the police is just standard procedure. We can tell 'em she was crazy, practically stalking you, going way beyond the editor role, you know? That'll be credible. She was kinda nuts. She was damn near stalking me, and I was just her contractor."

Merc looked around the living room.

"Once we get her situated, the workers can carry off the debris, which will be business as usual with all the changes we've been doing around here. My guys are all clean, no priors or nothing, we always make sure of that." Merc turned to Penn. "But you and I are gonna handle the body. The hardest part will happen in the bathroom."

"In the bathroom?"

"Yeah."

"We're gonna have to take her to the tub and handle all the dirty business there. We'll clean up the tub when we finish, and the crew can haul it out tomorrow with the rest of the shit. It won't be a big deal. We've brought three new tubs in since we started rehabbing this place."

———

They were in the bathroom. Beryl's naked body was in the tub.

Mercury kneeled beside her and turned on the faucets. Penn stood by the bathroom door and watched him.

"I'll have the guys take up all the flooring tomorrow in all the rooms and put new material down over the next few days. We'll paint. Do everything. We have instructions to rebuild anyway."

"People will be looking for her," Penn said, "won't they?"

"Not necessarily. She could have taken a vacation. Maybe she wanted to be left alone for a week."

"A week?"

"Yeah. I figure that's about how long we've got. Maybe two. She got a lot of friends?"

"No. She doesn't have any. She has a lot of acquaintances in the entertainment and business worlds, but she's pretty much a loner."

"Was a loner," Mercury said, getting up.

Penn watched his best friend's muscular girth and heavy feet seem to glide without effort throughout the apartment. He wandered around in silence until he found the kitchen. He could hear Mercury opening cabinets and poking around.

He was still standing when Merc returned with a sky-blue bucket filled with two big tan sponges, a small green one, some 409, a bottle of Mr. Clean, something with a black handle, and something with a cord. He took the items out and put them on the bathroom counter. The cord was attached to an electric knife with a serrated edge. The black handle belonged to a large stainless-steel knife, one of those never-needs-sharpening infomercial wonders, the kind used to carve mammoth turkeys and thick cuts of prime rib. A rubber handle was sticking out of Mercury's right pants pocket. He reached for it and pulled out a silver-headed hammer and set it on the counter beside the rest. He opened the bottle of Mr. Clean, poured some into the bucket, put it in the deep sink at an angle, and turned on the faucet in the sink.

"I had an idea while I was in the kitchen." Merc held the bucket as it filled with water. "You know how I got into the building tonight?"

"The doorman let you in."

"No. That's what usually happens. He wasn't around when I came through, so I went in behind somebody."

"I did the same thing. The doormen here are kind of iffy. So what? They've got security cameras, so they can easily track who comes and goes."

"Yeah, but that's not a problem. It won't be odd if we show up on security tapes. You're one of her writers. I'm doing work on her place. But that's not what I'm getting at."

Merc turned off the faucet and lifted out the bucket.

"My bad," said Penn. "Go ahead."

"So what if some kids got in here and vandalized a bunch of shit on a few floors, started a fire or two. Fucked this apartment up and a couple more somewhere else in the building. Something that seems entirely random."

"I don't get where you're going," Penn said.

"If there's a fire, the guys won't have to repaint and put down new floors. Everything in here will be destroyed. Any traces of blood we might have missed, DNA evidence, fingerprints."

"Oh."

"We'll wait a few days, maybe three, four. There's a holiday coming up. We can take advantage of it."

Penn considered Merc's words. He closed the lid on the toilet and sat, in awe of such a brilliant suggestion.

"We could send an e-mail from her computer," he said.

"What kind of e-mail?" asked Merc.

"Something to her boss, her assistant, and her authors saying she had an emergency and needed to take some time off."

"When would we send it?"

"It's Tuesday. Tomorrow morning, I could send an e-mail from here to her assistant Shecky saying she's going to be in meetings outside the office. That won't come as a surprise to anybody. She does it all the time." Penn leaned his elbows on his knees. "I can do the same thing on Wednesday and Thursday. Everybody will take off early on Friday since it's Labor Day weekend. Beryl said they do half-days on

Friday in the summer, so I imagine most of them will be out of the office anyway, trying to take advantage of the last big weekend."

"So that gives us a good time to start the fire. I could get some kids I know in the Heights, some bad muthafuckas who do scandalous shit like this all the time. They can come in here over the weekend with fireworks, matches, gas, maybe graffiti up the floors a little. We'll make sure Beryl's place is one of the first ones they hit, so the fire damage'll be greater."

"I like this," Penn said. "But we don't want anybody else to get hurt. How can we manage that?"

"A lot of people will be away. Since the doorman tends to leave his post so often, the tenants won't find it far-fetched the way the vandals got in. I'll make sure the kids are careful. As careful as a buncha kids with fireworks, matches, and gas can get."

Merc set the bucket on the floor.

"The kids won't show up on the tapes," he said. "Not their faces. They'll have on the usual shit. Hoodies, clown masks, gloves, shit like that. The kinda stuff you'd expect from vandals."

"Perfect," Penn said, nodding. "So on Friday night I'll send the e-mail about the emergency and her needing to take some time off."

"No one will ever connect the fires here with her disappearance," Merc said. He smiled. "That's good, that's good. I see why your ass writes books."

"No shit. This would make a damn good story. Nobody would believe it, though."

"Niggas in the Heights would."

The ammonia-sweet scent of Mr. Clean wafted from the bucket. Mercury grabbed the three sponges from the counter and threw them in. He sat on the edge of the tub again, took a deep breath, wiped his brow, and turned off the faucets in the tub, now that Beryl's body was halfway submerged. His eyes were clear and direct as he spoke to Penn.

"All right, take that bucket and go scrub up that bit of blood and brains on the living room floor."

"Cool."

"I'll start on Beryl," Merc said. "I'm gonna cut the veins on her wrists the right way, vertical, all the way down, then I'll slice her jugular and open up both of those carotid arteries in her neck, and then I'm gonna need your help. We're gonna grab those bony ankles of hers and let her drain."

"Okay."

"We're gonna get as much of that blood out of her as we can. And then we're gonna chop her."

"We're gonna what?"

"We're gonna chop her," said Mercury, cool, even. "We'll cut her up into chunks, then saw and hammer through the bones. I'll do it in the tub, that way we can control any flying pieces of meat. Shouldn't be too hard to break her down, she's kinda slight. Then we're gonna bag up the chunks and throw 'em down the garbage chute. You'll get them out at the other end. Then we'll take her to a furnace and burn her. I already know a spot."

"We're going to burn her."

It wasn't a question.

"Yes. And then the hard part will be over. The vandalisms will be easy."

"I doubt they'll go that easy."

"Trust me, buddy," Merc said. "It will."

"I want to keep the ashes," Penn said.

Merc looked up at him.

"Not keep them, per se," he corrected. "I want to bag them up and spread them around the city. Kind of like a tribute."

Merc's eyes narrowed.

"You serious?"

"Yeah. That's the least we could do, don't you think, seeing as how she went all out for me. I figure we could make it fun, since she was all about being such a New Yorker. We can flush one down a toilet at the Port Authority. Dump another one into a bathroom sink at a McDonald's in the Village and rinse it down the drain. Mix some into the soil at Central Park. Spread the Beryl wealth. Uptown, downtown, midtown, West Side Highway, FDR. Columbia. I'll leave a little bit by CarterHobbs. You know . . . respect due. Like a tribute."

"I thought you said you spent most of the day freaked out."

"I did a lot of thinking," Penn said.

"Apparently. I thought I could come up with some shit, but you topped me on that one."

An hour later and Beryl's bloodletting was done. The tub was rinsed and she lay at the bottom of it, pallid and clammy. Penn had cleaned up the minor mess in the living room and had cleaned out the bucket. He was sitting on the toilet now, watching Merc.

"Hand me that electric knife."

He gave Mercury the narrow appliance.

Mercury dried the end of the cord with his pants leg and plugged it into a nearby socket. He hit the power switch and the thing made a buzzing sound like a miniature chain saw. The blade moved back and forth in a sawing motion.

"Oh, hell yeah," he said. "This is gonna make it easy." He turned to Penn. "Wanna watch the first cut?"

Penn came over and stood next to the tub.

"Where should I start?" asked Mercury. "You make the call."

The hairs on Penn's arms, legs, nape of his neck, and back were standing at attention. This was thrilling. His very first kill. It was almost operatic. What would Jessye Norman think?

"I dunno. Do something easy."

Mercury gazed up at him. "News flash, dude. None of it's easy."

"All right, all right . . . do her hand. The wrist. That shouldn't be too bad."

Mercury lowered the humming blade onto Beryl's left wrist. The serrated edges sawed effortlessly through the skin, then, seconds later, ground down to a halt when the blade met bone. Penn leaned closer to watch.

"Hmph," Merc muttered. "Not as easy as I figured."

He got up from his knees and grabbed the blade and the hammer from the counter. He knelt back beside the tub.

"Maybe we'll just use the electric knife to cut through the meat. We'll have to use these to get at the bone."

He held the blade in place on Beryl's wrist with his left hand, then lowered the hammer with his right with one solid, powerful stroke. The blade cut clean, snapping straight through the bone. He leaned down and glanced at the tub. Penn leaned over and peered in. Merc angled his neck and looked up at him. He held up the blade. "This thing is no joke."

Penn walked over to the bathroom doorway as Mercury fired up the electric knife and began sawing into thigh. Penn could hear the gentle resistance of metal against flesh as he closed his eyes and considered his life. Beryl was gone. Gone, gone, gone. Soon to be an ash mosaic scattered across the lovely Manhattan landscape.

But there was Sharlyn, sweet, sexy, helpful Sharlyn. And the *New York Times* bestseller list. And *TRL*. and *Billboard*. And next week, Katie Couric.

As he considered all this, his mind was transported several blocks south to Times Square, to the magnificent, gigantic, godlike image of himself nude, holding his book. Each of his abs was five feet across, easy, rippling cords of sinewy muscle. His golden skin, blonde hair and crystal-blue eyes were all vivid, even though the billboard was in classic black and white. His body was beautiful—all six-foot-three of it—particularly when viewed on such an epic scale. He was a work of art, WASP perfection. His body was as flawless as his beautiful mind.

The left corner of his lip pirouetted into a perfect letter C as he listened to his best friend hack away at Beryl's femur with the hammer and blade. Mercury was the ideal soldier, he mused. Penn didn't even have to give him instructions. All he had to do was make the call, and there Merc was, presto, pronto, taking charge, barking orders, chiding, cajoling, encouraging, supportive, organizing everything into seamless science. He didn't even demand that Penn help with the cutting.

Penn took a deep breath.

To Beryl, he toasted in silence. *To being number one.*

This was all for the best. Beryl could have never accepted his relationship with Sharlyn. She could have never dealt with the fact that he had no plans to marry, not any time soon, and definitely not her. Her life wouldn't have been the same knowing what she knew.

Killing her had been an act of kindness.

She was better off dead.

———

"Bring all the sheets that go with those pillowcases."

"Why?"

"So it won't draw any attention."

Penn stopped drying the chunk of shoulder in his hand.

"But why would that draw attention?" he asked.

Mercury kept packing meat.

"Just take them. We'll burn them with the rest of her. I just don't want anything that might draw attention from the right kind of investigator."

He grabbed another piece of meat from the tub.

"Do you think there'll be an investigation?" Penn said, surveying the squeaky-clean carnage.

"I don't know. She was a major editor. It depends on if anybody cares enough to take things further."

Penn glanced around at the scope of what they had done. Nothing about it made him nervous. In fact, he was confident things were going exactly his way.

"Our shit is tight," Merc was saying, "so don't sweat it. Everything'll be cool, as long as we pay attention to all the details."

Penn was half-listening, his thoughts still hanging on Mercury's comment about the sheets and the missing pillowcases drawing the attention of "the right kind of investigator."

Excitement palmed the back of his neck like a cold hand. The fine hairs stood on end.

He realized that it was happening, right now, this very moment. He was no longer just a man.

He was creating his legend.

By midnight, Beryl was cooking in a furnace at a meat warehouse in Hoboken owned by Mercury's Uncle Zezer.

"Do it with zest," Penn's father, once told him. *"Do it with zest, or don't do it at all."*

This was zest to the nth power. How heady it was.

"Hey," Merc said, "why were you whistling when we were first bagging her up?"

"When?"

"Back at her apartment. You were whistling some song, it was kinda creepy. I don't know where I've heard it before."

" 'Träume'?"

"Fuck if I know," Merc said. "It sounded like you were skipping and whistling."

"I was trying to catch a beat."

Merc laughed.

Penn began whistling the tune.

"Yeah, that's it!" Merc said.

"It's Wagner."

"Of course. You and your damn Wagner."

The two of them sat there, listening to the crackling of the fire and the popping of meat. Penn was surprised at the almost-pleasant aroma of it.

Beryl Unger was gone. In a puff of smoke.

"You know I got you, right?"

"What are you yapping about now?" said Merc.

"Moneywise, I'm saying. Now that you're out of a steady gig."

"I'm good. My uncle's always getting new jobs."

"I don't want to hear it. Effective right now, you're on the payroll."

"As what?"

"My crew."

Mercury laughed loud and hard.

"I can have a crew," Penn said. "Who said it's gotta be more than one person? Snoop's got Bishop Don 'Magic' Juan. I got you."

" 'long as you don't expect me to wear no money-green suits and carry gilded goblets, we cool."

"Don't knock Bishop. He's the most well known pimp in the world."

"I don't know," Mercury said. "I'm starting to think right now, that might be you."

Penn smiled.

The two men let their conversation fall off as they listened to the last of Beryl snap, crackle, and pop.

They remained at the warehouse another three hours, emptying out the cool ashes in the middle of the night. When they left Hoboken, Penn had the best of Beryl poured into an emptied Ocean Spray Cran-Apple bottle. He got Merc to stop at a store on the Jersey side so he could grab a box of Ziploc bags.

A few hours later, around eight A.M., he sent the first e-mail from Beryl's computer.

By late that afternoon, he had spread most of Beryl around the city. He paid great attention to each spot where he left some of her ashes so that he could record it in his journal later.

A few hours later, he was deep in the throes of an apology fuck, making amends for having shirked Sharlyn two nights before.

"What'd you do while I was out?" he asked.

"Nothing," she said. "Got drunk, a little high. Fell asleep. I dreamt I called you and left a bunch of rambling messages on your machine."

There it was. The thing that had set Beryl off.

He wasn't upset about it. Sharlyn had inadvertently done him a favor. He would have had to deal with marriage demands from Beryl eventually. She wanted to quit the business, have kids, be a family.

Sharlyn had saved him from something that would have been more disastrous than what had occurred. He would miss Shar when he headed out for the tour next week. Oh well. He'd just have to find other warm bodies to tide him over until he got back.

He looked down at her adoringly, pounding her with renewed, appreciative vigor.

Five random units caught fire at Beryl's building the following Saturday night. Two of them, one of which was Beryl's unit, were gutted by the time the fire department arrived. Everyone got out safely. Two-thirds of the residents were out of town.

The fire would have made bigger news in the papers if it weren't for other fires that weekend in Harlem, Canarsie, and Dumbo, each competing for their fifteen minutes. A fire in Riverdale claimed unanimous first place when a restaurant burned to the ground, taking several lives.

Summer went out in a few blazes of glory.

New York City was hot, hot, hot.

Shecky had stared at the e-mail, her heart daring to dance.

Beryl needed to take some time off?

She glanced around, watching people buzz about the halls, fresh from the long weekend.

So was Beryl leaving? Was that what this meant?

Shecky rejoiced inside. This could be her chance.

She knew how to do everything. She was familiar with everyone's manuscripts. She'd even found a promising tale among the slush pile ruins and Beryl had been considering buying it. This could be her moment in the sun. Wasn't that how things had happened for Beryl? Her editor at PaleFire had decided to leave and Beryl was given a chance at the job.

Shecky stared at the e-mail. Beryl might have to leave. Or take leave. Whatever. Same difference, maybe. No matter.

This could be a good thing.

Her window of opportunity was finally opening up.

"Any news?"

Kitty Ellerman was standing in front of Shecky Lehman's desk.

"No, Ms. Ellerman. She hasn't called or anything."

"Just that e-mail."

"Yes, Ms. Ellerman."

"This is so not like her. Beryl's always been such a professional. I'm really worried for her now. Perhaps someone in her family is very ill. Do you have her parents' contact information? Someone who might know how to reach her?"

"No, Ms. Ellerman. She never talks about her family. Beryl's very private. I don't know much about her other than what I see here at work."

Ellerman stood at the desk, thinking.

"The authors are fine, Ms. Ellerman. I've been following up with all of them, going over their edits. Penn's on tour and everything is going great. I check in with him every day at his hotels to make sure he's aware he has our utmost support."

Kitty Ellerman smiled.

"Good job, Shecky. I really appreciate it. I know this has been a tremendous burden on you."

"Not at all, Ms. Ellerman. I love my job. I think publishing is the greatest business in the world."

The big boss contemplated the enthusiastic girl's face.

"I think so, too, Shecky. I think so, too."

You've been

. . . doing what?!"

"Feeding her fatty foods so she'll gain weight and you'll finally leave her."

"Oh, Brookie, that's just absurd."

Miles was frowning. Brookie rolled away from him, fearing it was an expression of wrath. She didn't know from the wrath of Milestone Tate. But that wasn't what she had seen. Miles was angry with himself. That explained why Sharlyn was softer in the middle. Brookie was pushing food on her. He was screwing with the lives of two women. It was time for him to be the man he kept insisting he was.

Enough already.

He was just going to have to face things. He wanted to be with Brookie. He didn't want to sneak around.

He was leaving Sharlyn.

It was time to start a new life.

"You want a divorce?"

Sharlyn was sitting on the tan Philippe Starck couch. Miles was sitting next to her, calm, objective, as though he were handling another business deal.

"I'm prepared to provide you with a financial package that offers you total comfort for the rest of your life. I'm leaving you with all the residential property, although I would like the ranch in Montana. You were never very fond of it."

"You always make everything about money," she said.

"I'm not making this about money. Money will ultimately become a real factor in our divorce." He saw her flinch at the word. "I preferred to deal with it up front, to make this as smooth a transition as possible."

"But what about the papers? It'll be all over the papers."

Miles stared at his wife.

"What?" she cried. "Don't look at me like that. You know how these magazines and news rags are. They'll drag all our business in the street."

"There's nothing to drag," he said. "We can issue a press release that says we agreed to part company as friends and will continue to support each other with treasured respect for the rest of our lives."

The sound stopped coming out of Sharlyn's mouth. It hung open for a long moment before she could find the wind to speak again.

"Press release? I'm nothing but a footnote in a press release?"

"Sharlyn," Miles said, fingering a manila folder, "it doesn't have to be like this. We've been growing apart for some time now. We don't even vacation together."

"Whose fault is that?" she said. "You're always gone."

Miles exhaled.

"Just let me go, Sharlyn."

"No!" she said. "I will not have you humiliate me!"

"If you fight me on this, it will get ugly. We both have reputations at stake. We can do this amicably. That will be the best for everyone concerned."

"But Miles," she said, her voice thick, "I don't understand. Why couldn't we try to work through this? You've never indicated we were having any problems."

"I didn't see it coming. You can't control love."

"Love?" she sobbed. "You're in love? With who? Someone at work? Someone in Finland? Is that why you were there so long?"

Miles cleared his throat and braced himself.

"No, Sharlyn, I'm not in love with someone in Finland. It's Brookie."

She was frozen for a long, long moment. Then the words came out slow, impossibly slow, as she tried to process their meaning.

"Brookie? Your cousin Brookie? My assistant Brookie? That Brookie?"

A vein was bulging in the middle of her head.

"She's your fucking cousin!"

That f-bomb sealed it for him. He was out of there. He thrust the manila folder in her hand.

"She'll be coming with me. She obviously won't be working for you anymore. The terms of the divorce are in there. I would like to do it quickly. We want to marry right away."

Sharlyn flung the folder across the room.

Miles was stone.

"I advise you to have your attorney review the terms of the financial settlement, and then you should sign it. Or I will make your life a living hell, Sharlyn. I've loved you half of my life. I still love you now. If you were asking to be free, I would grant it. That's all I want. Friend to friend, Sharlyn . . . just set me free."

Sharlyn was smashing things.

Lamps. Cordless phones. China, crystal. A plasma screen was destroyed when a vase went flying across the room. At one point, she'd taken a knife and had gone on a literal ripping tear, stabbing the steel into couch and chaise cushions, gouging out feathers, filling, anything that could be gutted, anything she could use as a substitute for Miles.

He was leaving her! Leaving *her*! For Brookie! How long had *that* shit been going on?

She'd given all those years of her life to him. He'd plucked her when she was her most vivacious, in her early twenties, fresh from college and living as a free spirit in New York. She came from a family of men who loved strong independent women, beautiful women who were confident in every way, unafraid to express themselves.

That's how her parents had raised her, to express herself and to live life with gusto and appreciation of all her senses. Yet she had fallen for Miles with his Southern ways and no cursing and ladies-should-be-like-this shit. It was quaint. It was different. They'd built a world together, a world she believed, for the most part, had worked. She'd done her best to do his little donkey dance of feminine obedience, as much as it was in her to do. And after all that, he was leaving her for Brookie!

Sharlyn plunged the knife into a portrait of Miles that hung above the fireplace in their bedroom. She slashed the thing frontways and sideways, slicing his face into a jigsaw of hanging shreds.

Splitsville

Media mogul Miles Tate and his wife, sexy bestselling author Sharlyn Tate, have hit the skids. Seems the intense billionaire has finally had his fill of the free-spirited writer, who's been seen partying it up all over the city. According to our spies, Tate has set his sights on the younger, shapelier, green-eyed beauty who was most recently his wife's personal assistant. She and Tate were spotted two days ago looking at rings in Tiffany's. The young girl had her eye on the biggest rocks in the room after the much older Tate told the sales staff to "give her whatever she wants." Chi-ching!

"So what are you going to do?" Penn asked. He was on a break from his tour. He'd been away for two weeks and was back for the weekend.

"I have my reputation and a career to protect," she said.

"Were you still in love with him?"

They were in bed at her suite at the Sherry. He was playing footsies with her under the sheet.

"No. I haven't been in love with him for a while now."

"Then what's the problem?"

"I just didn't see it coming. Twentysome-odd years together and then this. This is the stuff you read about all the time in the tabloids,

but you never think it's going to be you. I'll be the first wife, the old
hag who gets dumped for the pretty young thing. It's so clichéd, it's
pathetic. Our friends are acting so awkward. No one's calling.
Nobody wants to have to pick sides."

Penn traced his finger along her thigh.

"Fuck 'em. They're not your friends if they won't stand by you.
And you aren't remotely close to being a hag. Stop being so melodra-
matic. You'll be single, extraordinarily rich . . . correction, richer, and
it's all happening at an age when women really start to hit their sexual
stride. Miles is the loser here. Not you."

She rolled on her side, facing him.

"You think so?"

"I know so. My Shar is a hot babe if there ever was one. No one
has ever made me as hard as you."

He reached for her hand beneath the sheet and placed it on his
rock. She moaned.

"I'm so glad I have you," she said. "Everything is turning upside
down all at once. I haven't heard from Beryl in two weeks. She won't
return my e-mails or calls. They said she had some kind of emergency.
Have you talked to her?"

"No."

"I don't know," she sighed, "I'm thinking maybe I'll take a year off.
Maybe a couple. No writing, no touring, no partying. I'll just lay low
in the cut. Chill for a while. Maybe do some traveling overseas."

She was looking in his face, searching for something. He held her
gaze. What's she looking for? he wondered. Was this a fishing expedi-
tion? Was he supposed to say "don't go"?

"I love you, Penn," she whispered, a tear running down the side of
her face.

"I love you, too, Shar."

It was the second time he'd said it. He meant it. He did.

Didn't he?

He felt something for her. He didn't really know what love felt like,
so who was to say that this wasn't it.

He knew he loved her pussy.

Hey, that was love.

———

Penn was spooning Sharlyn as she slept. The room was dark except for the twinkling city lights coming into the room. His eyes were wide open.

The tour had been going fabulously. Standing-room-only signings, lines around buildings, both for his book and the CD. No one was outraged by the content of his novel. It was being universally hailed as a masterpiece.

Penn was getting the dream just like he had imagined, through being celebrated as a literary genius, even though his fame had begun first with the Calvin Klein billboard and the video with On Fiyah. That wasn't a part of the original plan, but no matter. He was still on a magical ride that he didn't want to end.

"You're my favorite writer!" a short, pasty-faced woman in Chicago had screamed. "I was the first in line. I've been camped out for two days. Could you sign it 'To my dearest friend Irma'?"

"I'm sorry, ma'am," the Kittell Press publicist had interrupted. "We already announced that Mr. Hamilton's doing signature only."

Penn had smiled helplessly at the woman and shrugged.

"But I love you!" she cried with near-hysteria. "I have your CD! I know all the words to the songs! I'm your number one fan!" She lifted up her shirt. "See?"

Emblazoned across her very-rotund roadmap of a belly was the phrase "Penn is god."

"Oh my," said the publicist, shrinking back.

Penn gazed at the inked flesh of the woman, then looked up into her shining eyes. He reached for her palm and kissed her on the hand.

The woman was momentarily stunned, then exploded into a firestorm of tears. She had to be led away. Against his own protocol, a delighted Penn signed her book "To my dearest friend Irma," and sent the publicist off to catch up to the woman and give her the personalized book.

He thought about all that as he lay behind Shar now. He thought about Beryl. Not a peep since they'd minced her to meat mulch. He'd never realized it was this easy to kill. It was actually thrilling, the seamlessness of it all. From the way Mercury acted, it was something he did practically every day.

Penn found himself fascinated by the whole murder-death thing. He had yet to feel any remorse about it. He knew that he never would.

This could be the topic of his next book.

Writer murders editor and chops her to pieces. Burns the body. Throws the ashes around the city.

He needed to tweak it a little.

Writer murders agent. He'd keep the chopping-burning-ashes part.

He thought about what Mercury had said about the right kind of investigator possibly figuring things out. He would include that in the book. Something to give it a little more juice than what had actually happened.

The public would love it. It'd be another home run.

He fell asleep thinking of what kind of rap song he and On Fiyah could do about murder.

Maybe this time he'd do something with Snoop.

The right

. . . kind of investigator sat at his desk, eyeing a gunky cheese Danish.

It was enormous, the Danish, half a day old, as sexy as cancer. The cheese was a glutinous clump of thickness that screamed "Eat me and die!"

What the hell, he thought. He was already dying, perhaps even dead. Nothing else could explain this pitiful existence.

It certainly wasn't living, that was for sure.

He reached for the Danish, undaunted, and raised it to his lips.

It was just after midnight in the garden of not much good and mostly evil, better known as the Twentieth Precinct—the Two-Oh—proudly serving the areas between West Fifty-ninth Street and West Eighty-sixth and Central Park West to the Hudson River. Detective Jameson Rex's front teeth were halfway through the pastry's viscosity, his taste buds racing a message to his brain that he'd just made a terrible, terrible mistake, when a large hand slid a file across his desk. Jameson glanced up as he attempted to pry his mouth free.

"Jesus Christ," said the man who'd passed him the file. It was the boss, his old friend Captain Alan O'Hearn. "What the hell are you eating?"

Jameson's front teeth were coated with a thick white film, a god-awful substance that nestled in the crannies of his tongue and made itself at home. He breathed through his mouth as he looked around for a napkin. O'Hearn grabbed one from a nearby desk.

"Here. Jesus."

The detective took the napkin and wiped the goop from his teeth. O'Hearn picked up the Danish with a grimace and tossed it in the trash.

"What are you trying to do, Rex, kill yourself?"

"It looked all right."

"The hell it did."

Jameson swiped at his teeth once more and ran his tongue around his mouth. He reached for the file.

"What's this?"

"Missing person maybe," O'Hearn said, sitting in a wooden chair facing the desk. "Some big-shot book editor who hasn't shown up for work. She's not answering her phone or returning anybody's e-mails."

"Who called it in?"

"Her boss," he said, pointing. "It's there in the file."

Jameson opened the folder and scanned the first page.

"Hmmm. So why hasn't her family reported her missing?"

"They don't have any info on her family."

"Nothing?" Jameson asked.

O'Hearn's brow crunched and he threw up his big-knuckled hands.

"I don't know. Her boss said she sent an e-mail the Friday before Labor Day saying she had an emergency and needed to take some time off."

"So there you go. Why's there a report?"

"It's a big-time publisher, Kittell Press, and this missing lady—"

"Doesn't sound like she's missing to me."

"Well, apparently she never takes any leave. Hasn't in all the years she's been working there."

"Shit happens," Jameson said. "Maybe she finally needed a break."

"Maybe."

"She married?"

"Nope. No husband, no boyfriend, no kids, no nothing. She was always working, supposedly. Who the fuck knows? Maybe she's gay and was trying to hide it from her coworkers. These artsy types always turn out to be gay. She's probably off on a rug-rubbing caper."

A rookie in uniform, a young woman whose smooth face had yet to be introduced to the etchings of cynicism, sat at a desk doing paperwork just a few feet away. She seemed to sense a pair of eyes upon her. She raised her head and glanced in their direction. Jameson offered a nervous smile, nodded, and turned back to O'Hearn.

"C'mon, Captain," he whispered. "Do you hear yourself? What, are you fishing for a sexual harassment suit?"

O'Hearn leaned back and shoved his hands in his pockets.

"Yeah, yeah, all right already. I figured it was just us guys talking, old friends, so I took a little liberty."

"That's still pretty harsh. Even for you."

Jameson studied the report as he ran his tongue over his teeth. O'Hearn yawned and stretched.

"So now, after two weeks, they think something might be up?"

"J. Rex, I already told you what I know."

"But you're the one who took the call."

"It was a short conversation. Nobody's seen her, not even the doorman at her building. People were starting to get concerned. She lived in that building where we had those arson incidents Labor Day weekend. Her unit was torched pretty bad."

Jameson's tongue and teeth felt like they had been dipped in lard.

"Uh . . . doesn't that seem like it might be related?"

"Not necessarily. Other units got hit. There was another one torched worse than hers. This girl was already away when the vandals hit her building."

The detective walked over to the watercooler, guzzled a drink, crumpled the paper cup, and threw it toward the trash. He missed.

"A missing girl and a torched apartment."

"You got it."

Jameson picked up the paper cup and this time hit the mark.

"Interesting."

The detective sat back at his desk.

"So it doesn't sound fishy to you? The fire and the girl being gone?"

Captain O'Hearn shrugged and rubbed his bald pate. His stomach growled.

"Sounds like a coincidence and nothing more. Now stop grilling me. The only reason I took that report is because it got routed to me by Mabel, that fucking cunt up front."

"Hey, hey, hey," Jameson said, eyeing the rookie. "Put a lid on that. You're a superior, you're supposed to be setting the tone around here. What's the matter with you?"

"Yeah, yeah, yeah," O'Hearn said in a lower voice. "But that Mabel got me so fucking heated. Fucking rabble-rousing bitch." The edge had returned to his voice. "That call shouldn't have come to me. Mabel knew exactly what she was doing. She's done it at least three times a day since I called things off. You wouldn't believe the shit she's routing my way. She knows I can't do anything about it. I'd have to admit I was nailing her, and God knows what kind of Pandora's box that would be. IA'd be all over it."

"So you are fishing for a sexual harassment suit."

"It was just a piece of ass," O'Hearn spat as he sat back in his chair.

The rookie was staring right at them. Jameson coughed and leaned toward O'Hearn.

"So of all the asses in Manhattan," he whispered, "you had to go after one that worked for you."

"She works for the precinct."

"Which includes working for you."

O'Hearn's belly rumbled. He rested his palms on top of it, jiggling the meat. It was a beachball, an unnatural feature on an otherwise normal build.

"Listen, J. Rex," he said, "never nail a broad over fifty. They don't take letdowns too easy. Buncha vindictive bitches, they are."

"Didn't you say the same thing last week about that twenty-something you dumped?"

"Fuck 'em. They're all crazy. Broads. If it wasn't for fucking, I'd leave 'em alone."

The rookie got up and left.

"You think she heard us?" O'Hearn asked.

"I almost think you wanted her to. That's your ass on the line if she did, not mine."

The captain waved it off.

"You got the right idea, Jameson, staying unencumbered and all."

"It's not by choice."

"Still, better they should leave you than you leave them. You might get your heart broke, but at least you get to keep all your shit."

O'Hearn's stomach roared with impatience. He laughed as he patted the gelatinous meat.

"My better half calls."

"Paula took everything," said Jameson. "The whole place was empty when I came home."

"Yeah? Well, fuck stuff. You can always get more. Least you have your dignity."

Jameson pressed his lips together so tight, the blood drained away. He picked up the file.

"Mabel's been off for hours. When did this come in?"

"This afternoon. I been sitting on it, waiting for you. I figured you'd be pulling another one of your double shifts. Seeing as this precinct seems to be your favorite place these days. Cheers."

"Right. Thanks."

O'Hearn stood. His stomach popped. He tapped the edge of the desk.

"Gotta go feed the beast. Want I should get you something?"

"Where you going?"

"That place around the corner with the hot bar. What do you want?"

"Some soup would be good."

"What kind?"

"Anything, as long it's not something creamy or with cheese."

"Done."

The captain was just about to disappear when Jameson called out.

"And a Pepsi. Cold." He ran his tongue across his teeth again as he fingered the file and studied the name scrawled across the top. Unger, Beryl.

"Damn," he muttered, dropping the file on his desk as he got up for another drink of water. "I can't seem to get this fucking taste out of my mouth."

————

Jameson needed something to pour himself into.

This had an odd feel to it. A missing girl and a fire? Unlike O'Hearn, he didn't believe in coincidences.

Who was Unger, Beryl?

All he had was a photo, a clipping from a recent society page. Something in her twisted face spoke to him, begging his attention.

She deserved that much. Besides, he was curious. He was determined to find out who Beryl was and why she would suddenly just disappear.

There were no real leads at her apartment. Everything had been destroyed. He was hoping forensics could have salvaged something, maybe the hard drive on her computer, but the place was ruined. The computer had been melted to nothing. There were no leads on the teens who allegedly vandalized the building and set the fire.

"They were black," said one resident who hadn't seen anything firsthand, but was merely repeating a rumor in the building. "There were a bunch of them. They were looking for crack."

Jameson contacted the contractors who had been working on Beryl's apartment.

"How long have you been on this project?"

"At least three months," said the lead guy, Mercury. "I've got all the permits, licenses, and paperwork, if you need to see them. It's been a tough job. She changed her mind a lot."

"How's that?"

"As soon as we'd get everything done the way she wanted, she'd make us rip it out and do it again."

Jameson scribbled on a notepad.

"Did she seem disturbed, troubled, anything like that?"

He could see Mercury thinking about it.

"Not really. She was just kinda high-strung. She changed her mind a lot. I guess you really can't hold that against a person. We were on this job a lot longer than expected, and I know it must have been pretty annoying to her neighbors, even though we did all our work during the day."

Jameson gave Mercury his card.

"Would you call me if you think of anything I might need to know?"

"Sure. What's going on? We've been concerned. I'm used to her calling me at least once a day."

"She's been missing for a couple of weeks. We're just investigating things to make sure there's no foul play."

"I need some help with this," Jameson said.

"What kind of help?" asked O'Hearn. "What've you got so far?"

"Not much. Basic background stuff, but nothing really out of the ordinary." He slid into the chair in front of his boss's desk. "I've got a shitload of e-mails that she's sent from her computer at home to people at her office, but nothing rings odd in any of it."

"That's it?" O'Hearn crammed a whole cruller into his mouth, talking around the words. "A bunch of fucking e-mails?"

"She had contract work going on at her apartment. I talked to the guys who were doing the work. Nothing there, either. I talked to all the doormen. Nobody really knew much about her, but they didn't notice anything strange, either."

"What about her coworkers?"

"Same thing. This Beryl chick was apparently pretty intense, always caught up in putting together the next book with one of her authors."

"So what kind of help are you asking me for here?"

Jameson scratched his head, eyeing the sugary crumbs around the edges of O'Hearn's mouth.

"I'm thinking maybe you can let me have a couple of guys on this," he said. "I need some more legs. Maybe I can come up with something."

"Can't do it," O'Hearn said, inhaling another cruller. Five more sat in a box on his desk, awaiting inevitable slaughter.

"Why not?" asked Jameson. "It's not like this is some bullshit situation. This is a fairly high-profile person we're talking about here."

"A person who sent an e-mail that said she was taking leave. A person who's got a right to do that. Think about it, Rex . . . her boss reported her missing. Who knows what kind of hard-ass broad her boss is? Some people don't like being left in the lurch."

"That's silly, Captain, and you sound silly saying it. You know you do. This woman's mail is piling up. She had a fire in her apartment. Don't you think it's odd she hasn't had her mail put on hold or contacted her building and insurance company about the damage done to her property?"

"Sometimes people just walk away."

"Captain."

The big man pawed another cruller.

"I can't justify more men," O'Hearn said, clobbering the dough-nut. "I don't care how important this Beryl girl was. Vandals trashed her building. Yeah, so what? Her apartment wasn't the only one that got worked over. And she quits her job on Labor Day weekend. I still say she's run off with another Beryl. Two Beryls on a bush hunt, that's what I think."

Jameson stood.

"I can't believe I report to you."

"Believe it, buddy. I know from whence I speak. We got twenty-five reports of missing persons on our website, and that's just in Manhattan. Most of 'em have been missing for years. We do what we can. I can't have guys running around chasing theories. Gimme something to go on and I'll think about it. That's the only way I'll give this some heat, unless the order comes down to push it further. Otherwise, wrap this shit up. I can't have you chasing AWOL writers all fucking day."

"She's an editor," Jameson growled.

He snatched up a cruller and walked away.

He was able to trace Beryl back to Galena, Ohio, and from there learned that her parents were dead. That was more than her acquaintances and coworkers knew. He talked to people who had worked with her at PaleFire, then he went back to Kittell Press for a second round of what he hoped would be greater details.

"Did she date a lot?" he asked Beryl's assistant, whom he found unusually attractive. "Did she have a boyfriend?"

"I've never seen one," Shecky said. "But then, I didn't know a lot about her outside of the office. She was pretty guarded about her personal life."

Jameson scribbled on his pad, sneaking peeks at the girl.

"So no men ever called here for her?"

"Sure, but it was always business. I mean, um, have you seen a photo of Beryl?"

"Yes, I have," Jameson said, looking up from his note-jotting, taking in the smug expression on Shecky's face.

"Well . . ."

"Well what?" he asked, putting away his pad and pen.

"Well . . ." Shecky dragged, "she was rather sophisticated, in a put-on kind of way, I guess . . . not naturally . . . but it's not like guys were knocking down her door."

Jameson squinted.

"Sounds like you have some issues with your boss, Ms. Lehman."

"No, no, not at all," Shecky said, full of sugary brightness. "It's just . . . I mean, you know . . . everybody thought that. Page Six even joked about it."

"What did Page Six say?"

Shecky giggled, shook out her lustrous curls, flashed some sort of oddly coy look at the desk and then at Jameson, then showed her ultrabrite, ultrawhite pearlies. She leaned forward a bit, her voice almost a whisper.

"They called her face 'the ultimate contraceptive.' "

Jameson studied Shecky with growing dislike, watching the smile widen so much, it threatened to slice her head in half. He could tell she was waiting for him to join her in the derision. He jotted the comment on his notepad instead.

Shecky shook out her hair again and leaned back, serious again.

"She spent the most time with her authors. If anybody got to know her better, it would be one of them."

"Thank you, Ms. Lehman. I appreciate your efforts. Do you still have my card?"

"Yes, I do."

"If you come across anything you think is important, even if it doesn't seem important, any details . . ."

"Of course," Shecky said.

He talked to Canon Messier, a misanthropic, self-indulgent, insufferable character who was not much help.

"That fucking cunt just abandoned me! Selfish bitch! She knows how I feel about public appearances. She knows it. You would think, as much as I've done for her career, she would at least take me into consideration. You'd think that, wouldn't you? Doesn't that just make sense?"

Jameson jotted and nodded, starting to believe that perhaps Beryl had indeed just bailed, if this guy was any indication of the stress she'd had to deal with.

They were at Jean Georges at the Trump International in Columbus Circle, Jean Georges Vongerichten's venerable establishment that consistently ranked among the best restaurants in the world. Messier had insisted this was the only place he would meet Jameson, and only over a meal plus drinks, as much of both as he wanted, all of which he expected Jameson to cover.

"You're lucky I don't charge an honorarium for this," Messier said. "I can do that, you know. I'm very spare with my public appearances. Very spare. I can get very Salinger when I want to. If it wasn't for the money, I'd never set foot out—"

"This isn't a public appearance," said Jameson. "I'm conducting an investigation."

"Doesn't matter. Time is money, and my time comes pretty high."

As evidenced by the way he proceeded to eat.

They were meeting too late for the prix fixe lunch. Jameson watched the entire food chain pass across their table as Messier sucked down Mexican papaya with microbasil, roasted squab, fennel-glazed skate wing, beef tenderloin with Japanese eggplant, a loin of lamb, some kind of dessert with rhubarb in it, and at least three bottles of wines selected to complement the flavor collision going on in his mouth.

Jameson, in an attempt to keep costs down, only had the tomato fennel soup.

Meanwhile, Messier was a Visigoth, sacking the menu with unbridled fervor. Teams of waiters scurried about the room, rushing to meet his demands.

"Forks! Forks! I need more forks! I can't keep mixing tastes with the same fork!"

Diners looked on at the spectacle of gluttony, many recognizing the beast at its center. Most were just annoyed at his cretinous behavior.

"Hey! Where's that fork!"

A waitress arrived with a stack of fresh utensils. Messier immediately snatched one from her and examined it.

"There's a spot on this. Bring back clean ones. And make sure they're hot, that way I can tell they've been sterilized. Just forks. Why do I need all those fucking spoons?"

Jameson jotted in his pad.

"So how long have you known Beryl?"

"I don't know," Messier said, slugging his wine. "Forever, I guess. That's why this whole thing pisses me off. That cunt!"

Jameson was ringside at a freak show. He made more notes.

"Did you ever meet her family?" he asked. "A boyfriend? Any of her close friends?"

"Friends! Beryl? She didn't have any friends! Not outside of work. Her writers are her life."

"What about boyfriends?"

"Boyfriends!" he croaked, shoveling skate in his mouth. "Have you seen Beryl?"

"I have a newspaper clipping. She looks very well put-together."

"She is," said Messier, "but I wouldn't fuck her. Not with that face. Fork! Where's the fucking forks!"

People in the restaurant began to stir uncomfortably. The waitstaff apologized, offering up complimentary desserts to compensate.

Tony DiSalvo, one of the two esteemed chefs de cuisine that ran the kitchen, brought the hot forks himself.

"About time!" Messier barked.

DiSalvo apparently knew this drill. He smiled, nodded, and placed a friendly hand on Messier's shoulder.

"Is everything to your satisfaction?"

"Yes, it's great," said Messier, much calmer now that he was being indulged by someone he deemed more worthy.

"Just let us know whatever it is you need," said DiSalvo, "and it will be taken care of."

"That's what I'm talking about." Messier turned to Jameson. "This guy"—he jerked his thumb toward the chef—"he knows how to treat me. That's why I always come here. I love this fucking place!"

The chef offered a humble smile.

"Thank you, Mr. Messier." He looked at Jameson. "And how is your soup?"

"Excellent."

"Very good."

DiSalvo had barely taken his leave before Messier was swearing again, hurling more "cunts!" "selfish whores!" and other delightful terms across the table at Jameson as he expressed his absolute disgust with Beryl's unannounced departure.

Three full hours of orgiastic eating, with Messier never once offering to share with his patron the items he'd ordered.

The meeting cost Jameson over five hundred dollars, an amount he knew he could never submit to the department for reimbursement, so it would have to come out of his pocket. He departed with no more insight into Beryl than the fact that she was surrounded by a conspiracy of idiots.

He'd gotten nothing.

Messier, however, for all intents, had gotten his honorarium.

It was the same with Sharlyn Tate. She was going through a divorce and was emotionally volatile. The mere mention of Beryl's name had sent her reeling.

"It's been more than a month now. Why can't you guys find her? Are you the only person they've got on top of this?"

"I'm just doing the groundwork. Once we get more leads, others will join in a wider search. We don't have much evidence to go on. She sent an e-mail from her home saying she needed some time away. You can't really mount too heavy a search based on that. The missing persons report didn't come from a relative. It came from her boss."

"But she's family to us!" Sharlyn screamed.

"Then why didn't you report her missing?"

"Huh?"

"Why didn't you report her missing?"

"Because I thought she was away dealing with an emergency."

"Even though she's never done anything like that before?"

"How would I know that? We're not that close."

"Right."

Jameson gave Sharlyn Tate a card and went on his way.

He found his lucky break with a tenant in the apartment building of another of Beryl's authors. A three-hundred-pound man who happened to be returning just as Jameson was about to leave after interviewing other tenants in the building. He was holding a paper bag teeming with Subway sandwiches.

Jameson showed him a photo.

"Sure I've seen her," the man said, struggling to breathe. "All the time. She's real sophisticated, you know, elegantlike, but kinda homely. She practically lives with him, she sleeps over so much. I hear them down there late at night with their stupid giggling and loud opera music and loud sex, not so much that anymore, but it's rude, all of it. It comes right up through the floor and keeps me awake."

"So they're dating?"

"Yes. He's all big and famous now with his books and billboards and On Fiyah shit, so I guess he'll be moving, thank God, but yeah. They're a couple. I've seen them plenty of times kissing and holding hands."

Jameson was noting it all on his pad.

"She shrieks like a hyena when they have sex."

Jameson looked up. He put his pen and small pad back in his shirt pocket.

"Thank you, Mister . . ."

"Chapman. Brad Chapman."

"Thank you, Mr. Chapman."

"Is he in trouble?"

"The girl is missing."

"Ha!" grunted the guy. "I'm not surprised. He's a troublemaker. He's got no respect for other human beings. I thought that was why I hadn't seen her around lately, that maybe she caught on to what a loser he is and dumped him. So what, he's famous. An asshole is an asshole."

Jameson gave him his card.

"Please give me a call if you think of anything else."

"Sure thing," said the guy. "I hope you nab him. He's probably involved somehow. Fucking jerk with all his stupid opera music. He's probably secretly gay!"

Penn was singing, practically screaming, hanging note for note with Jessye Norman.

He'd been drinking Defibs and listening to his iPod. He didn't hear the banging at the door. The only reason he became aware of it was because he turned around and noticed it vibrating from the impact of the knocks.

He opened it. He'd been expecting this guy.

"Penn Hamilton?"

"Yes."

"Jameson Rex, NYPD. May I come in?"

Jameson was on the couch, drinking something called a Defibrillator. The young man had two cups of the stuff sitting on the counter and had offered him one. It was skinning his throat on the way down, but it was just the jolt he needed to really examine the man.

He had seen the Calvin Klein billboard in Times Square a million times or more, but was impressed to find the guy was naturally handsome, not airbrushed.

Not that he was attracted to Penn. It was just a detail he noted that might factor into Beryl's case. Jameson was straight. Very straight. Lonely, but not that lonely.

"I understand Ms. Unger wasn't just your editor."

"What do you mean?"

Penn was standing, leaning against the counter. Jameson noted how towering and golden he appeared. The blue eyes were trained on him with laser intensity.

"I understand the two of you were dating."

"Dating?" Penn repeated.

"Yes."

"Beryl is a good friend and a great editor. She worked tirelessly on my book. I've never seen anyone with such an incredible work ethic."

Jameson took a tiny sip of the scalding blackness.

"So you're saying the two of you weren't dating?"

"Beryl's so work-focused. Her mind was always on how to make the book better, how to publicize it, stuff like that."

"So you weren't dating her?"

Penn was drinking his Defibrillator. Jameson waited for him to respond, but he didn't. Jameson jotted in his pad.

"Are you sure you can't tell me anything more than that?" he asked, looking up.

"I'm certain. I don't know what more to tell you. I hope she decides to come back. I feel like I lost a really good friend, not to mention the best editor I'm sure I'll ever have."

"Right," Jameson said, standing, putting his pad and pen away. He was just about to reach into his pocket for a card when Penn spoke.

"I could take a lie detector test if you want," he said. "If that'll clear me. I don't like this kind of thing hanging over my head."

Penn failed the lie detector test.

He wanted to.

He felt the need to push his luck a little further, see how far he could go. He'd been journaling, putting together more ideas for his next book. He needed the material. Wagner would have done the same. It was artistic research.

————

"You're under arrest for the murder of Beryl Unger," Jameson said, unable to disguise what Penn realized was a smile of victory. "You have the right to remain silent. Anything you say can and will be used against you in a court of law. You have the right to an attorney . . ."

Penn wasn't listening. He was picturing his mug shot on the Smoking Gun website. They'd be talking about him even more on *The Today Show* ("he was just here!"), *The View,* Regis, O'Reilly, *Anderson Cooper 360, On the Record with Greta Van Susteren.* All the usual suspects would be hauled out, the cast of motley characters who earned their wages sitting in cable roundtables whining about the ruin of American civilization at the hands of people like him.

This was perfect. It was the next phase of the plan. Earlier than expected, but here nonetheless. This was the best part of his Gesamtkunstwerk theory. The yin of the yang that ensured his absolute media domination.

He was trying not to smile.

"You get a phone call once we've booked you," Jameson said.

It would be to Sharlyn.

Natch.

"What's going on?" she asked, her skin flushed with panic as she clutched the phone to her ear. "Why were you arrested?"

"They think I have something to do with Beryl being missing."

"What!"

"I need an attorney. There's a guy I used for the contracts with—"

"No," Shar said. "You need a real attorney. Somebody who knows how to handle this kind of thing. This is a criminal allegation we're talking about." She was shaking as she said the words. Criminal. Penn was no . . . criminal. He was all sweetness and love and passion and beauty and . . . and . . . and he was in jail!

"Shar . . ."

"Yes." The bones of her knees clacked as she sat on the edge of the bed.

"Relax. It's going to be okay. I'm not panicking—"

"You should be!"

"No I shouldn't. I'm innocent. Now is the time for calm, rational behavior. So who's this attorney you're talking about?"

She heard someone mumbling in the background.

"I've gotta go, baby," Penn said. "Can I trust you to handle this?"

"Yes! Of course! Don't worry, baby, we'll get this all straightened—"

Her ear was flooded with dial tone.

Shar dropped the phone. Her face exploded into tears.

The Upper Manhattan Empowerment Zone (UMEZ) was established in 1994 with a federal grant of some one hundred million dollars. One of nine such zones, its purpose was to revivify the district encompassing all parts of Harlem (Central, East, and West), Inwood, and Washington Heights. So inspired was the state of New York by this grand effort to breathe life and industry into the once-regal, long-suffering area, the governor kicked in another hundred million. So did the mayor. And, just like that, the UMEZ had three hundred *meeeeeeeeeeelyun dollars*. A king's ransom.

Then a king moved in. The Pride of Hope, Arkansas, that human vortex of infinite charisma, William Jefferson Clinton, himself.

His arrival put the *E* in the Empowerment Zone. It was the real deal, nots to be fucked with. Harlem was on the rise again, big-time, and had, arguably, the most beloved leader in living history holding court within its midst.

The map was unofficially redrawn. If Manhattan was the Center of the Universe, the Center now had a Center.

Its address was 55 West 125th Street, and the throne occupied some eight thousand square feet on the twelfth floor.

In the same building as the Center of the Center of the Universe, there was a smaller, less formidable presence, although, on its own, it could never be considered small or anything less than formidable.

It was about six and a half feet and stocky, with a receding wavy hairline, brown skin, a curious splotchiness raging across its back, and impeccably clad—a miasmic block of concentrated atoms with the power to purify the corrupt and disinfect those with implied taint. A messiah-for-hire who could wash sins away in the court of public opinion and state and federal jurisdiction, thereby saving careers and fortunes, and making a mountainous career and fortune for himself in the process.

He was the root rot of righteousness, the ruination of good. But he was the Man, and those with the capital to conjure the Devil called upon him posthaste, the moment the scent of a possible debacle hit the air.

Joshua Champineau Cougar.

A man who loved himself a vortex. Vortices. He wasn't against two or three of them going at a time. Any kind of situation with enough centrifugal force to create chaos was good enough for him. High-profile, of course. He worked best in high-profile chaos.

As long as he was in the center.

As long as he emerged as the calmer of the storm.

Joshua Champineau Cougar—J.C. to his friends, J.C. "Set 'em Free" Cougar to the world at large: master litigator, wordsmith, phrase-turner, law-tweaker, judge-baffler, jury-breaker, prosecution-scorcher, mind-boggling-settlement-getter, shaman, showman, Lord of the Legal Dance.

Expert at Criminal and Civil Law.

Family man.

Mistress-taker.

Moneymaker.

Don King of the Docket.

Provider of infinite second chances.

Professional sin-eater.

Wrangler of riches.

Mind-fucker.

Media whore.

Devil.

J.C. Cougar loved himself a vortex.

As fate would have it, a new one was just starting to form, with the promise of swirling into something massive and magnificent.

Murder!

Celebrated author/rapper/Calvin Klein model/Starbucks-shill Penn Hamilton was arrested on suspicion of murder in the case of his Kittell Press power editrix Beryl Unger, who's been missing for nearly eight weeks. Police have nothing to go on other than general suspicion and a failed lie detector test, which is inadmissible in court.

"I admit, we have no physical evidence," said Detective Jameson Rex of Manhattan's 20th precinct, "but he voluntarily took the lie detector test and he failed it. We have witnesses who've made sworn affidavits saying they've seen him and Ms. Unger together as a couple, which was something no one knew about. It was enough for us to bring him in on probable cause."

"This matter will be cleared up very quickly," said the author's attorney, celebrity legal eagle J.C. "Set 'em Free" Cougar. "They need to pin this on somebody, and my client's all they can come up with. You want to know what I think? I think Beryl Unger is somewhere in Ibiza, shaking her butt in the club or lying on the beach. People burn out in publishing all the time. She sent an e-mail saying she was taking leave. Folks walk away from their jobs. I imagine that's what's happened here."

Hamilton has been released on a one-million-dollar bond. Best-selling author Sharlyn Tate, whose editor was also Ms. Unger, posted his bail.

———

Ripkin was eating his morning crumpet when he saw the paper. The *Post* was more a guilty pleasure for him, not a regular read. The maid had left it on the tray this morning when she'd brought in his breakfast.

He perused the article, his pulse quickening. Beryl was missing. *No!*

This was the very thing he had feared. She'd terminated her therapy too soon. She was in no way ready to have a functioning romantic relationship. He tried to tell her that, but she didn't want to listen.

This wasn't why he'd gone into practice. He hadn't spent all those years trying to save her life, only for her to lose it once she was no longer under his care.

He had to do something. He'd practically raised this girl. He picked up the phone and dialed.

"Hi, this is Joan, what city and state please?"

"Manhattan. May I have the phone number of the . . ."—he reached for the paper, bringing it closer to his fading eyes—"yes, the Twentieth Precinct of the New York City Police Department."

"Please hold for that number."

"Of course."

He would do something about this. He would speak to this Mister . . . he looked at the paper again . . . this Detective Rex.

He would tell him what he knew about Beryl and Penn.

"So how long was she your patient?" Jameson asked.

"Sixteen years and counting," Ripkin said, sitting across from the detective. He had made the trip to the precinct, so determined was he to help.

Jameson was jotting on a pad.

"What kinds of things did she talk about? What was wrong with her?"

"Well, sir, uh, I'm not at liberty to say. That's doctor-patient privilege."

"Then why did you come here?"

Ripkin bristled.

"I came here to help. That girl is almost like a daughter to me. I know for a fact that she was dating that young man, she was so excited about it."

"Did she talk about their relationship a lot? Did she tell you the things they did day-to-day? I just need to get some kind of a profile here. Something to help us build a solid case."

Ripkin suddenly felt silly. He didn't even know how to answer the man.

"Well? I know you can't divulge much, but did she at least give you updates about the status of their relationship?"

"She terminated her therapy two days after she met him."

There. He'd said it. He felt such the fool.

"What do you mean? She stopped treatment? She didn't come back anymore?"

"Yes, that's what I mean."

"Well, did she give you a reason? Did she say he told her she couldn't see you anymore?"

Ripkin was piddling around with the mahogany handle on his plaid umbrella. This was awkward now. He was ready to go.

"No, she didn't say he told her to stop."

Jameson Rex's fingers were tapping the desk. Ripkin was furious. Stupid arrogant American cop.

"So the reason was . . ."

"She said that she'd found the love of her life, she didn't need me anymore."

Jameson was staring at him. Why on earth was he staring at him?

Jameson stood and held out his hand.

"Thank you, Dr. Ripkin, for coming in with this information. I'm not so sure it can help us, seeing as you haven't told me any more than I already know, but I appreciate your valiant efforts."

Ripkin stood. He stared at Jameson's outstretched hand. He wasn't going to take it.

Jameson traded the hand for a card.

"Give me a call if you remember any information you feel you can give me without violating doctor-patient privilege."

Ripkin snatched the card.

"Good day, sir!" he huffed, and turned on his heel and walked out of the precinct.

He stopped to catch his breath once he was outside. His eyes were stinging. Something wet was streaking down his face. He reached up and wiped it. Tears. He couldn't remember the last time he'd shed them. Probably more than thirty years.

That was it.

He was retiring.

Effective today.

"So now what?" Penn asked.

"It was on the cover of the *New York Post,*" Spanky said. "This is bad, Penn. Career-ending. I'll be honest with you . . . we need to brace ourselves for the crashing sound of terminated contracts. Sex tapes are one thing. Murder is another."

Apparently murder wasn't.

The crashing contracts never happened.

Within twenty-four hours of the *Post* cover, sales of iPods, Calvin Klein products, Defibrillators, *Wonder Boy,* and *Book* had skyrocketed. Overnight. Nationally, not just in New York. The article in the *Post* had stormed the Internet and everyone became more fascinated with Penn Hamilton than ever.

"They want you on *Hannity and Colmes,*" J.C. said. "I think you should do it."

They were at Cougar's office in Harlem, sipping Defibs.

"But I thought you wanted me to do O'Reilly first." Penn had his feet up on the coffee table in J.C. Cougar's overaccessorized work chamber. Cougar was behind his desk, contemplating the ceiling as he rubbed his very pointed goatee.

"We'll do O'Reilly next, after Howard Stern. Howard's loving this. He's stirred up the people in your favor more than anybody."

"Then why *Hannity and Colmes*? I don't get it."

"I think we can really work this."

"How? Hannity'll be all over me."

"Does that bother you?" Cougar said, his left brow raised.

Penn smiled.

"Of course not. I relish it."

"Good," said Cougar, looking at Penn, his mouth curled up at both ends. "Then you're going to relish it even more."

"Why's that?"

"Ann Coulter's going to be on."

Penn was sitting between Sean Hannity, the ultra right-wing conservative cohost of *Hannity and Colmes,* and Ann Coulter, ultra right-wing conservative-at-large. Left-leaning host Alan Colmes, who, theoretically, was Penn's designated ally, was tucked off to the side, way at the other end of the desk, far enough away to not be of much use to Penn. J.C. Cougar was sitting to Alan Colmes's left.

Hannity and Coulter had made a wicked right-wing sandwich of Penn. Their daggers were out. The stabbing had commenced.

"So what kind of message do you think it is you're sending to the kids?" Hannity asked. "How can you look at yourself in the mirror every day with your, your, your hip-hop music and your naked billboards and negative messages and feel like you're contributing anything worthwhile to society?"

Penn smiled.

"You're not going to answer him?" asked Coulter. "You're just going to sit there with a big grin on your face? This is your chance to explain yourself—"

"Yes," said Hannity, "explain yourself. You're accountable to the American public. Aside from all the other deplorable activities you're involved in, you're now being accused of murder—"

"My client has not been officially charged with that crime," Cougar interrupted.

"That's right, Sean," Colmes said. "Let's keep things in perspective here."

"Perspective?" Coulter half laughed, half jeered. "Perspective? This guy is everything that's wrong with America right now. This is why kids are heading down the wrong paths, killing each other and laughing about it . . ."

"He still hasn't said anything," added Hannity, leaning toward Penn. "Speak up, Mr. Hamilton. Defend yourself. We didn't bring you on this show to be a mute. Oh wait, you're not speaking up because you can't defend yourself. Because what you do is indefensible."

"C'mon, Sean," said Colmes. "He's not speaking up because you guys aren't giving him a chance to get in half a word."

"Did you sleep with Beryl Unger just so you could get a book deal?" Hannity asked. "What kind of self-respecting man would do that? Don't you have any pride?"

"Be careful, Sean," Cougar said. "You're making slanderous statements on national television."

"Uh-oh," Hannity laughed. "Now the legal pit bull's gonna get me!"

Cougar and Colmes laughed along with him. Penn maintained his impervious smile.

"Are you a Christian, Mr. Hamilton?" Coulter had thrown her best right hook. She was just inches from Penn's face.

"Good question, Ann!" chimed Hannity. "That ought to put things 'in perspective,' as Alan said." He zoomed in on Penn. "Well? Are you a Christian?"

"Do you believe in God?" Coulter asked.

She was thisclose to Penn. He could see himself, in all his glory, twin Penns dancing in her pupils. He was the perfect deity. Even in her disapproving eyes, he shone with great light.

"Well?" she pressed.

In his head he heard music. His theme song, Wagner's *Träume*.

"Yes," he said, beholding his reflected self. "Yes. I believe."

"I say we all gather out in Times Square beneath his billboard," Howard Stern joked. "This guy's a rock star. C'mon! So what, he put some homely editor out of her misery. That's community service. Long live Penn-fucking-Hamilton. Let's march on Times Square!"

"*Howarrrrrrrrrrd,*" chided Robin Quivers. "Don't encourage that kind of behavior. People might take you seriously."

"Let's do it!" said Artie Lange.

"What do you know, Artie?" Baba Booey snarked. "Like you ever marched on anything."

"He's right," Howard said. "Penn Hamilton's my freaking hero. Imagine the ass this guy gets. Good-looking kid like him. Posters in Time Square. Secret books about giant pricks. Bumping off editors—"

"She's missing, Howard," Robin said. "You should be saying 'alleged.' He's innocent until proven guilty."

"Innocent, my ass. I hope he did it. I'd respect him more. One less skanky publishing leech walking the earth. Besides, it's about time men started screwing their way to the top. Women have been doing it for years. It's time for the guys to have a crack at it."

"That's what I'm talking about," Artie said.

"Seriously," said Howard, "I like this guy. We need to do something to help save his image before the rest of the media tries to run him out on a rail. You see the way he handled Ann Coulter the other day? I love this guy. Let's party for Penn!"

"In Times Square?" asked Robin.

"In Times Square!"

Thousands of fans gathered in Times Square beneath Penn's Calvin Klein poster. Several forward-thinking vendors had printed T-shirts with Penn's picture and the word BOOK and was selling them for ten bucks a pop. The crowd bought them, donned them, and partied on with an assortment of posters inscribed with their credos.

KEEP PENN FREE!

PENN HAMILTON IS MY BABY'S DADDY!

MAKE ME DISAPPEAR!

PENN IS GOD!

Riot squads were dispatched. People were teargassed. Arrests were made.

"He's the muthafuckin' man!" a black kid with locks shouted as he was kneed against the ground and handcuffed.

"So you're gonna go to jail for a white boy who doesn't even know you exist," the arresting officer smirked.

"Fuck you," said the kid. "Penn's an Everyman. If I don't stand up for him, who's gonna stand up for me?"

The next day, J. C. Cougar held a press conference. Penn was at his side.

"The New York City Police Department has officially dropped their bogus charges against my client."

The crowd was a sea of cheers. The sound of clicking cameras and journalists shouting over one another folded into the din.

Cougar knew how to wait for the valley of silence. He'd had years of playing a moment for maximum mileage. He smiled and nodded, biding his time.

One by one, the people stopped crowing.

"The information they had was shaky, at best. And the lie detector test, which my client, Mr. Penn Hamilton—"

More crowing from the crowd.

Cougar raised a hand. The silence was instant.

"My client submitted freely to the lie detector test. He didn't have to. It's inadmissible."

More applause, cheers, stamping, clicks.

"A woman—"

Stamping.

"A woman—"

Clicks.

Cougar raised his hand.

"A woman quit her job and walked away from the stresses of her life and profession. Happens every day. People get tired, fed up, take off for quieter parts where they can get some peace, get their heads together. That's a natural reaction to pressure. You can't arrest their friends for it."

Stamping. Clicking. Clapping. Cheers.

"This was someone who'd lost both of her parents when she was just a girl. She had no family. She was on two different types of medication, for narcolepsy and obsessive-compulsive disorder. These are things her colleagues didn't even know. She was under an extreme amount of pressure to succeed. Can you blame her for walking away?"

"*Noooooooooo!*" said the people.

"It's absurd," Cougar said. "Human beings have the right to go somewhere else and start over. Penn Hamilton is not a criminal. Beryl Unger was just exercising her right to be free."

Cougar stood above the people, the media, the world, looking down upon them with bold authority.

"That is our basic human right. This is America, after all."

A smother of clicks, claps, cheers, and stamping powered the air.

"Which is why we're suing Detective Jameson Rex and the New York City Police Department for defamation of character."

Cougar looked directly into the nearest television camera, which happened to belong to CNN.

"And we will win."

PENN HAMILTON IS MY BABY'S DADDY, MAKE ME DISAPPEAR, PENN IS GOD, and WWPD? (What Would Penn Do?) T-shirts were flying out of stores. I FUCKED PENN HAMILTON shirts, sold direct from the scandalous website, were the most popular of all.

He was young.

Rich.

Powerful.

Murderous.

And free.

Jameson had flamed out before he could barely get started. Even as a detective in the NYPD, possibly the most powerful police force in the country, he was nothing against the tide of celebrity and fame. All those people in Times Square cheering for Penn. J.C. Cougar's press conference. And now he was being sued.

It was scary. What did it all mean?

He had a lot of time on his hands. He'd been placed on paid administrative leave pending this lawsuit thing. He didn't know what to do with himself.

He went out and bought a copy of *Book*.

"Have a seat, Shecky."

Shecky sat in one of the chairs in front of Kitty Ellerman's desk. She was impeccably dressed, impeccably pretty. She had been doing everything just right, to the letter. She'd been putting in long hours, making sure every author had everything they needed. She'd been assistant and editor, without being asked. Nothing had suffered from Beryl's absence. Shecky had made sure of that.

"How are you today?" Ellerman asked.

"I'm great, Ms. Ellerman. Everything is just great. Thank you so much for asking."

Ellerman smiled.

"I believe you have the single most upbeat personality I've ever seen, Shecky. You never say no, and you never seem to have a bad day."

"I believe in being positive about everything I do, Ms. Ellerman. That's how I was raised."

"I like that. It's very professional."

Kitty Ellerman ruffled the papers in front of her, searching for something.

"Do you know why I called you in here?" she asked.

"I assumed it's because you need my assistance. Whatever it is, I'm happy to oblige."

Ellerman found what she was looking for. She handed it to Shecky. It was a memo. Shecky took the paper and scanned the page.

> TO: Staff
> FROM: Kitty Ellerman
> SUBJ: Editorial Promotion
>
> Effective immediately, Shecky Lehman has been
> promoted to the position of editor. She will

assume the author list previously managed by
Beryl Unger. Please do your best to assist her
during this period of transition.

Shecky stared at the paper, her eyes glazing over. Her heart
pumped in slow-mo, beat-beat, beat-beat.

"You're making me an editor, Ms. Ellerman?" she asked, choking
on the words.

"You deserve it, Shecky. We've all been impressed by your excellent
work ethic. You've got a great career ahead of you. It may as well start
now."

Tears coursed over Shecky's lovely cheeks.

"Ms. Ellerman, thank you. This is a dream."

"Congratulations, Shecky," Kitty said, standing. "Make me proud."

Shecky stood, reaching across the desk for her boss's hand.

"I will, Ms. Ellerman. You'll never regret this. I'll never let you
down. I give you my word!"

Penn was among the first of her authors to wish her well. He did it in
person, unannounced.

Shecky was in her new office, Beryl's old space, getting settled in.
She had her back to the door as she hung her college diploma on the
wall.

"People still do that?" Penn asked, standing in the doorway.

Shecky breathed in silently. She hated surprises. But he was her
author now. She must always be gracious. Yes. Always be gracious.
She turned toward him.

"Hello, Penn. Did we have a meeting scheduled?"

"No," he said, sauntering in and taking a seat. "I came by to congratulate you. It's good to see management's paying attention around
here. I didn't know who I'd get assigned to. I'm glad that it's you."

Shecky could feel his blue eyes course hotly over her body. She was
appropriately clothed in a camel-colored pantsuit that flattered her
figure but was very professional. Penn's eyes traveled over her bosom
then made their way up, back to her face.

What was that, she thought, an appraisal? He was smiling now, so she supposed he approved. How ridiculous. He'd never behaved like this before. He'd always been so formal, especially whenever Beryl was around. But now that he was officially her author, he acted as though that gave him a license to flirt.

"Have a seat," he said, pointing at her chair. "You can hang diplomas later. Let's talk. I want to get to know you better."

Shecky graciously pulled out her chair and sat.

"I apologize, Penn, I can't stay for long. I have an editorial meeting in five minutes. I was just taking advantage of the time to organize some of my stuff, but I'm more than happy to schedule an appointment for us to talk. I want to make sure everything is going well for you. Perhaps we can discuss ideas for the next book."

Penn sat across from her, staring in silence. Shecky continued to smile, but she was seething on the inside.

Who does he think he is? Is this eye-contact thing supposed to be turning me on?

"You're all about business," Penn said with a broad grin. He leaned forward, his arms on the desk. "I like that. But all work and no play, Shecky—"

"I take my work very seriously, Penn. Beryl was an excellent editor with an excellent reputation. I learned a lot from her. I want to make sure that you and the other authors feel just as secure and comfortable with me. It's important to everyone at Kittell Press that you're happy here."

He was gazing at her with those eyes again and that golden face. Girls fell over themselves just to get a few seconds of a look from him. Shecky didn't see the big deal. He was just another handsome guy. Yes, he was really handsome. And? She would never let herself fall under the spell of someone's good looks.

She glanced at her watch, then pushed back her chair. She stood.

"I'm so sorry, Penn, but I have to get going. Do you want to schedule a time for us to sit down and talk?" She flipped through a date book on her desk. "I don't have a permanent assistant just yet, so I'm booking some of my own stuff."

She reached for a pen and glanced up at him.

"How about tomorrow?"

"How about dinner?" he said, still sitting.

Shecky's eyes held his.

"I'm sorry," she said, "that won't be possible."

"Why not?" he asked. "We could have dinner, see a show, I could bounce some ideas off you. It'll be fun."

"Dinner's not possible," she said, her eyes still on his. "But I do have lunch free. Would you like me to put it down?"

Her pen was poised over the page.

Penn's eyes twinkled. He reached over and patted her hand.

"Let me get back to you on it," he said.

"Okay. Sure. Just let me know."

She was one thousand percent sweetness.

Penn stood.

"It's going to be fun working with you, Shecky. I can see that already."

"I hope so, Penn," she said, reaching for her notepad and walking toward the door. "We are so excited about you here. I can't wait to see what you're going to do next."

"Right," Penn said, watching her sidelong. "It'll be mind-blowing, you can bet that."

"Oh, I'm sure of it," Shecky said. "You're such a talented writer."

She stood in the doorway, waiting for him to pass. He moved slowly past her, his chest barely, deliberately, grazing hers.

"See ya," he said.

"Good afternoon, Penn."

She watched him walk down the hall.

Cocksucker.

Who the fuck did he think he was?

Penn turned when he got to the end of the hallway. He watched Shecky sashay away, her voluminous chestnut hair bouncing against her back.

She was beautiful today, stunning even, bedecked as she was in her foxy pantsuit. He wasn't used to women being impervious to his

charms, but Shecky hadn't flinched. She was warmly aloof, all business and shit. He didn't quite know what to do with that.

He had time, plenty of time.

Shecky wasn't so special. Sure, she was gorgeous, but so what?

She was just a woman.

Any woman could be cracked.

They'd been

. . . at the Hotel Plaza Athénée for the past three days.

Penn had finally moved out of his place and was waiting on his new loft in Tribeca to be completed. She had offered him a place in her home, but he didn't think that was a good idea. She agreed.

They'd spend days together in spurts, at least two a week, sometimes three. She had suggested he stay at the Plaza Athénée until his place was done. There was an intimacy there, though still not quite intimate enough, as the paparazzi were constantly at his heels. Privacy came at a premium these days. Now that Penn's star had arrived, there would never be enough.

Sharlyn had kept her word. She wasn't writing. She was taking time off. Finding out that Shecky would be her new editor made it even easier. Spanky had been duly advised to leave her alone until she was ready to resurface again.

No matter how sweet the potential deal, she just wanted out of the public eye.

All she'd done for the past six months, since "the Beryl situation," was hang with Penn and watch his star soar higher and higher. There'd been no more celebrity parties, no hanging with her celebrity friends. No more cocaine. Well, maybe just a little. And some Dom here and there. Not much. She didn't even go to parties with Penn anymore.

She was reconnecting with herself. Funny, when she stopped all the partying and celebrity-moshing, the people of that world stopped calling.

She had a theory about it. For every celebrity that fell off the scene, there were ten more waiting to take his place. Twenty, if you threw in the reality rabble.

She didn't want to be one of those twenty-four-hour-party people.

She was relieved to have vacated their space.

She was sitting on the bed with her laptop.

"What? Are you writing?"

She chuckled.

"Nooooo. I'm reading the news on Google."

"Google," he said. "Pretty soon those guys are gonna own the world."

"Perhaps. But for now they give me more news than I can handle. That's good enough for me."

Penn was getting dressed for yet another party. First there was dinner with the coheads of GreeneStreet Films, Fisher Stevens and John Penotti. They'd won the rights to *Book*. Twentieth Century Fox would coproduce and distribute. Penn would be writing the screenplay with author/screenwriter Michael Chabon, the *real* original Wonder Boy. And Penn was going to star.

He would be Gregor Balzac.

He would be the dick. A dick of his own making. It was Gesamtkunstwerk on steroids.

Fame was a dream.

After the dinner meeting, he was off to a party at Kos, with Denzel and Lenny, and Fiyah, of course.

He came over to the side of the bed, grabbed her face, and kissed her hard.

"Bye, baby," he said.

"Bye, sweetie. Have fun. I'll probably be asleep when you get in."

She ordered the chilied ahi tuna and foie gras for dinner, with a crab and celeriac napoleon as an appetizer and the tarragon panna cotta for dessert.

She was full but not overstuffed as she strolled over to the window with her glass of port. She stared out at the city. No matter where she went in the world, New York was the only place that ever felt right. This was where, when the time came, she would one day be buried. Ashes to ashes, dust to dust, she forever wanted to be connected to New York City.

Such morbid thoughts, she mused. She needed to put her mind to better use.

She walked back over to the bed, almost tripping on something sticking out from underneath. Her port flew out of the glass onto the sheets as she tried to regain her balance.

"What . . . ?"

The corner of something had stopped her. She kneeled and pulled it from under the bed.

It was a light gray messenger bag with black piping. She opened the flap. Penn's stuff. What was that, a script? Something an agent had given him. A book by Chuck Palahniuk. A small plastic bag of some sort of white-gray dust. She opened it and sniffed. She stuck her pinky in and tasted it. She snorted a bit. Whatever it was, it wasn't drugs. She threw the plastic bag back in. There was an *Us* magazine with him on the cover. A pack of Twizzlers. A small book with nothing on the cover. What's that? A journal? She pulled it out and opened it to a random page.

Sharlyn Tate has the best pussy I've ever had.

Her hand flew to her mouth, unable to stop the giggle bursting through.

She flipped to another page.

Fiyah's cool.

She kept reading.

It's amazing how easy it was. You can watch movies all day long, but nothing can ever match the sensation of cutting flesh, human flesh, and watching it burn. She had a smell, like a premium pork roast. It was all so easy. I have to work it into a story.

Sharlyn's heart began. pumping. very. slow.

It should have sped up, but it was being tugged down with every word on the page.

She flipped another.

I put some outside her building last night. Just a small bit at the foot of a tree. Maybe it'll fertilize it better. Powdered bone is good for that.

Another page.

Places I've Scattered or Placed Her Ashes:
1) Inside the pages of Canon Messier's books in the Barnes & Noble at Astor Place
2) In front of Mitali East
3) The dirt outside the Carter&Hobbs building
4) Central Park, two feet away from the entrance to Tavern on the Green
5) A potted palm in Bungalow 8
6) The Harlem River
7) The bathroom at Scores
8) Riverside Park
9) The bowling alley at Chelsea Piers
10) Barney Greengrass
11) The African violet she gave me; it's been blooming like gangbusters!

Sharlyn dropped the book, feeling faint. She glanced over at the nightstand.

There was an African violet.

A flourishing African violet.

She raced to the bathroom, dropped to the floor, and vomited and vomited until she believed her entrails would surely come out.

She was sitting in the dark when he came in.

It was four forty-eight.

The book was on the bed beside her, along with the plastic bag of white-gray stuff.

He tried to come in without much noise. He gingerly closed the door and tiptoed across the room, his eyes not quite adjusted to the dark.

"You killed her."

It was a soft dagger of sound, cutting the night wide open.

"What?" He was whispering.

"You killed Beryl. I read it in your journal."

She flung the thing at him. He could hear its velocity turning on the wind and managed to fake a move to the right, barely missing getting his head taken out. The journal hit the wall, the pages wide and bent as it fell to the floor.

She ran toward him, trying to take him down.

Sharlyn could feel the blood racing through her head, her arms, the fronts of her thighs. She was hot with rage, not fear. She wanted to hurt him for what he'd done to her and Beryl. She wanted to take everything away from him, everything she and Beryl and every stupid, willing woman who'd been drawn to the superficial had given him, had made easy for him, had paved the way for him to have. She hadn't thought it out from the legal side. She hadn't even considered the police. She was on pure emotional fumes now, and she was blinded by it. All she could see was striking out.

She dove onto him, knocking him to the floor.

"Sharlyn, stop it! Get off me!" They were rolling on the floor.

He somehow managed to get on top and pin her down. Sharlyn thrashed beneath him.

"Let me go!" she screamed.

"Stop it," he hissed. "It's the middle of the night!"

"No!"

More than any feeling she'd ever had, she wanted to see Penn Hamilton dead. She'd lost everything because of him. Everything. Her husband, her life, her editor, her desire for her career.

She wanted him dead.

He had her arms immobilized. She adjusted her butt and tried to knee him in the groin.

"Ooph," he grunted.

Good, she thought. Good.

She saw a blue flicker in his eyes as they seemed to light up in the darkness. He was breathing hard, angry now, his hands around her neck.

Shar pushed and squirmed and thrashed, trying desperately to cough, but unable to get any air past the clench of his hands. Her face was growing hotter and hotter. Her eyes were burning. She kicked and wriggled and grunted and moaned.

The twin blue flames were bearing down on her, even as his grip grew stronger around her neck.

She stopped fighting against him, focused only on the flickering blues.

They grew hazy at first.

Then the lights went out.

Merc came by late the next afternoon. Things were already situated when he arrived.

They brought her out in a Louis Vuitton trunk. The unsuspecting bellman helped them load her into the back of Merc's Navigator.

Penn gave him a hundred-dollar tip.

Upstate New York was nothing like New York City. It was a far-off hinterland of thick forests, wineries, finger lakes, arctic winters, and blue-collar ethics. It was real life, the workingman's world, unlike the ultraslick, mythical Manhattan, filled with its mix of the unfathomably rich and the desperately poor, all equally aware that, despite the vast differences in their lots in life, they were living in the Center of the Universe.

It wasn't like that upstate. There, people dealt with real issues that hit them real hard, with no glint and glamour to buffer the view. In the Uticas and Buffaloes and Elmiras and Binghamtons of the world, people struggled, ate spiedie, got dirty, had calluses, worked in factories, vineyards, breweries, garages, Roy Rogers, and fought like hell against the travails of nature and existence as though their lives depended upon it.

Which, in most cases, they did.

———

The drive up to Rochester was a quiet one. Not much to say. Both men had their own things to contemplate. Conversation had never been a mandate between them.

The Rochester Embayment was made up of thirty-five square miles of Lake Ontario and the last six miles of the Genesee River. It was nasty, as nasty went. Filthy. Rotten. A mutant-making cesspool.

They took her out of the Louis Vuitton trunk and flung her in.

Her body hit the water with a hard splash, plunged rapidly for a few feet, then settled into a gentle rocking drift that laid her gracefully at the bottom.

Penn and Mercury stood next to each other, watching moonbeams alight on the wavy surface, twinkling like so many stars.

"You all right, man?" Mercury asked.

"Please."

"That's good," Merc said with a nod. "Gotta do what you gotta do. Besides, her husband left her for what, his cousin? That's what it said in the paper. No telling what a distraught bitch'll do behind some shit like that. It would make perfect sense if she turned up dead."

"It would, wouldn't it?"

"Sure," Merc said. "There's all kinds of possibilities. He could have done it. She could have done it to herself. Not that anyone will come up here looking for her. She'll be way out in Lake Ontario before long. The natural pull of the river will drag her off. If the crabs don't eat her first."

"Nice, Merc. Nice."

"I'm serious, man. Catfish, trout, whatever the fuck is down there. She's gon' get some chunks bit out her ass, you can bet on that."

Penn was chuckling.

"Man, you're crazy."

"I'm just saying."

They listened to the croaking of infinite frogs, miniature witnesses to a night of magic, horror, secrets. Just one of many such secret horrors the creatures had witnessed before.

"How'd you find this place?"

"My uncle used to talk about it. I looked it up on the Net a few years back."

"I suppose I shouldn't ask why you were looking it up."

"A lotta shit's been dumped in here over the years," Merc said. "This was once ranked the second most polluted river in the country. I mean this shit is mad toxic. I'm talking 'take the skin off your bones if you even touch the water' kind of shit."

"You and your hyperbole."

"Seriously. Dioxin's in there, pesticides, who knows what else. Now that I think about it, those crabs might never even get a crack at her. She probably dissolved on the way down."

They stared at the water for a long moment, each with their own imaginings of a Sharlyn buffet versus a Sharlyn smoothie. Eight-eyed catfish. Three-headed trout.

"You're a good friend, Merc," Penn said.

"You know we don't even have to talk about that."

"I know. I just don't want it to go unsaid."

Merc stooped and picked up a pebble, threw it at the shiny water, watched it skip along the surface.

"So do you think you could handle being a manager?"

"A manager?" Merc asked without turning his head.

"Yeah. A general always needs a good lieutenant."

"I like to see it as a don needing a good consigliere."

Penn nodded.

"A good consigliere knows about places like the Genesee River," said Merc. "Plenty of bodies have been thrown in here. Who the hell's gonna want to fish them out? I figure if it's good enough for the mob . . ."

Penn turned and shook his consigliere's hand.

"Good job."

Merc smiled.

"What's the most polluted river?" Penn asked.

"The Mississippi, nigga. By leaps and bounds."

"Right."

They went back to the car.

———

He was scribbling in his journal, even though the cover was bent and some of the pages were crumpled from the way it had hit the wall when Sharlyn threw it across the room.

It was easy throwing her in. I thought I loved her, but at the end, I felt nothing. Maybe I can't love.

Maybe there is no love.

Maybe there's just feelings in a moment that, like ripples on the sea, rise, fall, and then disappear into something else. Disappear into nothing. Like water. Water's not love. Water's just water.

Whatever. What else.

That can be my next book.

Deus Ex Machina:

(Translation: "god from the machine") A device used in Greek and Roman theater where a crane made of wooden beams and elaborate pulleys lowered a god or what appeared to be the hand of a god onto the stage to physically remove the hero from the midst of an impossible difficulty.

A literary device where the author uses the surprise intervention of an improbable person or event to get a character out of a difficult situation or to bring the story to a convenient conclusion.

Metafiction:

A work of fiction that self-consciously examines itself while telling a story, blurring the lines between reality and fiction within the levels of narrative. Fiction about fiction. Also known as "surfiction."

We live inside an enormous novel.

—J. G. Ballard, Introduction to *Crash*

Deus Ex Meta

Penn was dozing in the upper-class suite of Virgin Atlantic Flight VS004, en route to London for a round of signings and an appearance on the popular BBC music countdown show *Top of the Pops*. He was sitting upright, having fallen asleep as soon as his butt hit the seat, long before the plane was finished boarding. The flight attendants were buzzing around in a useless huddle near the bar, debating whether to wake him so he could flip his seat into a bed for a more comfortable trip. They could hear the gentle curdle of exhaustion every time he took a breath. None of them had gathered the nerve to approach him yet.

"He's so beautiful," one whispered as she prepared a round of drinks.

"Can you Adam and Eve it?" said another. "If I didn't 'ave me George Michael right now, I'd flash 'im a bit o' Khyber just for kicks."

"You never let it stop you before, you slag," said a third.

"You think I should flirt with him when he wakes up?" piped another. "Wouldn't that just be insane? Flirting with Penn Hamilton! I mean, what if he's a murderer after all? You never know. It's so damn sexy. Imagine the kind of orgasm you'd have knowing the man inside you might have killed someone."

The flight attendants stared at her.

"I mean, yeah, it sounds sick," the girl reasoned, "but c'mon, it's a bit like a rape fantasy, don't you think? All that danger lurking just beneath the surface of such a pretty package."

"A famous package."

They turned toward Penn.

"That'd be a shag worth dying for."

"I dunno, there's something dodgy about the fact that he might . . . ugh . . . I can't even say it."

"Imagine 'avin' 'is teapots."

"Wicked."

"I'll bet they'd be gorgeous."

"They'd be a bunch of bloody killers is what they'd be."

"Look at him. If none of you plan on going over, I will. That's not the face of a murderer. That's the face of an angel."

"Lucifer was an angel."

"Penn Hamilton is not Lucifer. The charges were dropped. That's good enough for me."

"Bollocks. People get away with murder all the time."

"He's not like that. You can tell. It's in the eyes."

"His eyes are closed, you nit."

"What if he doesn't wake up at all during the flight?"

"I'll wake him. I can show him something worth lying down for."

"What a scrubber. You've already got a boyfriend. Don't you think it's a bit greedy to set your sights on him?"

"Sod off. You just want him for yourself."

"And what if I do? You're just jealous because Keith Richards made eyes at me on that last flight and not you."

"You bloody cow. Who the hell wants that trout face gaping at 'em?"

"I'm going to go wake him and tell him to let me dress his bed. I wonder if he'll want the complimentary sleep suit. I can help him change into it."

"Karen, don't you dare!"

Karen was indeed about to dare, but before she could take a step, the plane hit a patch of turbulence and did a quick radical drop. Penn awoke at once, startled and disoriented. He looked around. The very first face he focused on was a smiling Harold Gersh, the head of Brecker Books, in the suite right next to him.

"We meet again," said the perennially upbeat Gersh. "I was wondering what it was going to take to finally rouse you. That was some pocket of air we just hit."

"Sure was," Penn groaned as he rubbed the sides of his mouth and stretched his face. "How long have we been flying?"

"A couple of hours at least," said Gersh. "The flight attendants have been circling you like roadkill."

"Really?" Penn said, perking up. He spotted them across the way. When they noticed him looking, they giggled nervously and turned away. A couple of the daring ones glanced back, eager to be turned into pillars of salt.

"You get that everywhere, don't you?"

Penn shrugged. "You get used to it after a while."

Gersh laughed. "You're so cavalier. I love it!"

Penn flashed his multimillion-dollar grin. As if on cue, the flight attendants traipsed by, one after the other, still not daring to interrupt the publishing executive and the golden boy. They were as inconspicuous as elephant's balls.

"You hungry?" asked Gersh. "I was about to order dinner."

"I'm starving," said Penn.

"Mind if I come over there?"

"Sure."

Gersh ambled out of his suite and slid onto the ottoman in Penn's.

"We probably need to be diplomatic about this."

"What's that?" asked Penn.

"About which one of these flight attendants gets to come and take our order. I get the feeling a fight might erupt."

Karen was pouring their second glass of Selak's sauvignon blanc.

"So what's next for the amazing Penn Hamilton?" asked Gersh. "Have you started working on your next bestseller?"

"I've been kicking around some ideas."

"I imagine half the city's wooing you."

"More like all of it."

"Brilliant." Gersh chuckled. "I think your immodesty is what I like best."

"Is it abrasive?"

"Not at all. You've got the charisma factor. You don't see that kind of thing very often. Clinton has it. I'm afraid to admit it, but I think Paris Hilton has it, too. The public is very forgiving when you've got the charisma factor."

"I like that description. I've grown tired of hearing the press call me 'smug.' "

"So tell me about this next project of yours," Gersh said, getting right into it. "Will it be another modern take on a classic?"

"I've been toying with ideas. I thought I had a good one, but now I'm not so sure about it. Nothing's grabbing me just yet."

"Really." Gersh lingered over his glass. "It's funny because, you know, it really bothered me that we never got a shot at that first book of yours. It was great stuff. The whole Balzac thing. Kafka meets the Valley. It was amazing."

"Thank you."

"I've actually been coming up with some ideas on my own. Kind of an if-I-could-get-Penn-Hamilton-this-is-the-kind-of-thing-I'd-like-to-see-him-do wish list, if you will."

"Do tell."

Gersh took a sip of wine first, then readied his lungs for the pitch.

"All right, Penn. Here's my take. You're a damn good writer. That's obvious to almost everyone by now. You know the craft, and you know how to manipulate it for the betterment of a story. You've got this whole genius angle going. And the way you worked in the concept of Gesamtkunstwerk was priceless. And let's face it, men, women, children, everybody gets taken in by your looks. You know how to brand yourself as the ultimate product better than anyone I've ever seen."

Penn drank it in. He loved this part, the wooing. It spoke to his most basic need. There was a fine line between wooing and pandering. Fortunately, Gersh was nowhere near it.

"You went through something most people don't come out of clean. Anytime someone is accused of murder, even if it's just implied, and then it's played out in the media on the level yours was, the person is usually left with this . . . taint . . . a stigma that ends up following them forever. The public will forgive a lot of things, but the stench of accusation lingers on in cases of murder, rape, and crimes against children."

Gersh waited for Penn to respond, but he didn't.

"So what I'm saying is, I've never seen anyone emerge more beloved, more emulated, more celebrated than you after being trotted out in front of the world as a possible killer. You still got all your endorsement deals?"

"Apple and Starbucks both just sweetened the pot."

"That's what I figured. So here's what I propose, here's what's on my wish list for you. Imagine this, if you can: Penn the character. Still Penn the man, but also Penn the character."

"Go on."

"Imagine books being written with you in mind, with a fictional-ized Penn Hamilton, an antihero navigating the literary landscape as the best of the best writers take him on."

"So I'd be writing myself taking on other writers?"

"Yes and no. Sometimes. Maybe. And sometimes others will take on the task."

"Others like who?"

"Others like premier commercial and literary writers. Patterson could have Alex Cross hunting you down," the publisher enthused. "John Grisham could take a swipe at you in one of his novels. You could turn Washington, D.C., on its ear in one of Brad Meltzer's books. Patricia Cornwell, Dennis Lehane, Stephen King could make you a monster. Mosley could come after you with EZ Rawlins. There's so many possibilities! Sue Grafton, Updike, Irving, Wolfe." He caught himself. "Strike those last three. They'd never do it."

"Huh?"

"Yes, yes, this could be huge," Gersh said. "We could get Elmore Leonard, hell, Nick Sparks could even wrap a love story around you. That'd really catch the public off guard. It'd be awesome. We can get totally meta with this!"

"How's that?"

"The layers, Penn, the layers! They'll be endless. On the one hand, it'll be camp, but at the same time, it'll be serious. We'll be reshaping the fictional realm. It'll be the book that knows it's a book, and every-body reading it will know it's a book about a guy who wrote a book in real life who may or may not be a villain, even though he's a vil-lain in the book, and he'll be chased for fictitious crimes by fictitious characters who know they're after a real guy but don't know they themselves aren't real, they're just part of the book! When you come to a project with that many slants, it challenges the reader, the writer, the art!"

Penn smiled as he sipped his wine. Gersh was on a tear, and it was all making sense. Just a few feet behind him hovered Karen, at the ready for whatever they might need. She blinked coyly. Penn held her gaze long enough to unnerve her, then rose from his seat.

"Excuse me, Mr. Gersh. Nature calls."

"Sure!" the big man said, jumping up to let him pass. "Go right ahead. Am I rambling? I'm not rambling, am I? I don't want to scare you off. I'm just so excited about what we could do. I've been turn-ing this over in my head for a while now. I don't think it's an accident that we're meeting like this."

Penn put his hand on Gersh's shoulder.

"It's not easy to scare me off. Besides, where would I go? We're thirty thousand feet in the air. There's only ten suites in upper class, and I refuse to travel in any other section of this plane. I usually don't fly Virgin at all. Branson's a megalomaniacal blowhard. At any rate, I'm trapped up here for a while. But then again," he said with a wink, "so are you."

Gersh laughed heartily as his quarry walked away. The flight atten-dant gave a slight nod to Penn as he passed, then followed him qui-etly into the john.

Ten minutes later, Penn returned.

"The wine"—he smirked—"it goes right through you."

Gersh went along with the ruse.

"No problem. It gave me a chance to collect my thoughts."

"More about the metanovel thing?"

"Yes. I'm pretty excited about it. Think about it, Penn. This could

be a chance to do something really different. We're talking about spinning a character based on a real person, a celebrated personality, a genius,
an award-winning writer, an accused murderer who was wrongly
charged . . . maybe . . ." He cleared his throat, took a sip of wine.
"We're talking about spinning that character—you—into the works of
other bestselling authors. Across several genres! It's a home run all the
way. Even if it doesn't work in all the books we try it with, there's a
strong chance it'll stick with a few. The ones that get it right will soar.
Readers will be dying, heh-heh, dying to see how a particular author
takes on the next Penn Hamilton tale."

"Really?"

"Of course they will. And we'll have you, I mean, we'll have the
fictional you killing real people, not Hollywood types or publishing
figures or fashion icons. It'll be man-on-the-street kinds of characters,
and we'll have you knocking them off at random."

"Why not have me bump off celebs? The public might love it."

"Nooooo," Gersh said, vigorously shaking his head, "readers hate
that kind of insider stuff."

"How so?"

"Movies about life in Hollywood, books with characters in the
world of publishing, that stuff never does too well. It's all a bunch of
self-celebrating garbage. That's not the kind of thing we're going for."

"I liked that movie *Adaptation*," Penn said. "It was an insider story,
but it was great."

"Of course you liked it. You're a writer. People love stories that
relate to their own struggles. *Adaptation* got critical acclaim and Oscar
notice, but it wasn't a blockbuster."

"I see."

"Just remember this: most people aren't in Hollywood. Most people don't write books. Even fewer are drop-dead models with seven-
figure contracts. People might like celebrity-watching and may want
to write a book or be a model, but they sure as hell don't want to sit
around and listen to the people that do it whine about their lives or
pat themselves on the back about it. But everybody, everybody . . ."—
he let the word hang in the air—"everybody lives with the possibility
of murder, and everybody loves sex and money, despite what they say.

People like villains versus heroes, class struggle, and the pursuit of love. They like intrigue, drama, and suspense. That's why movies and books like that sell so well. Murder, sex, and money are always home runs, and right now, you've got high ratings with all three."

Penn mulled over his words.

"What if I bumped off O.J.?"

"Oh," Gersh said, rubbing his chin. "That's actually quite clever. But it would split your audience. You'd be heroic to some and despised by others. It'd play the race card, and that's not what we're looking to do."

Penn gave a slight nod, his lips pursed.

"But it was an excellent thought," Gersh added encouragingly.

"So how do you think the authors you mentioned would feel about doing this?" Penn asked. "You can't just impose an alien element into their work."

Gersh leaned forward with intense conviction.

"Let me tell you, Penn . . . we work really hard for the writers we publish and we pride ourselves on not interfering with the creative process, but I get the feeling the authors will see the merit of what I'm proposing. I'm not casual about stuff like this. When I fall in love with an idea, I fall hard. That doesn't mean I think it's foolproof. What it does mean is that, over the years, I've learned to look at things from every angle, pick my battles wisely, and make calculated moves. I think I'm able to recognize what's worth fighting for. I think we can make this work, Penn."

"But the authors you talked about are all at other houses. They're not at Brecker Books."

"So what? All the best writers will be lining up for a chance to take a crack at you on the page. It's just a matter of getting you on board."

"This is starting to sound like the branding of a partnership," Penn said. "It's got imprint written all over it."

"Penn Books, maybe?" Gersh was on it.

"Fifty-fifty share?" Penn asked.

"I don't see why not."

Penn whistled. This guy was a bona fide closer. The real deal. He

had to give the man that. And he was so damn likable. All that effu-
siveness was rubbing off.

The two-hour nap Penn had taken was refreshing. The wine had
given him a pleasant kind of mellow. And the trip to the bathroom.
The bathroom had been quite special, indeed.

"His willy is right proper," Karen whispered to the clusterfuck of
idling flight attendants. "It's like a nice, thick banger."

The owl-eyed girls peeked in Penn's direction.

"Did you take it with cream?"

"Clotted, of course."

A round of devilish sniggles could be heard across the room.

"So tell me something, Mr. Gersh," Penn said, looking at the flight
attendants.

"Please call me Harold."

"Okay . . . Harold." He turned his attention to the publisher. "You
think somewhere in all these metabooks we can arrange it so that my
character gets a decent helping of meta blow jobs?"

Gersh's brow shot up.

"You know," Penn continued, "kind of like a blow job within a
blow job within a blow job, where the fictitious women in the books
don't realize they're giving a real person a real blow job, and the real
women in the real world are aware that some of the blow jobs they're
giving are fake."

Harold howled.

"You are bad."

"I figured since we're making meta wish lists and all."

Gersh finished the last of his wine.

"You could be the antidote to 007," he said, brimming with excitement. "Imagine, a suave supervillain. Sleek, well-spoken, a mastermind who's got a way with the ladies. People won't know who to root
for, especially if the character pitted against you is a schlep. Readers
might even prefer it if the author lets you get away."

"With murder, you mean?"

"With everything."

Penn's gleaming smile lit up the cabin.

"I like that."

"So do I."

"So what do we do about it?"

"Let's make a deal."

A few hours later, he was in the bathroom. Everyone else was asleep.

The other flight attendants were scattered throughout the plane. Some were sleeping. No one had seen him get up.

No one but Karen, the flight attendant who had serviced him before.

No one saw Karen follow him into the bathroom.

She was with him now, leaning over the sink. He was taking her from behind.

She was grunting. He placed his right hand over her mouth.

"Keep it down," he whispered, pulling back.

"Don't stop," she moaned, "don't stop."

"I will unless you keep it down."

Karen quieted, pressing her backside deeper into him.

He increased his tempo, pounding into her as the plane made a dip. Karen grunted.

He slid his hand from her mouth, down her neck, wrapping his fingers around its delicate grace. It was a beautiful neck. He could feel the ridges under his fingers as he pumped and pushed her against the sink.

The flesh of her neck was so soft. The more he clutched it, the more Karen moaned and tilted back her head.

It was an overpowering sensation, the feel of fragile bone beneath the power of his fingers. He pulled against her neck, tilting it back even further. Karen gasped and moaned more, her breathing impeded as she escalated toward incredible ecstasy.

He could snap a neck like that. It would be so easy. Just a quick tug beneath her chin and it would all be over. No fingerprints, nothing.

"Do it with zest, or don't do it at all."

His father's words rang in his ear as he pulled the girl's throat back a little bit further. Karen coughed, still pressing her backside into his thrusts.

He pumped harder, faster, simultaneously pulling her throat, his hand now under her chin. He could feel the tension building in his groin.

They hit a patch of turbulence, and the impact made him shove harder against her, inside her, her head tilting back even more. A bell dinged as the Fasten Seatbelt sign lit up.

Karen moaned.

Penn pumped with urgency, his hand clasping her chin. Tighter, tighter. The plane and Karen lurched and rocked. So much power was about to explode out of him at both ends. From his hand at her neck. From his loins.

He would come any minute.

Do it with zest, or don't do it at all.

Do it with zest, or don't do it at all.

Do it with zest, or don't do it at all.

Do it.

Do it.

Do it.